I FOUND YOU

Surrey: Twenty-one-year-old Lily Monrose has only been married for three weeks. When her new husband fails to come home from work one night, she is left stranded in a new country where she knows no one. Then the police tell her that her husband never existed . . . East Yorkshire: Alice Lake, a free-spirited single mother of three who earns a living by making art out of old maps and selling it on the internet, finds a man on the beach outside her house. He has no name, no jacket, and no idea what he is doing there. Against her better judgement, she invites him in to her home. But who is he, and how can she trust a man who has lost his memory?

I Found You

Lisa Jewell

LARGE
PRINT

First published in Great Britain 2016
by
Century

First Isis Edition
published 2017
by arrangement with
Century
Penguin Random House

A catalogue record for this book is available
from the British Library.

ISBN 978–1–78541–401–5 (hb)
ISBN 978–1–78541–407–7 (pb)

Published by
F. A. Thorpe (Publishing)
Anstey, Leicestershire
Set by Words & Graphics Ltd.
Anstey, Leicestershire
Printed and bound in Great Britain by
T. J. International Ltd., Padstow, Cornwall
This book is printed on acid-free paper

This book is dedicated to Jascha
(see, I do love you more than I love the dog)

Acknowledgements

Thank you to Selina Walker, my editor. Thank you for the dozens of paperclips and bulldog clips, sticky arrows and Post-it notes. Thank you for Selina-ing my manuscript in the thorough, loving and totally unannoying way that you always do. Thank you for making my book so much better than it was.

Thank you to Jonny Geller, my agent. Thank you for your honesty and thoughtfulness and the really long email that showed me how much you care about my writing. Writing first, career second, as it should be.

Thanks to all at Arrow; Beth, Najma, Georgina, Celeste, Gemma, Cassandra, Asian — and Melissa Four for the drop dead gorgeous cover of the Random House edition.

And thanks to all at Curtis Brown; in particular, to Catherine, Melissa and Luke.

Thanks as always to Richenda Todd for copy editing. You are a pleasure to work with.

In the US, thanks to my former editor at Atria and my new editor at Atria, both called Sarah, both amazing. And thanks to Ariele, my extraordinary US publicist. And last but not least, my publisher, the inimitable Judith Curr, for faith and passion and lovely dinners.

Thanks to all my lovely readers, all the booksellers, book buyers and librarians who make the world of books go round and allow me to sit around in cafés making up stories. And thanks to my family, my friends, my neighbours, the people who form the fabric of my life, without whom etc.

Lastly, never leastly, my many writer friends, on the Board and elsewhere. Writers make the best friends, they really do.

PART ONE

CHAPTER
ONE

Alice Lake lives in a house by the sea. It is a tiny house, a coastguard's cottage, built over three hundred years ago for people much smaller than her. The ceilings slope and bulge and her fourteen-year-old son needs to bow his head to get through the front door. They were all so little when she moved them here from London six years ago. Jasmine was ten. Kai was eight. And Romaine the baby was just four months old. She hadn't imagined that one day she'd have a gangling child of almost six feet. She hadn't imagined that they'd ever outgrow this place.

Alice sits in her tiny room at the top of her tiny house. From here she runs her business. She makes art from old maps, which she sells on the internet for silly money. Silly money for a piece of art made from old maps, perhaps, but not silly money for a single mother of three. She sells a couple a week. It's enough, just about.

Beyond her window, between Victorian street lights, a string of sun-faded bunting swings back and forth in the boisterous April wind. To the left there is a slipway where small fishing boats form a colourful spine down to a concrete jetty and where the great, dreadful froth of the North Sea hits the rocky shoreline. And beyond that the sea. Black and infinite. Alice still feels awed by the sea, by its vast proximity. In Brixton, where she lived before, she had a view of walls, of other people's gardens, of distant towers and fumy skies. And suddenly, overnight, there was all this sea. When she sits on the sofa on the other side of the room it is all she can see, as though it is a part of the room, as though it is about to seep through the window frames and drown them all.

She brings her gaze back to the screen of her iPad. On it she can see a small square room, a cat sitting on a green sofa licking its haunches, a pot of tea on the coffee table. She can hear voices from elsewhere: her mother talking to the carer; her father talking to her mother. She can't quite hear what they're saying because the microphone on the webcam she set up in their living room last time she visited doesn't pick up sound in other rooms properly. But Alice is reassured that the carer is there, that her parents will be fed and medicated, washed and dressed, and that for an hour or two she won't need to worry about them.

That's another thing she hadn't imagined when she'd moved north six years ago. That her spry, clever, just-turned-seventy-year-old parents would both develop Alzheimer's within weeks of each other and require constant supervision and care.

On the screen on Alice's laptop is an order form from a man called Max Fitzgibbon. He wants a rose made out of maps of Cumbria, Chelsea and Saint-Tropez for his wife's fiftieth birthday. Alice can

4

picture the man: well preserved, silver-haired, in a heather-coloured Joules zip-neck jumper, still hopelessly in love with his wife after twenty-five years of marriage. She can tell all this from his name, his address, from his choice of gift ("Big blowsy English roses have always been her favourite flower," he says in the "Any other comments" box).

Alice looks up from her screen and down through her window. He is still there. The man on the beach.

He's been there all day, since she opened her curtains at seven o'clock this morning: sitting on the damp sand, his arms around his knees, staring and staring out to sea. She's kept an eye on him, concerned that he might be about to top himself. That had happened once before. A young man, deathly pale in the blue-white moonlight, had left his coat on the beach and just disappeared. Alice is still haunted by the thought of him, three years later.

But this man doesn't move. He just sits and stares. The air today is cold and blowing in hard, bringing with it a veil of icy droplets from the surface of the sea. But the man is wearing only a shirt and jeans. No jacket. No bag. No hat or scarf. There's something worrying about him: not quite scruffy enough to be a drifter; not quite strange enough to be a mental health patient from the day-care centre in town. He looks too fit to be a junkie and he hasn't touched a drop of alcohol. He just looks . . . Alice searches her mind for the right word and then it comes to her. He looks *lost*.

* ★ ★

An hour later the rain comes down. Alice peers through the spattered windowpanes and down to the beach below. He's still there. His brown hair is stuck to his skull and his shoulders and sleeves are dark with water. In half an hour she needs to collect Romaine from school. She makes a split-second decision.

"Hero!" she calls to the brindle Staffy. "Sadie!" she calls to the ancient poodle. "Griff!" she calls to the greyhound. "Walkies!"

Alice has three dogs. Griff, the greyhound, is the only one she deliberately went out and chose. The poodle is her parents'. She is eighteen years old and should by rights be dead. Half her fur is gone and her legs are bald and thin as a bird's but she still insists on joining the other dogs for a walk. And Hero, the Staffy, belonged to a previous lodger, Barry. He disappeared one day and left everything behind, including his mental dog. Hero has to wear a muzzle on the street, otherwise she attacks prams and scooters.

Alice clips their leads to their collars as they circle her ankles and notices something else that Barry left behind in his midnight flit, hanging from the coat hooks next to the leads: a shabby old jacket. She automatically wrinkles her nose at the sight of it. She once slept with Barry in a moment of sheer stupidity — and intense loneliness — and regretted it from the moment he lay down on top of her and she realised that he smelled of cheese. That it emanated from every crevice of his slightly lardy body. She'd held her breath and got on with it but ever after she associated him with that smell.

6

She plucks the jacket gingerly from the peg and drapes it over her arm. Then she takes the dogs and an umbrella and heads towards the beach.

"Here," she says, passing the coat to the man. "It's a bit smelly but it's waterproof. And look, it has a hood."

The man turns slowly and looks at her.

He doesn't seem to have registered her intention, so she babbles.

"It belonged to Barry. Ex-lodger. He was about the same size as you. But you smell better. Well, not that I can tell from here. But you look like you smell nice."

The man looks at Alice and then down at the jacket.

"Well," she says, "do you want it?"

Still no response.

"Look. I'm just going to leave it here with you. I don't need it and I don't want it and you may as well keep it. Even if you just use it to sit on. Shove it in a bin if you like."

She drops it near his feet and straightens herself up. His eyes follow her.

"Thank you."

"Ah, so you do talk?"

He looks surprised. "Of course I talk."

He has a southern accent. His eyes are the same shade of gingerbrown as his hair and the stubble on his chin. He's handsome. If you like that kind of thing.

"Good," she says, putting her free hand into her pocket, the other grasping the handle of her umbrella. "Glad to hear it."

He smiles and clutches the damp jacket in his fist. "You sure?"

"About that?" She eyes the jacket. "You'd be doing me a favour. Seriously."

He pulls the jacket on over his wet clothes and fiddles with the zip for a while before fastening it. "Thank you," he says again. "Really."

Alice turns to check the locations of the dogs. Sadie sits thin and damp by her feet; the other two are scampering at the water's edge. Then she turns back to the man. "Why don't you get indoors, out of this rain?" she asks. "Forecast says it's set to rain till tomorrow morning. You're going to make yourself ill."

"Who are you?" he asks, his eyes narrowed, as though she'd introduced herself already and he'd momentarily forgotten her name.

"I'm Alice. You don't know me."

"No," he says. "I don't." He appears reassured by this.

"Anyway," says Alice, "I'd better get on."

"Sure."

Alice takes up the slack in Sadie's lead and the poodle gets unsteadily to her feet, like a freshly birthed giraffe.

Alice calls for the other two. They ignore her. She tuts and calls again.

"Bloody idiots," she mutters under her breath. "Come on!" she yells, striding towards them. "Get here now!"

They are both in and out of the sea; Hero is covered in a layer of green-hued mulch. They will stink. And it is nearly time to collect Romaine. She can't be late again. She'd been late yesterday because she'd over-run on a piece of work and forgotten the time, so she'd had to retrieve Romaine from the school office at three fifty where the secretary had looked at her over the top of the desk screen as though she were a stain on the carpet.

"Come on, you shitbags!" She strides across the beach and makes a grab for Griff. Griff thinks a game has been suggested and darts playfully away. She goes after Hero, who runs away from her. Meanwhile, poor Sadie is being dragged about by her scrawny neck, barely able to stand upright, and the rain is coming down and Alice's jeans are sodden and her hands icy cold and the time is ticking away. She lets out a yell of frustration and takes an approach she used with all the children when they were toddlers.

"Fine," she says, "fine. You stay here. See how you get on without me. Go and beg for scraps outside the fucking butcher's. *Have a good life.*"

The dogs stop and look at her. She turns and walks away.

"Do you want some dogs?" she calls to the man, who is still sitting in the rain. "Seriously? Do you want them? You can have them."

The man starts and looks up at her with his ginger-bread eyes. "I . . . I . . ."

She rolls her eyes. "I'm not being serious."

"No," he says. "No. I know that."

She strides towards the slipway, towards the steps carved into the sea wall. It's three thirty. The dogs stop at the shoreline, glance at each other, then back at Alice. Then they run for her, arriving at her feet seconds later, salty and pungent.

Alice starts up the steps and then turns back when the man calls after her.

"Excuse me!" he says. "Excuse me. Where am I?"

"What?"

"Where am I? What's the name of this place?"

She laughs. "Really?"

"Yes," he says. "Really."

"This is Ridinghouse Bay."

He nods. "Right," he says. "Thank you."

"Get inside, will you?" she says softly to the man. "Please get out of this rain."

He smiles apologetically and Alice waves and heads towards the school, hoping he'll be gone by the time she gets back.

Alice knows she's something of an oddball in Ridinghouse Bay. Which, in fairness, was already pretty full of oddballs before she arrived. But even in a town this strange Alice stands out with her Brixton accent and her Benetton family and her slightly brusque ways. Not to mention the dogs. They make a show of her everywhere she goes. They will not walk to heel, they bark and snap, they whine outside shops. She's seen people cross the street to avoid her animals: Hero in particular with her muzzle and her huge muscular shoulders.

Ever since she got here Alice has played the role of the enigmatic, slightly scary loner, though that is not at all what she is. In London she had friends coming out of her ears. More friends than she knew what to do with. She was a party girl, a come-over-later-with-a-bottle-of-vodka-we'll-put-the-world-to-rights girl. She'd been the kind of mum to stand at the school gates after drop-off and say: Come on then, who's up for a coffee? And she'd be there at the heart of them all, laughing the loudest, talking the most. Until she pushed it too far and blew her life open.

But she has a friend here now. Someone who gets her. Derry Dynes. They met eighteen months ago, on Romaine's first day in reception. Their eyes met and there was a flash of mutual recognition, of shared delight. "Fancy a coffee?" Derry Dynes had said, seeing the film of tears over Alice's eyes as she watched her baby girl disappear into the classroom. "Or something stronger?"

Derry is about five years older than Alice and about a foot shorter. She has a son the same age as Romaine and a grown-up daughter who lives in Edinburgh. She loves dogs (she's the type to let them kiss her on her mouth) and she loves Alice. Early on she learned that Alice was prone to making terrible decisions and letting life run away with her and now she acts as Alice's moderator. She sits and counsels Alice for hours about issues she has with the school over their handling of Romaine's learning difficulties but stops her storming into the office to shout at the secretary. She'll share two bottles of wine with her on a school night but encourage her to stick the cork back into the third. She tells her which hairdresser to go to and what to say:

"Ask for stepped layers, not feathered, and a half-head of highlights *with foils*." She used to be a hairdresser but now she's a reiki therapist. And she has more of an idea about Alice's finances than Alice herself.

She's standing outside the school now, under a huge red umbrella, her boy Danny and Romaine nestled together underneath.

"Christ. Thank you. Dogs went mental on the beach and I couldn't get them back."

She leans down to kiss the crown of Romaine's head and takes her lunch box from her.

"What on earth were you doing on the beach in this weather?"

Alice tuts and says, "You don't want to know."

"No," says Derry. "I do."

"Are you busy? Got time for a cup of tea?"

Derry looks down at her son and says, "I was supposed to be taking this one into town for shoes . . ."

"Well, just come via mine then, I'll show you."

"Look," she says, standing by the sea wall, peering down through the cascade of rain pouring off her umbrella.

He was still there.

"Him?" says Derry.

"Yeah. Him. I gave him that jacket. One of Barry's."

Derry gives an involuntary shudder. She remembers Barry, too. Alice gave her a very thorough and evocative description of events at the time.

"Did he not have a coat then? Before?"

12

"No. Sitting there in a shirt. Soaked. Asked me where he was."

The two children pull themselves up on to the edge of the wall by their fingertips and peer over.

"Where he was?"

"Yes. He seemed a bit confused."

"Don't get involved," says Derry.

"Who said I was getting involved?"

"You gave him a jacket. You're already getting involved."

"That was just an act of simple human kindness."

"Yes," says Derry. "Exactly."

Alice tuts at her friend and heads away from the sea wall. "Are you seriously going shopping?" she asks her. "In this?"

Derry peers into the dark skies overhead and says, "No. Maybe not."

"Come on then," says Alice. "Come to mine. I'll light the fire."

Derry and Danny stay for a couple of hours. The little ones play in the living room while Derry and Alice sit in the kitchen and drink tea. Jasmine returns at four o'clock, soaked to the skin with a wet rucksack full of GCSE coursework, no coat and no umbrella. Kai comes back at four thirty with two friends from school. Alice makes spaghetti for tea and Derry stops her opening a bottle of wine on account of her having to go home. She and Danny leave at six o'clock. It is still raining. Small rivers of muddy rainwater pour down the slipway to the beach and cascade off rooftops. And now a howling wind has set to, sending the rain onto the perpendicular, driving it into everything.

From the top floor of the house Alice sees that the man is still there. He's no longer in the middle of the beach. He's moved back towards the sea wall and he's sitting on a pile of rope. His face is turned up to the sky and his eyes are closed and something inside Alice aches when she looks at him. Of course he may be mad. He may be dangerous. But she thinks of his sad amber-brown eyes and the softness of his voice when he asked her where he was. And she is here in her home full of people, a pile of logs burning in the fireplace, warm and dry and safe. She can't be here knowing that he is there.

She makes him a cup of tea, pours it into a flask, tells the big ones to keep an eye on Romaine and goes to him.

"Here," she says, passing him the flask.

He takes it from her and smiles.

"I thought I told you to go indoors."

"I remember that," he says.

"Good," she says. "But I see you didn't take my advice."

"I can't go indoors."

"Are you homeless?"

He nods. Then shakes his head. Then says, "I think so. I don't know."

"You don't know?" Alice laughs softly. "How long have you been sitting out here?"

"I got here last night."

"Where did you come from?"

He turns and looks at her. His eyes are wide and fearful. "I have no idea."

Alice pulls away slightly. Now she's starting to regret coming down here. *Getting involved*, as Derry said. "Seriously?" she says.

He pushes his damp hair off his forehead and sighs. "Seriously." Then he pours himself a cup of tea and holds it aloft. "Cheers," he says. "You're very kind."

Alice stares out towards the sea. She's not sure how to respond. Half of her wants to get back indoors to the warm; the other feels as though she needs to play this out a bit longer. She asks him another question: "What's your name?"

"I think", he says, gazing into his tea, "that I have lost my memory. I mean" — he turns to her suddenly — "that makes sense, doesn't it? It's the only thing that makes sense. Because I don't know what my name is. And I must have a name. Everyone has a name. Don't they?"

Alice nods.

"And I don't know why I'm here or how I got here. And the more I think about it the more I think I've lost my memory."

"Ah," says Alice. "Yes. That makes sense. Do you . . . Are you injured?" She points at his head.

He runs a hand over his skull for a moment and then looks at her. "No," he says. "It doesn't look like it."

"Have you ever lost your memory before?"

"I don't know," he says, so ingenuously that they both laugh.

"You know you're in the north, don't you?" she asks.

"No," he says. "I didn't know that."

"And you have a southern accent. Is that where you come from?"

He shrugs. "I guess so."

"Jesus," says Alice, "this is crazy. I assume you've checked all your pockets."

"Yeah," he says. "I found some stuff. Didn't know what to make of any of it though."

"Have you still got it?"

"Yes." He leans to one side. "It's here." He pulls a handful of wet paper from his back pocket. "Oh."

Alice stares at the mulch and then into the darkening sky. She pulls her hands down her face and exhales. "Right," she says. "I must be mad. Well, actually, I *am* mad. But I have a studio room in my back yard. I usually rent it out but it's empty right now. Why don't you come and spend a night there? We'll dry out these bits of paper, then maybe tomorrow we can start putting you together? Yes?"

He turns and stares at her disbelievingly. "Yes," he says. "Yes, please."

"I have to warn you," she says, getting to her feet, "I live in chaos. I have three very loud, rude children and three untrained dogs and my house is a mess. So don't come with me expecting a sanctuary. It's far from it."

He nods. "Honestly," he says. "Whatever. I really don't mind. I'm just so grateful. I can't believe how kind you're being."

"No," says Alice, leading the wet stranger up the stone steps and towards her cottage, "neither can I."

16

CHAPTER
TWO

Lily's stomach is clenched as hard as a rock. Her heart has been beating so fast for so long that she feels as though she might pass out. She stands and heads for the window as she's done every couple of minutes for the past twenty-three and a half hours. In thirty minutes she'll call the police again. That's how long they said she had to wait before she could report him as officially missing. But she'd known he was missing within an hour of him not coming home from work last night. She felt it like a slick of ice down her spine. They only got back from their honeymoon ten days before. He'd been racing back from work, sometimes early, and certainly never more than a minute late. He'd been coming home with gifts, with "two-week anniversary" cards, with flowers. He'd spring through the door and say, "God, baby, I missed you so much," and then breathe her in, desperately.

Until last night. He wasn't there at six. He wasn't there at half six. He wasn't there at seven. Each minute felt like an hour. His phone rang and rang for the first hour. And then, suddenly, it stopped ringing, no voicemail, just a flat high-pitched tone. Lily was filled with blind, raging impotence.

The police . . . Well, Lily had not had an opinion either way about the British police before last night. Much in the same way as you wouldn't have an opinion about your local laundrette if you'd never had to use it. But she has an opinion now. A very strong one.

In twenty minutes she can call them again. For what good it will do her. She knows what they think. They think: Stupid young girl, foreign accent, probably a mail-order bride (she is *not* a mail-order bride. She met her husband in a real-life situation, face-to-face). She knows the woman she spoke to thinks her husband is messing about behind her back. Having an affair. Something like that. She could hear it in the slackness of her tone of voice. "Is it possible that he just got way-laid after work?" she'd said. "In the pub?" She could tell that the woman was doing something else as she talked to her, flipping through a magazine maybe, or filing her nails.

"No!" she'd said. "No! He doesn't go to the pub. He just comes home. To me."

Which had been the wrong thing to say, in retrospect. She'd imagined the sardonic lift of the policewoman's eyebrow.

Lily doesn't know who else to call. She knows Carl has a mother, she's spoken to her on the phone, just once, on their wedding day, but she hasn't met her yet. Her name is Maria or Mary or Marie or something like that and she lives . . . well, God, Lily doesn't know where she lives. Something beginning with S, she thinks. To the west? Or maybe the east. Carl told her once; she can't remember and Carl keeps all his numbers stored in his phone. So what can she do?

She also knows that Carl has a sister. Her name is Suzanne. Susan? She's much older than him and lives near the mother in the place beginning with S. They are estranged. He hasn't told her why. And he has a friend called Russ who calls every few days to talk about football and the weather and a drink they really should have one day soon but it's so hard to organise because he has a new baby.

Lily is sure there are other people in Carl's life but she's only known him since February, only been married for three weeks and only lived with him here for ten days so she's still new to Carl's world. And new to this country. She knows no one here and nobody knows her. Luckily Lily's English is fluent so there's no communication issue to deal with. But still, everything is so different here. And it's strange to be completely alone.

Finally the time ticks over to 6.01 p.m. and Lily picks up her phone and calls the police.

"Hello," she says to the man who answers the phone, "my name is Mrs Lily Monrose. I'd like to report a missing person."

CHAPTER
THREE

"Sorry," says the woman called Alice, leaning across a small table to open a pair of navy-blue curtains. "It's a bit musty. It's been weeks since I had anyone in here."

He looks around. He's in a small timber room with a Velux window in the roof and a glazed door which opens into Alice's back garden. It's furnished spartanly. There's a camp bed on one side, a sink, a fridge, a Baby Belling, a plug-in heater, the table, two plastic chairs, grimy rush matting on the floor. But the timber walls are painted an elegant shade of green and hung with an assortment of very attractive artworks: flowers and faces and buildings seemingly made from tonal slivers of old maps, skilfully collaged together. And by the camp bed is a pretty beaded lamp. The overall effect is quite pleasant. But she's right, it does smell: an unhappy blend of must and damp.

"There's an outdoor toilet next door. No one else uses it. And you can use our downstairs bathroom during the day; it's just off the back porch. Come on. I'll show you." Her tone is clipped and slightly scary.

As he follows her across the gravelled back yard, he takes in the form of her. A tall woman, slim enough, if a bit heavy around the middle. She's dressed in narrow-fitting black jeans and an oversized sweater, presumably to camouflage the heavy middle and accentuate the long legs. She's wearing black boots, slightly in the style of DMs, but not quite. Her hair is a springy mass of caramel and honey and treacle and mud. Bad highlights, he thinks, and then wonders how he has an opinion on such things. Is he a hairdresser?

The tiny door at the back of the house sticks as she attempts to open it and she gives it a well-practised kick at the base. Ahead and down three steps is a galley kitchen, to the left is a cheap plywood door leading into a rather sad bathroom.

"We all use the one upstairs so you'll pretty much have this one to yourself. Shall I put a bath on for you? Warm you up?"

She turns screeching taps before he has answered either way. She pulls up the sleeves of her oversized jumper to stir the water and he notes her elbows. The wrinkled misshapen pockets of them. Forty, forty-five, he thinks to himself. She turns and smiles. "Right," she says. "Let's get you something to eat while that's running. And get these things on the radiator." She takes the damp bits and pieces she found in his pockets from him and he follows her again, into the galley kitchen: walls painted magenta, pots hanging from racks overhead, handmade units in soft oak, a sink full of washing up and a corkboard pinned with children's scribbles. There's a teenage girl sitting at the tiny table wedged into the corner. She glances up at him and then looks questioningly at the woman.

"This is Jasmine. My eldest. This" — she gestures at him — "is a strange man I just picked up on the beach. He's going to sleep in the studio tonight."

The girl called Jasmine raises a pierced eyebrow at her mother and throws him a withering look. "Excellent."

She looks nothing like her mother. She has dark hair hacked — deliberately, he assumes — into a brutal bob, the fringe too high up her forehead, but somehow framing well her square face, her full vermilion lips and heavy eyes. She looks exotic, like a Mexican actress whose name he cannot possibly recall.

Alice throws open a red fridge and says things to him. "Ham sandwich? Bread and pâté? I could heat up some cauliflower cheese? Or there's an old curry. From Saturday. Where are we now? Wednesday. I'm sure it'll be OK. It'll be OK, won't it? That's what curry was invented for, wasn't it? To preserve meat?"

He's finding it hard to assimilate information. To make decisions. This, he suspects, is why he ended up sitting on the beach for more than twelve hours. He was aware that there were options. He just couldn't put the options into any kind of order. Instead he'd sat stultified, inert. Until this strident woman had come along and made a decision for him.

"I really don't mind," he says. "Anything."

"Fuck it," she says, letting the fridge door shut. "I'll order in pizzas."

He feels a surge of relief at another decision being made for him. Then discomfort when he remembers that, bar a loose coin or two, he has no money.

22

"I'm afraid I don't have any money."

"Yeah. I know," says Alice. "We went through your pockets, remember? It's fine. My treat. And this one" — she nods her head in the direction of her daughter — "she lives on fresh air. I always end up throwing hers away anyway. I'll just order what I'd normally order. If you weren't here."

The girl rolls her heavily lined eyes and he follows Alice into a tiny sitting room, bowing his head to miss a low beam. Here sits a small girl with white-blonde curls, nestled into the side of another teenager, this one lanky and of Afro-Caribbean descent. They are watching the television and both turn and look at him with alarm.

Alice is rifling through a drawer in a desk. "This is a man I found on the beach," she says without turning around. She pulls a leaflet from the drawer, closes the drawer and passes the leaflet to the teenage boy. "We're having pizzas," she says. "Choose something."

The boy's face lights up and he sits up straight, unhooking the small girl's arms from around his middle.

"Romaine," says Alice, pointing to the small girl, "and Kai." She points at the tall teenager. "And yes, they're all mine. I'm not a foster parent. Sit down, for goodness' sake."

He lowers himself on to a small floral sofa. It's a nice room. There's a fire burning in the grate, comfortable furniture veering towards the shabbier end of shabby chic but generally well chosen, dark beams and dark-grey walls and Vaseline-glass shaded wall lights.

There's a Victorian street light hanging just outside the window, beyond that a necklace of fat white lights, beyond that the silvery shadows of the sea. Atmospheric. But this Alice is clearly no housekeeper. Dust furs everything, cobwebs hang from the beams, surfaces are cluttered with flotsam and jetsam, and the carpet has possibly never been hoovered.

Alice begins to arrange the things from his pocket across the top of a radiator.

"Train tickets," she mutters, peeling them apart. "Dated yesterday" She peers closer. "Can't make out the time. Kai?" She passes the damp ticket to her son. "Can you read that?"

The boy take the ticket, glances at it, passes it back. "Seven fifty-eight."

"Last train," says Alice. "You would have changed at Doncaster. Got in really late." She carries on sorting through the papers. "Some kind of receipt here. No idea what it says." She adds it to the top of the radiator.

Her face is what he might call handsome. Strong features, a slight dip below each cheekbone, a good mouth. She has the smudged remains of this morning's eyeliner under her eyes, but no other make-up. She's almost beautiful. But there's a hardness to her that sets her jaw at the wrong angle, makes shadows where there should be light.

"Another receipt. Another receipt. A tissue?" She holds it out towards him. He shakes his head and she drops it into the fire. "Well, that's kind of it really. No ID. Nothing. You're a complete mystery."

"What's his name?" asks Romaine.

"I don't know what his name is. And *he* doesn't know what his name is. He's lost his memory." She says this as if it is normal and the small girl furrows her brow.

"Lost it where?"

Alice laughs and says, "Actually, Romaine, you're good at naming things. He can't remember what he's called and we can't call him nothing. What shall we call him?"

The small girl stares at him for a moment. He assumes she'll come up with something childish and nonsensical. But she slants her eyes, purses her lips and then very carefully enunciates the word *Frank*.

"Frank," says Alice, appraising him thoughtfully. "Yes. Frank. Perfect. Clever girl." She touches the girl's curls. "Well, *Frank*" — she smiles at him — "I reckon your bath's run. There's a towel on your bed and soap on the side. By the time you're done, the pizzas should be here."

He can't remember choosing a pizza; he's not sure if Frank is his real name. This woman is making him dizzy with her officious certainty about everything. But he does know that his socks are damp, his underwear is damp, his skin is damp, that he is cold from the inside to the outside and that he wants a hot bath more than anything in the world right now.

"Oh." He remembers something. "Dry clothes. I mean, I'm happy to put these back on. Or I could . . ."

"Kai can lend you some joggers. And a T-shirt. I'll leave them by the back door for you."

"Thank you," he says. "Thank you so much."

As he stands to leave the room he sees her exchange a look with her teenage son, sees the mask of crisp nonchalance slip for a moment. The boy looks worried and annoyed; he shakes his head slightly. She responds with a firm nod. But he can see fear in her eyes, too. As if she's starting to doubt her decision. As if she's starting to wonder why he's in her house.

After all, he could be anyone.

CHAPTER
FOUR

"Tell me a little about your husband," says the policewoman called Beverly. "How old is he?"

Lily pushes down the hem of her top, flattening the fabric against her skin. "He's forty," she says.

She can see the WPC's eyebrow arch, just a fraction. "And you're?"

"I'm twenty-one," she says. It's no big deal, she wants to shout. Nineteen years. In a life of maybe ninety years. So what?

"And his full name?"

"Carl John Robert Monrose."

"Thank you. And this is the address where he lives?" She indicates the small living room of the purpose-built flat where she and Carl have lived since they got back from their honeymoon on Bali.

"Yes," she says. "Of course!" She knows as she says it that she has been rude. She is aware that sometimes her manner can be quite harsh for British people's tastes.

The policewoman gives her a look and then scratches words on to a form with a noisy pen.

"And tell me about yesterday. What time did you last see your husband?"

"He left at seven o'clock. Every morning he leaves at seven o'clock."

"And he goes to work where?"

"He works in London. For a financial services company."

"And have you spoken to his company?"

"Yes! It was the first thing I did!" This woman must think she is an idiot, to call the police before calling his office.

"And what did they say?"

"They said he left work at the normal time. Just as I expected they would say. Carl takes the same train home every day. He can't leave work late or he would miss it."

"OK. And did you speak to him at all? After he left work?"

"No," she said. "But he sent me a text. Look." She switches on her phone and turns it to face the WPC, the text already there, ready to be displayed.

You know what's crazy? This is crazy: I love you more now than I did this morning! I'll see you in an hour! If I could make the train go faster I would! xxxxx.

"And look," she says, scrolling up through their text exchanges. "This from the day before."

How can it be true that I have a wife like you? How did I get so lucky?! I can't wait to be holding you in my arms. Fifty-eight minutes to go!

"See," she says. "This is a man who wants to come home every night more than he wants to do anything else. Do you see now why I know that something bad has happened?"

The WPC passes the phone back to Lily and sighs. "Sounds like he's got it bad," she says, laughing.

"It's not a joke," says Lily.

"No." Abruptly, the policewoman stops smiling. "I didn't say it was."

Lily breathes in hard. She must try harder, she reminds herself, harder to be pleasant. "Sorry," she says. "I'm feeling very stressed. Last night was the first time we've spent a night apart. I didn't sleep. Not one minute." She waves her hands about, desperately, before bringing them back into her lap.

The WPC softens when she sees the tears filming across Lily's eyes and squeezes her hand gently.

"So." She takes her hand back. "You got the text at five last night. Then . . .?"

"Nothing. Nothing. I rang him first just after six, then again and again and again until his phone ran out of charge."

The WPC pauses for a moment and Lily gets the feeling that it is finally sinking in, that for the first time since Carl didn't come home last night someone believes that he might actually be missing and not in another woman's bed.

"Where does he catch his train from?"

"Victoria."

"And always the same one?"

"Yes. The five oh six to East Grinstead."

"Which arrives in Oxted at?"

"Five forty-four. Then it is a fifteen-minute walk from the station to here. So he is home at five fifty-nine. Every night. Every night."

"And do you work, Mrs Monrose?"

"No. I study."

"Whereabouts?"

"Here. It's a correspondence course. Accounting. It's what I was studying at home, in the Ukraine. I left college to be here, with Carl. So, now I finish what I started." She shrugs.

"And how long have you been here? In the UK?"

"One week. And three days."

"Wow," says the WPC. "Not long."

"No. Not long."

"Your English is excellent."

"Thank you. My mother is a translator. She made sure I could speak it as well as she does."

The WPC puts the lid on her pen and looks at Lily thoughtfully. "How did you meet?" she says. "You and your husband?"

"Through my mother. She was translating at a financial services conference in Kiev. They needed people to look after the delegates — you know, show them about, get them taxis, that kind of thing. I needed the cash. I was put in charge of Carl and some of his colleagues. It was obvious from minute one that I would marry him. From minute one."

The WPC stares at Lily, seemingly mesmerised. "Wow," she says. "Wow."

"Yes," says Lily. "It was very wow."

"OK." The policewoman slips the pen into her pocket and folds up her notepad. "I'll see what I can do. Not sure we've got quite enough yet to open this up as a missing person. But call again if he doesn't show up tonight."

Lily's heart drops, brick-heavy inside her. "What?"

"I'm sure it's nothing sinister," the WPC says. "Honestly. Nine times out of ten it's just something completely innocuous. I'm sure he'll be home before bedtime."

"Really?" she says. "I know you don't believe that. I know you believe me. I know you do."

The WPC sighs. "Your husband, he's a grown man. He's not vulnerable. I can't open a case. But I tell you what, I'll check his details against our database, see if anyone matching his description has been brought in for any reason."

Lily clutches her heart. "Brought in?"

"Yes. You know. Brought into the police station. For questioning. And I'll cross-reference with local hospitals. See if they've treated him."

"Oh God." Lily has been picturing this all night long. Carl under the wheels of a bus, stabbed and left for dead in an underpass, floating face down in the dark water of the River Thames.

"It's all I can do for now."

Lily realises that the WPC is doing her a favour and manages a smile. "Thank you," she says. "I really appreciate that."

"I'll need a photo, though. Do you have a recent one?"

"Yes, yes, of course." Lily fumbles with her handbag, opens her purse, pulls out the photo-booth snap she has in there: Carl looking serious and handsome. She passes it to the WPC, expecting her to pass some kind of comment on how incredibly good-looking he is. Maybe say something about his resemblance to Ben Affleck. But the policewoman doesn't; she merely tucks it into her notebook and says, "I'll get it back to you, I promise. In the meantime, speak to his friends and family. His colleagues. Maybe someone there can shed some light."

After the policewoman leaves, Lily stands for a few minutes and stares out of the window. Below her is a small car park. Carl's black Audi A5 is there, where he parked it after their trip to the supermarket on Sunday. Just the thought of supermarket shopping with Carl makes her want to curl herself into a tight ball and howl.

Then she turns to face their home. The flat that Carl chose for them, a brand-new flat in a brand-new development, the kitchen never used before they used it, the toilet still with a paper band across the lid. A brand-new place to start their brand-new life. With a heavy heart she starts opening drawers and searching through paperwork, trying to find the one small thing she didn't know about her husband that might unlock the mystery of where he has gone.

CHAPTER
FIVE

The rain finally stops at five in the morning. The sun's gentle ascent turns the sky silver-grey and the insolent clamour of birdsong and rasp of boats being heaved down the slipway brings Alice to consciousness. It's a rough awakening. She fell asleep only an hour ago, having spent the preceding five hours in a state of heightened alertness, aware of every tonal shift in the background hum, every creak of the old house, every flicker of moonlight ricocheting off the surface of the sea beyond her window.

It isn't the first time there's been a strange man sleeping in the studio. She's rented it out to many strangers over the years. And to strangers much stranger than Frank. But at least she knew who they were, where they came from, why they were there. They had a context.

But this man, "Frank", he'd entered stage left, silently, without a script. Charming as he is — and he is, actually — it's unnerving. The bits and pieces in his pockets revealed nothing other than that he'd travelled to Ridinghouse Bay from King's Cross on Tuesday night and that at some other point in his recent history he'd spent twenty-three pounds in Robert Dyas and bought a bagel and a can of Coke from Sainsbury's.

He'd appeared in the kitchen after his bath, in Kai's clothes, looking pink and raw and deeply embarrassed. His thick hazel hair was damp and wavy and he was barefoot. Lovely feet, Alice had noted. For the record. She'd watched him eating his pizza, seen him trying to control the impulse to stuff it down his throat with pure, wild hunger. She'd offered him beer and he'd looked confused for a moment, possibly trying to decide whether he was a beer-drinker or not. "Go on," she'd said. "At least we'll know that about you then." So, he'd had a beer and it had been a tiny bit awkward, the four of them standing around eating pizza with a big scared man in a teenager's hoodie. Hard to know what to say, really.

When he'd gone to bed her children had all turned and looked at her with cold disapproval.

"What", Jasmine had managed eventually, "are you doing? Mum?"

"Where's your compassion?" she'd said. "Poor man. No jacket. No money." She'd gestured at the kitchen window, at the fat, angry rain pounding off the glass. "In this."

"There's other places he could have gone," Kai had added.

"Yeah," she'd said. "Like where?"

"I dunno. A B and B."

"He's got no money, Kai. That's the whole point."

"Yeah, well, I don't see why that's our problem."

34

"Jesus," Alice had groaned, despite knowing that her children were right, "you kids. You've got no human decency, have you? What do they teach you at school these days?"

"Er, about paedophiles and conmen and voyeurs and rapists and—"

"They do not," she'd interjected. "The media teaches you all that and I've told you all a million times: people are fundamentally good. He's a lost soul. I'm the Good Samaritan. He'll be gone this time tomorrow."

"Lock the back door," Kai had said. "*Double*-lock it."

She'd pooh-poohed his concern at the time but later, after calling out goodnight into the dark space between the back door and the studio, she'd locked the door behind her. Bolted it too. And then barely slept. She'd imagined, at intervals, a big man-hand held tight across the soft jaw of her sleeping baby girl, her green eyes stretched wide with terror. Or the *pad pad pad* of a strange man in her living room, silently opening drawers in search of gold and iPads. Or her older daughter being watched in silhouette as she absent-mindedly undressed in front of the window. Even though her window faced the wrong way. And she would never do that anyway because the ridiculous child thought she was *fat*. But still.

Alice gives up on the notion of sleep and decides to capitalise on the early start. She crosses the room and unplugs the iPad from the charger, switches it to the webcam app, watches her parents' empty living room for a while. Since they both became . . . well, *ill*, is how she prefers to refer to it, rather than demented, loop-the-loop, bat-shit nuts, they have started to rise later and later. Their morning carer comes at ten and has to lure them out of bed like a pair of sleep-starved teenagers.

She turns off the iPad and pulls open her curtains. The sea is blanket-flat after the rain, pink and yellow as the sun rises over it, as lush as the Caribbean. The fairy lights are still lit, as are the street lights. The pavement below is petrol-black and gleaming. It couldn't be any prettier.

Alice showers, moving quietly around the house, not wanting to rouse anyone any earlier than necessary. In her room she appraises herself. She never normally has time to appraise herself. Normally she rises too late to do any appraising, rises with just enough time to make sure she doesn't leave the house naked. Her hair, she realises, is verging on bizarre. Her last set of highlights were quite bold, or, as Jasmine said at the time, *stripy*. And now the roots are coming through in vivid salt and pepper. And being out in the rain a lot the day before has done it even fewer favours.

She wipes away the shadows of yesterday's quickly applied eyeliner and starts hunting through the top drawer of her dressing table for her make-up bag, the one she usually gets out only on special occasions. She tells herself that she is doing this because she has the time to do it. That it has nothing to do with the handsome man in her studio room. She pulls the crazy badger hair up into a bun, finds clean jeans, a checked shirt that skims her tummy but clings lightly to the outline of her breasts, a favourite pair of earrings with greeny-blue stones that echo the colour of her eyes.

Alice is a woman often described by men as sexy. Dirty, too. She's never traded on being pretty. Never thought she'd do better in a tight dress and high heels (although when she does make the effort it doesn't seem to hurt). Generally Alice lets it all hang out. But not this morning, for some strange reason.

Romaine appears at her bedroom door, blonde ringlets in a disaster, drooping jersey pyjamas sagging at the crotch. Together with Griff, they tiptoe down the narrow, open-tread staircase that leads to the hallway. The other dogs greet them silently with mouths stretched into black-lipped smiles and tails beating against the flagstones. Alice holds her breath vaguely as they enter the kitchen, aware of what lies beyond the back door, nervous of the unknowingness of the day ahead. She loads the dogs' bowls with meat, makes Romaine a toasted bagel with peanut butter, herself an oversized mug of tea and a bowl of All Bran. All the while she has half an eye on the back door. Wondering. Unsettled.

But by eight thirty Kai and Jasmine are on the school bus and she is gone from the house with the dogs and Romaine and there is no sign of him. The studio is still and silent, as though there is no one in there at all.

Derry looks at her curiously at the school gates, which are only just being unlocked by the caretaker. "You're early," she says. "And . . ." She peers more closely at her, ". . . you're wearing make-up."

"Whatevs," says Alice.

"What's going on?"

"The man came in," says Romaine. "The wet man from the beach."

Alice rolls her eyes. "He didn't *come in*," she corrects. "I asked him in. To dry off. To have a bath, something to eat. I'm pretty sure he's already gone."

But when she gets home forty minutes later the curtains are pulled open in the studio and she can see movement inside. She rubs the dirty puddle speckles from the dogs with an old towel, checks her reflection briefly and switches on the kettle.

His dreams were remarkable last night. After so many hours of blankness, of a head full of nothing, to be plunged suddenly into this ethereal world of people and experiences and places was quite exhilarating. He clutches on to the fading fragments as he comes to, knowing that there might be something there, a clue to tie him back to himself. But they float away, hopelessly, intangibly.

He sits up in bed and rubs his face hard. The curtains in this room are gossamer thin and the light outside is the particular acid-blue of a morning after rain. He can hear scuffling at his door and peers through the curtains into the earth-dark eyes of a dog. The dog looks as if it is about to smile, but then the mouth stretches further until its teeth are revealed and then its gums and the dog snarls and he lets the curtain

38

drop. At least he can remember where he is now, he thinks. At least he can remember tea in a thermos and pizza in a kitchen and a leggy woman with thick blonde hair and a hot bath in a mouldy, echoing bathroom. And he remembers the name *Frank*, bestowed on him last night by the little girl with the golden ringlets.

He wants to go to the toilet, he wants to brush his teeth, but the dog is going mental outside the door and he has no idea if it's the kind of dog that just barks for fun. It's a . . . He searches for the name of the breed, but it's gone. Assuming he ever knew. But it's the sort of dog that thugs have. Muscly and square with a huge jaw.

He opens the curtains and stares at the dog. The dog barks louder. And then, from the tiny door at the back of the house, Alice appears. She looks cross and shouts something at the dog, and grabs it by its collar; then she sees his face and she walks towards him.

"Have you remembered who you are yet?" she asks, handing him a mug of tea with one hand, keeping hold of the dog with the other.

He takes the mug and says, "No. Still no idea. Had lots of weird dreams but I can't remember any of them." He shrugs and rests the mug on the table by the door.

"Well," she says, "come inside when you're ready. I'll leave the door open. I can make you some breakfast if you're hungry. I've got fresh eggs."

It's quiet in the cottage when he bows his head down to pass through the back door a while later. No children. Alice is looking at something on an iPad and sighing a lot.

"Where is everyone?" he asks.

She looks at him as though he's simple and says, "School."

"Ah, yes. Of course."

She switches off the iPad and folds over its case. "Do you reckon you've got any children?"

"Christ." The thought had not occurred to him. "I don't know. Maybe. Maybe I've got loads. I don't even know how old I am. How old do you reckon I am?"

She examines his face with her grimy, green-blue eyes. "Somewhere between thirty-five and forty-five, I reckon."

He nods. "How old are you?"

"You're not supposed to ask a lady that."

"Sorry."

"It's OK. I'm not really a lady. And I'm forty-one."

"And your children," he says. "Their father?"

"*Ers*," she says. "Fathers. I've totally failed in the providing-a-conventional-family-unit-for-my-children department. Jasmine's dad was a holiday romance. Brazil. Didn't know I was pregnant until I'd been home for two weeks and had no way of tracking him down. Kai's dad was my next-door neighbour in Brixton. We were — excuse the expression — fuck buddies. He just disappeared one day, when Kai was about five. A new family moved in. That was that. And Romaine's dad was the love of my life but . . ." She pauses. "He went mental. Did a bad thing. He lives in Australia now. So." She sighs.

He pauses, trying to find something to say that won't sound like he's insulting her. "Have you never been married, then?"

She laughed drily. "No. Never managed to snare a man."

He pauses again, looks down at his hands. "I'm not wearing a wedding ring."

"No, you're not. Doesn't mean you're not married though. You might be one of those bastards who refuses to wear one."

"Yes," he says vaguely. "I guess."

She sighs and pushes the sleeves of her checked shirt up her arms. She has a long dip between her radius and the flesh of her forearm, which reminds him of someone.

And there! Immediately, overpoweringly. His mother. His mother has that dip. She also has that little pouch of crinkled flesh at the nib of her elbow that he noticed yesterday on Alice. He has a mother. A mother with arms! He smiles and says, "I just remembered something! I just remembered my mother's arms."

"Oh," she says, brightening. "That's good. Can you remember any other bits of her?"

He shakes his head sadly.

"Listen," she says. "I went on to Google last night, to look up your symptoms. Apparently, unless this is all a massive wind-up, you are in something called a 'fugue state'."

"Right."

"Does that mean anything to you?"

"No."

"OK." She runs her hand over her forehead. "Well. It's a kind of amnesia, but it's not brought on by head trauma or alcohol or drugs or anything like that. It's usually caused by an emotional trauma. Or a shock to the system. Often it can be caused by seeing or remembering something from your past that you might have been repressing. And the brain kind of shuts down, like a self-protection mechanism, and people do just what you've done. Turn up in random places with no memory of who they are or where they come from or what the fuck they're doing there. It's pretty fascinating actually."

"What happens to these other people? I mean, will I get better?"

"Well, that's the excellent news. Well, sort of excellent. They all recover. Sometimes within hours, usually days, occasionally a few weeks. But it is temporary. You will get your memory back."

"Wow," he says, nodding slowly. He feels numb. He knows he should be pleased. But the concept of remembering who he is is hard to grasp when he can't remember who he is.

"And look," she continues, "you just remembered your mother's arm. I mean, it's not exactly a *revelation*. But it shows it's all still there, just waiting to be unlocked. So, the big question is: What now?"

"What do you mean?" *What now.* It's a phrase that holds no meaning for him.

"I mean, we should probably take you to the police, shouldn't we?"

His response to this suggestion is visceral. All his muscles contract, his fists curl tightly inwards, his breathing quickens, his pulse speeds up. It's the strongest onslaught of sensation he's had since he found himself on the beach two nights ago.

"No," he says, as softly as he can, but he can hear the . . . what is it? Anger? Terror? He can hear it in the bass of his voice. He has a sensation of pushing someone, pushing them hard against a wall. He feels hot breath against his cheek. "No," he says again, even more softly. "I don't think I want to do that. I think . . . Can I just stay here for one more night? See if I get my memory back first. Maybe we can go another time. If . . ."

Alice nods, but he senses that she is unconvinced. "Sure," she says after a short pause. "One more night. Sure. But after that, if you still don't know who the hell you are, you know. Because that room, I usually rent it out, extra income, so . . ."

"I understand. One more night."

She smiles uncertainly. "Good. But in the meantime, keep 'em coming. The memories, I mean." She stands up and reaches for a box of eggs so fresh that there are feathers stuck to the cardboard. "Fried?" she says. "Scrambled?"

"I have no idea," he says. "You decide."

CHAPTER
SIX

Lily sits in the waiting room at the police station. She is clutching a carrier bag containing a small album of wedding photos and Carl's passport. She found nothing else in her search of his drawers and filing boxes. Nothing at all. No baby photos. No birth certificate. No identifying paperwork of any kind. There was one locked drawer but when she put her hand into it from the drawer above, it seemed to be empty. It was rather strange, she thought. But she assumes that everything must be at his mother's house. Carl is a tidy man and a minimalist. It makes sense that he would not want to clutter up his beautiful new flat with things he has no use for.

In her other hand she holds a paper cup of coffee. She shouldn't have bought it; she has thirty-eight pounds in cash in her purse and no access to a bank account. Carl paid for everything, He was setting up a separate bank account for her, was going to put money into it for her every month until she finished her accountancy course. She will have to ask her mother to send her some money. But she knows it will take time for her mother to do that. So. Thirty-eight pounds. She should not have bought the big coffee. But she needs it. She has not slept at all.

The big policewoman called Beverly appears with a small smile. "Good morning, Mrs Monrose. Do you want to come this way? I'll find us a room where we can have a chat."

Lily follows her down a corridor and into a small room that smells of stale cake.

"So," the WPC says as they both sit down. "Still no sign of Mr Monrose, I assume?"

"No. Of course. Or I would not be here."

"It was just a turn of phrase, Mrs Monrose."

"Yes," says Lily. "I understand."

Beverly smiles a strange smile. "So, you want to make an official missing-person report." She clicks a pen and turns a page in her notebook.

"Yes. Please."

"I did run your husband's name through our system yesterday, Mrs Monrose. Nothing came up. He's not in any of the London hospitals; nothing came up at any of the Met stations."

Lily has no idea what a "met station" is but nods, because she's already sure this woman thinks she is an idiot. "And what about the police stations?" she says. "Did you check there?"

Beverly gives her an odd look. "Yes," she says. "Like I said. Nothing."

Lily nods again. "Anyway," she says, "I searched the flat. For anything I could find. And, you know, it's a new flat. We only just moved in. I think, probably, he has left all his paperwork with his mother."

"And have you been in touch with his mother?"

"I have not. I do not know where she lives. Her phone number is on Carl's phone. It is not written down anywhere."

"Her name?"

"Maria. Or something like that."

"So, Maria Monrose?" She looks at Lily for confirmation before writing it down.

"And where does she live?"

"I don't know. Somewhere to the west. Beginning with an S."

Beverly grimaces. "Slough?" she suggests. "Swindon?"

"I don't know," say Lily with a shrug. "Maybe."

"OK. And what about other family? Brothers? Sisters?"

"He has a sister called Suzanne. Or something. She lives in the same place."

"Married?"

"I don't know. Yes. I think. I think there is a nephew."

"So, possibly Suzanne Monrose. Possibly not?" She writes this down.

Lily pulls the carrier bag on to her lap and feels for the passport. "I found this," she says, placing it in front of Beverly.

Beverly flicks though it and says, "It's current. That's good. At least we can eliminate the possibility that he's gone abroad."

Lily snorts. "Of course he has not."

She sees Beverly roll her eyes very slightly and take in a small breath of impatience. "I'll need to keep this," she says, touching the passport, "run it through our system."

"Sure. And then there is this." Lily slides the photo album across the table towards Beverly. "Some better photos of him. Ones where he is smiling so you can get a better idea of what kind of a man he is. So you can see that he was happy and not about to run away from me."

She watches Beverly flick through the album. "And this was in . . .?"

"Kiev. Yes. He wanted to marry me in my home country, to be surrounded by my family and my friends. He wanted me to be happy and relaxed. Not stressed out in a strange place. With strange people. He is the best man in the world. My friend, my father, my lover, my husband. Everything." She finds she has her fist clutched against her heart and that there are tears in her eyes. "I am sorry," she says.

"Don't be sorry," says Beverly. "It's understandable for you to feel this way. Now, is there anyone you can call? Any relatives in this country? Anyone who can stay with you for a while? Take care of you?"

"No." She bunches her hands together in her lap. "No. There is no one here."

"Oh," says Beverly. "That's a shame. Well, maybe you could ask someone from home to come over for a while?"

"Yes. Maybe."

On the staircase up to her flat later, Lily is subsumed by a horrible blend of excitement and dread. Might he be there, she thinks, on the other side of the door?

Sitting in his rumpled shirt and tie with some story of woe? But she knows with every fall of her step that he will not be. She pushes open the door into a vacuum of aloneness. The stillness is appalling. She has never been alone before. Never. She stands for a moment, rocking slightly as though the emptiness has a hold of her, is trying to shake reality into her. She hears a single drop of water hit the bottom of the kitchen sink, the rumble of the fridge, the sound of the front door downstairs being opened and closed. And then she jumps at the sound of the phone.

She runs to the phone and grabs it up. "Yes."

"Hi, it's WPC Traviss. Is that Mrs Monrose?"

"Yes. Yes it is."

"I'm calling because . . . well, this is quite strange, but we've run your husband's passport through our system and, well, to put it quite plainly, Mrs Monrose, your husband doesn't technically exist."

"I beg your pardon?"

"His passport is fake, Mrs Monrose. There is no Carl John Robert Monrose."

PART TWO

CHAPTER
SEVEN

1993

They rented the same house every year. A higgledy-piggledy coastguard's cottage in the town of Ridinghouse Bay in East Yorkshire. It was, perversely, not as nice as their own actual home in Croydon, which was modern and clean and had shiny white bathrooms and cream carpeting and double-glazing.

Rabbit Cottage was damp and ill-furnished. The kitchen was small and the walls were nicotine-beige. There was a tiny bedroom off the kitchen and two even tinier bedrooms on the top floor; the mattresses were lumpy and all the bedding was worn and holey. Things leaked when it rained and there was a strange odour about the place: briny and mackerely, damp and smoky. But for some reason Gray and Kirsty's parents were entranced by the place. Something to do with the atmosphere, they said, and the people. Not to mention the views and the air and the walks and the fish. They'd loved the place as children, all wellies and crabbing and funfairs and chips. But now Kirsty was fifteen, Gray was seventeen and Rabbit Cottage was virtually the last place on earth either of them wanted to be. They arrived on a damp July afternoon in poor spirits after what felt like a much-longer-than-it-used-to-be journey up the M1, during which Tony, their dad, had refused to let them put on their own music and did the thing he always did of chasing local radio stations in and out of frequency to keep himself abreast of traffic reports.

Parking restrictions had changed in the years since they'd first come to Ridinghouse Bay. Back then you could park right outside the house and unload all your stuff in the middle of throngs of holidaymakers. Nowadays you had to park your car in a car park on the edge of town and walk in. So here they were, unloading cardboard boxes packed with breakfast cereals and long-life milk, toilet rolls and Heinz soups, and trudging up the hill into town with suitcases and rolled-up towels and duvets. A light summer drizzle fell upon them as they walked and by the time they'd emptied the car and closed the door of Rabbit Cottage behind them they were steaming like New York pavements and all in rather bad tempers.

"Christ," said Gray, resting a cardboard box on the Formica-topped table in the kitchen and looking about. "Is it possible that they have actually painted Rabbit Cottage?" It was true that the walls had lost their tarry patina and there were also "NO SMOKING" signs attached here and there about the place that had not been present before.

He heaved his rucksack up the narrow staircase and dropped it on to the single bed (unmade, sheets and blankets left in a folded pile at the foot of the bare bed). His room overlooked the sea. His parents liked the room at the back because it was quieter; the street below could get quite noisy during these summer months: there were three pubs on this road alone, not to mention the steam fair that came to town every summer with its loud pump organ music, which carried up the coast on the slightest breeze.

But Gray didn't mind the noise. It made a nice change to the silence of the quiet street they lived on in Croydon, where the only noises at this time of year were droning lawnmowers and honey bees. He liked the sound of drunk people calling out to each other, the echo and reverb of footsteps on the cobbles in the dark.

They were here for two weeks. Gray had tried to persuade his parents to allow him to return home a week early; there was a party he wanted to go to, there was a girl he liked. Plus the weather forecast for the south was glorious in comparison. But they'd said, "No." They'd said: "Next year. When you're eighteen." And Kirsty had looked at him with searing, beseeching eyes, a look that said: *No, please don't leave me here alone*.

They were reasonably close, as far as brothers and sisters went. She'd played him well as a small child; gone to him with sore knees and unlaced shoes; left him alone when he asked her to. They looked out for each other in a rather detached way, like well-meaning but somewhat reserved next-door neighbours. So, he'd agreed to the full two weeks and hoped that the girl he liked would still be available when he got back.

Downstairs, Gray's dad was building a fire and his mum was unpacking food into cracked Formica-covered kitchen cabinets. Kirsty was on the sofa folded into a pile of gangly limbs and cheap knitwear, reading a magazine. Outside, the rain was still spritzing against the windowpanes but a band of hopeful brightness sat on the horizon forcing a gap between the clouds.

"I'm going out," said Gray.

"Going where?" asked his dad.

"Just for a walk up the prom."

"In this?" His dad indicated the rain-spattered windows.

"I've got a waterproof. And anyway, looks like it's brightening."

Kirsty looked up from her magazine. "Can I come?"

"Yeah, sure."

She raced to the front door, pulled on her trainers and grabbed a cagoule from the coat pegs.

"Don't be long," Mum called from the kitchen. "I'm making a pot of tea and there'll be cake."

Away from the claustrophobia of Rabbit Cottage, Gray felt his temples relax, his jaw loosen, the cool rain freshen his travel-worn skin. She was almost as tall as him now, his sister, all legs and hair, not quite grown into herself but almost there. The resemblance between them was startling enough, he hoped, for it to be obvious that the gawky, scruffy girl in a damp cagoule, patterned nylon jumper and faded baggy jeans walking alongside him was not romantically connected to him in any way. She was a slow developer. She'd worn her hair in a plait down her back until only recently and still didn't wear make-up. But she was suddenly quite desirable, he could see that, raw and new like a half-blossomed flower, embarrassingly beautiful in fact.

He felt a surge of awful fear rise through him, a strange mix of disgust and tenderness. Disgust at himself for being a man, for every bad thing he'd ever thought about a girl, for his base instincts, his low-level throbbing urges, predatory needs, filthy mind, for all of it. Disgust at the knowledge that now men like him would look at his sister and think things and feel things and then purge themselves over her. And tenderness because she did not know.

They walked in silence for a few moments, Gray absorbing and processing, the rain drying, and there, at last, a blade of sunshine at their feet.

"Have you got any money?" asked Kirsty.

He felt his pockets for coins, pulled out a pound and some mixed change. "A couple of quid. Why?"

"Sweets?"

He rolled his eyes, but tipped the coins into her upheld palm. She'd had her braces off a few weeks ago and was celebrating by eating as many hard, chewy sweets as she could. He watched her shuffle into a gift shop, one of those with cone-shaped bags of floss hanging by the door, carousels of postcards, garrotted nets of buckets and spades. He turned and watched the sun filter through the striated clouds over the sea, the light changing from gold to silver, the sea glittering in response. Further ahead he saw the steam fair. It was empty; no one came to the fair in the rain — all those damp seats.

Kirsty returned, offered him a paper bag of Cola Cubes and some of his coins. He took a sweet. She put her hand to her forehead to shield her eyes from the sharpness of the sun. "Two weeks," she said with a sigh.

"Exactly."

"Shall we go and see if they're showing anything half-decent at the cinema?"

Gray nodded and followed her away from the sea-front towards the high road. The cinema was housed in a damp, one-storey breeze-block cave just off the main road. It showed one film at a time and seated a hundred people.

"*Cliffhanger*," he read from the poster outside. "Fuck's sake. I've already seen it."

Kirsty shrugged. "I haven't."

"Well, I don't want to see it again. It's all about not knowing how it ends."

Gray looked closer to see if the programme was set to change at all over the next two weeks. Behind him stood his sister, sucking a Cola Cube, one hand in the pocket of her cagoule, entirely oblivious to the young man who'd just stopped on the other side of the street, his eye caught first by her long legs and then by the way her brown hair fell in damp waves around her face, framing high cheekbones and narrow brown eyes, her pretty mouth clamped around a sweet, sucking hard on it, her gaze neutral, placid, soft.

He continued to stare at Kirsty as she followed Gray towards the high street. He had inventoried everything about her by the time they turned the corner. Her big feet, slightly turned in. Her bust, larger than expected, cocooned beneath her shapeless jumper. Her face, devoid of make-up, natural, unlike so many girls his

56

age. No earrings. A paper bag of sweets. The awkwardness of her gait as she followed behind that boy (her brother? There was a resemblance and she didn't seem to have any need to be physically close to him).

Kirsty and Gray continued on their way and the man thought about following them, but in a town this small their paths would be sure to cross again so he walked on, a small smile pulling at the corners of his mouth, as though enjoying a private joke with himself.

CHAPTER
EIGHT

Alice feels strange in her room at the top of the house. All day yesterday she'd felt strange because that man was sitting on the beach in the rain. Now she is feeling strange because that same man is in her shed. His presence is benign but somehow unnerving. The emptiness of him. All the spaces and gaps. But more than that, the pure maleness of him. Somehow his lack of identity has distilled him down to an essence of raw masculinity. The fact of his gender is irrefutable and Alice . . . well, Alice has not had sex for a long, long time and Alice is a woman who likes to have sex. Her whole life has been shaped — virtually destroyed — by her sexual desires.

She pulls on her reading glasses and she positions a map of Saint-Tropez under the Anglepoise lamp. She has already sketched out the pieces of the rose petals and she slices through them now, slowly, adeptly, with a scalpel. The thought of Saint-Tropez, of steamer chairs and chilled champagne by an aqua pool, of waiters in white linen and tanned men in swimming trunks, is stirring her. She can almost hear the background murmur of muted conversation, feel the hands of some unknown lover rubbing cream into her shoulders, and soon enough those anonymous hands become the hands of the man in the shed and Alice is thinking of those same hands as they used a knife to saw effortlessly through the thick slab of farmhouse toast she'd made him earlier. Good hands. Good wrists. And then she is thinking of all of him, because clean and dry in Kai's hoodie, he cuts an impressive figure. Not too tall, probably just an inch or two taller than her, but solid. No weak points in his physiology. And his hazel eyes, soft with need and confusion.

Apart from that moment, when she'd suggested taking him to the police station. She'd seen something entirely different pass over him then. A wash of fear and anger, gone before she'd had a chance to analyse it, leaving her wondering if she'd imagined it.

She pushes the thought of him from her mind. Men are no longer on her agenda. Her children are her priority now. Her children and her job. She excises the petal-shaped pieces of map from the sheet and places them side by side. Avenue des Canebiers. Chemin de l'Estagnet. Rue Cavaillon. Names that talk of palm trees and open-top cars, hotels with striped awnings and valet parking. She shouldn't feel jealous, though. She has so much here. There are even palm trees on the other side of the bay. Two of them.

A ringing of the brass bell above her front door below makes her jump slightly. This is followed by the clatter of three sets of dog claws against the wooden stairs and some exuberant barking. She peers over her desk and looks downwards where she sees the distinctive hennaed topknot of Derry Dynes.

"Coming!" she calls out. She has to part the dogs forcefully at the front door to reach the handle and then hold them back to prevent them from knocking Derry down.

"Hello, friend," she says. "To what do I owe the pleasure?"

Derry is peering over Alice's shoulder with body language that doesn't appear very social. "I saw Jasmine earlier," she says. "She told me that man is in your house."

Alice sighs and pushes some hair behind her ear. She's angry with herself for not briefing the children to keep Frank a secret. She doesn't mind Derry knowing, but if anyone else found out . . .

"He's not *in the house*," she snaps. "He's in the shed."

She holds the door open and the dogs back so that Derry can pass through.

"You're mad," Derry says, looking this way and that as she passes through to the living room. "Jasmine says he has no memory."

She turns, satisfied that "the man" is not in the living room, and heads for the kitchen.

Alice sighs again and follows her. "It's not as bad as it sounds."

"I told you not to get involved," Derry says. "You said you wouldn't." She peers through the window in the back door across the courtyard towards the shed. "Christ, Al, what if the school find out? What if . . ." She stops and sighs. "Come on. After last year, Al. You can't just bring strange men into the house."

60

Alice knows exactly what Derry's talking about, but she's not in the mood to hear it. "I told you. He's not in the house. He's in the shed. And we kept the back door double-locked last night."

"That's not the point. It all sounds really dodgy. This whole 'memory loss' thing. Sounds like a scam."

Now Alice tuts. "Oh, for God's sake. It is not a scam. You are such a conspiracy theorist."

"Is he out there now?" she asks, pulling two of Alice's mugs from a hook and flicking on the kettle.

"As far as I know," says Alice. "I haven't heard him leave."

"Get him in here," says Derry, dropping a green tea teabag into her mug and an Earl Grey into Alice's.

Alice doesn't move for a moment.

"Go on," says Derry. "Tell him the kettle's on."

"You do know I'm supposed to be working, don't you?"

"Later," she says, "you can work later. This won't take long."

Alice doesn't argue. The basis of her friendship with Derry is that Derry is always right.

She touches her hair before opening the back door, checking that it's in place. She cups her hand to her mouth and breathes into it; she grimaces. Tea breath. The curtains are open in the shed and she knocks gently at the door. "Frank," she says, "it's me. Alice. Just taking a break from work, wondered if you fancied coming in for a cuppa."

There's no reply, so she knocks again. "Frank?" She pushes open the door and peers through the gap. The bed is made, Kai's hoodie and joggers are folded into a neat pile on the end. The room is empty.

"Well," she says to Derry a moment later, "looks like you can stop freaking out. He's gone."

"Gone, gone?"

"I don't know," she says. She looks around the kitchen, notices the mug she'd made his tea in earlier, sitting on the draining board, upside down. She scouts for a note of some kind, but there's nothing. Sadness plummets through her; she feels heavy-limbed with disappointment. And then she feels concern, a burn of anxiety and fear. She thinks of his hazel eyes, his woolly schoolboy hair, his utter vulnerability. She cannot imagine him out there, alone. She really cannot.

"Well," says Derry, "let's hope so. The last thing you need."

"Yes," says Alice, "he probably was."

He feels as though he's on a conveyor belt, being carried along by external forces. He feels like a sack of dust being dragged down the street. He sees a bench ahead and he veers towards it, almost getting knocked over by a woman on a bike with a pannier full of fruit. She looks at him strangely and he wonders if maybe he looks as mad as he feels.

As he lay on the bed in Alice's shed after breakfast this morning he had experienced not memories as such, but strong sensations, much like the one he'd had when Alice had suggested taking him to the police station. Terrible dark waves of doom. A sense that something somewhere was horribly broken and that there was nothing he could do to fix it. But more than that, there were flashes of bright whiteness, like the ricochet of sunlight off a passing car, momentarily blinding and unbalancing, and behind the flashes were pictures, he knew, pieces of the jigsaw, if he could only see them.

He needs to keep walking. He needs to find the thing that brought him to this northern seaside town. But as he gets to his feet he has another flash of whiteness and falls back on to the bench. He squeezes his eyes closed tight, desperately trying to find the edges of the hidden image. And then he sees it. A barley-twist pole, a pastel-coloured horse, a girl with brown hair; she goes up, she goes down, she's smiling and waving and then she's gone.

He laughs at the power of it, after all these hours of nothing. "Shit!" he says to himself. "Shit!"

He jumps up from the bench, feeling himself drawn towards the seafront across the road. He looks down at the crescent of the beach, empty on this brisk April day, and tries to pull something from the view, some essence of the moment he just remembered. But nothing comes and he heads down the steps built into the seawall. He runs his hand down the painted metal handrail; a few flakes of peeling paint come off under his grasp. He fits his feet carefully into each narrow step, breathing in the smell of fish-guts and brine. Has he been here before? Is it possible? And if he has, then why? And when? And who is the girl on the carousel, the smiling, beautiful girl with chestnut hair, lost in her moment, oblivious to his eyes upon her?

At the thought of the girl he feels another wave of doom wash over him. His body, no longer his own it seems, reacts by regurgitating the eggs and toast Alice cooked for him earlier on. Afterwards he is shaky and weak. He returns to the position he'd adopted during his first hours in Ridinghouse Bay, on his haunches, on the beach, staring out to sea as though waiting for the ocean to bring him something.

CHAPTER
NINE

1993

After the damp start to their holiday, there followed three days of warm sunshine. And sunshine meant days on the beach. Beneath Rabbit Cottage, the beach was narrow and gravelly, full of glittering rock pools and fishing boats. As children they'd spent their days down there, picking their way across the slimy rocks in plastic boots and sou'westers. But now they were older they preferred to take towels and sun cream, a windbreak and folding chairs and walk a quarter of a mile across town to the wider sandy beach below the high street. Here there was a café hewn from the cliff face serving fast food and ice creams and beer in plastic cups. There was a shower and a lifeguard and various rides for small children. It wasn't exactly Blackpool Pleasure Beach but it was fine for a small town like Ridinghouse Bay. So here they were, Tuesday morning, not yet warm enough for swimwear, Tony wearing a short-sleeved shirt unbuttoned over denim shorts, Pam in cycling shorts and a baggy T-shirt with a cartoon dog on the front, Gray in Hawaiian-print surfer shorts and Kirsty in a black halter-neck bikini top and a denim skirt. And there he was. That guy. Gray couldn't quite think of him as a "man". He looked around eighteen, Gray supposed. But unlike himself, he was not shackled to a family.

He'd been there on Sunday, and yesterday too: alone, stretched out on a white towel in black swimming trunks, black sunglasses, a paperback novel, a Walkman. Every now and then he would sit up, wrap his arms around his legs and stare out into the sea, moodily. He was sitting close enough for Gray to be able to see the towelling indents in the skin of his back, close enough to catch the smell of aftershave on every breeze, to hear the tinny beat of Cypress Hill through his earphones. It was a matter of a few inches, his infringement of their personal space, but Gray could feel it in every fibre of his being, like a Chinese burn.

The man stood up now, his back facing them, and stretched ostentatiously, letting each set of well-formed muscles ripple in turn. Then, feigning nonchalance, he rubbed at the stubble on his chin as if he alone possessed sufficient testosterone to produce such rough facial hair. Slowly he walked past them, and headed for the beachfront café where he bought himself a small beer and drank it standing up, his elbow against the bar, his legs crossed at an angle, his gaze fixed unabashedly on Kirsty.

"I see your admirer's back," said Tony, talking over the top of a *Daily Express*.

Kirsty shrugged and looked at the sand. "He's not my admirer," she said unconvincingly.

Tony just smirked and went back to his newspaper.

"He's very good-looking, Kirst," said Pam, and Kirsty shushed furiously at her.

"He can't hear," said Pam. "He's way over at the bar."

"Looks like a creep to me," said Gray.

Pam looked at him admonishingly. "No need to take everything so seriously, Graham."

"I'm not 'taking things seriously'. I'm just expressing an opinion. I just think he looks like a creep. That's all."

Gray saw him from the corner of his eye, crumpling up his empty beer cup inside his fist, letting it drop into a bin, as though demonstrating again his superior levels of male hormone. He was good-looking, Gray could concede that. Good-looking and fit. Only a year or so older than Gray but far removed in degrees of physical maturity. But Gray had to question his motives. Why Kirsty? There were girls scattered across the beach, girls matching this man's levels of preened attractiveness, girls in proper bikinis, girls with highlights and big earrings and pink lipstick. Girls not sitting with their mum and dad and big brother eating cockles out of a plastic cup with a toothpick.

The man returned slowly to his white towel, passing within inches of Kirsty as he did so, and Gray had to control an impulse to stick out his foot and trip him over. In fact he extracted a few moments' pleasure from picturing the scenario and replaying it in his mind over and over until he found himself stifling a chuckle.

"What?" said Kirsty.

"Oh, nothing."

And no, Gray wasn't jealous. What would Gray have to be jealous of? Gray was tall, reasonably good-looking in a boyish kind of way, somewhere between slim and average. Girls told him he was cute. Girls told him all sorts of things in fact. Mainly about other boys, but that wasn't the point. The point was that he had their confidences. Girls liked Gray and he liked girls. Sometimes probably not in the way that the girls thought he liked them. Sometimes probably in a slightly darker way, under his covers, alone at night. But still, this guy, he reckoned, this guy wouldn't know how to talk to a girl if his life depended on it. Gray wasn't sure he could talk, full stop. He looked like the kind of guy who could grunt. Beat his chest. At a push.

And it was at the very moment that this thought passed through Gray's head that the guy turned, looked at him, looked at Kirsty, looked at their parents and said in a voice straight from a James Bond movie: "Lovely when the sun's out, isn't it?"

Every member of the family turned like startled animals at this unexpected conversational opening. His mother put her hand to her collarbone and said, in a voice that Gray had never heard her use before, "Why, yes, it is."

He saw Kirsty flash his mum a terrible look and then cast her gaze downwards, her face burning red.

"You here on your holidays?" he asked, somewhat superfluously.

Tony nodded. "Up from Surrey," he said, which was Dad's posh way of not saying Croydon. "How about you?"

"Harrogate. I'm here to keep my aunt company. Her husband just died and she couldn't face coming alone."

"Oh," said Pam, her hand moving to her heart, "your poor aunt. And good for you. Not many young boys would sacrifice their summer holidays for a relative."

"Well, she's a good person. She's been there for me a lot. Plus, well, her house is kind of amazing." He smiled then and pointed across the bay towards the other side of town where the houses got bigger and bigger the further you went until his finger came to rest upon what looked like a stately home: pale walls and tall windows, surrounded by poplars and yew trees.

"Oh!" said Pam. "We always wondered who lived in that one, didn't we, Tony?"

Tony nodded. "Thought it might be royalty."

"Not quite. My uncle made his fortune out of pig farming. Bacon, basically." He smiled. "And that's just their summer home. You should see their place in the country."

Gray's parents nodded reverentially.

"Oh," said the man, moving towards them, his hand outstretched. "My name's Mark, by the way. Mark Tate."

"Nice to meet you, Mark." Tony wheezed slightly as he leaned forwards in his deckchair to reach Mark's hand. "I'm Antony Ross — Tony. This is Pam, my wife; Graham, my son; and Kirsty, my daughter."

"Gray," muttered Gray. "Not Graham. Gray."

But the man called Mark wasn't listening. He was holding Kirsty in his gaze, a smile on his face of what looked to Gray suspiciously like triumph. As though this "spontaneous" conversation with his family was not just a passing moment of friendly human interaction but the first brilliant stroke of a much bigger master plan.

He watched his parents chatting animatedly to the young man as though he was in fact Prince Charles on an official visit rather than just a plummy-voiced stranger with absolutely no reason whatsoever to be talking to them. And then he looked at Kirsty. She was — and it really was the only word Gray could find to describe it — blooming. Before his very eyes. It was as though attention from this man was somehow pushing her out from within, everything about her becoming plumped up and fully extended. Her eyes seemed dewy and more heavy-lidded. She was glowing.

"You know," said Mark, "you should come up to the house. Have a look. My aunt will make a cake."

"Oh, we can't intrude on your aunt like that, not when she's grieving," said Pam.

"Oh no, she'll love it. Honestly. She's such a sociable person and she gets lonely up there. In fact, why don't you come today? Come at four."

What? thought Gray. What?

His parents were smiling and saying things like: Well, if you really don't think your aunt will mind and Is there anything we can bring?

And then there it was, a plan.

Gray couldn't believe it.

Mark pulled on a pristine T-shirt and chino shorts; then he rolled up his towel with military precision and tucked it into a cloth bag. Before he left he turned to them, bowed slightly and said, "Four p.m.? Yes?" to which his family nodded furiously and said, "Yes, yes, thank you."

And then he left.

"Well," said Pam, "that was a strange turn of events."

"Certainly was," said Tony. "But looks like we've got ourselves a free tea."

Gray sat, his jaw clenched, thinking that there was no such thing as a free tea, that there was bound to be some price to be paid and his family were too stupid to see it.

CHAPTER
TEN

Lily's mother wires her a hundred pounds. She uses some of it to take a train into London on Friday afternoon, to go to Carl's office, to retrace his steps. It's the first time she's been into London alone. She's flustered at the ticket machine: what does it all mean? She waits in a small queue to speak to a man behind a window.

"Yes," she says when she finally reaches the front, "I need to go to London. Can you help?"

The man does not smile. "Return?"

"Yes," she says, "I will. Later on."

Now the man smiles and she knows she's said something stupid.

He takes her twenty-pound note, prints her off two tickets, passes them to her with her change and says, "Platform three. Seven minutes."

She snatches the tickets and the money and says, "OK."

On the train she watches her new world passing in fleeting vignettes: squares of scrubbed green and acid yellow, back ends of industrial estates, rows of red-brick houses with identical children's toys on narrow scraps of grass. She does not know this world. She only knows

Carl. She plugs her mouth with two knuckles, holding down a throb of grief. She cannot cry. Not here, on a train, with strangers. She stares hard through the window, hard as steel.

She's been to Carl's office before. It was during one of the weekends they'd spent in London, before they got married. They'd stayed in a West End hotel and eaten dinner in a sky-scraping restaurant with sparkling views across the capital. He'd said, "Want to see where I work?" She'd shrugged and said, "OK then."

It's a short building, symmetrical and fronted with black glass and brushed steel. In the centre is a large electronic revolving door, and beyond that a black and chrome foyer with a stainless-steel water feature on the back wall. She checks her watch. It's four forty. Twenty minutes until the time that Carl would have left work. She will wait here and play some Candy Crush.

At five to five she pictures Carl switching off his computer, pulling his jacket from the back of his chair, clicking the metal clasps on his briefcase, calling out goodbye to some colleagues (would he? Would Carl say goodbye? Maybe not. Carl is not the type to call out goodbye. Maybe a raised hand. Or a brusque *See you tomorrow*). She sees him waiting for the elevator, checking his phone, checking his hair. She counts to twenty in her head and then pictures him walking into the elevator, the quiet *ping ping* of the floors as they pass, exiting into the foyer, and then into the revolving doors and then she starts to walk. Victoria is not far, just two minutes. She scans the boards for Carl's train,

73

the 5.06 to East Grinstead, and heads towards platform four. She looks at the faces of the people heading the same way. Do they know him? Would they recognise him? The same train at the same time every day?

She boards the train and sits down. Opposite her is a man. She draws in her breath and feels inside her handbag for a photo of Carl. "Excuse me," she says, her voice emerging more harshly than she intended. "Could you help me?"

He looks at her with unguarded suspicion and she knows that he thinks she is about to ask him for money. "This is my husband," she says, sliding the photo across the table between them. "He takes this train every day and now he has gone."

The man recoils slightly. He still thinks she is going to ask him for money She swallows down an urge to tell him to fuck off. "He is a missing person," she continues. "Officially. The police know."

He raises an eyebrow and says, "Ri-ight."

"Do you recognise him?" she says grimly.

He peers at the photo and shakes his head. "Never seen him before."

"Thank you." She snatches back the photo and forces it into her handbag. Her face is flaming red and she can feel angry blotches forming on her collarbone. She walks to the next free seat and finds herself sitting alongside three female friends who have been drinking and smell of wine and cigarettes. She cannot possibly ask them, they are talking so loud and so fast and anyway, they are not commuters and commuters is what she wants. To her right is a man in a suit. She pulls out the photo, draws in her breath. "Excuse me," she says, talking quickly to get to the point, not wanting to leave him any time to jump to prejudicial conclusions. "My husband is missing. He used to get this train every night. Do you recognise him?"

The man pulls reading glasses from his jacket pocket, picks up the photo, examines it and passes it back. "I'm afraid I don't." His voice is soft and deep and gentle. She feels herself relax. She smiles, warmly, says thank you and then makes her way from carriage to carriage, from commuter to commuter, her confidence building with each encounter. People are generally kind, she finds, and a smile seems to go a long way with the British. It is not in her nature to smile without cause. Smiles are for friends and babies and jokes and family. Not for strangers on trains. But she smiles and she smiles and soon the train is pulling into Oxted and she has asked at least thirty people and at least thirty people have said, "No, I'm really sorry" And a few have even asked her more. "What's his name?" "When did he go missing?" "I wish you all the luck, I really do."

At the ticket barrier she looks for the last person who would have seen Carl leave the station. The ticket person. But there is no ticket person, just a barrier. She sighs. She'd been pinning all her hopes on a person she could ask. And then she starts the long walk home. The walk takes her past some shops and, feeling buoyed by the nice people on the train, she goes into a couple, smiles the smile, shows the photo, asks the question. The man in the beer shop recognises him, says he used to come in for a bottle of wine occasionally.

"Good-looking fella," he says and Lily nods and says, "Yes. He is."

When the shops peter out she crosses the main road and takes the little roads of red houses that crisscross each other in a confusing grid, left right, left right, and then on to the other main road where the supermarket is and the chain stores, where she comes out for her lunch sometimes when she is lonely in the flat, where she sits in Starbucks and reads a newspaper so that she has something to talk to Carl about when he comes home from work. The last stretch of the walk is quieter. Widely spaced short houses which Carl says are called bungalows, with driveways. No shops. No people. And then a short section of road where they have been building yet another new housing development; it will be called Wolf's Hill Boulevard, according to the big hoarding outside. Carl laughs every time he sees it. "Boulevard," he says. "In Oxted. What a load of crap."

Lily stops for a moment and stares at the development. There's nobody there. There hasn't been anyone there since she came to live here. She can see that the first of the blocks is all but built. It has been glazed and clad. The builders have moved along to the next block, which is all skeletal girders and flapping plastic sheets. The sun has gone, the early-evening sky is velvet-blue, cars pass her in golden streaks and she is alone on this road. A strange chill runs through her. She looks again at the new block of flats and sees a flicker of light from a first-floor window.

She turns and heads home. The flickering light is bothering her for some reason. She will tell the big policewoman about it. It might be something; it might be nothing. But right now the flickering light is all she has.

She calls the policewoman the minute she gets home.

"Hello, Mrs Traviss?"

"WPC Traviss."

"Yes. Sorry. WPC Traviss. This is Mrs Monrose. The wife of Carl Monrose."

"I know. And actually, you must be psychic. I was about to call you. We need to bring your husband's computer in. His passport looks like it's probably a dark net passport. We'll want to check his browsing history and his email account."

"I don't know what you're talking about."

There is that pause at the end of the line, the one the big policewoman always leaves, the one that says that she thinks she is a nuisance and a fool.

"These passports, they're bespoke, incredibly expensive, made to order by people in the darkest, deepest corners of the internet. Your husband would have been communicating with some fairly nefarious types. And probably for quite a while. So we need to find these people. And we need access to your husband's computer to help us do that."

"But what do these people have to do with finding my husband?"

That pause again. "Well, actually, it's not a direct lead but they might know something. And it's even possible they might be involved in his disappearance.

Say, for example, if he owed them money or was threatening to expose them."

The image of the flickering light in the new-build apartment window flashes to the forefront of her mind again. Her blood feels cold and then hot. *Gangsters. Criminals.* These things had not crossed her mind in the dark of night. "You know," she says, "it may be nothing, but last night I noticed, in the new building that has been built next to our apartments, a light. Just one light. In just one window. With no one living there. It made me think . . ."

She pauses. What did it make her think? She has no idea. It made her feel creepy. That was all. Creepy and cold.

"I don't know," she continues. "It seemed strange."

"Right," says Beverly, hurtling straight past her comments and on to the next thing. "Are you there now? Can I come now? And collect the computer?"

"Well. Yes. Of course. But you know, I don't have his password."

"We can get the guys on to that. That's not a problem."

"Well, then, fine. And maybe, when you come, we can go to the building site? We can look at that flat? With the light?"

"Not sure there'll be time for that. But I'll see what I can do."

Beverly arrives with a young man wearing plain clothes and big glasses, carrying a filing box. He spends an inordinate amount of time in the spare bedroom where the computer lives and Lily sits anxiously at the edge of the sofa, cupping her elbows and checking the clock on the wall. "What is he doing in there?" she asks Beverly.

"Oh, you know, just procedure. We can't just walk in here and unplug it."

Lily nods. A few more minutes pass. She hears drawers being opened and closed. Then the man appears at the door and looks at Lily. "Do you have a key?" he says, "For the bottom drawer of the cabinet?"

"No," she says. "I have been looking for it for two days. I think it must be on his key ring." She shrugs.

"Do you mind if I drill it out? See if there's anything in there? Memory cards, that sort of thing?"

Lily stiffens. She thinks of Carl walking into the flat, seeing his brand-new filing cabinet from Ikea with a dirty big hole in it, his personal effects plundered and rifled. But then she thinks: Carl has lied to her. She does not even know what his real name is. He has kept a locked drawer in their shared home. Taken the key to work with him. There must be a reason for that.

"Yes," she says. "Fine. But please don't make a mess."

The young man smiles and heads back into the spare room. Ten seconds later she hears the high-pitched wail of wood being ground away. A moment after that the young man appears again, holding the card box.

"Well," he says, lightly, as though what is happening here is completely normal, "all done here. Have you finished . . .?" He looks down at the sheet of paper he gave her earlier, the one with personal questions on it:

memorable dates, pets' names, parents' names, nicknames, significant place names.

"Yes." She slides it across the table to him and he adds it to the contents of the box.

"Awesome," he says. "OK." He says this to Beverly, who gets slowly to her feet.

They go together to the door and Beverly says, "We'll be in touch."

There is no mention of the empty apartment with the flickering light.

Lily stands still for a while after they've gone. She looks about the flat, as she's done a hundred times since Carl didn't come home on Tuesday night. At first all she'd seen was Carl's absence. Now she sees his deceit. She walks slowly to the spare bedroom and kneels down to examine the contents of the locked drawer.

CHAPTER
ELEVEN

"Oh," says Alice, "you're back."

It's nearly ten o'clock at night and he's standing in the doorway in Barry's jacket, backlit by a cloud of sodium glare, looking like the weariest person in the world. He's been gone for thirty-six hours.

"Yes," he says. "If that's all right."

"Well, it'll have to be really, won't it? Where've you been?" she says.

"On the beach."

"All this time?"

"Yeah, well, most of it. I slept there last night."

"What is it with you and that beach? I thought you'd got your memory back and gone home."

"Well, that's the thing." He looks over her shoulder, wistfully. "I remembered something. Something big." He looks again and she relents and opens the door properly so that he can come in. She gets them both a beer and they sit side by side on the sofa, Sadie at their feet, Hero on Alice's lap, Griff keeping a polite distance.

"Kids all in bed?" he asks.

"Small one in bed, the others on their beds. Doing things with screens." As she says this her phone pops.

She glances at it fleetingly. Jasmine has left Alice's phone logged on to Instagram. Someone, somewhere, has liked something that Jasmine has posted on Instagram. This means that Alice's phone will continue to pop for the next ten minutes or so as everyone Jasmine knows likes the thing she posted. Alice pictures a sea of disembodied thumbs senselessly pressing hearts. She sighs.

"What's that?" asks Frank, looking at the iPad.

"That's my parents' living room," she says. "In London."

He nods. As though that makes sense.

"They've both got dementia," she explains. "They have visiting carers but no one to watch them 24/7. And, believe me, they need someone to watch over them. My sister's got the same set-up. So hopefully between me and her and the carers we can keep them at home for a while longer. Because the alternative is, well . . . unthinkable."

She smiles tightly, hardly able to believe that less than two years ago her parents were planning a trip to the Great Wall of China and now neither of them is capable of planning even a trip to the bathroom.

"My life is very strange," she says.

"So is mine," he says and they both laugh.

She can't believe how relieved she'd felt to see him standing there in her doorway just now. She'd tried very hard to sound stern but had had to resist the urge to throw her arms around him and say, *Thank God you're back.* So now she is being circumspect and cool because that is her default approach to life and throwing her arms around people is not.

"So," she says. "What've you been up to?"

Frank smiles and turns his beer bottle around in his hands. "I had this theory that I must have chosen this town for a reason. You know, I bought a ticket to come here. I found my way to the beach. It can't be random. So I thought if I walked around for a while, something might jog my memory."

"And it did?"

"Yes!" His hazel eyes light up. "I remembered a girl on a carousel. One of those old-fashioned ones with horses going up and down?" He looks at her uncertainly as though unsure that he has made any sense, so she nods encouragingly.

"The steam fair," she says. "It comes every summer."

"Oh!" He looks pleased. "So it might be real?"

"Yes. It might be. And who was this girl?"

"I don't know. But she had brown hair and she was very young, a teenager I'd say."

"No idea at all who she might be?"

"Well, no, but a weird thing happened. I went down to the beach, up by the high street, because I had a strong feeling that that was where I'd seen this girl on the carousel . . ."

"That's where they have it. Exactly."

He smiles. "The fair?"

"Yes, on the beach, beneath the high street! So, what happened when you went down there?"

"I threw up," he says.

"What, literally?"

"Yes. Just out of the blue. And then after that I couldn't move. It was like Wednesday again. I sat down and looked out to sea and my mind just went kind of opaque and people came and people went but I was just zoned out. And then, just now, when it got dark, I remembered something else. I remembered . . ." His hands were shaking. "I remembered a man, jumping into the sea, here. It was definitely here. And it was dark and I could see the moonlight on the water and the man kept swimming and swimming and I needed to follow him but I couldn't because . . . I don't really know why . . ." He massages his right wrist with his left hand. "I just couldn't."

He looks up at Alice and blinks and she thinks of that young man she'd seen a few years ago walking out into the sea. "I saw that, too," she said. "Three years ago. I saw a man walk into the sea. He took his clothes off and folded them up in a neat pile and then just walked until his head went under. I wonder if . . ."

"No." He shakes his head. "No. This man was clothed. He was wearing jeans. And a shirt. And he had . . . he had something with him. Something big, in his arms. And he didn't walk in. He jumped. Like he was trying to get away from someone."

"From who?"

"I don't know," he says, "but it felt like it might have been me."

CHAPTER
TWELVE

1993

Mark's aunt's house was, by any measure, the grandest privately owned house that Gray had ever set foot in. It was decorated in a style that his mum referred to as "chichi", which seemed to consist of lots of gilt-framed mirrors and towering vases of stargazer lilies. A trio of terriers of some description greeted them at the door, followed by Mark in a white shirt with upturned collar and neat blue jeans. As they filed through the enormous front door, he greeted them all effusively like friends of old and led them, barefoot, across a circular hallway and into a palm-filled conservatory, which he referred to as "the orangery", where a very attractive middle-aged woman with severely coiffed blonde hair sat behind a low table laden with cake and teacups.

She rose to her feet and smiled and said, "Hello! You came! I wasn't sure if Mark had made you all up or not! Honestly. Funny boy. Came back two hours ago with a bag full of flour and eggs and said we had to make cakes because we had guests coming!"

She had a soft, well-spoken accent, like her nephew, but there was, Gray couldn't help but notice, a slight ring of hysteria about her manner. He wondered if it was part of her normal persona or a response to having a strange, somewhat sunburned family suddenly appear in her immaculate house.

"But anyway," she continued, cementing Gray's impression, "you're here and you're welcome. And please, please sit down."

She smoothed the seat of her pleated skirt and sat back down. "My name's Kitty, by the way." She shook their hands and they introduced themselves and Gray noticed her gaze linger a little longer on Kirsty than on the others. She sliced a Victoria sandwich with tremulous, manicured fingers and asked about Rabbit Cottage and their plans for the rest of their stay, and Gray fidgeted in his rattan chair and stared through the windows at the immaculate gardens beyond and wondered why they were here.

"Mark is a very good boy," Kitty was saying. "Woe is me, I had no children of my own" — she pressed her hand to her porcelain collarbone — "so I used to borrow Mark and his sister all the time. They feel like my own children and Mark certainly knows how to look after me." She patted his hand and he smiled indulgently at her and then the first of a few awkward silences fell across the group.

"Well," said Tony, breaking it. "I must say, this house is every bit as stunning inside as it is from the outside."

"Thank you, Tony," she said. "The venue for many, many happy times over the years." She looked sad, no doubt thinking of her recently deceased husband.

"How long have you owned it?" asked Pam.

"Oh" — her fingers felt their way to her golden necklace — "twenty years or so now, I suppose. We bought it from a romantic novelist. In fact, if you pop into the library on your way out, you'll see we kept a shelf just for her books. As a kind of memorial. Not that I've read any of them. Not really my kind of thing. Bodice-rippers, I believe they're called." She looked vaguely appalled by the concept. "So, Graham."

"Gray," he said, "everyone calls me Gray."

"Except me," said Pam.

"Gray. How old are you?"

"Seventeen."

"So you're still at school?"

"Sixth-form college."

"And you, Kirsty?"

"I'm fifteen."

Kitty arched a fine eyebrow. "Young," she said absently.

Kirsty nodded and blushed.

"What about you, Mark?" asked Tony. "How old are you?"

"Nineteen."

"And what do you do?"

"I'm at college. Business studies."

"That's nice," said Pam. "What do you hope to be?"

"A millionaire."

He said this with an entirely straight face and it was all Gray could do not to spit out a mouthful of tea.

"Well," said Pam.

"That's great," said Tony. "Nothing like ambition."

Kitty's mouth set into a straight line, giving away nothing.

"Oh!" said Pam, turning in her chair to peer through the windows of the orangery. "A peacock!"

And sure enough, there, on the lawn, fluttering its iridescent fan of feathers like a showgirl, stood a peacock.

"Well, that just puts the cap on it," chuckled Tony. "Peacocks!"

"I know," said Kitty tiredly. "It's a cliché, I suppose. But the novelist had a pair and I got used to having them around. So when they died I got a new pair. They're surprisingly good company. I have other animals," she said. "A donkey. A Shetland pony. It just seems pointless having all this space and not putting something in it."

Kitty noticed Kirsty's face light up at the mention of donkeys and ponies and said, "Mark, why don't you take the kids down to the animals?"

"Er, no thanks," said Gray, appalled at being referred to as a "kid".

Mark glanced at his sister. "Kirsty?"

She nodded and got to her feet, her fists curled into her sleeves, looking every bit a "kid". And as Gray watched Mark lead his sister from the room, watched them vanish through the door, heard their voices trailing into inaudible echoes and then disappear altogether, he felt a violent ache of anxiety. He looked from his mother to his father and back again but they were both preoccupied by the effort of making a half-decent conversation with a woman with whom they had nothing in common.

What was it, he wondered, about that guy? What was it that kept setting all his alarm bells jangling? It was all in the detail, he decided. The bare feet, the carefully combed and set hair, the unlikely bond with the glacially grieving aunt, the precocious talk of being a millionaire. Not to mention the blatant staring on the beach and the inexplicable invitation to tea. None of it gelled. None of it consolidated itself into a type of person that Gray could recognise. And Gray knew some strange people. Croydon was full of them.

He glanced at his parents again and then through the window across the lawn where he saw the receding figures of his sister and Mark, strolling companionably, Mark laughing, his sister turning to smile at him. Then they were gone but the peacock still stood, holding his ground, shimmering his tail feathers, staring, Gray felt, straight into his soul.

CHAPTER
THIRTEEN

The beers go quickly. Alice had a thirst and so, it appears, did Frank. She gets two more and when they are gone and there are no more beers left in the fridge, she crouches to her knees and pulls a bottle of Scotch from the bottom of the dresser. It's pushing midnight and normally Alice would be watching the clock, imagining her precious seven hours being whittled away. But tonight she has no interest in the time. Time is irrelevant.

She stretches to her feet and reaches up for tumblers.

"Mum?"

She turns at the sound of Jasmine's voice.

"What are you doing?"

"Getting drinks," she replies.

"For him?"

"For Frank. And me."

Jasmine arches her left eyebrow. "His name's not even Frank."

"No," she says patiently, "but it's better than nothing."

"Why is he even here? I thought he'd gone."

"Yes, well, so did I. But he came back."

Jasmine nods, and then bites her cheek before saying, "Let's hope no one finds out."

Alice looks at her questioningly.

"Kai and Romaine. And Derry. You should probably tell them not to tell anyone about him. In case, you know . . ."

Alice nods briskly. She doesn't want to have this conversation now. "Anyway," she says, "it's late. You need to get some sleep."

"No school tomorrow," she says, stifling a yawn.

"Yes. But still. It's late." Alice clutches the tumblers between her fingers, holding the bottle of Scotch in her other hand. She wants her daughter to go now. "Go on then," she says, mock sternly. "Off you go."

Jasmine stares at her strangely for a long moment, as though she has something important to tell her, as though her young mind is whirring with unfathomable thoughts. But then, finally, she shakes her head and sighs and says, "Night, Mum. Be careful."

The words still echo in Alice's head as she carries the Scotch and glasses through to the living room. *Be careful*. She's not sure she wants to be.

Hero has crawled on to Frank's lap during her absence and he looks slightly overwhelmed by the sensation of six stone of solid Staffy.

"Do you like dogs?" she asks.

He smiles. "It looks like it."

"Well, don't be too flattered. Hero likes everyone. She's a total attention-junkie. He's the one you want to work on." She gestures at Griff sitting guarded and watchful, chocolate-drop eyes going from Alice to

Frank and back again as though he knows he's being talked about. "He's *very* fussy. Do you want me to get her off your lap?"

"No." He shakes his head. "It's quite nice. She's . . . reassuringly substantial."

She pours them both a heavy measure of Scotch and passes one to Frank. "Cheers," she says, raising her tumbler. "To remembering."

Frank clinks his glass against hers and he smiles. "And to you," he says. "For being so generous."

"Oh," she says. "I don't know about generous. Stupid more like."

"Maybe both," he says.

"Yeah. I'll go with that. Story of my life. Generous and stupid."

"So." Frank takes a mouthful of his drink and grimaces. "What is the story of your life, exactly? Since we can't talk about the story of mine."

"Oh Christ," she says, "you'll wish you hadn't asked."

"No," he says simply, "go on. Tell me about the maps."

"Ah." She looks into her drink. "The maps." She looks up again. "That's my job. My business. My *art*." She laughs wryly.

"They're beautiful."

"Thank you."

"Where did you get the inspiration?"

"You know, it all started with one of those huge road maps for cars, you know. My dad had one. A map of the whole of the United Kingdom. Gigantic thing. I used to leaf through it on long journeys, look at all the places I'd never been. I loved the textural contrasts, you know, between, say, the centre of London and the Highlands of Scotland. London was black with road markings. Scotland was white. Then Dad gave me his old car when I was eighteen and when I sold it a few years later I found the old road map in the glove compartment. Brought it in, found myself leafing through it again. Stuck at home with a baby, bored out of my mind. Decided to make something out of it. That, in fact." She gestures at a likeness of a very young Jasmine on the wall opposite.

"That's made out of maps?"

She nods.

"Wow," he says. "It looks like a drawing. It's amazing!"

"Why, thank you. So, after that I bought up old map books whenever I could. I mean, you should see my room upstairs: I'm virtually hoarding them. And when I moved up here from London, I needed an income, so I started taking commissions. And then I opened a little online shop on the side for personalised birthday cards and stuff. And now I'm a professional full-time cutter-outer and sticker-oner of tiny bits of maps into flower shapes." She looks at him. "Told you my life was weird," she said.

"Well, speaking as someone with *no life whatsoever*, I'd say that sounds pretty great."

"Yeah. It's good. It's weird, but it's good. And means I can work round the kids, which is brilliant."

"Not to mention this lot." He indicates the dogs. "And them." He gestures at the iPad with its sinisterly glowing vignette of an empty room. "You've got a lot on your plate."

"Yes. I do. But no more than a million other women. Women are amazing, you know." She smiles and he smiles back.

"I'll have to take your word for it. Since I can't actually remember any women."

"Well, you know me, and take it from me, I am completely amazing."

He doesn't laugh but he does smile. "OK. You are Woman A and from now on will be the benchmark for every other woman I meet."

"Oh Christ, I've become your mother!"

This time he laughs and as he rocks back his leg presses briefly against Alice's leg and she feels it open up inside her, the big gaping hole of loneliness and neediness she's been trying to ignore for six years. Outside the low-slung window a lightbulb on the string is fizzing and flickering. Finally it extinguishes completely and the room is suddenly a degree darker. She hears the floorboards creak overhead as a child makes its way to the bathroom. And then something remarkable happens. Griff, who has been watching their conversation from the other side of the room, suddenly unfolds his elegant legs and wanders towards them. Alice expects that he is coming for some fuss from her but instead the dog stops at Frank and rests his chin on Frank's knee.

"Oh," says Frank, cupping his hand over the dog's skull. He looks up at Alice and smiles.

Alice looks from her dog to Frank and then back at her dog. Her stomach eddies. Griff, unlike Sadie and Hero, is *her* dog. She chose him from a rescue centre when he was a year old. He's been with her since her London days, since before she had Romaine. He is the kindest, nicest dog in the world. But he is not a friendly dog. He keeps his distance from people. But here he is, offering himself up to a stranger, echoing, in some poetic way, Alice's own subliminal desires.

"You must be a good guy," she says. "Dogs always know."

"You reckon?"

"I reckon." And then she feels something softening deep inside her, something that had once been tender and, over time, without her even noticing, became hard. She puts her hand over Frank's hand where it rests on Griff's tightly domed head. Frank brings his other hand to cover hers. And there it is. An exquisite moment of suspended existence beyond which lies the potential for everything. *Remember*, they might say in years to come, *that night. When we first touched*?

But for now there is the clank of the plumbing upstairs as a child flushes the toilet. Then there is the sound of footsteps coming down the wooden stairs. And there is Romaine in glorious disarray, eyes puffed with sleep, pulling at the sides of her off-white night-dress and saying, "Mummy. I keep waking up."

Alice takes her hand from beneath his and sighs and says to him, "I'll be back in a minute."

But he's already shifting in his seat, trying to dislodge Hero from his lap, putting down his tumbler of Scotch and saying, "You know, I'm shattered, actually. Is it OK . . .?"

"Stay as long as you like," she says. "Any friend of Griff's is a friend of mine."

She takes Romaine's outstretched hand and walks her up the stairs. "I'll leave the back door unlocked," she calls down to him. "See you in the morning."

CHAPTER
FOURTEEN

1993

That night they went out for dinner. The impromptu tea at Kitty's mansion had slightly upended their day and there'd been no time to go shopping for food so Kirsty had said, "Why don't we eat by the beach tonight? It'll be really nice."

It was a lovely evening, cool but golden with a brilliant blue sky, so Tony suggested the smart seafood restaurant at the other end of town with the covered terrace overlooking the beach. "No starters though," he pre-instructed.

Gray appraised Kirsty over the top of his menu. She looked different.

"What?" she said, spotting his gaze on her.

"Nothing," he said. "What are you having?"

"Scampi," she said, closing her menu.

Mascara. That's what it was. She was wearing mascara.

"What are you having?"

"Minute steak," he said.

She mock yawned. Gray always ordered steak.

"What did you talk about?" he asked. "You and the weirdo?"

"Oh, Graham," his mum interjected. "That's not nice."

"Well," he countered, "he's not exactly normal is he?"

"Well, no," said Tony, "but then, who is? Really? It's something you realise the older you get. Everyone's a bit strange."

"Yes, but not everyone takes your fifteen-year-old daughter off to the bottom of the garden to look at 'donkeys'."

"There was a donkey!" Kirsty cried.

Gray sighed.

"It was called Nancy It was beautiful. And he's not weird. He's just . . . posh."

"He's posh *and* weird. I mean, who invites a group of total strangers round for tea?"

"He's bored," said Kirsty. "He told me. He offered to come here to keep his aunt company because he thought some of his friends from the old days might be here and they're not and now he's stuck here with no one to hang out with."

"So he decides he wants to hang out with the Rosses from Croydon?"

Kirsty shrugged.

The waitress appeared and took their order and Gray looked down from the terrace on to the steam fair below. It was a pleasant evening and the seafront was heaving with bodies: clusters of teens and families. Gray did a double-take at a fleeting glimpse of a head of slick dark hair. He followed the head as it passed through the crowds. It wasn't, was it? Was it Mark? The figure circled the dodgems, then stopped and bought an ice cream. Then he started walking towards the near side of the fairground, and as he got closer he looked up and Gray whispered, "Jesus," under his breath.

"What?" said Kirsty.

Mark caught Gray's eye and raised his ice-cream cone towards him.

"*Jesus*," he muttered again, raising his hand to return the greeting.

"What?" Kirsty got up from her seat and came to see what he was looking at. "Oh!" she said. "It's Mark!" She waved and Mark waved back and then Pam joined them and waved and Gray folded his arms across his chest and sighed.

"Come down," he heard Mark call up. "After dinner. I'll wait for you!"

Kirsty was flushed when she retook her seat.

"You're not going to go, are you?" he asked, incredulously.

"Why not?"

"Because you're fifteen! Because he's nineteen! Mum, Dad, you're not going to let her, are you?"

Pam and Tony looked at each other and then at Gray, and Pam said, "I don't see any reason why not? Do you?" She glanced at Tony again.

Tony shook his head. "Long as you're home by ten."

The rest of the meal was tainted for Gray. He stole glances off the terrace every now and then, staking out the unnaturally shining crown of Mark's head. Who went to a funfair by themselves? Who hung around for an hour waiting for a teenage girl to finish her dinner?

His minute steak was tough and chewy, the chips were too greasy and the ketchup wasn't Heinz. He put down his knife and fork halfway through the meal.

Kirsty, he noticed, was racing through her scampi, putting two in her mouth at once at one point. She slapped her knife and fork together, gulped down the dregs of her Coke, accepted a five-pound note from her dad's wallet and left.

Gray turned and watched. He saw his little sister, her feet suddenly not so turned in, her gait suddenly not so gangling, stride down the steps and towards Mark, who was waiting for her by the entrance. Mark greeted her with a brief embrace and a kiss to her cheek. Then he stood with his hand upon her shoulder and smiled at her for a moment, before taking her arm by the elbow and leading her gallantly into the crowds.

And then Gray thought about the mascara and he knew that this had all been pre-planned. Down by the donkey paddock. He tried to imagine the conversation; he saw Mark smiling conspiratorially and saying, "Eight o'clock. Find a way to get away." And his sister, his gorgeous, stupid, never-been-kissed sister, saying, "I'll be there!" as if this was a scene in some stupid Disney Channel show.

And then he stood up and said to his mum and dad, "I'm going for a walk. I'll see you back at the cottage."

"No pudding?" asked his mum.

"No." He rubbed his stomach. "I'm not feeling too good actually. Think it was all that cake earlier."

"Oh." His mum made a *poor baby* face and stroked his hand. "Well, you get some fresh air and we'll see you later."

He smiled at them both and left, heading towards the steam fair. He found a good vantage point on a wall just above the fair, lowered his sunglasses, sat down and watched.

CHAPTER
FIFTEEN

Lily sits on her bed, the bed she shares with her husband. A husband who is not here. A husband who is not in fact a husband. A husband who is a cardboard cut-out of a husband. Like one of those life-size film-star figures they have in cinemas to give the impression that you are in the presence of celebrity. The bed still smells of him, it smells of them, of the sheen of their bodies when they are together, the heat of them and the joy of them. It has been three days now since she felt him. Three nights since their bodies tangled together under these sheets. The smell will fade soon. And then the sheets will become stale and she will need to wash them. And after the smell goes, everything that remains will be false, including this flat that was designed to look expensive with its fake wooden floors, its flimsy walls and cheap flat-pack furniture, its door handles and plug sockets that are coming loose and chrome taps that are already losing their bright shine.

She looks down into her hands at the objects she found in the locked drawer after the WPC and the computer forensics boy left. Two golden rings, one set with a large diamond. A key fob with three door keys on it. A thick wodge of banknotes: £890. So now she has money. But no answers.

The rings are very small. Maybe they belonged to his mother? The key fob is a brass sphere, heavy and satisfying in the palm of her hand. The notes are comprised of twenty- and fifty-pound notes, used, but neatly stacked as though from a bank. So. This is what he was hiding from her. Not so much. Nothing that any other man wouldn't keep locked in a drawer, for safekeeping.

The phone rings and she jumps. It will be the WPC, calling with more news to rock her world. To tell her, maybe, that her husband was once a woman. That his name is really Carla. Ha. She smiles grimly to herself and picks up the bedside phone.

"Is that Lily?" asks a man with a gentle, almost effeminate voice.

"Yes."

"Oh, hi, Lily. We haven't spoken before. My name's Russ. I'm a friend of your husband's? Of Carl's?"

Lily sits up straight and grips the phone harder. "Yes?"

"Listen, I've been trying to call him the past couple of days. His phone seems to be dead. Called him at work earlier and they told me he hasn't been in since Tuesday. I hate to bother you at home, but I wondered if maybe I could have a word with him." He stops and she hears him licking his lips. "If he's there?"

"No," she says. "He's not here."

"Ah, OK. When are you expecting him home?"

"I don't know. He is missing."

She hears him pause between breaths.

"He has not come home since Tuesday night. I have not seen him since Tuesday morning. The police are aware."

He breathes sharply. "Wow," he says, "*missing*. That's . . . I don't know what to say. I mean . . . Do you mean you literally haven't seen him?"

"Yes. He left on Tuesday morning. He texted me on Tuesday evening when he left work. He never came home. And now it is Friday night. So. Yes. I am being literal."

"Bloody hell. Christ. That doesn't sound like him. I mean, I know I haven't seen him for a while but from what little I gleaned he was completely potty about you. Deliriously happy. You know."

"He was the happiest man in the world." She pauses and looks down at the wedding rings and the keys on the mattress by her side. "Russ, how long have you known Carl?"

"Gosh, I don't know. A few years, I guess. I used to work with him at Blommers. We both joined around the same time: 2010? I think?"

"And where had he been working before that?"

"Well, I'm not sure exactly. Another financial services company I suppose. He probably told me but I don't remember."

"Do you know his family?"

"No. God, no. I've never met anyone he knows. We always just used to meet up for a pint or two, you know, just the two of us, whenever I found myself in town. And I'd been trying to get the pair of you over for dinner. So hard to get out and about with a baby, you know. But I got the impression he didn't really fancy a night with a screaming baby" He laughed nervously. "Kept finding excuses. So, what with one thing and another, I haven't seen him for at least a year."

"Where do you live, Russ?"

"Putney."

"Where is Putney?"

"It's south London. On the river."

"I want to come and see you. I want to ask you some questions. Please."

"Oh. Of course. Yes. I mean, we're busy tomorrow, seeing Jo's parents for lunch."

"I can come early. I don't sleep, so I can come any time."

"I suppose. I mean, mornings are quite hectic here what with the baby and everything."

"Half an hour. I just need half an hour."

"OK. I'll talk to Jo. Hold on . . ." The sound muffles as he cups his hand over the phone and she hears him call out. She hears "Carl's wife . . . missing . . . early . . . half an hour." Then a cross woman's voice saying, "Not here though. Go to Antonio's."

He comes back on the line. "OK, that'll be fine. There's a coffee shop, a deli kind of thing, just round the corner. Antonio's. I can meet you there at nine. Give me your phone number and I'll text you the postcode."

She reads it out to him and says, "So. What do you look like?"

"Oh, nothing much," he says apologetically. "Normal height. Normal build. Brown hair. Glasses. What do you look like?"

"I look like Keira Knightley," she says. "Except not so thin."

"Ah," says Russ. "Good. That helps. I'll see you tomorrow."

"Yes," says Lily. "I'll see you tomorrow."

CHAPTER
SIXTEEN

Frank swipes back the curtains and is greeted once more by the snarling dog. The very same dog that had lain upon his lap last night like a big sack of love. He smiles at the dog and the dog stops snarling and wags its blunt stick of a tail. He has no idea what the time is but the sun is still fairly low in the sky and the lights in the back of Alice's house are all turned off. He opens the door and the dog bounds in and leaps straight up on to his bed.

"Morning, girl," he says, scruffing her under her chin. She rolls on to her back and presents him with her stomach. Frank sits next to her and scratches her belly and thinks about the night before. He mustn't confuse his feelings of helplessness with his feelings about Alice. He is like a newborn baby latching on to the first person to show him any affection. But still. There is something about her, something magnetic. Whenever he's with her he finds himself pulled towards her as if the very air around her is cambered. And it's not just that she's self-assured and physically attractive. It's her resilience, her artistry, her generosity of spirit that draws him to her. Alice had told him last night about the dog, Hero, how she'd been left behind by another tenant, how Alice had taken her in, unquestioningly. And then when her parents had become too ill to look after Sadie, how she'd taken her in, too. And now here he is, in her cramped house, another body to house, another mouth to feed. And she genuinely doesn't seem to mind.

"Hero!" He hears a small voice calling in the courtyard. "Hero!"

The dog jumps from his bed and ambles out of the door. It's the little girl. Romaine.

She stops when she sees him standing in the doorway.

"You're up early," he says.

"I know," she says in a broad Yorkshire accent. "Mummy told me to go back to bed but I couldn't."

"And you were up late last night, too. You must be tired."

She shrugs, her arms looped around Hero's giant neck. "I don't get tired."

"Oh, well, that's lucky."

She shrugs again and kisses Hero's head.

"So, what are you going to do now?"

"I think I might go and try and wake Mummy up again."

He starts at this suggestion. He thinks of the shadows under Alice's blue-green eyes, the way she grabs her hair in her hands and pulls it away from her face as if trying to stretch herself awake. It's Saturday. It's early.

"How about I make you some breakfast and then we can put the telly on. Or something?"

"OK," she says. "I have a toasted bagel for breakfast. With peanut butter. Can you make that?"

Frank tries to envisage a bagel. He knows the word but is finding the associated object hard to locate. He sees a dog with silken ears. But that's not right. It's something that goes in a toaster. So it must be something bread-like.

"If you show me where everything is I'm sure I can manage it."

"OK then."

He follows her into the narrow kitchen. The clock on the microwave says 5:58.

"Here," she says, lifting the lid of a wooden bread box and pulling out a tubular bag of — yes, *bagels*! He remembers now. "And the peanut butter is up there," she points at a high shelf.

"Do you like butter too?"

She shakes her head.

"Good." He claps his hands together. "Right."

He pulls a plate from a wooden plate rack and finds a knife. Romaine sits on the chair at the kitchen table and watches him as he tries to force the bagel into the toaster.

"No!" She laughs. "You have to cut it in half!"

"Of course you do," he says. "Silly me!"

"Silly you!"

He cuts the bagel in half and slides both sides into the toaster.

"Why can't you remember anything?"

"I don't really know," says Frank. "Your mum thinks maybe I had a big shock. A shock so big that it forced all the memories out of my head."

"Like an electric shock?"

"No. More like a life shock. You know. Like something bad happening."

"You mean like when my dad stole me."

Frank turned to look at Romaine. "Did he?"

"Yes. But then the police came and everything was OK."

"Wow. That must have been quite shocking. How old were you?"

"I was small. Three years old. But it did a different thing to my memory. Because I can't remember much about being three but I remember all of that bit."

"Do you still see your dad?"

"Not really. Only when he comes to England. And he lives in Australia now, so he doesn't come much. But I'm not allowed to go anywhere on my own with him in case he does it again." She suddenly leans forward in the chair and stares at the toaster. "That's enough!" she cries. "I don't like it too toasty!"

"How do I . . .?"

"That button! There! Quick!"

He pops the bagel up. It has barely changed colour. "OK?" He shows it to her.

"Yes." She looks relieved.

"So, why did your daddy steal you? What happened?"

"It was because Mummy moved up here when I was a baby and he was cross because he lived in London and he wanted to see me more. And Mummy said he couldn't because of . . . *things*. And he got really cross and shouted and stuff and then one time I went to stay with him in London he took me somewhere. I think it was, like, a hotel or something. And even though he was really nice to me and bought me loads of presents and sweets I knew it was bad and I was scared. And then the police came and it was so scary. And I remember everything. *Everything*." She turns to face the table as he places the bagel in front of her.

Frank doesn't know what to say. All the stories, he thinks to himself, the world is full of stories. But the one story he really needs to know is buried somewhere so deep inside him he's scared he'll never get to it.

"Oh!" Alice is slightly startled to see Romaine nestled on the sofa between Hero and Frank. The TV is on and they're watching *The Octonauts*.

"Good morning," says Frank. "We thought we'd let you sleep a while."

It's nearly nine o'clock and Alice can't remember the last time she slept this late. "How totally brilliant," she says, leaning down to greet Griff. "That's worth a night's rent on its own."

She glances at Romaine. She's a gregarious child, nothing like her older sister, who has always treated anyone not directly related to her with appalled disdain. But even so, it's strange to see her so comfortable with a strange man. And not just as in a man who is a "stranger", but a man who doesn't know who he is. Alice, feeling suddenly horribly culpable, goes to the sofa and pulls Romaine's head towards her mouth and kisses her crown. "Are you hungry?" she says.

"No," says Romaine, "Frank made me a bagel. Except he tried to put it in the toaster without cutting it. It was so funny!"

"Silly Frank," says Frank.

Kai appears at the gap in the door. His eyes are swollen with sleep and he looks slightly angry. He immediately throws his mum a look when he sees Frank on the sofa, a look that says, *What the fuck is he doing here?*

Alice chooses to ignore the look and instead says, "Morning, gorgeous, what are you doing up so early?"

"I heard voices," he says. "A man's voice."

"Yes," she says, "Frank turned up late last night. He's started remembering things!"

Kai clearly couldn't care less about Frank's lost memory and slouches away and back up the stairs.

"Sorry," says Frank. "I suppose when you're a teenager it's a bit weird finding some stranger in your house."

"Honestly, Frank, they're used to it. We've always got people in the house. And stranger ones than you."

"Remember Barry?" says Romaine.

"I most certainly do."

"He ran away," says Romaine. "He left all his stuff and his dog and he owed Mummy loads of money and he just disappeared."

"He was a nasty man."

"Yes," Romaine agrees. "He was a nasty man. Except he always bought me comics. And chocolate."

"He shoplifted it, Romaine." She turns to Frank. "He gave a tiny girl stolen chocolate. Can you believe it?"

"God, well, I hope I don't find out that I'm a nasty man who steals chocolate and gives it to little girls."

"No," says Romaine, nestling closer into his body. "You're definitely not a nasty man. You're a nice man."

Alice looks at her daughter, the way her tiny body is pressed against Frank's big man body. She's allowed Romaine to be hurt before. She's taken risks with the safety of all her children and she's come terrifyingly close to paying for it. She searches her psyche for some sense of alarm or primal fear. But there's nothing there but warmth.

She says, "I was thinking, after what you remembered yesterday, maybe I should take you for a walk around town. See if you remember anything else."

"Can I come too?" says Romaine.

"You can come too," she replies. "And also, Frank, we should probably pick you up a new outfit. Some new underpants, possibly."

She sees him flush a little at the mention of underpants.

"I'm not saying there's anything wrong with your underpants. I'm sure they're lovely. Just that it's always good to have a spare pair."

"But I don't have any money."

"Look," she says, "your shirt is from Muji, your trousers are from Gap, your shoes are from Jones, you have lovely teeth, a nice accent and a nice haircut. I am going to assume that at some point, when we've put you back together, you'll be good for it."

"But what if I'm not? You've got all this" — he gestures around the room — "to pay for. Three kids. I couldn't live with myself if I left you out of pocket."

113

"Let me worry about that. I'm a big girl, I can make my own mistakes. And if it makes you feel any better we can hit the second-hand shops. Apart from the underpants, obviously."

"Ew," says Romaine. "Second-hand underpants. Ew!"

CHAPTER
SEVENTEEN

The man called Russ is indeed as he'd described. A plain man with a kind face and no fashion sense at all. She sees him start as she walks into the cute little deli. She made an effort with her appearance this morning. After three days of not showering and not wearing make-up and pulling her lank hair into a ponytail, she'd felt a strange compulsion to look nice for Carl's friend. Make the same effort she would have made had Carl ever accepted his invitation to go for dinner at their house. She imagines what Carl might have said about her to Russ. He would have told Russ that his new wife was beautiful. That she was tall and elegant. That he was the luckiest guy in the world. She didn't want to let him down.

"Lily?" he says, rising to his feet.

"Yes," They shake hands and she sits down opposite him.

"Lovely to meet you," he says, passing her a menu. He is shaking slightly.

"Yes," she says, "thank you."

"I'm just having a coffee, but order whatever you want. They do good bacon and eggs here. And the focaccia is freshly made."

She scans the menu, realising that she is actually hungry. She has not felt hungry for days. "Toast," she says to the owner who appears at their table. She remembers to smile and adds, "please. White. With butter. And a cappuccino. And orange juice. Thank you."

"So," says Russ, "still no word from Carl, I assume?"

"No. And there will be no word from Carl now. I am quite sure of that."

"You mean, you think . . ."

"I think he is dead."

Russ blanches.

"If he was alive, even if he was locked in a casket beneath the sea, if he had lost his limbs, if he was mute and blind, he would find his way back to me. He would."

"Well, yes, but it might take him quite a long time . . ."

She sends him a warning glance. This is no time for jokes. "It is a feeling, in my gut, in my heart. He is dead. And not only is he dead, Russ, but he was never alive."

Russ looks a bit scared now. He looks like the man on the train the other day, as though he fears he is about to be scammed in some way.

She tones herself down and says, "Listen. Russ. The police took Carl's passport when I reported him missing. They ran it through their systems. They tell me that he does not exist. That there is no Carl Monrose. That his passport is fake." She rests her hands on the table and looks deep into Russ's pale eyes. "And you

116

are the only person who knew him. So tell me, how can this be?"

"Fake?"

"Yes. He bought it from bad people on the internet. There is no such person as Carl. He doesn't exist."

"But — you got married? I mean, surely the paperwork must have added up otherwise they wouldn't have issued you with the licence?"

She resists the temptation to tut. "Listen," she says, "when you have a passport, then everything else follows. You show it, the man looks at it, all done. Plus, this was Kiev. You see what I am saying?"

He nods and stares into the froth on his coffee.

"So, can you tell me what you know about him? About my husband? Please."

"Well . . ." Russ draws back from the table and raises his gaze to the window at the front of the deli. The owner brings Lily her toast. She butters it while he talks.

"I met him at work, as you know. Five years ago. Four and a half. Something like that. We were put on the same team, can't exactly remember what it was. Anyway. I always thought he was a cool guy. You know. Kind of reserved, but he had something about him. So I made it my mission to befriend him. The thing I worked out early on with Carl was that you needed to take two steps forward and then one step back. Make your approach and then give him some space. So if we went out for a drink, I'd always leave it a few weeks before I suggested it again. And when we did go out, I'd keep the conversation kind of general. Just talk football, office gossip. If the conversation got personal I'd be the one to draw it back to the neutral, so he wouldn't feel like I was prying. So really, crazy as it sounds, I hardly knew anything about him."

Lily nods. It doesn't sound crazy at all. "What about his family? Did he ever tell you anything about them?"

Russ frowns. "Not really. I mean, I knew he *had* a family. A mum. A sister. His dad had passed away, I think."

"Yes," says Lily, relieved that this matches with the facts that Carl had given her. "Can you remember the names? Of the mother and sister? Or the place where they live?"

"No, he never told me. Just said *my mum. My sister.* Have you not met them, then?"

"No. We only returned from our honeymoon two weeks ago. Carl said there was plenty of time for family but this was time for us. So." She shrugs. All the things that had felt so romantic at the time, so special, now reduced to symptoms of his subterfuge. "I spoke to her though, the day we married. Carl brought me to the phone and said, 'My mum wants to say hello.' It was a short call. A minute, maybe less. She sounded very sweet." (And very uncertain, she now recalls, as though keen to end the conversation, as though scared of saying the wrong thing.) "I just wish I could remember her name."

"Although," says Russ, "even if you could, it's possible that maybe her surname would not be Monrose? Assuming that Carl's surname is not

Monrose? So even if you could remember her first name, I doubt it would help."

"This is true. Yes. But it feels so strange that I don't remember. That this woman was my mother-in-law, that I had a conversation with her, yet I don't remember her name. It makes me feel as though . . . as though I've been in a dream. In a trance. Ever since I met him."

"Well, yes, that's what they say about being in love. It's a chemical state, isn't it? Messes with your mind."

"I suppose. And now, without him, alone, it is as though my mind is clearing. And all I am left with is questions, questions, questions. All the questions I should have asked when he was here."

"Well, hindsight is a beautiful thing."

Lily smiles grimly. She doesn't know what hindsight is. "Listen. Russ. Tell me, does this surprise you at all? About Carl?"

"Well, yes, of course it does. My God. People going missing, having false identities, it's not exactly everyday is it? But even so, Carl was quite a closed book."

"Why did you want to be his friend, Russ? With all his secretiveness? Why did you bother?"

Russ gently rests his coffee cup on to its saucer. "Good question," he says. "Jo always asks me that: 'What do you see in him?' She doesn't like him much." He laughs.

Lily feels mortally offended and takes an instant dislike to this "Jo".

"But I think there's just this kind of *mutual respect* between us. Chalk and cheese, but we get each other.

What it boils down to" — he leans towards her and she sees his body language relax as the kernel of the thing dawns upon him — "is that I would like to be more like him and he, I think, would like to be more like me." He leans back again, satisfied with the distillation.

Lily cannot imagine any way in which her Carl would want to be like this innocuous man, but she manages a smile and says, "Yes. I see."

"I think he wanted what I had, in terms of a settled relationship, a home, a solid family life. And I would have liked some of his freedom and glamour and good looks." He laughs again.

"Where did he live?" she asks, moving the conversation along. "Before he met me?"

"I have no idea." He smiles and shakes his head as though suddenly bemused. "Not south, I know that. At the end of the night I'd sometimes offer to share a cab and he'd always say, 'I'm going in the opposite direction.' But I never asked where that was exactly." He pauses and scratches his head. "Yeah," he says, "it's funny now, looking at it, how much time I spent with him and yet how little I knew about him."

"Did he have any girlfriends? Before me?"

"Well, yes, but nothing serious. Just . . ." He looks at her uncertainly. "It's a harsh thing to say, but I'd say he was a user. Well, at least that's the impression I got anyway. He'd use women for sex. Never any names, just *this girl I met on Friday* or *this girl I shagged on Saturday*. Came and went. He seemed almost . . . *disdainful?* As though they'd lessened themselves by being with him. He could be quite cruel about them. I often thought maybe he'd been hurt in the past? That hard shell, you know?" He taps his fingertips against the edge of the table, looking suddenly downcast. "But then you came along." He brightens. "And it was different. Totally different. He adored you. I think he thought that you were going to change everything. And now . . ."

"He is dead," she finishes for him.

"Well, I don't suppose he's dead. But he is in trouble. False identity. He must have done something bad. Or someone must have done something bad to him. Nobody changes their identity unless they really have to. Unless they're desperate. I'd like to help you — if I can?"

"Yes please," she says. "Please. I know no one in this country. No one. The policewoman hates me. And no one wants to help me. No one seems to care." She finds that she's crying and angrily takes the paper napkin that Russ offers her, rubs hard at her tears before anyone else sees them. "I am sorry."

"No, don't be sorry. Please. Listen, I'm going to talk to Jo when I get home, see what we can do. We might be able to . . ." He stops, clearly thinking better of sharing his next thought. "Well, I'll talk to her. We'll do everything we can. You must be in hell."

"Yes," says Lily, nodding hard. "Yes. In hell. That is where I am. That is exactly where I am."

CHAPTER
EIGHTEEN

What a charming family unit they make: Alice, Frank and Romaine. Alice, who has no experience whatsoever of being part of a conventional family, feels like a fraud. She wants to tell people that he's not her husband, that Romaine isn't his daughter, that she's not that normal, that she's not that good at making life choices.

The sunny morning has brought out half the town and it's fairly buzzing. There's a French food market setting up in the square and they stop to buy freshly baked croissants and strong, milky coffees. Alice feels strangely proud of her lovely little town — and then a glow of happiness at the idea that she now thinks of this place as *her little town*. She has felt like an outsider for so long.

"You know, they've filmed all sorts here," she says, wanting to prolong the fleeting sense of belonging. "They once shut the whole place off for two days to film *Pirates of the Caribbean*. Seriously. We weren't allowed in or out of our houses. For forty-eight hours. And not even a sideways glimpse of Johnny Depp."

She looks at Frank and realises that he has no idea what *Pirates of the Caribbean* is or who Johnny Depp is and she remembers that he is essentially an alien.

They're outside the Ridinghouse Grand. It's a tiny cinema, far from grand, built of breeze blocks and showing one film at a time. She notices that he is staring at the cinema intently.

"Are you remembering something?" she asks.

He half nods, half shakes his head. "I'm not sure. I think I might. It's . . ." He clasps his head by the temples and turns away abruptly. "I can see that girl again," he says. "The one with the brown hair. I saw her going in there." He points at the heavy glass doors. His hand moves from his head to his chest and he starts kneading at his heart. "I feel . . ." he said. "I don't know. I feel sick. I feel . . ." His skin is clammy and grey. Alice leads him to a bench and sits next to him. She takes his coffee cup and puts it by her side, then she takes his hand and offers him the brown paper bag that her croissant came in. He bats it away.

"Stay with me, Frank," she says. "Stay with me. We don't want you doing another overnight stint on the beach. Breathe. Breathe."

He grips on to her hand and she feels his breath slowing.

"That's it," she says. "I'm here. It's OK."

Romaine stands and watches, curiously. "Are you going to be sick?"

He shakes his head and forces a smile.

"You can be sick in that bin, if you want."

"No, thank you." His voice is shaking. "I don't think that will be necessary."

They sit for a while and wait for Frank to emerge from his panic attack. Because that is clearly what it is. Alice has had enough in her time to recognise the signs.

"OK?" she asks a few minutes later.

"OK." He smiles. She passes him his coffee and he gets to his feet. "Right," he says, "let's keep going."

"You sure? We can always come back later if you're not up to it?"

"No," he says. "This has gone on for long enough. It's all in there: I can feel it. It's there and I want to get it out. I want to know. Let's keep walking."

"Good," she says. "Fine."

She looks at him as they pass the cinema again, his gaze fixed upon the front doors. He looks terrified, she thinks. He looks distraught. What happened to Frank in this town? And what part did he play in it all?

CHAPTER
NINETEEN

1993

Kirsty and Mark were having a wonderful time. True to fairground cliché #1, Mark had won her a big, ugly soft toy, which she was clutching to her chest. They'd also had candy floss: fairground cliché #2. And he'd whacked the big weight thing with a mallet and made it go ding-dong: fairground cliché #3. And now, yes, right on target, just when Gray had begun to think it wasn't going to happen, they had emerged from the Tunnel of Love with their mouths attached. *Full house.*

Gray could barely stomach it.

It was half past nine. The sky was indigo with some lingering streaks of lilac. His sister was kissing a man. He was torn between going home and telling his mum and dad what was going on and not wanting to leave this spot in case something bad happened. And what, he wondered, did he mean by *bad?* He couldn't quite put the feeling into words, but it was there, like a lump in his throat. It wasn't just that he couldn't handle the prospect of his sister falling in love, of his sister having sex, of his sister growing up. It was more than that. It was darker than that. It was *him*. Mark. There was just something off about him. Something shadowy and cruel. There were too many angles in his face. Too much thought behind each gesture, each word, each action. Even his hair colour was too uniform, Gray felt, as though he could tug at it and Mark's whole face would come off to reveal his true identity, like a Scooby Doo villain.

He watched them climb out of the Tunnel of Love carriage and now they walked hand in hand, the ugly toy under Mark's arm. What would they do now? Gray wondered. They'd done the fair. Kirsty was too young to take to the pub. It was dark. They sauntered towards the exit; Mark threw back his head to laugh uproariously at something Kirsty had said. Gray couldn't imagine what. And then he watched with a growing sense of unease as Mark led Kirsty away from town and towards the sea. He slid down from the shelf he'd been sitting on and followed them. The lights from town barely shone here, and the music from the steam fair was a distant, slightly eerie murmur. All that lit the way was the creamy moon. Gray held back inside the silvery shadows and tried to hear what they were saying, but the smack and fizz of the tide against the sand muffled their voices. Eventually they stopped walking, silhouetted by the moon hanging dead centre between them, and Gray watched with horror as they turned to face each other and began to kiss, at first tenderly and then with increased fervour. He turned his head slightly not wanting to watch but also not wanting to stop watching in case he missed the moment that Mark did something to hurt his sister.

126

But a few minutes later, Mark pulled away from Kirsty, cupped her face with his hands, kissed the end of her nose and they both turned. "Come on," Gray heard him say, "it's getting late. I should get you home."

Gray was home ten minutes before Kirsty, slightly breathless from running the whole way.

"Where've you been?" said his mum, looking up from a thick second-hand novel with yellowed pages.

"Nowhere," he said. "Just walking."

"Nice dinner, wasn't it?"

"It was all right."

"And funny bumping into Mark. Of all people."

"That wasn't a coincidence, Mum."

"What do you mean? 'Course it was."

Gray rolled his eyes at her naïvety. "Don't you mind?"

"Mind what?"

"Kirsty. Going off with him. When he's so much older."

"Oh, come on. He's only nineteen. I had a twenty-year-old boyfriend when I was Kirsty's age."

"Yes. But we don't know him."

"We've been to his house, Graham! We've met his aunty! That's more than most parents get when their child starts a relationship."

Relationship?

His mum checked her wristwatch and as she did so there was the sound of laughter outside the front door and the clatter of the letterbox being opened and shut and Gray's dad came to the door and there were Kirsty and Mark and the ugly bear.

"Come in! Come in!" said Tony.

Mark looked curiously around the house. "Would you mind?" he asked. "I've walked past these little houses so many times and I've never been inside one."

"Of course not!" Tony held the door wider and gestured Mark inside. "Please."

"Wow," said Mark, "it's like a dolls' house! So tiny!"

"Well," said Tony, "they built these houses for tiny people. You know, back in the sixteen hundreds, when this place was built, we'd all have been giants!"

Mark bowed his head to go from room to room. Gray watched him curiously. Then he turned and glanced at Kirsty. Her face was pink and pinched with what looked like embarrassment.

"And up here?" Mark asked, peering up the staircase.

"Bedrooms," said Tony. "Want to see?"

Mark turned and smiled. "No," he said. "I get the idea."

"Can I get you a beer? Or something?"

"No." Mark looked at his watch. "Thank you. I'd better get back. Promised Kitty I'd clean up the kitchen after dinner. Didn't even tell her I was going out!" He laughed, a hard bark that seemed somehow unrelated to him. "But maybe I'll see you on the beach tomorrow? Forecast looks good."

"Maybe not tomorrow," said Tony. "We were thinking of a day trip."

Mark's expression blackened for a second and clouds of displeasure passed across his eyes. But then he rallied and said, "Oh! Great! Where are you going?"

"Not sure yet. Maybe Robin's Hood Bay. Maybe a castle. See how we feel."

Mark shrugged, sighing. "Ah, well. Maybe another time then."

"Yes," said Tony, "more than likely. You all right getting back up there?" He gestured towards the big house on the coastal path. "I can give you a lift?"

"Tony," said Mum. "You probably shouldn't. You've had a couple of beers."

"Oh, don't be so daft. I had two halves. Two hours ago."

"Honestly. I can walk. I've done it a million times. In all weathers. At all times. But thank you. You're very nice people."

He left a moment later in a flurry of good manners and cheek kisses, leaving them once again windswept and unsettled in his wake.

"So," Gray asked his sister over bowls of Frosties the following morning. "What did you talk about all night? You and *Mark?*"

"Why do you say his name like it's made up?"

He shrugged. "I don't know. He just feels like he's made up. Like he's working from a script."

She frowned at him. "What on earth are you talking about, you weirdo?"

"Never mind," he said, knowing that he wouldn't be able to explain it. "Anyway, what did you talk about?"

"Not much," she said. "Just about school and family and stuff."

"Do you still like him?"

She flushed with colour and stared into her cereal bowl. "Maybe. He's all right."

"You don't have to see him again, you know. You can say no, if he asks."

"Yeah, well, he probably won't. So."

"Did anything happen?" he asked, curious to see if she would lie to him. "You know, like kissing or anything?"

"What's that got to do with you?" she snapped.

"I'm your brother," he replied with more force than he'd intended.

"*I'm your brother*," she echoed him mockingly, using a deep voice and rolling her shoulders. She laughed.

"Yeah. Well. I just don't want you to do anything stupid."

She rolled her eyes and got to her feet. "You're just jealous," she said. "Because I've kissed someone and you haven't."

It was a light-hearted dig. She hadn't meant it to hurt. But it did. Gray had no idea why he hadn't kissed a girl yet, given how much time he spent with girls. He'd had lots of those Hollywood moments when it had looked as though he was about to kiss a girl but then they'd turn away or someone would walk in or he'd lose his nerve and make a joke out of it. And there were girls who liked him, he knew that. People told him. But it was always girls he didn't fancy. Sad, doughy-cheeked girls making desperate eye contact across the lunch hall.

He'd hugged girls and had girls sitting on his lap. He'd held hands with girls and kissed girls' cheeks and had fun with girls and gossiped with girls and had girls on the back of his bicycle. But for some reason he couldn't cross the line into physical intimacy. He would wonder if he was gay if it weren't for the fact that he knew resoundingly that he wasn't.

"Get stuffed," he said to his sister's retreating back. "What do you know?"

She ignored him and walked away.

Mark was sitting outside Rabbit Cottage when they got back from visiting Sledmere House six hours later. He'd positioned himself sideways on the sea wall opposite, turned towards the late-afternoon sun, in a crisp white shirt and faded jeans. He was holding a bunch of pink roses.

Gray noticed Kirsty stiffen slightly at the sight of him.

"Good timing," said Mark, sauntering towards them, "I just got here."

"Well," said Tony, "that's a bit of luck."

"Here." Mark passed the pink roses to Kirsty. "For your room. To brighten it up a bit."

"Oh," she said self-consciously. "Thank you."

There was an awkward silence, the sort of conversational void that needed to be filled with an invitation to come in. But nobody offered it.

"Did you have a nice day?" Mark asked.

"Super," said Tony. "Been a hundred times before, but it's always a good day out."

"I've never been," said Mark in a tone that suggested he wouldn't dream of it.

"So," said Pam, "what have you been up to? Been to the beach?"

Mark shook his head. "Not today. No."

His usual effortless charm seemed to have deserted him. Kirsty's body language was all wrong and he could tell.

Gray turned and headed to the front door of Rabbit Cottage. He felt very strongly that for some unknown reason his sister wanted to be rescued from this situation and that he needed to be the one to do it. "Keys, Dad," he called to his father.

Tony passed him the keys and smiled at Mark. "Well, maybe see you on the beach again?"

Mark looked at Kirsty who was heading away from him with her pink roses. "I wondered . . ." he said. "Kirsty, would you like to join me to see a film? Tonight?"

Kirsty looked at her parents beseechingly. But his mum missed the nuance and said, "Well, I don't see why not. We haven't got anything planned for tonight."

"Great," said Mark, all the uncertainty disappearing and his usual carapace of self-assurance re-forming. "I'll come at seven. If that's OK?"

"Yeah," said Kirsty, her gaze on the floor. "Sure. See you then."

CHAPTER
TWENTY

Lily slides the two rings across the counter towards the jeweller. "Please," she begins, "can you tell me the value of these rings?"

He looks at her curiously. He thinks she has stolen them. It is obvious. Probably from the bedside table of some married man she has been sleeping with. She manages a small smile and says, "Thank you."

He rolls the rings on to a black velvet tray and brings a small magnifier to his eye. "Well," he says a few moments later. "They're both eighteen-carat gold, bought as a set; the stone is a diamond, about a carat. Value of around eight hundred pounds for the wedding band. Somewhere between two and three thousand for the engagement ring. Do you want to sell them?"

"No!" she says sharply. "No. They belong to my husband's mother. They are an heirloom!"

The man stares at her for a moment. "I doubt it," he says. "These rings were hallmarked in 2006."

She nods, as though this fact is not at all surprising. "I know," she says, adjusting her handbag. "Thank you." She drops the rings into her purse and zips it shut. "Very helpful."

On the high street outside the jeweller's, Lily clutches her handbag against her chest. She'd taken the rings to be valued because she'd suspected they did not belong to Carl's mother. The style was too modern. But she'd hoped she might be wrong. Now she knows her instinct was right. And after her conversation this morning with Russ she is left with the knowledge that she has no idea where Carl was between his birth on 4 June 1975 and starting work at the financial services company in 2010. Thirty-five blank years. Might there have been a wife, a family even? Russ had said that Carl used women for sex. That Lily had been the first woman he'd wanted to settle with. But Russ had only known him for five years. Carl had come to him, as he'd come to Lily, as a book without words. Maybe before that he had been a different person, with different traits. Maybe he had been hurt by another woman, the woman who owned the rings.

She stares down at her left hand, at the rings on her wedding finger. A thin white-gold band, paired with a baguette-cut diamond eternity ring. Carl had chosen the engagement ring himself. She remembers how she'd felt a tiny pinch of disappointment when she'd opened the suedette box. She'd been expecting a solitaire diamond, the type of diamond that snags on clothes and glitters under halogens, the type of diamond that looks like it contains all the constellations of the universe. But she had hidden her disappointment, smiled and said, "It is beautiful," whilst silently wondering how much it had cost.

She would have liked a ring like this, like the one zipped away inside her handbag. The one that her husband may have bought for another woman.

She breathes in hard and heads down the high street, away from the shops, back to the silence and stillness of her empty flat.

There is a small fan of letters on the doormat. She collects them together and adds them to the other letters that have arrived since Carl went missing four days ago. She is tired. Beyond tired. She heads straight to the bedroom. The keys are still there, by her bed. She picks them up, rolls the brass fob around her palm, examines the grooves and nibs of the keys. One of them has a plastic head and a strange double-sided stem with a complicated pattern of indents. There is a key-cutter by the station. She will take it there, maybe; tomorrow, if it's open, or Monday. The man in there might know. It might tell her something. It might help. Because, Lily is now almost entirely certain, these keys are the keys that open the door to the house where Carl lived with the wife who wore the rings in her handbag.

She sits on the side of the bed and she takes off the high-heeled shoes she wore today to look nice for Carl's only friend. She pulls her hair away from her face and fixes it into a ponytail and she stares through the window, into treetops silhouetted by the bleached-out sky behind.

It's Saturday. She tries to remember what she was doing this time last week. They had lunch, she remembers suddenly, at a pub in the countryside. It was a smart pub. Painted shades of grey, menus on blackboards, newspapers hanging from poles and cutlery in wooden pots on the tables. Carl had had a burger; she'd had an Asian prawn salad with noodles. Carl had had a pint of cider; she'd had a glass of Prosecco. What had they talked about? She can't remember. Work, she supposed: Carl talked about work a lot. Her family. He always liked to hear the latest news about her family. The flat. They'd been planning to redecorate, put some new colours on the off-white walls and soften the lighting, get some new blinds. "Put our mark on it," Carl had said. Lily had not really seen the point in spending more money on the flat when it was already so perfect but she liked to see Carl's face soften as he discussed it, she liked the way he became so animated. They'd talked about the food, of course. Carl was obsessed with food. So many people in this country seemed to be obsessed with food. On the television, day and night, there were shows about food, and the shops bursting at the seams with food that had travelled thousands of miles to get there. And even there, in the country-side, surrounded by fields, by cows and sheep, in a pub, a place to drink, there was tuna sashimi.

So, they had talked — comfortably. They had laughed. Their feet had curled together beneath the table; between courses they had held hands across the table. A normal newly married couple. Then Carl had driven them home, stopping on the way to pick up some shirts from the dry cleaner's. There'd followed a movie, some wine, sex. She'd woken the following morning, as she did most mornings, to find Carl smiling at her. And, as she did most mornings, she'd said, "What are you smiling at?" And he'd traced the contours of her face with his fingertips and said, "You." And then they'd kissed and had sex again. And that was how life had been. A tight, almost suffocating cocoon of love. Sometimes Lily had wondered if it might be nice to go to a night-club or to meet friends for dinner. But as Carl himself had often said, they were "still on honeymoon". There was plenty of time to share themselves with other people, to dilute the intensity of their coupling. Lily had been happy to wait.

But now she is feeling the full force of their isolation. She pulls the duvet over herself, over her head, so that it is dark and airless and she curls herself into a small ball.

CHAPTER
TWENTY-ONE

Alice, Frank and Romaine return three hours later with a bag full of perfectly decent clothes from the Red Cross shop and a three-pack of boxers and a clutch of new socks from M&Co on the high street. It's past lunchtime and everyone is starving so Alice has picked up a ton of fish and chips from round the corner, which they unfold at the kitchen table and tip on to china plates.

"I do normally cook," says Alice as Kai squirts half a bottle of ketchup over his chips and puts three in his mouth. "It's just everything feels a bit . . . out of sequence right now."

"I'm sorry," he says.

"No! You don't need to be sorry! It's just — I'm not the most together person in the world and it doesn't take much to make all the wheels fall off. I'm only one unexpected house guest away from existential chaos."

"I'll go shopping for you," he says futilely.

"They make you pay for stuff round here."

"I know. I just thought . . ."

She squeezes his hand and smiles. "I know what you meant and it's very sweet of you. But I can send one of this lot out." She gestures at Kai and Jasmine, who both roll their eyes at her. "And tell you what, to prove that I'm not as *Benefits Britain* as you probably think I am, I'll cook us a lovely dinner tonight. Pasta. Something like that."

He nods. Her offer is genuine and warm but he still feels guilty. "Once I've worked out who I am, I'm going to take you all to the . . ." He searches for the name. It begins with R. It evokes thoughts of 1920s glamour. It's gone. He sighs.

Alice looks at him and chuckles. "Sounds great. But, seriously, you don't have to do anything. Just accept the hospitality. That's how we do things *oop north*." She puts on a northern accent and her children, who all have northern accents, tut at her.

"Well, I'll be paying you back for the clothes and the rent."

"That you can do," she says. She smiles at him over the top of Romaine's head. It's a worn-out smile, tired and faded around the edges. But there's still a kind of thrilling glamour about it. Something golden and intoxicating. Like an old hotel, he thinks. Like . . . *the Ritz.*

He smiles to himself at the satisfyingly recalled name and he adds it to his collection: a priceless coin dug up on a beach.

Derry is at the front door. She has Daniel by the hand and looks very stern. "What", she says, "is going on? Jules says she saw you in town this morning, shopping, with that guy."

Alice clutches her heart and throws Derry a look of mock horror. "Scandalous!" she says.

Derry grimaces. "But, Al, it's one thing giving him shelter, it's another spending your bloody money on him."

"Christ, Derry, I spent twenty quid in the Red Cross shop." This isn't strictly true. It was closer to forty once you factored in the pants and socks.

"Is he here?"

Alice sighs. "So far as I know. He's in the shed. Having a nap."

Derry is wriggling with frustration. This is the downside of allowing a friend to manage your life for you.

Alice holds the door open and says, "Come on then. Let's get this over with. And just for the record," she adds in a low voice, following her friend into the kitchen, "Griff loves him. And so does Romaine. And kids and dogs *know people*."

"And what about you?"

"What about me?"

"You know what I mean."

"He's nice," she says circumspectly. "What do you want me to say?"

Daniel finds Romaine in the back yard and Derry immediately starts tidying Alice's kitchen. She doesn't even know she's doing it. " 'Nice'," she mutters. "Well. I look forward to being able to draw my own conclusions." She drops a ball of chip paper into Alice's bin, washes her hands and dries them. Peering through the window of the back door into the back yard she says, "He's up."

"Up?"

"Yeah. Your man. Playing with the littlies."

Alice joins her at the back door. Romaine and Daniel have embroiled Frank in a game involving two dolls, a threadbare dog and a Transformer. He is on his haunches, following instructions very gravely.

"See," says Alice. "He's a fine man."

"That's as maybe," says Derry, hanging up Alice's tea towel and switching on the kettle. "But he's an unknown quantity. And given your history, I really think you should call the police."

Alice rubs the tips of her elbows. As much as she doesn't want to fuel Derry's paranoia, she does want to share. "I suggested it," she says. "When he first arrived. He blanched. Looked petrified." She shrugs.

"Well," says Derry. "That's not particularly reassuring."

"And there's other stuff. He's started remembering things. He remembers watching a man jumping into the sea and drowning. He remembers a teenage girl on the carousel at the steam fair."

"So," says Derry, "have you googled it?"

"Googled what?"

"Men jumping into the sea and drowning?"

"What? No. Of course I haven't. I don't even know when it happened."

Derry sighs. "Where's your laptop?"

"In my room."

"Bring it down."

Alice does as she's told. Jasmine is sitting at her desk in her room and turns when Alice walks in. "Sorry, love, I need the laptop."

"When's he going?" she asks, closing the browser and putting the laptop to sleep.

"Frank?"

"Whatever. Yeah."

"I don't know," she says. "Soon. When he remembers."

"But what if he doesn't remember?"

"He will, love. It says, on the internet. It's temporary."

Jasmine stands up, adjusts her black-framed glasses and shrugs.

"Griff likes him," she says to Jasmine's back.

"Right," says Jasmine. "He's a dog."

"A fussy dog!" she calls after her daughter, but she's gone.

"Man drowned in Ridinghouse Bay".

Alice and Derry sit, heads almost touching, side by side at the laptop. Derry presses enter and they wait for the results to come up.

It is immediately surprising how many men have drowned off Ridinghouse Bay.

"We need a year," says Derry.

"I told you," says Alice. "I have no idea."

"You said he remembered a teenage girl. So maybe this happened when he was a teenager. How old do you reckon he is?"

"Late thirties? Forty maybe?"

142

"Right. So, say he was eighteen. And forty now. Twenty-two years ago. Nineteen ninety-three. Roughly."

"Very roughly," says Alice.

"It's better than nothing." She adds "1993" to her search. "Check on them, will you?" she instructs Alice.

Obediently, Alice goes to the back door and peers through the window again. The game is still very much on. Frank is voicing the threadbare dog. Romaine has one bare, olive-skinned arm draped nonchalantly around Frank's shoulder, her hip angled against him. They look as though they could be father and daughter. No one would doubt it for a moment.

Alice sits down next to Derry. "He's murdered them both," she deadpans. "Cut them to ribbons, is eating their warm flesh off the ground with the dogs."

Derry nudges her hard. "Shut up," she says. "Look." She angles the screen towards her. "Not quite a drowned man, but the timings match."

There is a story on the screen, from the *Ridinghouse Gazette* archives.

The Coastguard was called out to Ridinghouse Bay at around 1 a.m. this morning after reports of three people struggling off the coast. Two of those involved have yet to be located and are feared drowned. The third, a man named locally as tourist Anthony Ross, suffered a fatal heart attack on the beach moments after being swept to shore. Another man, believed to be Ross's teenage son, was taken to hospital but released shortly afterwards. Police are investigating the incident.

Derry is already googling the names: "Anthony Ross", "Ridinghouse Bay".

Nothing else comes up.

They hear the back door clatter and the children run in, high on play. Frank follows behind them and stops shyly when he sees Derry sitting there.

"Frank," Alice says, "this is my best friend, Derry Dynes."

"Hi," she says, a softness in her voice that wouldn't have been there if she hadn't just read the story about a teenage boy's father dying on the beach. "Mother of Daniel." She points at her son.

"Nice to meet you," says Frank. "Great kids."

"Listen," says Alice, exchanging a look with Derry who nods, imperceptibly. "We've just been looking into things, on the internet, seeing what we could find out about drownings in the area. And we found a story from a good few years back. Two people feared drowned on a summer's night. A man and his teenage son found on the beach, just here." She gestures towards the front door. "Apparently the man died of a heart attack. But the son survived. Does that ring any bells? Nineteen ninety-three? Anthony Ross?"

She is talking and talking because Frank is not responding.

"I mean, it could be entirely the wrong time frame. We were just taking a punt. You know, you mentioned the teenage girl. So we thought it might have been something that happened when you were a teenager. If anything actually happened at all of course."

144

Still he does not respond. He is leaning against the kitchen counter, but as Alice watches she realises that he is not leaning but being held up, that he is sliding, that his face has lost all its colour. She sees his hands grip the sides of the work surface, his knuckles white and hard.

"Frank?"

Derry jumps to her feet. "He's fainting," she says. "Quick. Let's get him sitting down. Help me!"

But it's too late. He falls to the floor like a felled tree.

CHAPTER
TWENTY-TWO

1993

Mark returned two hours later. He was wearing a blazer. An actual blazer. To go to the Ridinghouse Grand.

"What's on?" Tony asked, seeing them off at the door.

"*Cliffhanger*," Mark replied, his hand in the small of Kirsty's back.

"Oh, yeah, that's supposed to be thrilling," said Tony.

"So I've heard," says Mark.

Kirsty was edging out of the door, looking keen to be on her way. She'd claimed under heavy questioning from Gray that she really did want to go to the cinema and that Gray was imagining things when he'd suggested that she hadn't looked that keen earlier.

At the sound of their voices disappearing up the street towards town he jumped to his feet. His mum was cooking spaghetti in the kitchen and he stuck his head around to the door to say that he was popping out to buy a bottle of Coke.

"We've got Sprite," she said.

"I want Coke."

"Well then, can you get a lump of cheddar while you're at it?"

Kirsty and Mark had been walking slowly and he was able to catch up with them halfway to the high street without running. They'd stopped to look in the window of an antique shop. There was a display of old china dolls and they were talking about how spooky they were. Mark again put his hand into the small of Kirsty's back and gently guided her onwards towards the cinema.

He watched from a distance as Mark held the doors open for his sister and gallantly ushered her through. And then they were gone.

Mark brought Kirsty home at ten. Gray could hear them from his bedroom over the street. There was a kind of heaviness about their voices, as though they were on the verge of an argument. He peeled his curtain back a little and peered down on to the crowns of their heads. He saw Mark try to kiss her and he saw Kirsty duck to avoid the kiss.

"Oh, come on," he heard Mark say. "Not one single kiss throughout that whole ridiculous movie. And now not even a little one outside your door? That's not very kind."

"I'm sorry," she said, "I'm really tired. I just want to go to bed."

"You can go to bed very, very soon, I promise," he said, looming towards her again with puckered lips.

She ducked away again and said, "Honestly. I'm shattered."

"Really?" he said in a disbelieving tone and Gray heard him tut under his breath. Then: "What about tomorrow?" He sounded sulky, petulant almost. "Or are you going on another *day trip?*"

And there it was, the kernel of everything that Gray had been feeling uncomfortable about all week. Mark thought they were amusingly provincial. He thought he was better than them. Yet he was pursuing his sister as though she was the love of his life.

"I don't know," he heard Kirsty reply. "I don't think so."

"Well then, shall I come and call for you? We could spend the day at my aunt's. I'll make you lunch."

"I don't know," she repeated. "I need to ask Mum and Dad."

"Can you ask them now?" His tone was clipped and impatient.

"I'll ask tomorrow."

"Why not now?"

"It's late. I'm tired."

He heard Mark tut again and then say, "Fine. I'll call round tomorrow morning. You can tell me then."

His sister hesitated and then said, "OK. See you tomorrow."

The door clicked shut behind her and Gray heard her talking quietly with their parents before going straight to bed. Through his bedroom window, Gray watched as Mark stood for a moment or two outside Rabbit Cottage, his hands in his pockets, staring darkly at the front door, the muscles in his hollowed-out cheeks twitching slightly. Then he turned and crossed the narrow cobbled street, looked out to sea for a moment before suddenly and fearsomely kicking the sea wall, once, twice, three times, then finally heading away from the cottage, a thin, angry silhouette disappearing from view into the misty summer's night.

CHAPTER
TWENTY-THREE

Lily wakes from her nap with a start. It's dark and the duvet is twisted around her legs. She looks at the clock by the bed: 8:09. For a moment she has no idea if it is morning or night. Then she remembers that it's still Saturday night. She'd been dreaming of her family. She'd been dreaming of home. She picks up the phone and calls her mother.

"Mama," she says, her voice full of sleep. "He is still gone."

"Come home," says her mother.

"I cannot come home. In case he comes back."

"If he comes back he will know where you are. He knows how to get here."

"He cannot get here. The policewoman still has his passport."

"He can phone you and you can come back."

"But what if he is hurt?"

"Lily. He is in his own country. If he is hurt there are people there who will look after him."

"I am not so sure, Mama. They came yesterday and took his computer. They said that the kind of fake passport he had comes from the criminal underworld.

150

So he may know dangerous people. He may have crossed them."

Her mother makes a strange strangled noise. "My God. Lily. You must leave! You're in the flat by yourself. What if they come for you? What if he comes for you and they follow him? You are a sitting target!"

"I have nowhere to go, Mama! I know no one!"

"Oh, I knew. I knew this was all wrong. I should have stopped it. I should have made you wait."

"I would still have married him and he would still have been lying to me."

"No. With more time you would have realised. It is like onions. People reveal themselves to you a layer at a time. That is why you should wait. Wait until you get to the layers near the bottom. Usually where the worst stuff is. And *then*, if the worst stuff is not so bad, then you marry."

"Carl is not a bad man, Mama! We don't know his story! I think it is possible he was married before. I found some rings. Maybe this other woman hurt him. Maybe something bad happened to him. Maybe he has a false identity to hide from this woman! We don't know anything."

She hears her mother sigh. "I want you to come home. I can pay for tickets."

Lily pauses. She can't deny that she wants to be at home now. She wants her mother and her brothers and her dog and her college friends and the bars and the lost Saturday nights. She wants to brush her hair in the mirror in the bedroom she left behind, still adorned with photos of her and her friends. She wants to link

151

arms with those friends and walk down familiar streets, speak a familiar language, see familiar faces. She wants to be somewhere where she can talk to a stranger without being misread and treated with suspicion.

But — Carl was her ticket to the UK. Without Carl, or whoever he really is, she may not be allowed back. And for some reason, as lonely as she is, and as scared as she is, she wants to be allowed back. She wants to keep the key to the door of this life she has had such a small taste of.

"I am not coming back," she says, "not yet. Not until I know for sure what has happened to Carl."

Her mother sighs and she hears her tongue make a clicking sound against her teeth. "You," she says, warmly. "I don't where you came from. This strong woman. This woman alone in a foreign country. You are brave and foolish. But I cannot stop you."

"No," she says, "you cannot."

"I miss you. I love you."

"I love you, too."

"And soon, when I have finished this big contract, I will come. OK?"

"Yes. Please."

"A week. Maybe ten days."

"Good. Thank you."

"And by then, maybe, you will know where your husband is."

"Please. Yes."

"For what it is worth, I think he is a good man."

"He is. Yes. I know." Her syllables become more and more clipped as she feels tears surging.

"I love you."

"I love you, too."

And then the phone line is silent and the room is silent and the only light comes from the crack in the bathroom door. Lily drops the phone into her lap and cries.

CHAPTER
TWENTY-FOUR

Frank sleeps all afternoon. When he awakens at just past six he feels as though he is rising from a coma. It's dark already and the lights in the shed are turned off. As his eyes grow accustomed to the darkness, he sees the warm glow of the lights from the back of Alice's cottage. There's loud music coming from one of the rooms upstairs and the sound of high-octane teenage discourse. The noise prickles his subconscious in some strange way and he closes his eyes, trying to locate the root of it. But it's not there. He remembers being in Alice's kitchen, with Alice and that woman, her friend. *Debbie?* He'd walked in and they'd both turned and looked at him with the same expression of uneasiness and concern. And then they'd told him about a man called Anthony Ross who'd died on the beach, out there, in the very same spot where he'd sat for all those hours this week. The name had hit his consciousness like a bullet and then he'd blacked out. As he rises from the camp bed he tries to retrace the impact of the name. *Anthony Ross*, he mutters to himself. *Anthony Ross*. But nothing comes.

His stomach grumbles and he tries to ignore it. He can't keep walking into Alice's house expecting to be fed. He spends a few minutes dreaming of all the things he will do for Alice once he has found his life again. He'll send them on holiday. He'll take them out for meals. And, Christ, if he turns out to be really wealthy, he'll pay off their mortgage for them.

A moment later he sees the garden lighten and hears footsteps crunching across the gravel. He instinctively touches his hair, pushing it into place.

Alice knocks gently at the door. "Frank?"

He opens it and smiles at her.

"Christ. Thank God. You're alive. I was getting really worried."

"I'm fine," he says. "Bit blurry. But fine."

"Thank God," she says again. "Anyway, here." She passes him a large carrier bag. "It's all the stuff we bought earlier. I gave it a wash for you. Even the clean stuff smells bad in charity shops, doesn't it?"

He takes the bag from her and says, "Wow. Thank you. I didn't expect you to do that."

"For my own benefit really. Don't want another stinky house guest." She smiles. "Listen. I've cooked an actual meal. Meat and stuff. Want to join us?"

He wants to say no, because of his guilt. But his stomach speaks for him. "That would be wonderful. If you're sure it's not an imposition."

"God, no, I'm feeding the five thousand anyway, so another mouth won't make any difference. About ten minutes," she finishes, pushing her hands into the pockets of a huge hairy cardigan. "But just come when you're ready."

Frank picks out a soft blue shirt and a pair of khaki trousers from the bag of fresh-smelling clothes, then snaps off a pair of brand new socks from a packet. Pulling them on feels like the most civilised thing that has happened to him since he lost his memory, and as he approaches the back door a few minutes later he feels almost like a proper person.

The house is full of good smells, and all the windows in the kitchen are steamed up. Romaine is standing on a step stool over the hob stirring a pan of gravy and Derry is slicing carrots at the kitchen table while Daniel sits on the floor rubbing Hero's stomach.

"Through here," he hears Alice call from next door. "Here." She passes him a large glass of wine. "What do you think?" She has cleared the piles of paperwork and homework and books and artwork from the dining table and laid it. There is a small cluster of candles flickering in the centre and purple linen napkins folded into triangles on orange dinner plates, and heavy crackled-glass wine goblets with indigo bases.

"It looks beautiful," he says.

"Yeah," she says, appraising it herself. "Pretty classy. If I do say so myself." She raises her wine glass to his and says, "Cheers. To you not being dead."

He smiles. "I guess."

"And you're sure you're feeling all right? You went down like a dead weight."

"I'm pretty sure," he says, feeling the red wine warming the lining of his empty stomach, bleeding pleasantly into his cold veins. "I feel normal."

"Nothing normal about you, Frank," she says.

He laughs. "That's true."

They are silent for a moment. Frank can feel Alice's next question hanging in the air between them. He smiles at her.

"So," she says. "Anthony Ross."

"Yeah. I know. It obviously means something. It's obviously connected to me. The fact that I came here, the fact I sat right there." He gestures at the beach. "The fact that I can remember something to do with a man in the sea out there. It's definitely part of my story. I just wish I knew in what way."

"So there's nothing there now? No recollection?"

He shakes his head, apologetically, realising the implications for Alice of his failure to remember.

"That's a shame," she said. "I'd been secretly fantasising about you waking up fully restored back to factory settings."

"Me too," he replies.

"Clothes look nice." She nods at the outfit. "You look . . . very fresh."

He looks down upon himself. "Thank you. I'm so, so grateful. Honestly."

She shushes him and tops up their wine glasses. A peal of raucous laughter echoes down the staircase. She tuts. "I'm afraid we've been infiltrated," she says. "Kai's off to a party later and half the town's population of fourteen- and fifteen-year-olds is convening in his bedroom. There's about thirty of them up there. In his ten-by-eight bedroom. Doesn't bear thinking about."

"Al!" Derry calls from the kitchen. "*Something pinged!*"

"Sprouts," she says to Frank. "Be back in a minute. Help yourself to wine."

Frank stands and observes the warm flicker of the tea lights on the table for a while. He realises that they are scented in some way. He struggles for the smell. Something floral. He sees a white flower, with small blossoms. Then he notices a box on the sideboard behind him.

Jasmine and lily.

A huge thump reverberates through the low ceilings of the dining room, followed by screams of hilarity. A door opens and closes. "Christ's sake! What the fuck are you doing in there?" And then there are soft footsteps on the stairs. Jasmine walks into the dining room and stops when she sees him standing there.

"Oh."

"Your mum's in the kitchen," he says, wanting to stanch her awkwardness for her.

"Great," she says, "thanks."

She's tiny, with a head slightly too big for her body. Her black hair is twisted into a small bun over each ear and she's wearing a fitted black mini-dress under a baggy grey cardigan that hangs down the backs of her calves.

"Mum!" he hears her complaining. "They're being mental up there. Seriously. You need to stop them!"

Frank can't hear Alice's response, but a moment later Alice reappears, followed by Jasmine, Romaine and Hero, and yells up the stairs: *Food! Food!*

Within fifteen seconds a dozen teenagers have stampeded down the stairs, slowing gently as they pass the grown-ups, filing in and out of the kitchen with paper plates piled with sausages and mash and onion gravy. They take the plates to the sitting room and close the door behind them.

Frank looks at Alice in surprise. "You fed all those children?"

"Lining their stomachs. They'll go out empty otherwise and puke up everywhere. Besides, just some cheap sausages, on special offer. No big deal. Don't worry," she continues, "nice rib of beef for us. And *vegetables*."

"I'd be happy with cheap sausages."

"Yeah, so would I. But after all the crap we've been eating the last few days I thought it was time for something decent. More wine?"

Derry appears holding two steaming bowls which she deposits on the table before disappearing back into the kitchen. Romaine and Jasmine pull out chairs and sit down. Hero and Sadie both settle themselves expectantly on the floor by the table, their noses twitching.

"Can I do something?"

"No," says Alice. "You've had a shock. You just sit down. Me and Derry will sort it."

A large piece of meat is brought to the table, a dish of buttered mashed potatoes, jars of mustard and horse-radish and ketchup. A teenager appears with a pile of used paper plates and asks Alice where they should go.

She tells him and then calls after him, "There's Oreos on the side. Take a couple of packets through."

Alice tops up glasses with more red wine and sends Jasmine into the kitchen to get a second bottle. One of the dogs is making a low-level whining sound, like a distant car alarm.

"Shut up, Hero," says Alice.

Frank sees Romaine drop a piece of sausage at her feet and watches Hero pounce on it stealthily. He looks at Alice but she hasn't seen.

They're talking about Alice's parents, who have been witnessed on the webcam trying to remember the names of their children. "'The nice one,' my dad kept saying. 'You know. Lovely girl.' And then my mum was saying, 'You mean Alice?' And my dad was saying, 'No, not that one. The other one. You know? What's her name?' And my mum just shook her head and said, "Well, there's two. I know that much.'"

Derry laughs and says, "At least they still know they've got kids. That'll go soon."

Frank watches and listens and wonders about his mother, the one whose arms he remembered. Is she alive? Is she well? Is she senile? Is she missing him? Is *anyone* missing him? He slices through the meat and puts it in his mouth.

"Lovely beef, Alice," says Derry, looking meaningfully at Frank.

"Mm," he says, through his mouthful. "It's beautiful. So tender."

Alice smiles at him and touches his hand. "Good," she says. "I'm glad you like it."

There's a small and slightly uncomfortable silence as Alice gives his hand a last squeeze before letting it go.

The gesture has been observed and, in the cases of Derry and Jasmine, disapproved of.

"I was wondering," he says. "It's been four days now. Has there been anything, do you think? Anything on the news about a missing man? I mean, I seem like a decent type. It seems strange that there's no one to miss me. Doesn't it?"

"I've been checking," says Alice. "National news and the local London news. There hasn't been anything. But that doesn't mean you haven't been reported missing. It just means that it's not a story. And you know, the only way we can find out if anyone's reported you missing is to go to the police."

"I really . . ." His fingers fluster with his cutlery and a prickle of discomfort runs through him. "I really would like to remember a bit more. For myself. Before, you know . . . ?"

"But what if you don't?" snaps Jasmine and everyone turns to look at her.

"Jasmine . . ." says Alice.

"No. Really. What if you don't remember anything and there's, like, a whole family down south missing you and wondering where you are and feeling sick with worry? It's not fair on them. Is it?"

"I don't think . . ." he mutters. "I don't know, but I don't think there is anyone. I just don't feel . . ."

"There must be someone," says Jasmine. "Everyone has someone."

"Well, not necessarily," says Alice.

"That's not the point. It's not the point and you know it."

"Then what is the point?" says Alice.

"The point is that 'Frank' belongs somewhere. And no one seems to be making any effort to find out where it is. The point is that 'Frank' doesn't belong here. You know, if you'd found a stray dog on the beach that day you'd have done everything you could to find its owners; you'd have taken it to the vet to see if it was chipped; you'd have put posters up. You wouldn't have just started treating it like it was your pet. Not without knowing."

"Jasmine," says Alice again, looking at her daughter with concern, "you have to trust me here. I've lived a long and peculiar life and I've known enough bad people in my life to recognise one when I see one. And trust me, Frank is one of the good guys." She glances at Frank, throwing him a reassuring look. "I just want to help him, OK? And clearly there is some mysterious reason why he ended up on our beach and if he's not ready to confront his real life then we have to give him some time to feel ready."

"It's nothing personal," Jasmine says to Frank with a flash of her heavily liquid-lined eyes. "Genuinely. I'm sure you're really nice. I just . . ."

Frank smiles. "I understand," he says. "I do. I feel . . ." He looks for words that won't make him sound ungrateful. "I feel bad being here. I feel bad for taking up your personal space. I feel bad for your mum spending money on me. I feel bad for not being a real person, for making you feel uncomfortable in your own home. And I feel bad that I'm so weak and so needy. I feel . . . *very strongly* . . . that I'm not really like this.

That the real me is nothing like this. But right now I have no gumption and guts. I'm like a . . . limp rag. And hopefully this will pass, this big blackout blind in my head will spring open and I'll remember and then I'll feel strong. And I'm hoping it will be really soon. I mean" — he turns to Alice — "your mum found something today . . ."

"I know," says Jasmine, "she told me. You fainted."

"Yeah. So, I don't know, that could be the start of unravelling my story."

Jasmine nods. "Like I said," she says, her eyes downcast. "Nothing personal."

Frank exhales. He has not uttered so many words in such short succession since he lost his memory. He feels simultaneously depleted and euphoric, as though he has grown himself a new layer of muscle. "Thank you," he says.

He notices Derry and Alice exchange a look and then Derry says, "By the way, after you passed out earlier, me and Alice, we kept on looking. Couldn't find anything else about the Anthony Ross thing, but I emailed the editor, asked if maybe they had contact details for whoever wrote the piece. Or if they had any other stories."

Frank catches his breath and waits for the rest.

"Haven't heard back yet. But then, you know, it's Saturday. Maybe we'll hear something next week."

He exhales. Nothing new, but the potential for something new, at least. As the conversation warms up again and moves away from him he gazes down at his hands folded around his knife and fork, examines the angles and the creases, the freckles and the hairs. He wonders where these hands have been, whom they've touched, what they've done. And as this thought passes through his mind, he suddenly feels it again, the heaviness of someone against him, the feeling of hot breath against his face and his hands, *these* hands, tight around a throat, squeezing and squeezing and squeezing. He sees the blurry beginnings of a face, a man's face. A thatch of black hair, dark-blue eyes bulging from a handsome face.

CHAPTER
TWENTY-FIVE

1993

"So," said Gray, "what happened last night?"

"Nothing," Kirsty replied defensively.

"You know my window is right over the front door, right?"

"Yeah. And?"

"I heard what was happening. I heard him being arsey with you."

"What do you mean, *arsey*?"

"He got all dark and twisted when you wouldn't kiss him. And after you went inside he kicked the wall. Really hard. Didn't look like the date of the century."

She shrugged. "I just wasn't really in the mood. You know."

"My point exactly. At this point in a beautiful new relationship you should be all over each other like a rash, unable to keep your hands off each other."

Kirsty tutted and raised her eyebrows at him. "What would you know?"

"I know what love's young dream is supposed to look like, I've seen enough movies, and it's not you two, that's for sure."

"Life isn't like the movies, Gray."

He sighed. "Listen, Kirst, I'm not trying to get at you, I'm just looking out for you. This is your first boyfriend and I'm getting all kinds of bad vibes about it. About him."

Kirsty blinked and stared at the floor.

"It's just, you need to know that you're allowed to say no. There's no law that says you have to go out with someone just because they asked you. He's a big grown-up guy, he can cope with rejection. He'll get over it. And he's going to be coming over here any minute now trying to persuade you to *spend the day* with him and you need to decide now what you're going to say to him."

"I *know*," she hissed and Gray knew he'd hit the mark.

"So?"

"Can you tell him?" she said. And there she was again, the baby sister coming to him with a scraped knee. "Can you tell him I'm ill?"

Gray held back a victorious smile. "Sure," he said. "I can do that."

"It's not that I don't like him. I do. It's just . . ."

"You're not ready."

She looked at him first crossly and then softly. "Kind of. I guess. I mean, he's maybe a bit old for me. And he's really intense. About everything. And maybe I should be with someone who's a bit more fun."

"I concur. Wholeheartedly."

"But it's just that he's so *good-looking*. I keep thinking about my friends. How jealous they'd be if they saw us together."

"So, not shallow or anything then?"

She frowned and then smiled. "I know. And it's not like they'd ever see us together anyway."

"No," he agreed. "I can't quite envisage Mark pitching up in Croydon somehow."

As Gray spoke they both became aware of a movement behind them, a shadow across the low window that overlooked the street. Kirsty gasped and clamped her hand over her heart. It was Mark, hands cupped against the glass, peering in at them. He smiled grimly as his eye caught Gray's.

"Oh, for fuck's sake," Gray muttered. He turned to Kirsty but she had slipped, fast as light, under the table and was crouching on the floor at his feet.

"Tell him I'm sick," she hissed.

"But he's seen you."

"He might not have."

"Of course he has!"

"Just go and tell him. Please."

Gray sighed and pushed back his chair.

Mark stood at the door in jeans and a baseball cap. The baseball cap looked like a rushed after-thought, something he'd thrown on at the last minute because maybe his hair hadn't looked plastic enough. "Yo."

"Er, yo."

"Can I have a word with your sister?"

"She's not well."

"But she's ..." He pointed behind Gray at the dining room to the right.

"She went back to bed."

"Oh, come on ..."

"I don't know what you want me to say. She was sick. She went back to bed."

"Do you really expect me to believe that?"

"Yes. I really do."

There was a dark silence, a few seconds long.

"She was fine last night."

"Yes, well, maybe she ate something that didn't agree with her."

Mark rolled his eyes and started to push his way past Gray and into the house.

Gray pressed his hands into Mark's chest. "Er, I don't think so."

"I just want to see her," Mark said, his voice reedy with annoyance.

"She doesn't want to see you."

"How do you know? Did you ask her?"

"Yes. I asked her. She said, 'I don't want to see him.'"

"I don't believe you. Kirsty! Kirsty!" He began pushing himself against Gray's body again.

Tony appeared on the bottom step then, wrapped up in a towelling dressing gown, his hair wet from the shower. "Morning, Mark," he said genially. "Everything OK?"

"I was hoping to see Kirsty," Mark said. "Your son seems to think she's ill."

Gray threw his father a warning glance.

"Oh," said Tony, clearly lying, but Gray didn't care. "Yeah. Bit of a sore throat."

"Oh, right," said Mark. "Two minutes ago it was that she'd been sick. For God's sake. I'm not an idiot."

"Listen, Mark," said Gray, "it doesn't matter if Kirsty's ill or not. The fact of the matter is that she doesn't want to see you. OK?"

Mark fell back a step, snatched the baseball cap from his head and rubbed his hair back into place. "Whatever," he hissed, the cap twisted inside his hands. "Seriously. Whatever." He backed away another step before taking one more forwards and saying, "Tell her I called. Tell her I'll be waiting for her at my aunt's. When she's *feeling better*."

"We certainly will," said Tony, still upbeat. "Sorry for the wasted journey."

Mark gave both of them a furious look before pulling the cap back over his hair and striding away from them, muttering loudly under his breath.

Gray and his dad looked at each other.

"See?" said Gray. "Do you see now?"

Tony shook his head disbelievingly. "What a total dickhead."

Kirsty appeared from her hiding place under the dining table and then their mum poked her head down the stairs. "What was that all about?"

"Nothing," said Gray, "just Mark not being able to take no for an answer. He's gone now."

The four of them stood together for a moment, gathered around the front door, the backdraught of Mark and his strange anger holding them together like fence posts.

CHAPTER
TWENTY-SIX

Lily puts on all the lights, even the ones beneath the extractor hood in the kitchen. She cannot bear the darkness for another moment. She switches on the television, finds a movie with a dog in it and then she makes herself eat something. It's nearly ten o'clock and she hasn't eaten since her breakfast with Russ. The bread in the breadbin is green so she microwaves herself a packet of basmati rice and eats it with butter. She watches the movie about the dog for a little while, but the couple in it make her feel sad so she turns over and finds a loud dating show instead. Then she pours herself a glass of wine and readies herself for the thing she has known she must do since she was told that her husband didn't exist. She arranges Carl's mail into a neat pile and stares at it for a moment. Then she picks up the first letter and she opens it.

Junk mail from an estate agent.

The second letter is a statement for his current account. She skims it, fast. Everything is recognisable to her. Payments for meals in Kiev, for the hotel where they'd spent their wedding night, then drinks in Bali, airport shopping, the off licence by the station, Marks & Spencer, the railway company, the dry cleaner's, the pub in the country where they'd had their lunch last weekend. Then more bits and bobs of local spending, ending with a contactless payment of £2.20 to a coffee shop in Victoria in Tuesday afternoon. Then nothing. No more spending. A flat line and a beep.

So, she thinks, lowering the statement to her lap and reaching for her wine glass. There it is. Proof. He is dead. How could he be living otherwise? Without spending money?

She opens two more letters, both junk mail. She opens a bill from the electricity company and a statement from the shirt-making company that he gets all his work shirts from. Then she opens the last letter. It's from their mobile service provider. An itemised bill, listing every call by number and duration. She draws in her breath and starts to read.

Nearly every call and text is to her phone number. This is no surprise to her. What's she's looking for is the call Carl made from her mother's house in Kiev, the call to his mother on the day of their wedding. And there it is: 4.46p.m. on 21 March. Three minutes and five seconds. She takes a pen and underlines it. Then she looks at the time. It's almost half past ten. Too late, she assumes, to phone someone for a chat. But is it too late to tell a woman that her son is missing? She taps in the number, her breath held hard. Somewhere, maybe east of here, maybe west, maybe in a castle, maybe in a damp flat, a phone is ringing. Somewhere, maybe, a woman is listening to the phone ringing and, for some reason, not answering. Maybe she is sleeping? Maybe she is out? Maybe she is looking at Carl's number on a caller ID screener and choosing to ignore it. After twenty rings, Lily hangs up. She'll try again in the morning.

CHAPTER
TWENTY-SEVEN

The night air swirls with sodium-lit sea mist. Griff and Hero have run ahead, disappearing into the darkness. Alice and Frank walk slowly behind. Up on the promenade, a few late-night revellers are strolling between pubs, singing and ribbing and calling to each other. Derry and Daniel went home an hour ago and the teens finally left for their party about ten minutes ago. They have left Romaine at home with Jasmine and Sadie while they take the younger dogs out for a quick walk. The fresh damp air is exhilarating after the claustrophobic heat of the cottage with all those bodies in it, the oven going for hours, the red-hot logs in the fire cradle.

Frank has been very quiet since they left the house, since halfway through dinner in fact.

"I'm sorry about Jasmine," Alice says. "That was very out of character for her."

Frank looks slightly confused and then shakes his head and says, "No, no, honestly. That was nothing. If anything it made me feel a bit better, let me get some stuff out of my system. Better than feeling like you're being resented but everyone's too polite to say anything."

"You're not resented."

"Well, not by you, maybe."

He quietens again after this and they walk in silence for a while.

The dogs have seen something along the coast. Both of them have picked up speed and soon they've turned the corner of the bay and are out of sight.

"Oh, fuck's sake," says Alice. "Christ, what the hell are they playing at? *Griff!*" she roars through cupped hands. *"Hero!"*

She picks up her pace and soon they are both running across the beach. As they round the corner it is immediately clear what the dogs had been distracted by. There is a small fox standing at the top of some stone steps leading to the promenade, staring down at the dogs, triumphantly and disdainfully. The two dogs stare up at him, panting and looking at each other as if to say *now what?*

"You fools," says Alice, approaching the dogs with their leads. But they've got the bug now. The moon is high and almost full. A couple of seagulls have swooped and are picking amongst the rocks near the tide. The dogs set off again. Alice turns to Frank and shouts out, "I'm really sorry about this. You can go back to the cottage if you like."

He smiles and follows her. The seagulls sense the approach of two large dogs and take flight, the moon's rays catching the pale undersides of their bodies as they glide away. But still the dogs run. Alice hollers at them and whistles through two fingers the way her dad taught her. Finally they come to a stop at the farthest end of the bay, where in the summer months the steam fair pitches and the tourists come to sunbathe. The café built into the sea wall is shuttered up, the kiddy rides covered over and padlocked. From above comes the clang and clatter of the penny arcade. It's where Frank says he was sitting all day on Thursday, where he remembered the girl on the carousel and a man jumping into the sea.

The dogs sit panting at Alice's feet while she clips their leads back on. "Well," she says, "I guess we worked off some of that huge dinner." She turns to smile at Frank, but he's not looking at her. He's staring up at the cliffs that curve away from the end of the bay. He's got that look about him again, that look she's starting to recognise. She moves instinctively to his side. "What is it?"

He's still staring into the distance. "That house," he says, "there." He points at the grand house on the furthest tip of the cliff, the one with the yew trees and the flat roof. "Whose house is that?"

He's heavy against her side; she's supporting a lot of his weight. "The big one? At the end?"

"That one." He points again.

"I don't know who lives there now, but Derry said a famous novelist used to. A long time ago."

He shakes his head, as though he thinks she's wrong.

"There's a peacock," he says.

Alice smiles. "Well, yes, there might well be, I suppose."

He turns and looks at her. His skin is clammy and the milky moon casts a ghostly light over him. "No.

There is. I remember it. And I think . . ." He brings both hands up to his mouth, begins vaguely gnawing at his knuckles. When he looks at her again his eyes are full of tears. "When we were eating dinner — I think I hurt someone, Alice. I think I might even have killed someone."

She can feel his entire body trembling against hers.

"I can't take this any more, Alice. I really can't. And that house." He glances up again, fearfully. "I know that house. I know that house more than I know anything. I think I used to live there."

CHAPTER
TWENTY-EIGHT

1993

They didn't see Mark for three days after his angry exit from their cottage on Thursday morning. Gray's family remained slightly on edge as they carried on about their lives. Mark had proved he had a knack for knowing where they'd be and when and for appearing silently from the wings. The house on the cliff stood white and alert, the eerie call of peacocks occasionally being blown down the coast to the beach. But there was no sign of him.

"Maybe he went back to Harrogate?" suggested Tony as they sat in their usual spot on the beach on Sunday afternoon. It wasn't quite beach weather; the sand was still damp from the rain that had fallen that morning, but the sun was drying it out fast and the beach was slowly filling up.

"I reckon," said Mum. "No reason for him to stay here really if the girl he liked isn't interested."

"He was probably embarrassed, too," said Tony.

Gray gazed up at the house and shook his head slightly. "I reckon he's there," he said. "Planning his next move."

"Don't," said Kirsty. "You're scaring me." She turned to glance at the beach café behind them. She'd been doing that every few minutes.

"You haven't done anything wrong," Gray said to her. "You've got nothing to worry about."

"I feel bad," she said.

"Bad?"

"Yeah. I feel like I led him on."

"Oh, come on, you did not lead him on. He virtually stalked you!"

"I know." She plucked at the frayed tassel on her handbag. "But, you know, he paid for me to go to the cinema. And . . ." She shrugged.

"And what?"

"Well, I don't know. Maybe I let him think I was really into him."

"Did you?"

"I don't know. A bit, I guess. And I was, at first."

"Kirsty that's what happens," said Mum. "You meet someone, you feel an attraction, then you spend some time with them and sometimes you realise that the attraction is only skin-deep. So you move on."

Kirsty looked up at them with wide eyes. "He told me he loved me," she said.

Gray groaned. "What a loser."

"And . . . I told him I loved him, too."

Gray groaned again. "Oh my God, Kirst. Tell me you didn't."

She nodded miserably. "I didn't know what to do. He said it and then he looked at me like he wanted me to say it back. So I did."

"Jesus. When was this?"

"On the beach," she said. "After the fairground."

"You total moron," said Gray.

Kirsty whacked him. "It was my first kiss," she said angrily. "How was I supposed to know what to do?"

"I would say that *not lying* is something you've known how to do for most of your life."

She dropped her gaze to the ground. "I didn't want to hurt his feelings," she said. "I didn't want him to feel embarrassed."

"Well," said Mum, drawing things to a close. "It's over now. He's got the message. He's gone. And Kirsty's learned a valuable lesson. Let's all just try and relax and enjoy the last few days of our holiday. OK?"

Kirsty threw Gray a tragic look and Gray shook his head disappointedly.

From the end of the bay came another plaintive call of a peacock.

That evening they went to the pub for dinner. It was an old smugglers' inn, just around the bay where colourful fishing boats lay upturned on the shingles and narrow lamp-lit alleyways twisted uphill between the houses. On Sunday nights they always had live music: not the slightly shabby tribute acts in shiny shirts that played in the pubs in town, but quality stuff — a flamenco guitarist, a jazz pianist or a light-opera singer. Tonight's performer was a young girl called Izzy, singing her own songs, while another young girl accompanied her on the piano.

179

Their table was right by the stage, and Gray was close enough to see the pins holding Izzy's blonde hair in a bun, the slight smudge of eyeliner beneath her right eye, the scuff on the toe of her ballet pump. Close enough for it to feel as though Izzy was singing for him alone. Gray was mesmerised by her. She couldn't have been much older than him, yet she was so poised and so talented. He'd left his steak virtually untouched, too embarrassed to chew food in front of this goddess.

"Thank you all so much," Izzy said into her microphone. "Harrie and I are going to take a little break now. But we'll be back with some more music soon. In the meantime . . ." She leaned down briefly to pick up a small jar, affording Gray a quick glimpse down her evening dress at her virtually flat chest. ". . . if you've enjoyed our music, we'd be so grateful for any spare change. Or even some not-so-spare change." The audience laughed and Izzy and Harrie stepped off the podium.

"Here," Gray called her over.

He pointed at the jar and she smiled and said, "Thank you so much," as he posted a five-pound note into the jar.

"You're brilliant," he said.

"Gosh. Wow! *Thank* you," and then she was gone and Gray's family were all staring at him in astonishment.

"Five pounds?" said his dad.

Gray's face flushed scarlet. "Yeah. Well, she's really talented. You know."

"Yeah," said Dad, rubbing his chin. "Very talented." He chuckled. "Now eat your dinner."

Gray worked his way through his steak without really tasting it. He was exquisitely aware of Izzy's presence in the small room, her husky, chalet-girl voice somewhere behind him saying, "Thank you so much. You're so kind. Thank you."

After a few moments he dared to turn round and saw her standing at the bar drinking a half-pint of lager with her pianist friend and two young men. One of whom, he realised with a sickening jolt, was Mark.

"Oh Jesus," he muttered. "I don't actually believe it."

His family turned and looked and then all snapped their heads back to the front.

"He's like a bloody virus, that boy," said Tony.

Kirsty's face was bright pink.

"You OK, love?" said Mum, squeezing her arm. "Want me to take you home?"

"You know what," said Tony, "it's getting on. Why don't we all go home?"

"No!" said Gray. "I haven't finished my dinner!"

His dad looked at him in surprise. "Come on," he said, "surely it's stone cold by now?"

"It's fine," he mumbled. "You go. I'll stay and finish it. Honestly. I'll meet you back at the house."

"You're not going to do anything, are you?" Kirsty asked.

"Do anything?"

"You know, say anything. To Mark."

"You're kidding, right? I just want to finish my dinner. Maybe listen to some more music. Have another drink."

"Promise?"

He rolled his eyes at her and sighed. "Go," he said. "I'll be home soon."

He watched his father at the bar, settling their bill. He saw him make brief eye contact with Mark, a subtle raised brow, nod of the head. Then they left, Mark's eyes following Kirsty across the room and out of the door before turning back to his friends and laughing loudly, aggravatingly.

Gray slowly finished his meal. He could feel Mark's eyes boring into the back of his skull. He reached across the table for the dregs of the lager his father had left behind. He drank it fast. Then he drank the dregs of his mum's gin and tonic. He pulled his wallet from his back pocket. Nothing left in there after giving five pounds to the singer. He felt his pockets for coins and wondered what he could get for £1.20.

Slowly, he stood and headed for the bar. There was a sea of heads between him and Mark, but he could hear him from here: the shrill self-consciousness of him; the girls laughing loudly at his every utterance. This was a scenario that made sense to Gray. A posh, handsome guy hooting and snorting in a bohemian pub with his posh, pretty friends. This made more sense than Mark stalking his gauche baby sister.

"I've got one pound twenty," he said to the barmaid. "What can I get for that?"

She frowned and shrugged. "Pint of bitter is one nineteen. Pint of lager is one twenty-nine."

He searched his pockets again for any loose change. He pulled out three pence and sighed. "Pint of bitter please."

As he spoke something skimmed past him and landed on the bar. He looked down at it. A ten-pence piece. He turned to his right. Mark smirked at him.

He ignored the coin and shook his head at the barmaid who was looking at it questioningly. "Bitter. Please." He smiled tightly.

He glanced back at Mark as he waited for the pint to be poured. Mark gestured at him. He toyed with the idea of ignoring the overture, but the prospect of having a legitimate excuse to talk to Izzy was too strong to resist. He took his pint and the ten-pence piece and walked towards them, his heart pounding.

"Here," he said, passing the coin over. "Thanks anyway."

"Graham," said Mark, clasping a hand on to his shoulder and squeezing it a little too hard. "Good to see you."

"It's Gray. Not Graham."

"Yes. I keep forgetting. Let me introduce you." He finally let go of Gray's shoulder, leaving an imprint of his fingers in his flesh. "This is Alex, a friend of mine from Harrogate, and this is Harrie, his sister. And this, as you know, is the remarkably talented Isabel McAlpine. Also from Harrogate. And Alex and Harrie's cousin. This is Gray. He's a guy I met on the beach last week."

They all laughed, revealing banks of perfect teeth. "Oh, Mark," said Izzy, "you are such an eccentric. Nice to meet you, Gray." She gave him a warm, limp hand to shake. "Listen, we're due back on stage. But Mark's having some people back to his aunt's place later — you should come."

"Yeah!" said Mark, over-brightly. "You should. And bring your sister."

"She's only fifteen," Gray said.

"That's OK." Izzy laughed. "We won't eat her!"

It's not you I'm worried about, Gray wanted to say.

He looked at Izzy who was regarding him encouragingly from under her eyelashes, and he said, "What time?"

"We'll go straight from here," said Mark. "Ten-ish? Why don't you stay? We can all walk up together."

"I'll need to let my parents know."

"That's OK," said Mark. "We can knock on your door on the way past, see if Kirsty wants to join us, too."

"She won't want to," he said, "I can assure you of that."

Then he looked at Izzy, who was smiling at him. She winked and Gray's pulse quickened. She was pretty much the best-looking girl he'd ever spoken to. Not only that but she was talented and sexy, too. And she was winking at him. The party he'd really wanted to go to at home had been and gone. His little sister had kissed someone before he had. And the bitter was clouding his judgement because he found himself nodding and saying, "Yeah, all right then."

"Oh, *great*." Izzy touched his arm lightly with her delicate fingers. "I'll see you after." She turned to head back to the stage but then stopped and turned. "Oh, and thank you so much for being so kind earlier. I saw

184

what happened at the bar just now. I really appreciate your generosity." She smiled and he knew that it was a smile of promise and of hope.

"You earned it," he said, and then flushed as he realised how crass that sounded. "I mean . . ." But she'd gone.

"Right," said Mark, clapping his hands together. "Tequila?"

His friend Alex made a strange braying sound and they high-fived each other.

Gray turned to face the stage, his eyes fixed on the cool blonde singing her beautiful songs, trying not to think too much about what he was about to do.

CHAPTER
TWENTY-NINE

Sunday is here. Lily wants Sunday gone so that it can be Monday, so that she can talk to the policewoman and the key-cutter and the people at Carl's office. All she can do today is try this number. The phone belonging to Carl's mother rings and rings and rings. There is no answerphone to break up the agonising incessancy of it. It just keeps on ringing until it runs out of rings and then the line clicks off scornfully, as if it's saying: *For Christ's sake, there's no one here, can't you take a hint?*

As Lily sits with the phone cradled beneath her chin pressing redial, redial, redial, she builds up a mental image of the woman who is not answering her phone. She has dark hair, like Carl, and his sharp cheekbones; she looks young for her age, is wearing maybe a silky blouse and tailored trousers. Again, she wonders, why does she not know what her husband's mother looks like? Why did she never ask? Why are there no photographs in this flat? Who is this man she married? What is she doing here?

After an hour of sitting cross-legged on the bed calling Carl's mother, Lily begins to feel a rage building deep within her. It comes from the same place that her tears come from: the soft pit of her belly. She hurls the phone across the room and watches as it hits the wall and splits in two, expelling a piece of plastic that rolls deep under the divan bed. She growls in frustration and gets to her hands and knees, her fingers clawing at the narrow gap between the thick new carpet and the underside of the bed. She can't locate it so she pushes the divan across the carpet until it reveals itself. There's the piece of plastic. And there's something else. It's one of Carl's smart little silk knot cufflinks, bottle-green and claret. She holds it in the palm of her hand and stares at it. She sees him standing there, as he does every morning, pulling down the cuffs of his immaculate business shirts, popping the knots through the buttonholes, smiling down at her. And she remembers how she used to feel: so proud of this handsome, grown-up man with his serious shirts.

She rests the silk knot on Carl's bedside table and concentrates instead on fixing the bloody phone. The piece of plastic appears to have snapped off from somewhere — she can't work out where — and the two sides of the phone refuse to click together without it. She holds it together with an elastic hairband and attempts to redial Carl's mother, but there's no connection. She has broken the phone. She lets it fall on to the bed and she groans. All the people who might try calling Carl — his mother, his sister, his office, Russ — have this number.

She showers, washes her hair and gets dressed. Then she picks up her mobile phone and texts Russ: *I have broken the house phone. This is my mobile phone.*

Please use this number if you need to speak to me. Thank you. Lily.

Then she taps Carl's mother's number into her mobile and waits for the incessant ringing to begin again. But instead, within three rings there is a click and then a woman's voice, uncertain and quiet, saying, "Hello?"

CHAPTER
THIRTY

The time is six eighteen. The house is silent. Alice tries to go back to sleep but it's impossible. She is too energised by the intense joy of waking with her hands entwined inside another person's hands, the reassuring warmth of a body lying by her side: not the body of a small girl in loose-fitting pyjamas, not the bony parenthesis of an ageing greyhound, but a man's body, contoured and solid, filling her bed from pillow to foot. The morning light catches the autumn tones of his hair, the glints of gold in his five-day stubble. He has a spray of reddish freckles across his chest, a soft covering of auburn chest hair, smooth arms, a deep dip down the centre of his back where there are more freckles. He smells of sea spray and her brand of fabric conditioner. He smells of them.

She thinks through the steps and stages that brought them together last night, the quiet walk back along the beach, the rawness of him after his revelation about thinking he might have killed someone. Alice's own immediate and completely instinctive certainty that he was wrong, that those big, soft hands could never have hurt anyone and that she is not making a mistake letting him into her life. Her hand finding his, just to reassure herself, and the way he'd looked at her: surprised and touched and scared. But he'd squeezed her hand gently with his and then he'd brought it to his mouth and he'd kissed it. Not just kissed it, but inhaled it. He'd been shaking slightly, the way Griff sometimes did when a strange noise unnerved him. She'd drawn him towards her and he'd buried his face into her neck and tightened his arms around her waist and they'd rocked together for a while. It had not been too many steps between there and her bedroom.

"You'll have to go back to the shed," she'd said after, "I can't have one of the kids walking in and seeing you here."

"I know," he'd said. "Of course." Then somehow he'd used this as an invitation to start all over again. She couldn't remember falling asleep. She doesn't know if anyone came in while they slept. She didn't hear Kai coming home and suspects that he didn't. Dawn is pink through her thin curtains and she can hear the polite click of claws outside her room: Griff, waiting patiently for her to let him in. Sunday morning. She should wake Frank up, ask him to leave before Romaine gets up. But the soft warmth of his body is too tempting. She tiptoes from the bed and jams a chair underneath the door handle. Then she scurries back, the morning air cold against her naked skin, and throws herself back into her still-warm bed.

"Hurry," she whispers into Frank's ear. "You need to go."

He rouses and grimaces and says, "Shit. Sure. Sorry. What time is it?"

"It's quickie o'clock," she says, pulling him on top of her and dragging the duvet over their conjoined bodies to hide them from unexpected visitors. "Be really, really quiet."

He kisses her, morning breath and all, and she kisses him back, as though her life depended on it, as though it was the last kiss of her life.

By the time Romaine wakes up it's quarter to seven and Frank is safely tucked away in the shed. Alice lies in her empty bed, sated and shell-shocked, Griff curled contentedly at her feet.

The atmosphere in the cottage that morning is hard to judge. Kai is hungover, Romaine is shattered, Jasmine is prickly and Frank is edgy. Alice, meanwhile, is full of sex; her whole body is wired with it. She's showered herself thoroughly but she knows she still smells of it. Her mind keeps replaying sections of the night before: his hazel eyes fixed on hers, his thumbs firm against her hip bones, gentle fingers pulling a loose hair from her wet lips, strong hands clamped against her skull pulling her face back to his, murmuring her name into her ear, the moon shining mercury-hot through the curtains.

The images are vivid and hot and pulsate through her as she stands at the hob, turning slivers of bacon and filling the kettle and drying her hands on the worn tea towel and throwing words at her children. She glances at Jasmine. Does she know? Did she hear? Can she feel it in the very air? Is she, as she's been told so many times, a bad mother?

"I'm going to walk up to that house," says Frank, bringing his used coffee cup to the sink and rinsing it.

"The one on the cliff?" she replies.

"Yes."

"I'm pretty sure it's derelict."

"I know. You said. But I think it's vital. I really do."

"I'll come with you."

She sees Jasmine arch an eyebrow.

"You don't have to."

"I really want to." It emerges almost as a groan; she's still so full of desire for him.

She ignores the poisonous energy radiating from Jasmine and grabs her bag and a coat. "We'll only be an hour," she says, not giving anyone a chance to say anything, not giving the dogs a chance to realise that there's a potential walk on offer. "I'll get some fresh bread on the way back. Bye."

It's almost ten but the morning still feels new; the metal railings are covered with dew, the moon is a fading, Vaselined smudge on the horizon. Alice wants to take Frank's hand, but all her bluster and bravura of the night before has dissipated and she's vulnerable and unsure and remembering why she hates this shit. They walk separately for a while, breathing in the new air, breathing it out again in clouds of vapour. She takes him the back route, away from the sea, up the cobbled alleyways and the winding lanes to the main road that leads out of town. They pass the Hope and Anchor, the oldest pub in town, a smuggler's inn that's been there since 1651. Frank stops.

"I've been to this pub," he says.

She looks at him with concern.

"I've been to this pub," he says again.

"Right," she says, "in which case, we'll come here for lunch. OK? They do a brilliant Sunday lunch. Yorkshire puddings the size of footballs. I'm not kidding."

He looks at her blankly.

"You don't know what a Yorkshire pudding is, do you?"

He squints. "Is it something to do with toffee?"

"God bless you." She laughs and the awkwardness shifts and he laughs and takes her hand and they walk like that all the way to the house on the cliff.

Frank feels nauseous: lack of sleep, too much red wine the night before, too much strong coffee this morning, and on top of all of that, the stomach-turning vertigo of remembering. All that steadies him is Alice's hand inside his, her strong presence at his side as they climb the hill outside the town together. It appals him how much he needs this woman. Was he like this before? he wonders. Would the "him" from before have had any interest in this slightly worn woman with bags under her eyes and a stomach that flops over her waistband? Maybe in his own life, the adult life he'd lived for twenty or so years before he washed up on Alice's beach, maybe he was a player. Maybe he had a young girlfriend — maybe more than one young girlfriend? Maybe he only liked a certain type of woman? Maybe the "real" him would laugh out loud at the thought of the "fugue" him rolling about in bed with a forty-something mother of three?

Or maybe he was a virgin?

No, he thought, remembering the previous night, no, he most definitely had not been a virgin.

Where will all this end? He's pretty sure he killed someone. And if he has, it's bound to come out eventually. It's inevitable. There'll be a body, or a missing person. There'll be a witness. The police will come for him. Then there'll be a wife, or a girlfriend, possibly a child, or even a dog. There'll be a flat or a house with his things in it, a job with a desk with more of his things in it. There'll be parents, siblings. There'll be a court case. He'll go to prison. And then what will happen to this sweet, vital thing between him and Alice? Where will it go?

He puts his arm round Alice's waist, pulls her closer to him, rests his cheek against the crown of her head. She yields to him; their bodies blend; they walk in sync.

The house is not quite derelict. It's dusty-looking; last year's autumn leaves are mulched on the gravelled driveway, cobwebs glittering in the hedges that surround it. The pale stonework is patched green and streaked brown. But there are curtains in the windows, flowers in the beds. It looks like a house that has been absent-mindedly forgotten about, rather than deliberately abandoned.

Frank stands for a moment at the entrance. There is a rusting, studded chain draped across each side of the carriage driveway. He steps over one and his feet crunch against the gravel. Alice follows him.

"What a pretty house," she says.

It is a pretty house. Symmetrical, with generous windows and good proportions, Coade stone mouldings and Doric columns, a half-cartwheel fanlight above the front door.

Frank searches his psyche for the part of him that remembered living here when they were on the beach last night. He feels neural trails fizzing through his brain, pathways trying to re-form, flickering like lightbulbs with loose connections, then dying. Then coming back to life. Then dying again. He starts to feel cross, kicking at the gravel with the toe of his shoe.

"You OK?"

"I'm so sick of this," he says. "So fucking sick of it."

"Not remembering?"

"Yes," he softens, "yes. Not remembering. I was so sure last night. And now . . ."

"Come on." She tugs him gently by the arm. "Let's go and look. You never know. The door might be unlocked. Maybe inside will open up some memories."

He follows her down the driveway and then they are at the door. He plants his feet firmly on the stone steps, trying to root himself into the energy of the place, as though stone has memory, as though it might remember his feet. He clasps the large brass hexagonal knob that sits in the centre of the door. He holds it for a while. He closes his eyes. And then he sees it: dead lilies in a vase; a beautiful girl in a blood-red evening dress, fine blonde hair in a falling-down bun. She's smiling at him, offering him her hand, pulling him through this door.

CHAPTER
THIRTY-ONE

1993

Tony opened the door of the cottage and peered at the small crowd of drunken people standing outside.

"Dad," said Gray, "I'm going to Mark's aunt's house. For a party. Kind of thing."

"Not a party," Mark interjected, sounding remarkably sober for someone who'd been drinking tequila shots for the last hour. "Just a gathering. Some friends."

Tony gave Gray a look of utter confusion. He looked from Mark to Gray and then behind himself at Gray's mum, who had just appeared.

"What's going on?" said Mum.

"Gray wants to go to a party. With Mark."

"Not a party, Mrs Ross. Just a gathering. Just us. These are old friends of mine from home. And my aunt will be there."

Tony stared at Gray incredulously. Gray stared back at him steadfastly, his jaw set hard. He was going to this party if it killed him.

Then Izzy cut in with, "Does your daughter want to come too? It would be so nice to have another girl."

Kirsty popped up then behind Mum and Dad and threw Gray a questioning look.

"Ah, there she is," said Mark. "We're whisking your brother off to a small gathering. At the house. And Izzy wants you to come, too."

"Er . . ." Kirsty gestured at her pyjamas. "I don't think so."

But Gray could see her looking over his shoulder at the two glamorous girls in their high-street evening dresses and Mark's equally handsome mate in his half-unbuttoned shirt and his Spanish tan. They made an impressive-looking group.

"Come on," said Izzy "It'll be fun."

Kirsty bit the soft part of her lip. "But it's late," she said.

"It's only ten. Not even. Come on."

"I don't know."

Tony and Pam exchanged a look.

"Please!" said Izzy. "We'll wait for you to get dressed. It'll be fun."

Tony looked at Gray sternly. Gray shrugged. If Kirsty wanted to come that was entirely up to her. He wasn't about to persuade her. But neither was he going to dissuade her. He just wanted to go now, get to the house, have another drink, carry on the conversation he and Izzy had been having in the pub just now, the conversation during which she'd barely lost eye contact with him, had allowed their shoulders and their knees to touch on several occasions without attempting to reposition herself and had told him he was both "adorable" and "fascinating".

"OK, then," said Kirsty.

Tony and Pam shot her a panicked look.

"What?" she said. "It'll be fine." Then she turned back to the group. "Give me two minutes. Actually, *one* minute."

"We'll get her home early," said Izzy.

"And safely," said Mark.

"Gray," said Dad, "I want you both back here by midnight. *Midnight*," he repeated.

Gray tutted. If Kirsty wasn't coming they'd be more lenient. "Fine," he said.

"And if you're not I'll be up at that house to humiliate you. OK?"

"God," he muttered, "yes. OK."

Kirsty appeared in a pink T-shirt, a hooded jacket and jeans, her hair combed to a shine and her mouth pink with gloss. "OK?"

Gray saw her exchange an awkward look with Mark. Then Mark looked at him and smiled.

"Come on," said Gray "let's go."

The lilies in the hallway were dying. Their heavy white heads had drooped, leaving dustings of yellow pollen on the pale tiled floor and a deathly, stagnant odour. No dogs ran to greet them. The house was still and silent.

"Where's your aunt?" said Gray.

"What?" Mark replied absent-mindedly.

"Your aunt. Where is she?"

"Christ," he said, "I don't know."

"You said she was here."

"Well, maybe she is," he countered. "Maybe she's asleep."

They all followed Mark through to a room at the back of the house. It was a small, square room with an open fireplace, a sofa and two big armchairs and there, in the corner, a fully fitted mahogany bar. Mark leaned down, lifted a flap on the panelling, hit a switch and the whole thing lit up. There were bottles of spirits attached to the wall, shiny cocktail shakers, shelves of cut glasses, a tub of drinking straws and glass swizzle sticks, an ice tub with silver tongs, a small sink, a small fridge filled with beers and wine, and three bar stools with red leather seats.

"Right," said Mark, standing behind the bar, his hands clasped together. "Who's for what?"

The girls asked for gin and tonics; Alex asked for a whisky sour; Gray asked for a beer.

"What about you, Kirsty?"

"Do you have any Coke?"

Mark laughed. "Whoa, little one, bit early in the night for that!"

"I meant, like — no, I meant Coca-Cola."

"I know what you meant," he said, smiling at her indulgently. He slid a CD into a player beneath the bar and hit another switch. Immediately the room was filled with the sound of A Tribe Called Quest. Gray looked around and saw four speakers, one in each corner of the ceiling. Mark turned up the bass and the beat thrummed though the floorboards, through his feet. He popped the cap off a beer for Gray using a bottle opener screwed to the side of the bar and passed it to him. Gray drank it fast. Izzy and Harrie were sitting at the bar on the stools, whispering and giggling conspiratorially into each other's ears while Mark made their cocktails. Kirsty stood at Gray's side, sipping her Coke through a straw, bobbing up and down slightly to the beat of the music.

"Why did you come?" he whispered in her ear, loudly to be heard over the deafening music.

"Because I felt like it," she whispered back into his.

"Yeah, but why?"

"I dunno. I suppose I didn't want you to sit there tomorrow morning telling me what an amazing time you'd had. Didn't want to be the loser at home in her pyjamas." She fixed him with a penetrating look. "Why did *you* come?"

He glanced at Izzy, just as Izzy looked away from Harrie and glanced at him.

Kirsty nodded knowingly. "She's way out of your league."

"I wouldn't be so sure," he said.

"Seriously. Look at her. And she's older than you."

"Only just. A few months."

She looked at him sceptically.

"A year," he said. "That's nothing."

"And where does she live?"

"Harrogate," he said. "Like Mark. They all know each other from posh world. Polo and stuff."

Kirsty rolled her eyes. "Well," she said, "good luck with that."

"I think she thinks I'm *different*."

"Well, that's for sure."

"Look, it's not as if we're fucking urchins, you know. We're not that different."

200

Kirsty gestured at the high-ceilinged room, the lit-up bar, the chesterfield sofa, the leather-topped fenders and the brass chandelier overhead.

"I mean, intrinsically," said Gray. "Inside. We live in a nice house, we go to perfectly OK schools, we have holidays and a decent car. Mum and Dad drink wine."

"Yes, but there's a big difference between that and this."

"Whatever," he said, "I just don't think it matters. Not when two people have a . . . *connection*."

Kirsty rolled her eyes.

"Cheers," said everyone as Mark passed out the cocktails. Gray turned and brushed his beer against Izzy's cocktail. She held his gaze for a split second and smiled. Then she looked away again and he followed her gaze to Mark, who was laying out a row of small white pills on the surface of the bar.

Izzy rubbed her hands together and said, "Oooh! Goody!"

Gray stifled a groan. He should have guessed. Posh kids and drugs.

"No, thank you," he said when Mark pushed one towards him with a fingertip.

Mark looked at him disapprovingly. "Oh, come on," he said.

"No, honestly. I'm fine with the beer."

Izzy nudged him. "Go on," she said. "It's only E. You can share one with me if you want."

"Seriously, it's not my thing."

"Oh, Gray. You're so adorable."

This time the "adorable" didn't strike him as a compliment.

"I'll share one with you," said Kirsty, gently touching his arm.

"What! No way! You're fifteen! I can't take you back to Mum and Dad off your tits on E."

"Tell you what," said Mark, leaning across the bar on his elbows, "why don't you two share half. A quarter each. You'll barely notice anything. And you'll be back to normal by the time you get home."

"Then what's the point?

"It'll just take the edge off. You know. Make the world seem a little nicer for a little while."

"Oh, please, Gray." Izzy held his arm. Then she pulled him to her and put her face right next to his: the smell of her hair, the softness of her skin, her bare arm around his waist. "Please."

"Seriously," said Mark, "it'll just be like an extra-nice hour of your life and then you'll be home safe in bed."

Gray shrugged, knowing he was losing the battle and feeling a small unfamiliar part of him telling him that, actually, it might be fun and that maybe the chemical boost might be what it took finally to get him across the line between being "adorable" and being a guy that Izzy might want to kiss.

He nodded and Mark smiled and cracked a pill into halves, gave one half to Izzy, halved the other and gave a tiny chunk each to Kirsty and Gray.

"Are you sure?" Gray mouthed at Kirsty. She nodded back at him and they swallowed the pill fragments down.

Mark passed Gray another beer and Kirsty another Coke and turned the music up even louder and the lights off, so that the room was lit only by the bar lights and a church candle burning on the coffee table behind them.

Gray and Kirsty watched the others for a while, the almost theatrical performance of their conversation, the hooting back and forth, the in-jokes and the banter. Gray was beginning to think he'd imagined the mutual attraction between Izzy and himself when suddenly Izzy's cousin turned to him and said, "So, Gray, do you have a girlfriend? Down in Croydon?"

Izzy nudged Harrie in the ribs and threw her a mock-horrified look. "Harrie!"

"What?" said Harrie. "I was just asking."

"No," Kirsty interjected, "he doesn't have a girlfriend. In fact, he's never had a girlfriend—"

Gray clamped his hand over his sister's mouth and wrestled her halfway to the floor. She fought back and resurfaced, pinning Gray's arms down to say, "He's never even kissed anyone, apart from our mum."

He pushed her back down to the floor and said, "That's not true. Seriously. She's just saying that because she hates me."

"You know what? I don't think I kissed a girl till I was seventeen," said the taciturn, slightly cross-eyed boy called Alex. "Or was it sixteen? Actually, might have been thirteen. I don't know. I do remember thinking it was a long time to wait, anyway."

"I'll kiss you," said Izzy, turning to Gray.

Gray let go of Kirsty and blinked. "What? Look, it's not true that I haven't, so you don't need to kiss me just to be kind."

"Oh, Gray, I promise you, kindness has nothing to do with it."

And then, before he could protest or even decide if he wanted to protest, she was kissing him, in front of everyone: her arms tight around his neck, her tongue in his mouth, her small breasts hard against his chest.

He struggled briefly against her embrace, but soon the animalistic thud of the music, the golden darkness, the raw atmosphere, the tequilas, the beers, the E and this girl, here, in his arms, the taste of her mouth, the genuine desire coming from her and into him, all combined to bring him to a state of oblivion where the two of them were all that existed. His head swam with kaleidoscopic images, changing, moving, diverging and converging and then pulsating in time to the music into what he suddenly realised was the unfurled fan of a peacock's tail. It shimmered in his mind's eye, the great span of it, the iridescent layers of green and indigo and purple, dancing and swaying. He lost himself for a moment in the beauty of the thing, losing consciousness for a while of the fact that he was kissing Izzy, that her hands were in his hair, that the others were watching and cheering and whooping and clapping, that this was crazy, what was happening, just crazy. When they finally drew apart he looked into her eyes and he saw the peacock markings there, in her irises, and he leaned into her ear and said, "You are

204

beautiful." And she leaned into his ear and said, "You are beautiful too."

On the other side of the bar Mark pulled a small bag from his pocket, lined up another set of pills on the counter. Again he broke one in half. He pushed one half towards Gray, the other towards Izzy.

This time Gray didn't need to be persuaded.

CHAPTER
THIRTY-TWO

"Hello?" Lily almost whispers. "Is that Mrs Monrose?"

"No," says the quietly spoken woman, "I think you may have the wrong number."

"No, I'm sorry, I know that's not your name. Of course. My name is Lily. I spoke to you a few weeks ago. After the marriage to your son."

There is a short, tense silence. "I'm sorry," says the woman, "I still think you have the wrong number. I don't have a son. I don't know anyone called Lily."

"But this number. It is on my husband's phone bill. It is the number he called when I spoke to his mother. After our wedding. It is *you*."

"I think there has been some confusion," says the woman. "A misprint, maybe. I don't have a son. I don't have any children at all."

"But I recognise your voice!"

"No," she says vaguely "no, I don't think so."

Lily can hear her voice becoming distant as she moves the phone away from her ear. She shouts, "You *are* his mother! Why are you lying?" Then she stops, reins in her temper. "He's missing, you know? He's been missing for five days. Please, when I go, will you take down my number, immediately? Write it down.

Somewhere safe. Please. If you hear from him, you must let me know."

The line buzzes and dies. The woman has hung up.

CHAPTER
THIRTY-THREE

The door to the house is locked. Alice and Frank walk towards the gate at the side of the house that leads into the gardens. This too is locked, with a rusting padlock and curls of barbed wire on top. They return to the front door and peer through the windows on either side through cupped hands; they see a curved hallway with tiled floors and a sweeping staircase up to a wide half-landing bathed in sun. Grand double doors lead off from both sides, and there are more doors behind the staircase. Frank sighs.

"Are you OK?" says Alice.

"Yeah," he says. "Fine."

"No more memories?"

"Not yet."

They clamber through the flowerbed outside the front-left window and reach awkwardly to look through into the room beyond. It's a dining room, with a long table covered in books and piles of paper, a brass chandelier, a fireplace with matching leather wing chairs on each side, other unidentifiable pieces of furniture hidden under dust sheets. They repeat the action on the right-hand side of the house. Here there is a grand sitting room with three dust-sheet-covered sofas in a U shape, an ornate fireplace with a gilt mirror above, more dust sheets and cardboard boxes. It looks almost as though the inhabitant had been halfway through moving house when they left.

Alice takes out her smartphone when she hears a ringtone nearby. She looks at the screen, but it's black. She puts the phone back in her pocket, and then starts slightly when she hears a phone ringing again. She takes her phone back out of her pocket, looks at the black screen again. The ringing continues and continues and continues. She looks at Frank.

"Where's that coming from?" she asks.

He turns his ear to the house. "It sounds like it's coming from inside."

They stand for a while in the flowerbed, statue-still, listening to the phone ringing. Finally it stops; then a moment later it starts again.

A chill runs through Alice and she looks anxiously at Frank. He has clearly understood the significance of the ringing phone in the empty house. Within days of Frank arriving in Ridinghouse Bay and within hours of him remembering having been in this house, a phone is ringing and ringing behind the locked door. It can't be unrelated.

They ring the doorbell once, twice, three times. And then both move away from the house to look up towards the windows on the upper floors. They're looking for shadowy movements, for any sign of life. But there's nothing. Drawn curtains, dark glass. And the eerie, haunting sound of an unanswered phone ringing into oblivion.

"Come on," says Alice, taking hold of Frank's shoulder, "let's go home."

He pauses, looking reluctant to move from this place. But then his shoulders soften and he turns to Alice and smiles and says, "Yes. OK."

"We can always come back."

"Yes. We can."

The phone is still ringing as they crunch back across the driveway, its desperate insistence fading to a distant complaint as they step over the rusting chains and then swallowed up completely by the roar of passing cars as they step back on to the pavement.

For a while they walk in silence. It's hard to know what to say.

"Any theories?" Alice tries as they round the corner and see the comforting jumble of town below them.

Frank looks blank, shell-shocked. He shakes his head.

She tries again. "Someone really wants to talk to someone in that house."

He nods vaguely. And then suddenly he turns to Alice, his expression stricken and terrified, and he says, "I think we should go to the police. I think we should go now. Seriously."

"What!"

"The longer I'm here, the more I know that I've done something really bad. That phone ringing — it was about me. I know it was. Someone was ringing about me. Someone who thought I'd be there. And maybe it was someone who loves me. Or maybe it was someone who wants to kill me. Or maybe it was someone I've hurt. But they were calling here. And here is close to you. And I cannot be in your house any more, not without knowing who I am. Because I'm really starting to think, Alice, really, really, that who I am is bad. Please, Alice, take me now. Take me and leave me there. Let the police sort this out. I mean it. I really do."

Alice inhales sharply. She feels a kick to her gut and a tiny burst of nausea.

She stares at Frank for a while, her eyes locked on to his. He looks genuinely terrified. She wants to hold him, but she senses that he does not want to be held, that he wants to escape. She sighs, softly, and says, "There are no police here. The nearest police station is eight miles away. And it will be closed on a Sunday. I could call the police, but I'm not sure what I'd say to them: *Hello, there's a man in my house who thinks he might have done something, to someone, somewhere. Please come immediately.*" She smiles tightly, desperate to be right about someone for once in her life, desperate to keep Frank and prove to herself and the world that this wasn't a mistake. And even if he's right, even if he has killed someone, he'd have a good reason for it; she knows he would. "So listen, stay one more night. Please. One more night, then in the morning, after I've dropped Romaine at school, I'll take you. OK?"

He looks unconvinced.

"And remember," she continues, "that pub? We were going to go there for lunch? To try their famous toffee

Yorkshire puddings and see what you could remember? Yes?"

He lets his head drop slightly and nods.

"Come on then. We'll go via home and book a table. It gets busy there on a Sunday. And we're a big group." She touches his elbow and begins guiding him gently towards town. "We'll just take Sadie. Give her some quality time without those two other buffoons. And if we're lucky, there might be some live music. They often have live music. I wonder what sort of music you like, Frank. Indie guitar bands, I reckon, by the look of you." She's blathering, deliberately, not wanting to give Frank a chance to think or talk, not wanting him to remember that he doesn't want to be here any more. Because Alice really, really doesn't want Frank to go. She doesn't want to leave him at a police station and get a smug call from him in few days saying, *Thanks for everything — my wife and I are so grateful to you.* Or a call from the police saying, *He's an axe murderer. We'll need to bring you in for questioning.*

She doesn't want anything other than to wake up in his arms every morning between now and the end of time.

"Elbow," he says vaguely.

"What?"

"Elbow," he repeats, with more feeling.

She looks at his elbow, questioningly. "What? You mean . . .?"

"That's what I like. I like Elbow. Are they real? Are they real music?"

"Yes," she smiles. "Yes, they are. They're really good."

"Can we listen to some? Later?"

"Sure," says Alice, taking his hand in hers. "Of course we can."

"Wow!" he says, his whole demeanour brightening. "I can't believe I remembered that."

Alice squeezes his hand and smiles at him. "Batter," she says.

"What?"

"Yorkshire puddings. They're made of batter. Big golden puffs of batter."

"Ah," he says. "I think I remember those. I think I do."

Then he puts his arm across her shoulder and pulls her to him and they walk towards the heart of town together, the dark shadow of the house on the cliff fading away behind them.

CHAPTER
THIRTY-FOUR

1993

More people arrived at about eleven, fresh from the Hope and Anchor. Mark swung the front door open to them and they trailed into the house. Gray watched from the door of the snug. He wasn't sure he liked the look of this lot. They were older, weather-worn, burly and rough around the edges. Most of them were drunk. Mark looked unfazed by their arrival.

"Come in, come in!" he called out, high-fiving and fist-touching and taking carrier bags full of beer. "The party's through there." He gestured towards the doorway where Gray was standing. The new arrivals looked around the house as they entered, checking out the ceiling heights and the sparkling crystal chandeliers. A small guy with his hair held back in a lank ponytail seemed to be the one responsible for bringing everyone to the house. "Hope you don't mind," he called out to Mark over the shoulders of the men in front of him, "we picked up a few stragglers en route."

"No, no, no," said Mark, clasping the man's hand tightly and then doing a complicated twisty handshake. "The more the merrier. Definitely. Come in, come in." He gestured the last few people in. There were roughly twenty of them, mainly men, a couple of younger-looking girls and a woman who looked about fifty with a shaved head and pierced eyebrows.

The three girls looked round curiously as the new guests arrived. Alex stood up smartly and said, "Good evening, ladies and gentlemen! Welcome!"

They lined up at the bar while Mark served them all drinks. Gray stood at the side of the room and stared at them. The guy with the ponytail was making a spliff on the bar. The shaven-headed woman was smoking one she'd made earlier. Two of the younger men were hitting on Izzy and Harrie, who appeared not to be at all unhappy about this. He turned to see what Kirsty was doing and saw her sitting on the fire fender staring into the dead embers.

"Come on," he said, joining her, "let's go home."

She turned to look at him and he could see immediately that something wasn't right. She was smiling at him lovingly, her eyes filled with sparkles. "My beautiful brother," she said, pulling him towards her and then holding his face between the palms of her hands. "Just look at you. Look at your beautiful face. You are such a good person. Such a *beautiful* person." She pulled him towards her and held him hard against her.

He pulled away and looked into her eyes. "Christ, Kirst. Did you have more E?" he demanded.

"I did," she said, nestling her head into the crook of his neck. "I truly did."

"Oh, fuck. Kirsty! How the hell am I supposed to take you home now? I can't take you home like this. Oh, for fuck's sake! How much did you have?"

"Just one."

"One what? One quarter? One half?"

"One whole," she said.

"You had a whole one! Plus the quarter!"

"God, I don't know. Who cares? It's all just so beautiful. This house. And these people. And you, Gray My beautiful brother. Let's go and see the peacock! Come on!"

She got to her feet and he stared down at her. "Fine," he said, thinking that actually some fresh air might be just what was needed. "We'll go and see the peacock. And then I'm getting you a cup of coffee and a pint of water and I'm taking you home. But fuck, Kirst, you've got to promise me you won't take anything else. Seriously. It's dangerous."

"It's not dangerous, my beautiful brother. How can it be dangerous? Look what happened to you! You kissed that girl! Seriously, Gray! It's the answer to everything!"

He turned to look at Izzy who was now sitting with her legs hooked over the lap of one of the men from the pub and playing with Harrie's hair; Harrie had her head in Izzy's lap. The man from the pub looked as if he was too scared to move, or even to breathe. Mark meanwhile was sliding beers and cocktails across the counter and passing out more and more of his white pills and the music was getting harder and harder and the chatter was getting louder and louder and the air was filled with smoke and shadows of people dancing and Gray was now fairly convinced that Mark's aunt was not in the house.

216

"Come on then," he said, "let's go and find the peacock."

The air outside was crisp, more October than the first day of August. A light mist hovered between the ground and the sky and the gardens glowed silver in the moonlight. The bass of the music was still loud out here, the beat insistent and raw, and Kirsty danced and spun ahead of him. Gray breathed in deeply, trying to clear his head. The effect of the E hadn't lasted long and in fact, apart from the manic bliss of his kiss with Izzy half an hour ago, he wasn't sure it had really done anything at all.

He scoped the gardens, looking for the peacock, and then there, in the distance, glimpsed a shimmer and flurry, a screech and a sudden movement. "There," he said to Kirsty. "There he is."

Kirsty put her hands to her mouth and whispered, "Oh, look. Look at him. Look at him, Gray!"

They tiptoed across the soft grass, then sat side by side a few feet away from him and watched. Kirsty nestled her head into the crook of Gray's neck and he felt a softness open up in his belly. She'd never been affectionate with him before. There'd always been that polite remove between them, but here she was, her heart wide open, holding on to him and loving him. He put his arm around her waist and he pulled her closer and he whispered into her ear, "Love you, little sis." And she whispered back, "Love you, too, big bro."

And there before them the peacock suddenly turned towards the light of the house, towards his audience, and he opened up his fan of plumage and he shook it in time to the music and Kirsty opened her mouth wide and said, "Wow! He's dancing! The peacock is dancing!"

"He is!" Gray laughed. "He really is!"

And as he said this he saw a shaft of light fall across the lawn and the shadow of a man stretched out before them. They both turned and saw Mark heading towards them with a handful of beers.

"Hello, you two," he said loudly.

Gray stifled a groan.

"What are you doing out here?"

"Just watching the peacock," said Kirsty. "He's dancing!"

Mark sat down next to them and passed them each a beer. "Dancing peacocks, eh?"

"Yes, look!"

But the peacock had disappeared.

"Oh," said Kirsty.

"So," said Mark, looking at Gray, clearly uninterested in the dancing peacock, "you appear to have lost Izzy to the charms of a local oik."

Gray shrugged. "She was never mine."

"She looked quite a lot like she was yours, earlier."

"It's just drugs, isn't it? It wasn't real."

Mark nodded. "Like dancing peacocks?"

Gray ignored him. "Who *are* all those people in there, anyway?"

"Locals. You know. People who actually live here all year. Christ. Just imagine."

"Do you know them?"

"Some of them, sure. I've been coming here all my life, remember. Since I was a kid."

There was a long silence, pierced by screams of laughter coming from inside the house.

"So," said Mark, a while later. "The other morning. What the hell was that all about?"

"What do you mean?"

"You know what I mean. I mean me basically being *dumped*, by you *and* your parents, on your *doorstep*. That wasn't very nice."

Neither of them said anything.

"I mean, I assume that that's what it was? Yes? I was being dumped by proxy?"

Gray held Kirsty closer to him. "She was just feeling ill. She wasn't in the mood."

"So, you and me, Kirsty. Are we still on?"

Kirsty didn't reply, just nestled closer to Gray.

"Are you feeling better now?" he insisted. "Well enough to come out with me tomorrow night?"

He plucked at the grass with his fingers as he talked. His voice was shrill. His energy was manic.

"I don't know," said Kirsty. "I'm not sure."

"What does that *mean*? You're either into me or you're not. You either want to go out with me or you don't. We're either on or we're off."

Kirsty said nothing.

"Well?"

"Listen, Mark, it's late. She's wired. I need to get her home. Let's have this conversation another day, shall we? When we're all a bit less . . . *chemical*."

"But don't you see? That's precisely why we should have this conversation right now. While all the emotions are running on the surface. While we're all feeling *real*."

"Mark," Gray sighed, "this is not real."

"Of course it's real. All of it's real. Whatever you're feeling, whatever you're seeing, it's real. It comes from in there." He pointed at Gray's head. "It comes from in there." He pointed at his heart. "Just takes little keys to unlock it, little keys like E and booze. So" — he turned sharply so that he was inches from Kirsty's face — "I'm asking you now, Kirsty, I'm asking you: what's going on? Huh?"

Gray got to his feet and pulled Kirsty up to hers. "Really, not the time, not the place, mate. I'm taking her home, OK?"

Mark grabbed at Kirsty's arm and brought her back down on to the grass. She landed on her bottom with a hard thump.

Gray pushed down on Mark's shoulders and said, "Get the fuck off her!"

He began to pull Kirsty back up again and Mark suddenly threw himself at Gray's legs, pulling him down into the grass, half on top of him. Gray's upper body hit Kirsty who cried out in pain and he pulled himself up and struck out at Mark, who caught his fist in his hand and gripped it. With his other arm Mark dragged Kirsty towards him and held her around the neck in the crook of his arm. Gray pulled at Kirsty's arms, but this just tightened Mark's hold around her throat, so he took hold of Mark's wrist and attempted to pull his arm away. Mark kicked out with the heel of his right foot and slammed it between Gray's legs, narrowly missing his balls. Gray rolled backwards and then came back up to sitting again, about to launch another attack on Mark, and stopping as the silver of a flick-knife caught the moonlight.

It was at Kirsty's throat. Mark was panting. His eyes were wide and he licked his lips.

"Now look," he said to Gray. "Now look what you made me do."

CHAPTER
THIRTY-FIVE

Lily showers and dresses. Her jeans are loose around her waist. She must eat. There is nothing in the kitchen that is edible, so she decides to go to the shops.

It's a pale, sunny day, almost warm when she catches the morning sun. She pulls down her sunglasses and enjoys the feel of it against her face. She walks past the building site next door and glances up at the window where the light flickers every night. It looks so innocuous by day. She can't imagine why it scared her so much the other day. As she walks she feels her lungs fill and empty, fill and empty, the sun on her skin, her pace wide and long, the paving stones solid beneath her feet. For a while her mind empties of all it's been holding on to for five days. Before Carl went missing she'd spent her days in limbo, living for the text messages, envisaging the trains coming and going, barely breathing until he was home again. And now, for the first time since she came to this country, she feels as though maybe she lives here. Not just in that flat. Not just in Carl's arms. But here. In this country.

She picks up some colour in her cheeks as she strides towards town. Blood surges through her. She grabs a basket at the entrance to the high street supermarket, breezes through the aisles collecting things: packets of solid, fibrous cereal, pots of soup, pizzas, bread, a box of doughnuts, milk, toilet rolls, biscuits, chocolate spread, hams and cheeses, bath soap and shower gel. No salads, no health drinks, no vegetables. She won't eat them. She chooses only what she needs and what she knows will sate her hunger without her having to think about it.

At the checkout she smiles at the girl and says, "It's nice weather today, isn't it?"

And the girl smiles back at her warmly and says, "Hope it sticks around till my shift is over. It's definitely beer-garden weather!"

Lily doesn't quite know what beer-garden weather is but she can make a good guess, so she smiles and says, "I hope so too!"

She swings the carrier bags off the checkout and starts to head home. But first she notices a dress shop, just two doors down, one she hadn't noticed before. In the window is a green dress, made of a silky-looking fabric. It has short sleeves and a full skirt. It's not something she would have looked at before. It's very grown-up. But it suddenly occurs to her that she has no summer clothes. That she came to this country at the tail end of winter, with just jeans and jumpers and small, clingy things to wear at night. The weather today reminds her that soon it will be May, and she has some of Carl's secret money in her bag.

She stops at the door of the dress shop, her hand against the door.

Then she thinks of the future. She thinks that Carl is most likely dead and she is alone and this money may be all she has to live on for a long, long time. Suddenly she is taken away from the clarity and peace of the moment and back into the dark reality of her situation. She walks home slowly, the shopping bags heavy in her hands, clouds gathering over the sun.

She quickly unloads the shopping bags. She eats a doughnut and drinks a Coke. Then she plumps all the cushions on the sofa, sits neatly on the edge and calls Russ.

"Lily," he says, clearly having programmed her number into his phone, "how are you?"

"Not so good."

"No sign of him then?"

"No. Of course not."

"No," he repeats, "of course not." Then: "Anything else?"

"Well, yes. I spoke to his mother. This morning."

"Wow! Well, that's a big development!"

"No, unfortunately it is not. She pretended not to be his mother. She said she had no children."

"Ah," he said, "I see."

"I want you to call her please. Call her for me. Pretend that you are the gas man, you know, or the satellite man." This was the thing that occurred to her as she walked through the high street this morning, feeling so light and clear-headed. Now she knew someone in this country, they could help her. "Ask her some questions. Maybe find out her name. Please."

There is a short silence on the other end of the line. "Gosh."

"Please."

He is silent.

She lets him think for a moment.

Then he says, "Give me the number. First thing I'll do is google it and see what comes up. Then I'll call you back."

"Fine," she says, although it's not really fine. What would be fine would be for him to do what she asked him to do. She gives him the woman's number and sits and waits. Her stomach aches, from anxiety and from the sudden hit of sugar after eating nothing but bread and rice for three days.

A moment later the phone rings.

"Right," he says, "I've googled the number and I've got the full address."

"What?"

"It came up on one of those websites for buying and selling other people's stuff. Someone at that address was selling a grand piano. It was a couple of years ago, but still."

"So, where is this place?"

"Somewhere called Ridinghouse Bay. In East Yorkshire."

"Where is that?"

"North," he said, "about four or five hours from here."

"Can we go there?"

"We?"

"Yes. You and me."

There follows a dense silence.

"It's still early, we can go now."

"Well, blimey. I don't know. It's Sunday. I'm with my family. We've got plans."

"What sort of plans?"

"Lunch. We're having lunch."

Lily inhales, holding back the urge to shout: *Lunch! Lunch! That is your plan? Lunch!* "He might be there, Russ," she says. "He might be in that house. With that woman."

He pauses again. "Yes," he says. "That's true."

"I would go on my own, but really, I am a foreigner, I would not know how to get to a place so far away."

"It's a really long journey, Lily. I don't think we could do it in a day."

It's eleven o'clock. She tallies it up in her head. If they left now they'd get there at four o'clock. Stay an hour. Be back by 10 p.m.

"We could, Russ. We'd be home by ten o'clock."

Russ sighs. "Lily. Lily, I'm really sorry. I really am. But I just don't think . . ."

"Ask your wife," she says. "Ask her now. Tell her your friend is in danger. Tell her it's life and death. Please!"

"I'll call you back in a minute, Lily. OK?"

"Yes," she says, "yes. Thank you, Russ. Thank you."

She turns off her phone and smiles.

An hour later Russ is in the car park downstairs in a people carrier. Lily climbs in gingerly. It's dirty and covered in crumbs, sucked-out sachets of baby muck, dried-out baby wipes, a drool-stained baby seat in the back.

"I would have had a clear-out if I'd known we'd be doing this today," says Russ, wiping away some crumbs on the passenger seat. "Sorry."

"No, it is fine. Here." She shows him the contents of a carrier bag. "I made us sandwiches. And I have doughnuts, and drinks. And look!" She pulls out a cylinder of crisps. "Pringles."

"Great stuff." He smiles and the corners of his eyes crinkle. "Jo gave me this." He shows her a Tupperware box full of raw pasta. "Or should I say *threw it* at me. Said, 'This is your lunch. You'll have to cook it yourself.'"

"Oh," says Lily, clipping in her seatbelt. "That sounds not good."

"No." He turns on the ignition and puts the car into reverse. "No. It was definitely not good. I'm in big trouble."

"Ah, well," says Lily, "when you come home you will tell her that you found your friend and that you are a hero and she will forgive you."

"Well," he says, pointing the car towards the car-park exit, "let's hope you're right, shall we? Otherwise I'll be on the naughty step for the foreseeable."

"Naughty step? What is this?"

"It's a . . ." He laughs. "It's a place for naughty children to go. For time out."

She widens her eyes and says, "Seriously? Russ? Your wife will make you sit there? Like a child?"

He laughs loudly, *boom*; it makes her jump. "No, no!" he says, still laughing. "It's just an expression. A turn of phrase."

"So she won't?"

"No, she won't. But she will sulk a lot. And I'll most likely be on the sofa tonight."

Lily nods and stops talking for a moment. Then, finally, she turns to Russ, appraises his slightly weak-chinned profile, his Sunday-morning stubble and his pale hairless hands upon the steering wheel and she says, "I am sorry. I very much appreciate what you are doing for me. You are a very good man."

He turns and smiles at her and says, "You are welcome, Lily. Really. It's nothing."

But Lily knows that it is not nothing, that in order to be here he has had to fight against his wife, a woman who sounds strong and terrifying. She sees now why Carl might have wanted to be in his company. For this mild-mannered man is clearly braver than he looks.

CHAPTER
THIRTY-SIX

The moment they set foot in the Hope and Anchor, Frank knows. He knows he has been here and this time the neural connections don't flicker and fizz, they stay clear and strong and yes, he was here and there was a singer with blonde hair and a girl on piano and there was . . . his throat fills with the acid of it . . . there was tequila and there was tension and that girl was here, the girl with the brown hair, and now, from nowhere, comes her name. It lands like a rock at his feet. Kirsty. The girl is called Kirsty and he loves her. He really loves her.

Frank manages to maintain consciousness, manages to keep his feet planted on the ground, to retain the contents of his stomach. He makes it to the table reserved in their name in a small room off the main pub lounge. He makes it to a chair and he sits down heavily. He closes his eyes, trying to chase the memory as it darts away into the dark corners of his mind. He keeps up with it for a second or two, long enough to see gentle green eyes, a cagoule, cheap trainers, a goofy smile. His heart aches so much that he has to grab hold of it with both hands and massage it.

Alice hasn't noticed his change of mood. She's too busy settling Sadie on a grubby sheepskin rug brought from the cottage, trying to work out what Romaine wants from the menu ("They don't have omelettes on a Sunday, fusspot"), trying to get Jasmine to take her earphones out and turn off her phone. By the time he has her attention, the moment has passed and he feels normal again.

"Beef, pork or chicken?" says Alice.

He brings his attention quickly back to the menu and turns to Romaine who has chosen to sit next to him, and says, "What are you having?"

"Roast potatoes."

"Just roast potatoes?"

"Yes." She's sulking. Her arms are folded across her chest.

Alice raises her eyebrows at him and sighs. "Don't judge me," she says. "She claims that meat tastes of blood. Unless it's got breadcrumbs on it, or comes in a bread roll with cheese, or is minced up and cooked with tomatoes."

Frank nods and says to Romaine, "Well, I was going to have what you're having but now I'm thinking I might have the chicken."

Romaine shrugs as though she couldn't care less and Alice and Frank exchange smiles over the top of her head.

"Tired," Alice mouths.

Frank nods and holds her gaze. "I remembered something," he says as the conversation between the three children picks up.

230

"Are you OK?"

"Yes." He smiles. "I'm fine. It was different this time. It was clear and clean. I saw a singer, standing out there." He points towards the main lounge. "With a pianist. And I remembered the girl. The one with brown hair. I remembered her properly. And Alice," he says, joyfully, "I remembered her name!"

Alice raises her brow. "Seriously?"

"Yes! Kirsty! She's called Kirsty."

Something passes over Alice's face then, something cloudlike. "Oh," she says, "wow! That's amazing, Frank!"

"I know," he says. "I think this might be it. I think everything's going to start coming back now. Just like you said it would."

"And who was she?" she asks pensively. "Do you remember who she was?"

"Not quite," he says. "But I remembered that I loved her. That I loved her very much. And that . . ." He clutches at his heart again. The ache has come back at the thought of that sweet-faced girl from his past. "And that I miss her. I really miss her."

Alice stretches her arm across the back of Romaine's chair and squeezes his shoulder softly. "Was she your wife?" she says, almost in a whisper.

"I don't know," he says. "I really don't know."

"Funny to think, isn't it, that you might have a wife?"

He shrugs. It's not funny, not really. It's awful. He remembers what Jasmine said last night over dinner, about how he was being cruel not finding out who he was, that there might be people worrying about him.

And until now he hasn't been able to imagine what that might really mean. He's felt nothing for anyone beyond the people in the room with him. Now, suddenly, he loves someone from before. He loves Kirsty.

He sees Alice force a smile. She rubs his shoulder and then swiftly brings her hand back on to her lap.

The waitress arrives with a notepad and Frank turns to her to give his order, but not before noticing Alice staring blindly into the middle distance, a film of tears across her eyes.

Alice doesn't seek out Frank's hand on their way home. The kids would freak out for a start, but beyond that she doesn't want to. It's coming, she realises, the end of this thing; it's sitting on the horizon and she doesn't like the look of it at all. It looks cruel and mean. It looks like her, sitting alone in her room, cutting up maps to make art for people to give to people they love. It looks like her watching TV on a crumb-strewn sofa, surrounded by stinky dogs and moody teenagers, and then going to bed with a greyhound and waking up the next morning with greasy badger hair and not caring and starting the whole thing all over again. It looks like this beautiful man with his autumn hair and his gentle eyes and his warm breath and his strong hands walking out of her life and leaving her here, in a life she was quite happy with before he turned up on the beach five days ago. It looks like the best thing that could have happened to her at this exact moment in her life being snatched away before she's even had a chance to enjoy it.

232

She's quiet on the walk home. Sadie limps along at her side. Jasmine has plugged herself back into her music and is walking ahead, looking moody and vulnerable: a stance purposely affected, Alice assumes. Kai is holding hands with Romaine and they're chatting about this and that. Gulls weave and swoop across the horizon where a giant cruise liner twinkles dully, so far removed from the smallness and ancientness of Ridinghouse Bay that it looks like something from another planet.

"Are you OK, Alice?" asks Frank, looking down at her with soft, concerned eyes.

"I'm fine," she says. "Just pensive. You know."

He nods and looks into the distance; then he turns back and says, "She might be dead, you know? The girl. Kirsty. Maybe she was my girlfriend when I was young. I mean, she looks really young. A teenager. It's unlikely I'd still be with her now, even if we were in love back in 1993. Or whenever it was I was here."

She genuinely doesn't know what to say. "Kirsty" could be anyone: his wife, his daughter, his first love, his sister. That's not the point. The point is that he loves her. Loves her *present tense*. Which means that she can no longer pretend that Frank exists in a bubble. She can no longer pretend that he is exclusively hers.

He sighs and says, "Well, whatever it is, we'll find out tomorrow and after that I'm not sure you'll have any desire to know me any more anyway. Whether I'm married or not."

She stops then, and turns to face Frank. He doesn't get it, she thinks, he really, really doesn't get it. "I'll always want to know you, Frank," she says. "One way or another. It's whether or not you'll want to know me, that's the real question."

CHAPTER
THIRTY-SEVEN

1993

Mark's knife made an indent in the flesh of Kirsty's neck. Her fingers pulled at his arm where it was wrapped tight across her chest.

"Don't fucking *move*," Mark hissed at her. "Just sit still. OK?"

Gray sat forward and made a swipe for the knife. Mark kicked him backwards again. "Do you want me to kill her? Because I really will."

Gray looked desperately at the back of the house, willing someone to come outside now. Anyone. He began to pull himself up. If he could just get into the house, tell the others what was going on. Mark wouldn't kill her. He couldn't.

"Don't even think about going anywhere, you little runt. You're part of this. OK? You're staying here. Or this slices through her jugular. And I wouldn't even blink an eye. OK?"

Gray nodded. He'd do whatever Mark asked. For now. For as long as the tip of his knife was making that painful-looking indent into his sister's throat.

"What the fuck are you doing?" he asked. "You're crazy."

"No," Mark replied bluntly. "I'm not crazy at all. I'm completely sane. You're the one who made this happen. You and your whole shitty little family."

"What!" Gray asked. "What did we do?"

"You know what you did. I could see you all on the beach, talking about me; I saw the way you all looked at me, sizing me up, wondering if I was going to be good enough for your *precious* little princess. I did everything I could — I baked you all a *cake*. A fucking *cake*. And you all sat there like I'd presented you with a turd."

"What!"

"I'm not stupid, *Graham*. You hated me then and you made it your goal to make sure everyone in your family hated me too. You turned them all against me. Including Kirsty."

Gray opened his mouth to say something, to tell Mark that he'd turned Kirsty against him all by himself just by being a fucking freak. Then he saw the knife pressing harder and harder against Kirsty's skin, Kirsty's eyes growing wider and more terrified. He decided to try empathy.

"I'm sorry you think that," he said mildly. "I suppose maybe I was just being an over-protective big brother. You know. Kirsty's never had a boyfriend before. I just wasn't that comfortable with it."

"And that episode last week," Mark continued wildly. "When I came to see Kirsty, to ask her out. And you all stood there in the doorway like a bunch of illiterate bodyguards. So offensive. In my whole life I have never been treated like that before. Never. It was disgusting."

"Again," said Gray, holding hard on to his urge to punch Mark in the face. "I apologise if you felt that way. Kirsty had told me that she was feeling maybe too young to be in a relationship. That she was nervous about hurting your feelings. She asked me to say she wasn't feeling well, so that she would have time to think about whether or not she wanted to continue with the relationship. I was just looking out for her. Complying with her wishes. I thought you'd respect that. I wasn't expecting you to try and muscle your way in. It took us all by surprise."

"Listen, mate," Mark snarled, "no one does that to me, OK? No one acts like they're better than me. Least of all a rancid little shit like you."

"I'm sorry, Mark. Seriously. I've been unfair to you and I apologise. Now please, please, will you let my sister go? You're scaring her."

"Do you know what I've been through in my life, shit-bag? Do you have any idea? Of course you don't. You live in your lovely, cosy little mummy-daddy-brother-sister bubble. Of cosy cottages. And pub dinners. Of *day trips*. So excuse me for falling in love with your sister. And, oh, excuse me for not understanding how your sister" — he shook Kirsty slightly, increasing the pressure of his hold on her chest — "can one minute be standing on the beach with me, *in my arms*, telling me she loves me and the next minute decide she's 'not ready' for a relationship. Eh?" He shook her again and she whimpered.

"Come on," Mark said, dragging Kirsty to her feet. "Get up."

"Where are you taking her?"

"Her? I'm not taking *her*. I'm taking both of you. Get up, you little runt. *Get up!*"

Gray couldn't move.

Mark's face twisted with disgust and for a brief moment he took the knife from Kirsty's throat to take a swipe at Gray. "Get the fuck *up!*"

Gray grabbed Mark's wrist and for a moment he had it firm within his grasp. "Kirsty!" he called out hoarsely. "Now. Run now!"

Kirsty tried to slip out from under Mark's arm, but he yanked her back by the hair and pulled her back under his arm. Then suddenly he'd shaken Gray's hold from his wrist and was twisting Gray's arm backwards, pushing his hand upwards against his wrist joint, harder and harder. And the world seemed to splinter into about a thousand black and red pieces as the bone cracked and pain arrived at the edges of his consciousness and sat there like a terrible dark bird waiting to swoop and carry him away. Gray looked down at his arm, at the appalling angle between the heel of his hand and his wrist, at the improbable bulge of bone through the skin. The sky seemed to darken around him and for a moment he thought he was going to pass out. But then the pain arrived, waking him up, fully, shockingly.

Mark had the knife back at Kirsty's throat.

"You try and run and I'll break the other one," he hissed. "Get the fuck up and come with me."

238

CHAPTER
THIRTY-EIGHT

Lily and Russ have left the south-east and are on a motorway heading north.

"So," says Lily, "how did you and Jo meet?"

"Oh, God, now you're asking."

"Yes," she says, "I am."

He smiles and says, "At work."

"The same place where you met Carl?"

"No, the place I worked before that. She was my boss."

"Ah," says Lily. "Yes. That makes sense."

"Does it?"

"Yes. Because she is bossy."

Russ laughs out loud. "She is not!"

"She is! She doesn't want you to have breakfast with me. She doesn't want you to take me to Yorkshire. She throws your lunch at your head!"

"Oh, seriously. That's just . . . she's just tired a lot. That's what that is. And she gets a bit kennel-mad during the week—"

"Kennel-mad?"

"You know, like a dog in a cage. Desperate to get out. She lives for the weekends, when I'm at home, so we can share the childcare. Do nice things together. Spend time with Darcy."

Lily shudders slightly. She does not want a child until she is thirty-five. She told this to Carl and he said he'd wait as long she wanted him to wait. But she can relate to this woman, Jo, now. She has felt "kennel-mad" too at times these past two weeks. She would have been extremely unhappy if Carl had left her for a whole day on the weekend to drive another woman across the country. And she doesn't even have a baby to look after. She nods and says, "I understand. Please will you tell her that I'm very sorry? That I am very grateful. And that I will buy her a gift."

"Oh, no need, no need. But I will tell her. She's not scary, really. She's a sweetheart. She's the best girl ever. I'm so lucky to have her."

"What does she look like?"

"She's beautiful," he says and she wonders if he means beautiful like her, or just beautiful compared to him. "Red hair. Green eyes. Stunning."

Lily looks at Russ, at the glow that emanates from him when he talks about his wife. This is how she feels when she talks about Carl. As though she has been enchanted.

"Here." He reaches into the inside pocket of his sensible jacket and pulls out a wallet. "There's a photo in there. Have a look."

She takes the wallet from him and opens it. The photo shows a nice-looking woman in spectacles holding a blob of a baby. She passes the wallet back to him. "Very beautiful," she says. "You are very lucky."

She feels inside her coat pocket for the keys she found in Carl's filing cabinet, for the reassuringly solid

240

sphere. And then her fingers find the roll of twenty-pound notes she'd brought, just in case she needed to take a room in a hotel or buy a train ticket home. In her carrier bag she has the wedding photo album to show Carl's mum and some pictures of her own family, back in Kiev. She is holding on to the hope that the woman will soften once Lily is there, on her doorstep. That she will invite them in, pour them tea from a pot, take an interest.

"How about you?" says Russ. "How did you meet Carl?"

"He didn't tell you?"

"No. Need-to-know basis, as with everything." He laughs. "Just got back from the Ukraine and told me he'd met someone special."

She tells him the story about the conference back in February, about the cash-in-hand job she'd taken as a favour to her mum, about the first time she saw him and how she'd just known.

"So when did he ask you to marry him? Was it then?"

"No. No, he came back a week later." Her face softens at the memory. "With a ring. It was the best moment of my whole life."

"And what . . .?" He hesitates, begins again: "What is he like? You know? Day to day? I'm just — I can't imagine him as a domestic being."

"Day to day he is wonderful. He brings me things, every day, a chocolate truffle, a rose, a hairslide. He sends me texts, with words of love. When he comes home he looks after me, he cooks for me, he runs me a bath and brings me towels. He worships me."

241

"Wow," says Russ, peering into the wing mirror and the rear-view mirror before pulling into the middle lane. "That's amazing. I kind of can't imagine."

"I can't explain it," she says, "it's like nothing I ever experienced. It's more than love. It's obsession."

"Which can be, well — there's a dark side to that, isn't there? To obsession?"

"There's a dark side to everything, Russ."

"Ha!" He smiles. "Yes, I suppose that's true. I suppose it is."

"I am a very dark person."

"Oh, I wouldn't say that . . ."

"No, because you don't know me. But it is true. I am dark. That doesn't mean I can't have fun. I can have lots of fun. But when it is just me, alone, with myself — there is no sunshine."

Russ nods and moves the car back into the fast lane. "Well," he says. "That's interesting."

"Yes," says Lily. "It is."

"In this country, I think, people spend a lot of time worrying about the darkness. We all want to be sunny. We're scared if we're not."

"You are sunny."

"Yes, I am, or at least I try to be. That doesn't mean that I don't have moments of . . . introspection."

"This word? Looking inside?"

"Yes, looking inside. Wondering who I am and why I'm here. Questioning everything."

Lily absorbs this and then nods. "I think Carl is also very dark," she says a moment later.

"Yes," says Russ, nodding emphatically. "Yes. I think you're probably right."

She turns then, to look through her window. The scenery is a blur of green fields and blue sky and occasional blasts of golden rape. A big green road sign says "THE NORTH". She thinks of Carl's darkness, of the moments when he would become silent, when he would shrug away her hand, or not reply to a question. She remembers the nights when he would talk in his sleep. Thrash from side to side. Call out. Once he strangled her, in his sleep. She awoke to find him above her, his eyes not looking at her, his arms raised, then his hands meeting together around her throat and squeezing and squeezing and her eyes filling with tears and the blood pulsating through her temples and her knee at his groin and then the shock in his eyes as he awoke and looked at her, the expression of sickening realisation, his hands loosening around her neck, his fingers finding her face, groaning, "I'm sorry, I'm so sorry, it was a nightmare, I was having a nightmare," kissing her, holding her, then making love to her more tenderly than ever before.

There was a necklace the next day, with a simple diamond pendant.

She knows nothing of his childhood, of his past. She knows nothing of his scars. But she knows they are there.

It's sunny as they pull off the main road towards the town called Ridinghouse Bay. But it's cosy in here, the radio tuned into something easy listening, the heater

243

breathing out warm air. And Russ is very good company. Lily feels relaxed with him, as if she can say anything. On the next bend the town comes into view: a C-shaped jumble of tiny houses spilling down towards the sea, small boats bobbing about in the sparkling harbour. But they turn away from the town and down a shadowy road where bowers of darkly nodding trees meet overhead like a corridor.

The lady on Google Maps says: "In fifty yards, on your left, you have reached your destination."

Lily feels nervous now. She grasps Russ's sleeve and says, "I'm scared."

"It's going to be fine," he says. "Chances are there'll be no one here. Chances are we'll be turning straight round and going home again."

"I am scared of that, too."

They pull off the road and have to stop because there is a rusty chain across the driveway. Lily jumps out of the car and unclips the chain, pulls it across and stands back to let Russ bring the car on to the driveway. She has never seen such a beautiful house. It is built from a cream-coloured stone, or maybe it has been painted cream. There are gargoyles and busts built into the plasterwork, fluted columns and a set of smile-shaped stone steps leading up to a huge black wooden door with a brass knocker at its centre. Behind the house is the sea and a royal-blue sky full of pale-gold puffs of cloud.

She goes to the door of Russ's car and waits for him to get out.

"This house is very beautiful," she says. "I have never seen a house like this before."

"Georgian," says Russ, brushing sandwich crumbs from his lap and stretching out his arms. "Or maybe neo-Georgian. Looks a bit neglected."

She follows him towards the front door, her heart thumping hard, the carrier bag with the photo album in it clutched tight in her hand. There is no sign of life and now that they are closer to the house Lily can see that the building is tired and scruffy, that the cream walls and the windows are dirty, that the rose beds outside the front windows are overgrown and filled with dead leaves.

It is not a fairy-tale palace after all. But still, it is a fine house. She cannot imagine why Carl would not have wanted to bring her here. To share this with her.

She rings the doorbell and it chimes, just as she had imagined it would, with the elegant sound of copper tubes. No one comes. No lights go on. No voice calls out. Russ rings it again. He looks at her and frowns, then rings again. They try for five minutes, until it is obvious that no one is here, or that if they are here, they do not want to come to the door. Then Lily puts her hand in her pocket and pulls out the key fob.

"This," she says to Russ, holding it out to him in the palm of her hand. "It was in Carl's filing cabinet."

He takes it from her and examines the keys. Then he looks at the keyhole carved into the big wooden door and says, "It might be."

He inserts the strange-looking key, the one Lily had been planning on taking to the key-cutter at the station

245

tomorrow, into the lock and turns it. There's a low click as it unlocks.

Russ and Lily look at each other. Lily nods. Russ pushes open the door.

CHAPTER
THIRTY-NINE

Alice leaves Frank to his own devices that evening. He'd gone straight to the shed when they got back from lunch, claiming to be tired. But she knew he was just looking for solitude, for space in which to ponder the memories unlocked today.

She goes up to her room to check on her parents on the iPad. They're sitting side by side on their nice John Lewis sofa, staring at the TV. She knows that neither of them has a clue what they're watching. If she called them up now and said, *What are you up to?* they'd struggle to find an answer. But even in the fog of their fading faculties, they are holding hands. There are their hands, clutched together between them. They don't know who the prime minister is; they don't know what day of the week, month or even year it is. They can't quite remember their daughters' names and they certainly can't remember if they had lunch today or what the plan is for supper tonight. They know nothing of any significance whatsoever. But they do know they love each other.

Alice turns to appraise her bed. The sheets are twisted into a very particular post-coital knot, the bedsheet wrinkled and ridged like a tide-rippled beach.

She doesn't linger over the memories of the night before. Instead she yanks off the bedclothes and rolls them into a large ball which she leaves on the landing outside her room so that they can go directly into the laundry. She tugs out a handful of clean sheets from the airing cupboard and redresses the bed, speedily and efficiently. From the corner of the room she retrieves the embroidered cushions she bought long ago to decorate her bed and which have never decorated her bed because she cannot be arsed to take them off and put them back and take them off and put them back and she is really and truly not a bed-cushion kind of person. She places the pretty cushions in a row against the puffed-up pillows and pulls the duvet smooth and then considers the effect. It is nice. It doesn't look like a bed for having intense, life-changing sex with potentially murderous strangers. It looks like a single woman's bed, like a place for reading novels and comforting children and talking to dogs as though they can understand what you're saying.

On the screen of the iPad on her desk she hears her parents talking.

"I love you," her father says to her mother.

"I love you, too," her mother says to her father.

Then: "I wonder if we're going to get any lunch today?"

Frank lies on his back, his hands clasped together over his stomach, his eyes taking in the detail of the wooden ceiling overhead: the cobwebs, the knots and whorls, the joints and cornices. His mind is clearing. It's

248

clearing fast. He can now remember the place where he lives. It's a flat in a big house, down some stairs, through a door, then inside and down some more steps; there's a living room ahead, a bedroom to the right, a hallway to the left that takes you to a kitchen and a bathroom. The walls are painted yellow. All his shoes sit in a pile by the front door. He owns trainers, and walking boots, brightly coloured football boots and several pairs of leather shoes with laces. Mostly brown. Above hang his coats. There's a pot with an umbrella in it. A table with some keys. The floor is made of laminated wood boards of a pale apricot colour. The living room is square and scruffy, with a big battered cream sofa — he thinks it might have been a hand-me-down from his mother — and a long thin coffee table covered in paperwork and empty mugs. There's a view through two sash windows of a wall, some white plastic garden furniture and the bulge of a green lawn above and beyond.

He's been searching and searching this newly remembered terrain for signs of a family or of a woman but there are none. He wants to rush upstairs and tell Alice: *There's no woman! I live alone!* But there's so much more he needs to know before he can assure of her of anything.

He can remember his job. He works in a school. He teaches thirteen- and fourteen-year-olds. He's mentally searched through the faces of the children sitting in rows in front of him, looking for the girl called Kirsty. He can't find her face, but he can see the book on his desk and the work on the whiteboard behind him and it appears, rather appallingly, that he is a maths teacher.

He hadn't felt like a maths teacher last night in bed with Alice. Last night he could have been anything and anyone, he'd been raw and vital, stripped down to the very essence of himself. He'd liked himself in bed with Alice, but now, with every memory, he's whittling himself down to a smaller and smaller thing. A maths teacher, living alone in a scruffy flat.

He can hear music coming from Jasmine's bedroom window across the courtyard. He can hear one of the dogs barking, the clatter of someone cooking in the kitchen. It would be so tempting to opt out of remembering, to stop the process right here, right now, crawl back into Alice's bed, be enigmatic, empty, needy Frank for ever and never find out anything else disappointing about himself.

He rolls off the bed and opens the door to the shed. He stands in his socked feet, the evening air cold and harsh against his skin, and he looks upwards into Jasmine's window. As he looks she appears there, framed in her window, a white-faced apparition, all eyes and hair and lips. She stares down at him for a moment; then she raises one hand at him before moving away and closing her curtains behind her.

Franks turns and goes back into the shed. No, he thinks to himself, I don't belong here. I can't be here, however much I wish I could. It's not fair on Alice and it's not fair on her children. The police will tell me who I am and then we can take it from there. He collapses back on to his bed, heavily, feeling a painful swell of tears in his gullet at the thought of leaving, at the thought of losing Alice. And then, suddenly, in his mind's eye, there's a red cat. A red cat called . . . *Brenda*. He sees the small brown bowl that sits in his galley kitchen, crusted with uneaten meat. He sees the cat rolled into a ball on the scruffy cream sofa. *His* cat, he realises, with a stab of surprise. Why would he call his cat Brenda? Then he is taken by a wave of concern. Who is feeding his cat? Who is taking care of her?

And this, more than anything, seals his resolve. This is over. Tomorrow he will know.

CHAPTER
FORTY

1993

Mark had locked Kirsty and Gray in a spare room somewhere near the top of the house where the ceilings were low and the furniture was tired and shabby. They could still hear the music from here; it pulsed through the soles of their feet and made the ill-fitting glass in the dormer windows shake and rattle. It was so loud that Mark had managed to get both of them up two flights of stairs without anyone hearing them. Kirsty sat huddled on the bed while Gray was trying to kick the door down. The door was Victorian, solidly made, and Gray's kicking was making no impact. He went to the window, tried to open it with his left hand, but it too was locked. He smashed against the glass with his fist, on the off chance that someone might be in the garden.

Kirsty began to sob.

"Listen," said Gray joining her on the bed, "it's nearly midnight. Remember what Dad said? He said if we weren't home by midnight he was going to come here and humiliate us. Yeah? So, he'll be here soon. OK? OK."

She nodded and sniffled and said, "But Mark'll just say we're not here. He'll just say we left."

"Well, then, Dad'll go and try to find us. And when he can't find us he'll come back here. OK?"

"But what if it's too late, Gray?"

He turned and smiled at Kirsty. "He's not going to hurt us, Kirst. I won't let him."

"But look at your wrist! He's already hurt us!"

Gray glanced down at his wrist, which hung at an obscene angle from his arm.

"He took us by surprise. We're prepared now. OK? We know what he is now. And we'll be ready for him.

"Here!" He got up from the bed and began opening the drawers in the bedside cabinets. "Come on." He turned to Kirsty. "Go and check out the wardrobe. There must be something in this room we can use."

"What sort of things?"

"Anything! A sewing kit, a toothbrush, an old blanket. Let's get it all out and see what we can do."

Sweat rolled down Gray's forehead and into his eyes. The pain of his broken wrist was diluted by the adrenaline surging through him, but still, his body was in shock. He breathed out with amazement when the first thing he found in the top drawer was a packet of Anadin. The pack had an expiry date of 1990, but he didn't care. He popped four in his mouth and swallowed them down dry. Also in the drawer he found a tourism brochure for the local area dated August 1988, some old train tickets and a pair of dry-cleaning tags with the safety pins still attached. He took the safety pins out and laid them carefully on the top of the cabinet; then he opened the next drawer down.

Here he found some Dioralyte tablets, a packet of playing cards, some used tissues, a half-empty pack of Handy-Andys, a leaflet from Sledmere House and there, tucked away at the very back, curled into a circle, was a slim leather belt of the type that fits through loops on ladies' dresses.

He put this with the pins on the cabinet and then went to the cabinet on the other side of the bed.

Here he found more flotsam and jetsam left behind by messy house guests: earplugs, old batteries, a word-search magazine, an elastic hairband, a Virgin Atlantic eye mask and some screwed-up sweet wrappers. He sighed and tutted.

"What have you found?" he asked his sister.

"Wire coat hangers," she said. "Loads of them."

"Excellent," he hissed through gritted teeth, waiting for the pills to kick in. "What else?"

"Some rank old-man trousers with stains. Blankets. A hairdryer. Moth balls. Plug-in heater. And some hats."

"Right." He began pulling wire coat hangers out of the wardrobe. "I reckon we could maim him quite significantly with these. What you need to do is snap the hooks off. Bend them backwards and forwards. Yeah, like that. Till they snap. Excellent. Now put a couple in your pockets. You could use them to take his eyes out. Maybe make the next one a bit longer. That's it. Brilliant."

He looked around the room again. There was a small wooden chair in the corner. He tried picking it up with one hand. It was too heavy to bring down on someone's head with just his left hand. Then he noticed an Anglepoise lamp on one of the cabinets. This had a solid base, definitely heavy enough to cause concussion. A plan began to formulate. He asked Kirsty to hold the lamp while he wrenched the wire out of it. Then he moved the chair to the door. "You're going to stand here," he whispered urgently, wiping the sweat off his brow with the back of his hand. "With this." He handed her a folded-up blanket. "When he comes in, drop it on his head. I'll do the rest, OK?"

Kirsty nodded, then shook her head, then nodded again and said, "But what if I miss? What if it goes wrong?"

"It won't go wrong. And if it does, I'll be here with this." He gestured at the lamp. "And this." He pointed at the ripped-out flex from the lamp and the plastic belt. "If the worst comes to the worst, just get off the chair and hit him with it. Then use the wire hooks to hurt him. Just use anything and everything. OK? The most important thing is that we get out of this room. Once we're out we can get help. So we need to be *animals*, Kirsty. Yes? Animals."

She nodded uncertainly and he took her in his arms and held her tight against him. "I love you, Kirst," he said. "Whatever happens, I want you to know that. You're the best sister anyone could ever hope for. I'm so proud of you. And I love you."

She pushed her face closer into his chest and he rested his chin on the crown of her head and stared hard at the ceiling rose above. The pills weren't working. His wrist screamed out at him, like a thousand electric shocks being pumped through his arm. He wanted to lie down and cry. But he needed to stay alert. He needed to keep his sister safe.

There was a noise at the door and they broke apart. Kirsty stepped on to the chair, unfurling the blanket. Gray stood to one side, the lamp held firm in his left hand, the pain in his right suddenly gone.

CHAPTER
FORTY-ONE

"Hello! Hello!" Lily steps slowly and cautiously across the tiled hallway. "Hello! Is there anyone here?"

Russ follows behind her, searching the walls for light switches. He finds one and when he turns it on a large crystal chandelier overhead slowly lights up, revealing a thick network of dusty cobwebs.

"Wow," she says, looking around her. It is like a stately home. Like the grand buildings in central Kiev: the banks and the insurance companies. Doors open up from four points off the central hallway; double doors to the left and the right, then smaller doors behind the staircase. Above is a glass dome through which she can see the burnished golden clouds. The air smells old and stale, but not damp. She turns right and pushes through the double doors there. They lead into a grand sitting room. It is full of elegant, thread-bare furniture and half-packed cardboard boxes. A door at the other end leads through to an anteroom: a vase of dusty dried flowers on the windowsill, a velvet moth-eaten armchair. They pass through here, quietly, nervously, into a remarkable room: it is made entirely of glass and ornate wrought iron and is filled with desiccated palm trees and dusty rockeries, dead rubber plants and shrivelled trees. It smells of earth and decay. But there at the other end is an arrangement of nice rattan furniture, a glass-topped coffee table, lamps with ragged shades, suggesting that this was once a fine room in which to sit and enjoy the greenery.

A door to their left leads into a kitchen, long and narrow with five windows overlooking the lawned garden. It is decorated in the style of the 1970s: rust-coloured Formica countertops and pine doors, low-hanging orange plastic lampshades, plastic-topped bar stools at a breakfast bar. Everything is covered in a fine layer of grease and dust.

They find themselves back in the hallway and explore the rooms on the other side of the house. A large dining room, a smaller room with clubby leather armchairs and a bar built into a corner, and a cloakroom with a painted porcelain handbasin and a cistern with a chain set high up the wall.

As they emerge once more into the hallway, Russ says, "Well, I'm pretty sure there's no one living here."

"But the woman!" she replies. "She answered the phone!"

"This is true. But seriously. Look at this place. You can just tell. It's got that air about it. Of abandonment."

"Come on," she says, "let's go upstairs."

She grips the mahogany banister and looks upwards. It's a staircase from an old-fashioned American movie, sweeping into two dramatic curves as it heads upwards towards the glass dome. The first landing leads to four large bedrooms. The second landing leads to two attic rooms. Each door opens at their touch; each room is empty. But on the top floor, a door is locked. Russ and Lily exchange a look. Russ tries the handle after Lily. It rattles in its setting, but doesn't budge.

"Hello!" Lily calls out through the door. "Hello! Lady! This is Lily! We spoke earlier on the phone. Lady? Are you there? Hello?"

She puts her ear to the door, but there is pure silence on the other side.

She turns to Russ. "Kick it in," she says.

"What!"

"Kick the door in. Please."

"I can't do that, Lily. That's criminal damage. I could be arrested; it could . . ."

Lily pushes him out the way and launches herself against the door.

"Lily!" He tries to stop her but she pushes him away from her.

The door feels solid, but not impregnable. She hefts herself against it again and again, until she can feel bruises forming on her hip. She uses her feet then, kicking and kicking, sending shockwaves from the soles of her feet through to her knee joints.

"Lily! Seriously! You can't do this!"

"I *can* do this," she snaps, turning to Russ angrily. "My husband might be in there. Anyone could be in there. We drove five hours to come here. I'm not leaving until we've been inside this room. OK?"

She starts to kick again and then Russ is at her side.

"Come on then," he says, "on three. One . . . two . . . three."

They kick at the door in tandem, once, twice, three times, and suddenly, finally, there is a sound of splintering wood; they kick again — the door loosens; then again and the door flies open.

Russ reaches for the light switch. He turns it on. They step inside.

CHAPTER
FORTY-TWO

Frank's face appears at Alice's back window at about six o'clock. It's become very cold very suddenly and his breath leaves his body in misty clouds.

"Hi," he says, rubbing his hands together. "Bit chilly, isn't it?"

"Get in front of the fire," says Alice. "I'll bring you something to drink. What do you want? Tea? Wine?"

"Actually . . ." He pauses and looks down at his feet. "I didn't come in to bother you — I know this is your busy time — I just came in to say I'm sorry. About earlier. I feel like I was a bit of a downer. And I didn't thank you properly for the wonderful lunch. So nice of you. And also, I made you this." He passes her a postcard-sized piece of card.

She looks at the card, and then up at him, and then down at the card again. "You did this?"

He nods, looking slightly embarrassed. "It turns out I can kind of draw," he says.

"Wow," says Alice. "That's just, God, it's beautiful."

It's a tiny pencil sketch of the three dogs on the beach, with the words "THANK YOU" in an elegant calligraphy underneath. The sea in the background and the fairy lights in the foreground are coloured in pale smudges of pastel.

"I hope you don't mind but I used some of your art stuff. I found it in a drawer."

"No, God, no. Of course I don't mind. I mean, wow, Frank, you're really talented. This is so beautiful."

"It was the weirdest thing, Alice. I wanted to give you something so much and I have nothing to give you and I might never see you again after tomorrow and I was scared that maybe I'd never have a chance to repay you, and I saw your drawer and I had this huge wave of wanting to draw something so I sat down and my hands seemed to know exactly what pencil to use, how to use the pastels and the dogs just suddenly appeared on the paper and I can draw!"

"You can draw, Frank," said Alice. "You really can."

"I know. And it's quite ironic really, because just before this happened, I remembered what my job is. And seriously, it couldn't be further removed from this." He gestures at the beautiful postcard.

"What?" she asks breathlessly. "What is your job?"

"Guess."

"You're an accountant."

"No, but not far off. I'm a maths teacher."

"Ha!" Alice hoots. "Seriously?"

"Yes. In a secondary school."

"Oh my God. Where? I mean, could you remember the name of the school?"

"Couldn't remember the name, but I remembered the uniform: black blazers, black jumpers with a red trim. Black and red striped tie. An emblem like a sort of castle thing, a turret."

Alice smiles. "You know," she says, "actually, I can just see you. I really can." She laughs. "And had we known this sooner you could have repaid me for my hospitality by giving Kai some extra tuition."

"I still could!" he says brightly. "I could do some with him now!"

Alice laughs again. "I think that might not go down *all* that well as a Sunday-evening suggestion. But if you come back from the police station tomorrow, I'll definitely take you up on the offer."

Frank nods and then sighs. "There's more, Alice."

She bites the inside of her cheeks and waits for some terrible pronouncement about children and wives.

"I'm pretty sure I'm single."

She starts and looks up at him. "You mean . . .?"

"I mean I remembered where I live. I could see the inside of my flat. All my stuff. And there was no sign of a woman. Just a cat. Called Brenda."

Alice feels her heart blossom and unfurl. This man, this remarkable stranger, this person who has made her feel ways she thought she might never feel again, is a single maths teacher with a cat. She laughs loudly. "Brenda?"

"I know! Brenda! What a wag I am!"

"What a wag you are, Frank." She smiles and hugs herself.

"And now, of course, I'm really worried about her."

"About Brenda?"

"Yes. I live alone. She must be hungry."

"Oh," she says, "cats are adaptable, resourceful. She'll find someone to feed her."

"Do you think?"

And his face is so stricken with concern that Alice can't help throwing her arms around him and hugging him. "Don't you worry about Brenda," she says into his ear. "If you get locked up tomorrow I'll personally go to your flat and collect her and bring her back here to live with me. OK?"

"A murderer's cat? Are you sure?"

"As you know," she says drily, "I have no problem with animals owned by criminals."

He pulls back from her and appraises her warmly. His eyes are taking in the detail of her and she feels raw and alive. "You", he says, "are amazing."

"I am not amazing," she says. "Really. Trust me. Ask anyone. I'm an idiot."

"How can you say that?"

"Because I am. Just look at me. Look at this house. It's chaos. And you know . . ." She stops, hovering with one foot poised on the edge of a conversational precipice. "You know, I've had the social services called on me. Twice."

He looks at her disbelievingly.

"Seriously," she said. "Once in London over Kai and Jasmine. Some busybody mother at the school decided I wasn't raising them properly, because there were people in my house who maybe shouldn't have been in my house, because they were late for school most mornings, because I couldn't get my arse out of bed in time, because I was so fucking depressed, because sometimes I had no food in the house and I sent them in with inappropriate meals. All that. And it was all true. I was a shit mother. I loved them, but I didn't have a clue how to mother them. That was a real wake-up call. I changed everything. I went to the GP, got myself a prescription for Prozac. Got rid of the stupid friends. Kept the good ones. Tidied the flat. I was allowed to keep them. But it was close. And it was . . ." She blinks slowly and swallows, ". . . it was the worst time of my life. But we got through it. And then, oh, you know, clever, clever me, I go and get pregnant again. By some man that any other woman wouldn't have touched with a bargepole. A psycho. So, that was great. Just when I'd got my shit together, suddenly I'm suffering with PND and a new baby and a controlling idiot of a man trying to tell my kids what to do, trying to tell me what to do, what to wear, what to think."

She stops and pulls her hair back from her face. "So, yeah — we ran away. Didn't tell Romaine's dad where we were going. I did all this covertly." She indicates the cottage. "Waited until he was in hospital, for his cirrhosis, because, oh yes, I forgot to mention, didn't I, that he was an alcoholic?" She laughs wryly. "He stopped drinking for long enough to be granted occasional access to Romaine. And then he kidnapped her. It was . . ." She gasps as tears jump up her throat. "It was a nightmare. Then, thank God, he fucked off to Australia and made a baby with another woman and everything settled down for a while. And then, oh joy, Romaine's reception teacher decides that Romaine is being neglected."

"What!"

"Yes. Because I never had time to comb her hair in the mornings. Because she had stains on her sweat-shirt. Because I was always late collecting her. Because she wet herself and cried a lot. Oh and because, once, *once*, she talked about a horror film she'd accidentally watched at home when I was out and Kai didn't know she was in the room. Because . . ." She sighs. "Because I took my eye off the ball. Because I'm a shit mother. And no, no action was ever taken. They came round here, I told them the story of her kidnapping — you know he kept her in a hotel room for nearly two weeks? Two weeks! On her own half the time as well and she was barely three years old. Fucking, fucking bastard. I was so cross with the school, with that po-faced little teacher with her fucking shiny little crucifix round her neck, who knew *nothing* about *anything*, I couldn't walk through the gates without getting in a row with someone. I was *that* mother. You know: the scary one that they all have to have meetings about. It was . . ." She pauses and rubs her face. "It was the worst time. Of all the worst times. I just wanted to sell the cottage and move somewhere else, Outer Hebrides, as far away from everyone and everything as possible. And that was when Derry stepped in. She turned everything round for me. Liaised with the school on my behalf. Helped me get a diagnosis of dyslexia for Romaine. Collected Romaine when I was running late. Smoothed everything over. Dear God, I'd be dead without her. Really I would."

Frank has been staring at her fixedly throughout her monologue.

"I still think you're amazing," he says.

"I haven't told you about sleeping with Barry yet though."

"Barry?"

"Yes, remember the dodgy lodger who stole chocolate and gave it to my kids? The one who left me with a six-stone Staffy and two months' of unpaid rent? The one whose jacket I gave you on the beach?"

He nods.

"Yeah. Him. I slept with him. He was physically repellent. But I did it anyway. Because I'm a fucking idiot. I've always been an idiot and I always will be an idiot."

"So," he says thoughtfully, "where do I fit into this litany of idiocy?"

"Oh, pretty high, I'd say. *Pretty* high. Yeah, imagine how this would play with the social services, with the mums at the school. A man who remembers nothing other than that he thinks he might have killed someone. Living in my back garden. Oh, yes, and in my bed also." She shakes her head despairingly. Then she smiles drily and says, "At least you're not married though, eh? That really would have put the cherry on top of the turd."

Frank puts his hands on her shoulders and looks hard into her eyes. She feels like an open wound. There's more she could have told him: all the one-night stands, the lost weekends, the cutting of the corners of parenting. She's still a work in progress. But that's enough for now. She's given him almost the bottom line

267

about herself. She doesn't want to say goodbye to him tomorrow and leave him with some golden, idealised fantasy of who she is. Taking in stray dogs doesn't make you a saint. Neither does taking in lost strangers. If it turns out that he's done nothing wrong — that he really is just a slightly vague maths teacher with a cat called Brenda and is free to leave and get on with his life — and if he chooses to come back here, she wants it to be in the light of full disclosure. He can't come back here expecting a saint and angel, expecting to be rescued. Because she's not capable of rescuing anyone.

His hand caresses the side of her face, his thumb finding the dip under her cheekbone. She waits for him to say something but he doesn't. He brings his hands to the nape of her neck and his lips to her forehead and he kisses her hard. The kiss feels like redemption, as though he's taking away all her sins, sucking them out of her. She feels weak with it and soft and she takes his hands in hers and holds them against his face.

And then there is a scuffle at the kitchen door. A dog, followed by another dog, followed by a child. "Is it teatime yet?" says Romaine. "I'm hungry."

Alice lets Frank's hands drop and takes a step away from him, her eyes still on his. Then she turns to Romaine and she says, "Well, yes, that'll be because you only had potatoes for your lunch."

"Shall I make you a bagel?" Frank asks and Romaine looks at him with wide eyes and says:

"Yes! Please! But don't forget to slice it first, Frank."

"I will never forget to slice a bagel again, thanks to you."

"I can do that," says Alice, opening the bread bin. "Seriously. You sit down."

"No," says Frank, cutting in front of her. "No. I want to. Honestly. More than anything.

Romaine picks up the postcard and says, "Wow, did you draw that, Frank?"

"He certainly did, angel," says Alice.

"Wow. It's really good. Will you draw me something? Will you draw me? And Mummy?"

"I'd love to," he says. "Let me make you this bagel and then I'll come back and draw you."

Alice stands, her hips against the kitchen counter, her arms folded across her stomach, and she watches this man in her kitchen, making food for her baby, the dogs sitting at his feet, looking at him hopefully for possible scraps of ham or chicken. He belongs here, she thinks, suddenly, dreadfully. Whoever he is. Whatever he's done. *He belongs here.*

And then she remembers that tomorrow she is taking him to the police and that chances are she'll never ever see him again. She turns to the fridge behind her and pulls out a bottle of wine.

CHAPTER
FORTY-THREE

1993

It had all gone horribly wrong.

Kirsty had managed to get the blanket over Mark's head but because Gray could not actually see the crown of Mark's head, the base of the lamp had landed somewhere innocuous around the side of his head instead. Within seconds Mark had scrabbled his way out of the blanket and bundled Kirsty on to the bed. Gray had launched himself at him, grabbed him around the middle with his one good arm and attempted to wrench him away, but Mark was twice as strong as Gray even without the broken wrist and batted him off with very little effort.

Gray staggered backwards against the door. It was unlocked. His hand found the handle and he began to turn it.

"You leave this room and I'll kill her," said Mark.

Gray stopped.

"You really don't seem to have got the message," Mark continued, "either of you. You're not going anywhere. The party downstairs is over. There's no one else here."

"Our dad will be here soon," said Kirsty breathlessly.

"Oh, yeah," said Mark. "Your dad. Been and gone. Told him you left an hour ago."

"He'll call the police," said Gray, "when he can't find us. They'll come straight here. They'll find your drugs. You'll be arrested."

Mark shrugged. "I doubt it. I told him you'd gone to the beach. With some new friends. That you were both wired. Off your faces."

He pulled Kirsty up to a sitting position by her arms and then turned to Gray "Sit down," he said, patting the bed next to him. "Now."

The knife was back at Kirsty's neck. Gray sighed and moved towards the bed. Mark dragged him down and then jumped to his feet. He found the cord that Gray had ripped from the lamp and used it to tie their hands together so that they were joined together back to back.

"My wrist," Gray called out, "please be careful with my wrist!"

Mark looked at Gray's wrist thoughtfully and said, "Yeah, sorry about that. I don't know my own strength sometimes," before slowly pulling the cord tight around it, his eyes never leaving Gray's as he did so.

Gray screamed. It felt like nails being driven into the marrow of his bones. It felt like every moment of pain he'd ever experienced blended together into one shocking, unthinkable sensation.

"Scream as much as you like," said Mark, adjusting the cord fussily. "No one will hear you."

Then he stood back to appraise his handiwork. "There," he said, "that should stop you both arsing about."

"Mark," said Gray, his voice desperate and hollow, "what are you doing? I mean, what is your plan?"

Mark adjusted his posture to that of someone giving something some very deep thought. "Gosh, good question. I really haven't decided yet. Let me get back to you on that one."

Sweat dripped into Gray's eyebrows and down the sides of his face as he struggled to deal with the pain of the cord digging into his broken bone. Kirsty wriggled slightly and he howled in pain.

"Sorry," he heard her whisper.

Meanwhile, Mark paced backwards and forwards, still maintaining his ridiculous "thinking" charade. Then suddenly he sat down next to Kirsty and Gray felt her breath catch and her back straighten. Gray couldn't see what was happening but he heard Kirsty say, "Don't."

"Get off her," he said hoarsely. "Don't fucking touch her."

He felt Kirsty's whole body twitch and buckle.

"Stop it," she said. "Don't."

"What's he doing, Kirst?" he asked.

"I'm touching her, Graham," came Mark's voice, calm and measured. "I'm touching her body."

Gray flinched; his stomach felt liquid. "Fucking *get off her*," he said. "Get your hands off her or I will *kill you*."

Mark laughed in that girlish, revolting way of his. "Will you now, Graham? Will you? I'm caressing her throat now, Graham. *Very* gently. With my fingertips. I think she quite likes it. Yes, she really does. She's virtually purring."

A dark red fire was building inside Gray. It was licking up the walls of his consciousness, melting his reason. He wanted to kill this man. Murder him. Stab him, batter him, stamp on his skull until it smashed, shoot him in the head and then in the heart, kick him, stone him, decapitate him, maim him and maul him until he was nothing but a lump of flesh and bone.

"Tell me, Kirsty, why did you come here tonight? Just out of interest."

"Because it sounded like fun." Her voice was tight and low.

"And is that why you told me you loved me? On the beach. Because it was fun?"

"No," she said. "I said it because I didn't know what else to say. Because I've never had a boyfriend and I didn't know what I was supposed to be doing."

"Well," said Mark, "you're certainly learning a life lesson tonight. You really, really can't go around telling people you love them, Kirsty. Not when you don't mean it. You could give someone the wrong impression. Oh" — he peered round at Gray — "by the way, I'm currently massaging your sister's breasts. They're absolutely lovely. Even better than I'd imagined. Two proper handfuls."

Gray felt Kirsty wriggling against him. He was blinded by impotent rage but breathed in and out until his mind cleared. Rage wasn't going to help anything. He rearranged his hands a fraction, ignoring the blast of pain in his wrist, and began to fiddle with the electric cord. It was tied tightly, as he'd known it would be, but if he could find the frayed end, there might be just enough slack in it to manipulate it somehow.

"Men are sensitive, Kirsty, that's what people don't realise. Easily hurt. And you really hurt me. The minute I saw you I fell in love with you. I told you that. It was like a thunderbolt. It was like nothing I've ever experienced before. And for you to behave the way you have behaved, to have so little respect for another person's feelings, it makes you less than human, somehow. Do you see what I mean?"

Kirsty's entire body jerked then.

"What did he do?" Gray shouted.

"I've got my hand between her legs, Graham." His tone was jaunty. "Right . . . between . . . her . . . legs. Oh yes. Yes, she likes that, big brother. She really, really does. And you see, this is the sort of thing that happens to people who don't have basic respect for other people." This was addressed to both of them, like useful advice for the future. Then, horribly, he groaned. "Mmmmm. Yes."

Gray's fingers fiddled harder and faster with the electric cord. The Anglepoise lamp was still there, where he'd left it. He could still do something. If only he could get this cord untied. Kirsty had worked out what he was trying to do and he felt her fingers start to work at the cord too.

Mark groaned again; Kirsty flinched. This was not going to happen. He was not going to let it happen. If it did their lives would be ruined. For ever.

274

He looked at the lamp. He licked his lips. He felt the cord. It was loosening. It was definitely loosening. Mark was talking to him. Telling him how good his sister felt, how wet she was getting, but he blanked it all out. He could not listen to it. He needed to focus. Forget the pain. Forget Mark's hand between his sister's legs. Just get this cord loose. Slip his hands out. Get that lamp. Bash it over Mark's head. Make this stop. Make this stop. Make this stop.

CHAPTER
FORTY-FOUR

Lily looks around the room. It is a large rectangle with a sloped ceiling and two dormer windows. There is a four-poster bed to their left, nicely dressed with white cotton bedding and satin cushions. It is freshly made, the duvet smoothed to a glacial sheen. It smells fresh in this room and the walls are papered with something quite modern: duck-egg blue with a pattern of chrysanthemums. The carpet is new and plush and there are smart fitted wardrobes. At the other end of the room is a door to an en-suite bathroom, a small modern kitchenette, two cream armchairs and a desk with a standard lamp. It looks like a room in an upmarket B & B. It looks nothing like any other room in this house.

"Well," says Russ. "This is interesting. It looks like we've found the lair of your mysterious phone-answering woman."

"I don't understand," says Lily. "In a house so big, why would you live in a room so small?"

"Saves on heating bills, I guess."

She steps into the room and begins to explore. Whoever lives in this room is a nice, clean person. The woman she spoke to on the phone sounded like a nice, clean person. She pulls open a wardrobe and there is the scent of jasmine, of clean clothes. The wardrobe is full of expensive-looking things: tailored trousers clipped neatly to wooden hangers, soft woollen jumpers folded into neat squares, handbags with golden chains, neat loafers with tassels, shiny court shoes with buckles.

"This woman is very elegant," she says to Russ, who is picking up and examining the objects on the desk. "She is classy. Like Carl. And also very tidy. She is definitely his mother. It is obvious." She closes the wardrobe door and joins Russ. "What have you found?"

"I reckon", he says, "that the occupant of this room left very recently and took a lot of personal effects with them."

"What do you mean?"

"It just looks like a couple of drawers have been emptied, and there's an empty jewellery box, an empty filing tray. Look."

The roman blinds over the two dormer windows are open and the daylight is just starting to fade. She sees Russ sneak a quick peak at the time on his mobile phone. Their mission has been unsuccessful. Lily must have scared the lady away with her phone call this morning. She is gone. The house is empty. Russ needs to leave. He needs to see his baby and his wife and sleep for eight hours before he goes to work tomorrow.

"You go," she says, sitting on the desk chair and swivelling round to face him. "It is late."

"But where will you stay?"

"I will stay here. In this lovely room."

"But, Lily, I wouldn't feel . . . I mean, this is a big house. You'd be all on your own. And what about getting home? You know I can't come back and collect you."

"I have money," she says. "Plenty of money. I can find my own way home."

"But you don't even know where we are!"

"I do know where we are. We are in Ridinghouse Bay. I have my phone. I have money. Please, Russ. I want you to go home. To your baby. And your wife."

"But if something happened to you . . ."

"Nothing will happen to me. This house is safe. The only person who can get into this house is the woman who answered the phone. And look" — she gestures around the room — "does this look like the room of a dangerous woman?"

Russ smiles and shakes his head. "No. I guess not. But still, I'd feel happier if you were in a hotel."

"I want to stay here," she says firmly.

Russ pauses, then breathes out. "I do need to go," he says.

"I know you do. So go."

He softens and relaxes. "Are you sure?"

"I am sure."

He smiles and steps towards her. "Please, please call me tomorrow morning, so I know you've made it through the night."

"Oh, yes, of course I will."

"And if you're scared in the night. Call me. I'll keep my phone by my bed. Any strange noises. Anything. Please."

She laughs. He looks so earnest. "Yes," she says, "I promise."

She steps towards his open arms and they share a long and heartfelt embrace.

"Did you leave anything in my car?"

She shakes her head.

"Fine then, I'll say goodbye."

He hugs her once more and then he turns and leaves the room, clicking it quietly shut behind him.

Lily sits down again on the swivel chair and lets it spin 360 degrees. It stops, slowly, and she finds herself facing her own reflection in a full-length mirror built into the wall. Here she is, she thinks, staring blankly at herself, here she is: already hundreds of miles from home, and now hundreds more. She thinks of the empty flat in Surrey. She thinks of the building site next door with its flapping sheets of plastic, its strangely flashing light. She thinks of tomorrow, of exploring the streets of this odd little town, of the answers she might finally find to all her questions.

But mainly she thinks of just maybe waking here in the night, the moon shining down on her through the high-set windows, and feeling the gentle touch of her husband, his hand against her cheek, his face above hers, smiling down at her and saying, "You found me. You came all this way and you found me."

CHAPTER
FORTY-FIVE

Alice rests the little postcard against the base of her bedside lamp and gazes at it. It is exquisite. A tiny pencil sketch of her and Romaine standing side by side with their arms around each other. They'd posed for him in the kitchen; it had taken him all of ten minutes, and he'd captured them exactly. Romaine's extraordinary curls, the pudge of her wrists, the crooked ends of her smile. And Alice's long legs, the way her hair springs back off her hairline, the tired glamour of her face. But mostly what he'd captured was the love between the two of them. The matiness. Because Romaine was very much her buddy. They lived life at the same rhythm; they danced to the same beat. If Romaine were thirty years older and not her kid, they'd probably be best friends. And that was what poured out of Frank's lovely drawing. Alice and Romaine. BFFs.

He'd spent the evening with them, wedged between Romaine and Kai on the sofa watching fifty greatest something or others on Channel Five. But by the time Alice had come downstairs from putting Romaine to bed (far too late, as always), Frank had gone to bed. The little postcard was all that had remained of him, and a small scrawled note that said: "Off to bed. School night! See you in the morning."

She'd felt both deflated and relieved. Of course he must sleep in his own bed tonight. Had she not just this morning made up her bed with man-repelling Monsoon Home cushions? But equally she's aching for him. She picks up the card and traces her fingertip over the pencil markings. He's made her look beautiful. Willowy and hollow-cheeked with a piercing gaze. Is that how he sees her? she wonders. Not a badger-haired housewife with a spare tyre and dark circles around her eyes? But a woman who could give Catherine Deneuve a run for her money?

She sighs and looks behind her, imagining Frank in her shed, on his bed. Possibly naked. Then she imagines that same bed tomorrow night, empty, the shed cold and locked. Life returning to normal. Who knew how long it would be before she would hold a man's body again? What were the chances of a single mum of three living in a small seaside town miles from anywhere, who left the house only to chase dogs around a beach and stand outside schools, meeting a half-decent man who wanted to have sex with her ever again?

She makes it as far as the back door before sanity reclaims her. She lets her hand drop from the door handle and takes a deep breath.

Kai appears behind her as she turns round.

"Hello, gorgeous," she says.

"What you doing?"

"Just locking up," she says. "What are you up to?"

"Nothing. Just getting some water."

He pours himself a glass from the tap.

"You all right?" he says, turning to appraise her.

"Yeah. I'm fine."

"You seem . . ." His eyes trace a thoughtful arc across the room, then zoom back to her. "A bit mad."

She laughs. "Mad?"

"Yeah. I mean, not, like, crazy mad. Just a bit distracted." He looks towards the courtyard. "Is it him?"

"Him?"

"Yes. You know. All this lost-memory stuff. Having to deal with it?"

"Well, yeah. I suppose, a bit. It's been strange, hasn't it? Having him around. But" — she steps towards her son and wraps her hand around the back of his neck — "this time tomorrow it will be over. He'll be gone. Life will go back to normal."

"Do you want that?"

She looks at him sharply.

"Do you want things to go back to normal?"

"I suppose. I mean—"

"I like him," he cuts in. "If it turned out that he wasn't a murderer. You know. Or even if he was." He laughs.

"Oh," says Alice. "Good."

"Night, Mum." He gives her a bear hug. "Love you."

"I love you, too, baby." She kisses his cheek and he smiles at her and then he's gone, leaving her alone in the kitchen with the buzzing fridge and the darkness and the dogs.

CHAPTER
FORTY-SIX

1993

The cord was now loose enough for Gray to remove his hands. He resisted the temptation to free himself, and gave himself a moment to plan his next move.

"I'm using the knife to slice through the front of your sister's T-shirt, Graham. Don't worry. I'm being very careful. Because I don't want to hurt her. At least, not yet."

Gray flinched again at the sound of fabric rending, his sister's intake of breath.

Then: "Wow. I mean really — wow. Those are about the most incredible tits I have ever seen. Truly. Have you ever seen your sister's tits, Graham?" Mark asked this conversationally, as you might ask someone if they've seen a certain movie. "Such a shame you can't see what I'm seeing. You're really missing out."

Gray breathed in deeply, holding down the flames of fury. He slipped his good hand gently from the cord and then used his fingers to locate one of the wire coat-hanger hooks Kirsty had put in the back pocket of her jeans earlier. She adjusted her position slightly to let him ease it out, which Mark misread as an indication that she was enjoying herself. "Oh," he said, "your sister seems to be getting into things now, Graham. Right, let's let these beauties free, shall we?"

Gray felt Mark's hands reach behind his sister's back and begin to fiddle with the fastening of her bra. He stilled his hands and stopped breathing. It seemed to take for ever.

"Have you never undone a bra before, Mark?" he asked.

"Shut up, you fucking dweeb."

"No, seriously. You appear to be a bit of an amateur. And actually, I'm starting to wonder, given the way you're behaving like a total fucking *freak*, if maybe you're a virgin."

He felt Mark's hands loosen from behind Kirsty. Then Mark was in front of him, his face twisted with disgust. He brought his arm back and slapped Gray hard across the cheek. "Just shut the fuck up."

And there it was, the moment. Swiftly Gray pulled his bad hand from the cord and then leaped to his feet and brought the wire hanger hook down on to the crown of Mark's head. He felt it puncture the flesh, felt it rip the flesh, saw Mark's hands reach up and meet together over his scalp, saw the blood ooze through his fingers, saw the heavy-based lamp on the floor at his feet, brought it up with his good arm, brought it down again, saw Mark's hands leave his skull and grab it midway, felt it come away from his one good hand like a flower plucked from a meadow.

"Oh my God," Mark was saying, the lamp in his hand, blood dripping down his face in three separate rivulets, "you've done it now. You've really, really done it now." His voice had changed, the high-pitched whine lowered to a bass rumble.

"The door!" Gray shouted at his sister. "Get out! Go!"

He caught a glimpse of her tear-stained face as she hurled herself towards the door, one hand holding the shredded flaps of her T-shirt together across her breasts, the other tucking something into her pocket.

"Go!" he shouted again.

Dropping the lamp, Mark stumbled across the room, almost grabbing hold of Kirsty's arm as she slipped through the door which she slammed hard in her wake, right on to his arm. Mark stopped, grabbed his arm, howled; then he flung the door open, setting off after her like a wounded animal. Gray followed in pursuit; he saw Kirsty hurtling down the staircase two steps at a time, stumbling, sliding down three steps on her backside before regaining her feet, but leaving a vital beat for Mark to catch up with her. Then Mark brought her down on to the stairs, landed with his full weight on top of her, began tugging at her bra, tugging at her jeans, blood dripping from his wound on to her chest. Gray grabbed the back of his collar and tried to yank him off her but he didn't have enough strength in his one arm and Mark easily pushed him away. But while he was distracted by Gray's lame efforts to manhandle him, Kirsty launched her left foot right between his legs, throwing him back into a foetal ball of pain.

"You fucking bitch," Mark wailed, clutching his crotch. "You disgusting, ugly bitch."

Gray grabbed Kirsty's hand and they ran, shouting out for help as they went, in case there was still someone in the house.

"No!" Gray said, pulling Kirsty away from the front door. "It'll be locked."

They ran across the tiled floor of the hallway and towards the back door. Gray turned once, to see how much of a lead they had, just in time to see Mark's blood-smeared face inches from his, to feel his hot, angry breath, and then he was down, hard, his jaw cracking against the hard tiles, momentarily winded, Mark on top of him. He felt Mark's hands meet tightly across the crown of his head, pick it up and then smash it against the hard floor, felt his brain bounce against the walls of his skull, his hearing fade to a drowsy buzz.

His sister was screaming, and then there was a strange and terrifying moment of silence. Mark suddenly rose away from him, then slumped again. His sister had stopped screaming and stood over them both breathing loudly, hyperventilating.

She was clutching a bloodied knife. Mark's knife. Blood dripped on to the pure white floor. Then they were both running, through the door at the back of the house, across the glorious, moonlit lawn, hand in hand.

CHAPTER
FORTY-SEVEN

Lily hadn't fully lowered the Roman blinds last night and a blush of dawn light is now breaking through the gloom of the room. It's five fifty-one. She's only been asleep for a few hours — three, maybe four. So many strange noises here by the sea. Seagulls cawing like haunted children, foxes wailing as though they are being slowly disembowelled. And the distant tide, like a mob of people, hushing and whispering, ooh and aahing, throwing itself against invisible rocks.

She peels back the thin blanket she'd covered herself with last night and swings herself to a sitting position. She feels numb with tiredness and strangeness, with the echoes of the dreams that had chased each other about in her head last night while she lay suspended just out of reach of deep sleep. She folds the blanket into a neat square and tucks it back into the cupboard from where she'd taken it. Then she smooths down the duvet cover and the pillowcase, restoring them to the state of perfection in which she'd found them. She pulls a single dark hair from the pillow and drops it on to the floor. She doesn't want this elegant woman to think of her, a scruffy stranger, lying on her beautiful white bed.

She pulls a can of Coke from the carrier bag she brought with her from home and drinks it down in a few short gulps. Then she swallows down the remains of one of yesterday's doughnuts. She sits for a moment, feeling herself re-form.

Her phone pings and she picks it up.

Good morning. Please text me when you get this. Russ.

She texts him back; *Hello. I am here. Everything is OK.*

He texts her back a smiley face and she smiles. He is a nice man. She almost texts him back with her own smiley face but stops herself. It is too much.

She goes to the window and winds up the blind. Then she gasps. Everything is pink. The sky, the sea, the grass, the trees. Even the undersides of the sea-gulls circling overhead are pink. She holds her hand to her throat and surveys the undulating, glittering lawns that fall in terraces down towards the sea, the peach-hued statues that dot the gardens, the ancient walls grown over with ivy and creepers, the small ponds and sundials.

She is truly in heaven now. She wishes her mother could be here to see this place. Her friends from home. She brings her phone to the window and takes some photos but not one of them captures the true majesty of this place.

Last night she'd gone through the woman's possessions but had found nothing to link her to Carl. Just clothes, jewellery, menus for local restaurants, a camera with no charge, a pile of local business cards, receipts from shops. She would take these into the town today, talk to local shopkeepers, ask them about the woman who lives in the big white house on the cliff. Ask them about Carl.

But first she wants to look around this house again. She waits until the sun is fully up, until the pink has turned to gold, then brightened to a stringent blue, and then she lets herself slowly out of the attic bedroom and tiptoes across the landing, a small paring knife held tight inside her hand.

Is this where Carl grew up? she wonders. Did he play in these magnificent rooms, run across those rolling green lawns? Did he kick off sandy boots in the small boot room by the back door and hurtle into the kitchen to beg for snacks? She finds dogs' leads hanging from coat hooks and imagines a small Carl and a large dog, jogging towards the beach together.

She spends an hour exploring and investigating the house. She goes through drawers in the living rooms, finds nothing more than spent matches, broken Christmas decorations, dead batteries and packets of fuses. She opens packing boxes and finds nothing more than cutlery and wine glasses, paperback books and knick-knacks.

Russ phones her at eight. "How are you getting on?"

Lily's heart warms at the sound of his voice. "It is fine," she says. "I'm looking through the house now, and then I will walk into town."

"Have you found anything?"

"No. Not one thing. Just . . . *crap*. Books and stuff." She sighs. "It is strange, I think, for a house to have no clues? Don't you think? To be so full of things, yet to hold nothing of itself?"

"It is strange, yes."

She pauses, imagines Russ in a suit, striding towards the Tube station. "How are you?" she asks.

"I'm fine," he says. "I'm great."

"I hope your wife, she wasn't still cross when you came home?"

"No. She was fine. I got home an hour earlier than I said — I think that helped. And the baby had gone down well. And she'd had a glass of wine. So . . ."

"So. Good. I am glad. And thank you."

"It was nothing. It was nice. I like driving."

"Good," she says again. "You are a good driver."

He laughs. "Thank you. I'll tell my wife you said that."

"Yes. Tell her."

She wants to say more to this warm, kind man. She has not met anyone like him before. She wants to tell him that he is special and that Jo is a lucky woman. Instead she says, "Well, goodbye, Russ. Have a good day at work."

"I'll call you later," he says.

"Yes, please."

She feels completely alone when Russ has hung up. The house looms around her, strange and silent. But soon the silence is replaced by the sound of traffic beginning to pass by the house on the main road outside. Monday morning. The town is awakening.

She returns to the attic bedroom and collects her coat and her belongings.

290

CHAPTER
FORTY-EIGHT

"I'll come with you," says Frank.

Alice is making packed lunches in the kitchen.

"Where?" she asks.

"To drop Romaine at school."

"Why?"

He shrugs. "To say goodbye. Say goodbye to Derry, too. And Daniel. Also . . ." He pauses. "I just wanted to . . . you know, hang out with you a bit longer."

Alice smiles and strokes his arm. "You funny boy."

She tears off a piece of cling film and wraps up Romaine's bagel. She'd been hoping that Frank might have woken up this morning with his memory restored. That he might burst through the back door and say: *It's all fine! I didn't kill anyone! And I know where I live! I'll be back tomorrow with my cat and all my stuff and we can start a new life together!*

Instead he seems more withdrawn than normal.

"Not funny," he says. "Just scared. And sad."

She stops what she's doing and looks up at him. "'Course you are," she says. "So am I."

"You are?"

"'Course I am." She feels her face flush and turns away from him, unzipping Romaine's packed-lunch box.

He doesn't ask her why and she's glad.

She decides to leave the dogs at home. She doesn't want to spend her last walk with Frank stopping to collect steaming turds from the cold pavement.

She calls the teenagers in to say goodbye to Frank before they leave the house and then at eight forty they set off. It's a startlingly beautiful day, not a cloud in sight and already some warmth in the platinum sun. Romaine holds one of Frank's hands in hers. Frank holds her packed-lunch box in the other. It has a picture of Olaf from *Frozen* on it and looks impossibly small in his big hand. Without the dogs holding her up, Alice finds herself at the school gates a few minutes early. Derry looks at her askance. "What's going on?" she says, looking at her watch, theatrically.

"Shut up," say Alice.

Derry looks at Frank impassively. "Morning," she says.

He nods and smiles.

"You off today, then?" she asks.

"I reckon," he replies. "It's been almost a week. It's time."

She nods. Then she says, "I was thinking — let's have a coffee, before you go. All three of us."

Alice and Frank nod at each other. Anything to prolong things.

"I'll check my email after nine, see if the editor from the *Gazette* has written back."

"Yes," says Alice, "good idea. You never know" — she turns to Frank — "depending on what they know, we might not have to go to the police at all."

292

"Assuming they reply," says Derry.

"Assuming they reply," echoes Alice.

They all nod. They all know it's a last chance saloon.

The school gates are unlocked and the children stream in. Alice catches the eye of Romaine's class teacher from last year, her nemesis. The teacher looks at her and then at Frank. She arches an eyebrow. Alice wants to punch her. Derry puts a soothing hand against her arm and says, "I'll walk them in. I'll meet you out here."

"What's her problem?" asks Frank, squeezing hold of Romaine and saying goodbye.

"She hates me." She shrugs. "And no doubt someone with nothing better to do with their sad little life has *informed the school* that I'm housing a deviant in my shed. So she'll add that to her little list of reasons to treat me like shit."

Frank sighs. "I'm sorry."

"No!" she says, more sharply than she'd intended. "No. Do not be sorry. Do not be sorry. That's her problem. It's not yours. It's not ours. We are *good*. Well, we *were* . . ." She trails off.

"We were," he agrees. And then he takes her hand in his and he holds it tight, right there in front of the school. Right there in front of the teacher. Alice squeezes it back.

The café is quiet on this Monday morning. A couple of other mums from the school sit outside at pavement tables, smoking and drinking coffee out of mugs; one of them has a Yorkshire terrier on her lap. Inside a young mum sits with her newborn in a pram and two elderly couples sit side by side, still in their coats, nursing mugs of tea, having quiet, broken conversations punctuated by moments of blank contemplation. Frank, Alice and Derry order coffees and bacon rolls at the counter and then sit down.

"Right," says Derry, pulling off her scarf, swinging her red coat over the back of her chair and switching on her phone, "let's see if our friendly local rag editor has come up with anything." She swipes the screen, her brow furrowed; then she switches it off again. "Nothing yet," she says. "But it's only just gone nine. I'll keep trying."

They all turn then as the door opens and a tall, attractive woman walks in. She's very young, with fine, dark hair tied back off her face and wide-set features. She's wearing a lightweight black Puffa jacket, jeans and high-heeled boots and carrying a plastic bag. She marches straight to the counter and says, fairly loudly and in a strong Eastern European accent, "Please, can you help me. I am looking for someone. I wonder if you know her. She is a lady, well dressed, probably middle-aged; she lives in the big house up there." She indicates the cliffs to the left of the café. "Do you know her?"

Alice and Frank exchange a look.

The man behind the counter says, "You mean Kitty?"

"I don't know her name," says the girl.

"Well, that's the only person I can think of. You mean the house around the bend? The white one?"

294

"Yes!" she says. "It is white."

"Well, yes, then it must be Kitty you're talking about. Very elegant woman."

"Yes!"

"What did you want to know about her exactly?"

"I don't know." She sounds excited. "Everything, I suppose. I'm married to her son, and—"

He breaks in. "Ah, well, no, in that case we're talking about different people. Kitty has no children."

The young woman stops. Her shoulders slump. Then she straightens again and pulls something from the carrier bag. It's a photo album. She opens it and passes it to the man. "Here," she says, "do you know this man?"

Frank and Alice watch with held breath as the man behind the counter studies the book. "No," he says. "Sorry. I can't say I do. Is that your husband?" He passes the book back to her.

"Yes!" she says. "My husband. And he has been missing now since last Tuesday. He told me this woman, this Kitty, was his mother. Do you know where she is?"

"Kitty?" he says. "Gosh, no. As far as I know she hasn't been here for years. I mean, you know that house is just her holiday home?" He laughs incredulously. "Apparently she lives in an actual stately home, over in Harrogate."

"But I called her yesterday. I called her here. And she answered her phone. Here."

The woman is beginning to sound aggressive and the man recoils from her slightly. "Well," he says, "I'm not the oracle. Maybe she's here. Maybe she's not. I don't know."

Alice gives Frank a questioning look. "Her husband is missing," she whispers urgently. "My God, do you think . . .?" She has to see the photos in that album. "Is she Kirsty?" she hisses. "Frank? Is that Kirsty?"

He shrugs and looks panicked. "I don't think so," he whispers back. "I don't know."

Alice gets up and approaches the woman at the counter. The woman spins round at the touch of Alice's hand against her arm and gives her a chilling look.

"Sorry," says Alice, "I couldn't help overhearing you and, well, I don't suppose . . . I mean . . ." She turns to the table where Frank and Derry are both watching her avidly. "You don't recognise that man, do you?"

The woman turns and gives Frank a withering look. "No," she says, "I have never seen that man before in my life."

Alice exhales a small deep-seated breath of relief. To say goodbye to Frank now, here, to hand him over to this hostile, impossibly young woman . . . She would rather take him to the police.

"Oh. OK. But, you know, it's interesting, because he just turned up here, late on Tuesday night. He came from London on the train. And he can't remember anything. And then a couple of days ago he remembered that house. The house you were asking about. He said . . ." She pauses. "He said he thinks he used to live there."

The woman has lost her expression of impatient disdain and stares at Alice now with her mouth hanging open. "Oh," she says, looking behind Alice to Frank and then back again.

"I wonder," says Alice, "would you join us? Just for a minute? We might be different characters in the same story. If you know what I mean?"

The woman nods, and follows Alice to their table, the photo album clutched to her chest.

"My name's Alice, by the way. And this is my best friend Derry. And this is . . . well, we call him Frank. But actually we haven't got a clue what his name really is."

Alice pulls a chair over for the woman and she sits down. "My name is Liljana," she says. "But people call me Lily."

"And where are you from?"

"I am from Kiev. In the Ukraine."

"And you're married to an Englishman?"

"Yes. His name is Carl. Although . . ." She pauses and looks at each one of them in turn. "Well, that is not his name either." She laughs nervously. "No, since I reported him missing to the police, they have told me that his passport is a fake and that no such person as him exists." She shrugs. "So. Two men with no name. It is weird."

Alice shivers. There is a dark pit of unknowable badness beneath her words. *Two men with no name. It is much more than weird.*

"This is him," says Lily, laying the photo album on the table in front of Alice and Frank and pulling it open. "This is my husband."

Alice looks at a photo of a nice-looking man, dark-haired with piercing eyes in a razor-sharp suit.

Then Frank looks at the photo and suddenly he is on his feet, his chair knocked backwards behind him, his face drained of blood, his hands bunched together in front of his mouth.

Alice grabs his arm. "Frank?" she says. "Frank. What's the matter?"

CHAPTER
FORTY-NINE

1993

Gray and Kirsty skidded down the terraces and pathways where Kitty's garden sloped sharply towards the sea. There was no light here, the treetops cancelled out the moon, and they were running virtually blind.

Kirsty was babbling.

"I killed him! Fuck! Fuck! Gray! I killed him!"

Gray placated her breathlessly. "You don't know that! We don't know anything! Just keep moving!"

He needed to pull her along to stop her from collapsing. She was hysterical.

He turned to look behind him, imagining heavy breathing in every rustle of leaves overhead, frantic footsteps in every crash of the waves on to the rocks below. He'd felt the lifeless weight of Mark's body on top of his but he was still far from convinced that he was dead.

They were at the edge of the grounds now, where a small metal gate opened on to a long and perilous wooden staircase attached to the cliff face. The moon reappeared and everything immediately turned silver. In this light Gray could see the state of them both. Their clothes were stained with blood, their hair matted, Kirsty's clothes virtually shredded. They looked like extras from a horror movie, stumbling down the precarious steps towards the rocky beach below. And then, from behind them, no longer an outcrop of Gray's adrenaline-fuelled imagination, but as real as the rocks beneath his feet, came the sound of a man breathing heavily and the thud of feet against the wooden steps.

"Faster," he hissed at Kirsty, "come *on!*"

The footsteps behind them grew closer and closer as they approached the end of the staircase. They clambered together over the slimy rocks, spray from the waves soaking them to the skin. On the beach around the bay they could see movement, the light of a torch, a figure moving jerkily.

"Dad!" Gray whispered. "Look. It's Dad."

He turned briefly to check behind them. A figure was lurching over the rocks.

"Dad!" he called through cupped hands, before moving on again. "Dad!"

The torch beam swung towards them, small and spindly from this distance, but definitely aimed at them.

The small figure on the beach called something out to them that got snatched away by the sea.

"Dad!" screamed Kirsty.

They both moved even faster now, and faster still as the figure on the beach headed towards them.

They were almost at the edge of the rocks when the figure clambered up and the light from his torch blinded them momentarily. At the familiar shape of his father behind the torch, Gray felt his heart slow down.

But Tony looked angry. "You two," he yelled, "Jesus Christ. You two. I've been ..." And then his gaze moved over them, taking in Kirsty's bloodstained, sliced-open T-shirt, her expression of sheer terror and then he looked behind them and saw Mark appear and he roared, "*What have you done? What have you done?*"

Mark froze. He was about ten feet away. Everything stopped completely for a moment; even the sea fell silent below as the next wave slowly built up its bulk. Then suddenly Mark ran towards Kirsty, ran right at her, hooked his arm around her waist and before Gray or Tony had a chance to move, he had jumped with her into the wildly frothing surf, into the rocks and the darkness and the swirl of the sea.

"No!" screamed his dad.

"Kirsty! Shit!"

And then they were both in the sea. The shock of it, the ice water against his sore body, the roar of the water closing over his head. Gray flailed around for something to hold on to. He heard his father's voice close by and headed towards it. He was beckoning Gray. Gray followed him, using his legs to push himself along, his bad arm held close into his body. His father pointed east. Gray saw two small shapes, moving across the bay. Mark was swimming fast, taking Kirsty with him. "Come on!" shouted his father.

"My wrist is broken!" he screamed out into the chaos. "I can't swim!"

His dad was silent for a moment. "Get out!" he roared. "Get out now!"

Gray stared helplessly at the shapes of Mark and Kirsty getting smaller and smaller. Then he watched his father begin a breakneck front crawl away from him, shrinking and shrinking until he could barely see him. He let the next wave deposit him against the rocks and crawled painfully, pitifully back on to a solid shelf where he lay on his back for a moment, unable to move. His heart hammered and jumped in his chest. His wrist throbbed and ached. He sat up and saw nothing. The distant figures had disappeared completely. He pulled himself painfully to his feet and scrambled awkwardly across the rocks until finally his feet found the solid floor of the beach and he began to run. The beach was empty. From high up above he could hear the thud of music drifting down from the town. He heard high-pitched female laughter and a car screeching away. He turned and saw the lights of Kitty's house behind him. But out at sea there was nothing.

"Help!" he screamed into the night air. "Help me!"

He ran and ran, shouting hopelessly as he went. Then suddenly he saw a shape crawling out of the surf. The shape landed heavily on the beach and lay for a moment, before pulling itself up. Gray picked up his pace and fell breathlessly on his knees by the side of his father.

"Dad!" he cried. "Where's Kirsty? Dad!"

His dad said nothing. He rolled on to his side and brought his knees up to his chest. Then he rolled on to

302

his back again and clutched his heart with his hands, kneading it. "Jesus Christ," he gasped. "Jesus Christ!"

Gray looked towards the sea. Large waves rolled in like unfurling carpets, spreading themselves as sparkling foam at his feet. The surface glittered and wriggled. An ocean liner sat on the horizon; a plane passed silently overhead. He stared desperately into the shifting shapes of the sea, aching for a sign of Kirsty.

"Dad! Get up! Dad! Where is she? Where's Kirsty?"

But his father was still clutching at his chest and now, Gray could see, his breathing was becoming more rather than less laboured. "Dad! Get up!"

He looked out to sea again, at the black nothingness, and then back at his father.

"I . . . I can't . . . breathe," his father panted. "My . . . heart."

"Oh Jesus." Gray pulled his hair back from his face and stamped at the sand. "Oh Jesus. Dad. Oh . . . fuck." He looked behind again at the tops of the buildings in town, scanning the promenade for people. He saw a couple, walking a dog, their arms hooped around each other. "Help!" he screamed out. "Oh, fuck, *help me!*" He knew even as he called out that it was hopeless, that they couldn't hear him. The couple kept walking, oblivious to the scene on the beach. Gray sank to his feet and pulled his father into what seemed something like the recovery position he'd learned about in the Boy Scouts. But there was so little he could do with one hand. He pulled his father's hands from his chest and started pounding at his heart with his left hand, counting the intervals under his breath. But it was pointless. CPR didn't work with one hand. He turned and screamed again at the retreating backs of the couple on the prom. And then he began to cry. "Dad," he wailed, "I can't do it! I can't do it! Oh, *shit*. Dad, what shall I do? What shall I do?"

His father's body was rigid and his hands had come back to his heart, which he scratched at as though he was trying to dig down under the very bone and pull it out. Gray jumped up and looked out to sea again. Nothing. Then he turned, yet again, to look up at the prom. More people were walking by, late-night drinkers, arranged in groups, singing and shouting. "Help!" he screamed. "Help us!"

His father had begun to wheeze now, pulling hard at the collar of his wet polo shirt.

He was dying, Gray suddenly knew. His father was dying and his sister had disappeared into the North Sea with a psychopath. And he couldn't do anything, not one single thing about any of it.

He pulled his father's head on to his lap and he caressed his forehead and he kissed his cheeks and he cradled him to his stomach and he looked out to the sea and up into the black, star-filled sky and behind him towards the oblivious town and he felt the life pouring out of his father, pouring so fast that he felt sick with it. "Oh no," he sobbed, "oh no, oh no, oh no. No, Dad. Not my dad. Not my dad. No, Dad. No. Please, Dad. Please. Oh God. Oh God. Oh God."

And then a few seconds later he knew it was over. No time for last words of love or reassurance. No time for anything other than to catch the last few rasping breaths of the man who'd brought him up, to suck them in and hold on to them, like droplets of precious essence. Gray dropped his head on to his father's chest and sobbed into his cold wet polo shirt. "Not my dad," he sobbed, "not my dad."

He raised his head to the sky and he wailed at the moon.

Behind him the sea rolled in, the sea rolled out, waves fizzed upon the sand, but the dark water beyond remained empty.

CHAPTER
FIFTY

"He drowned?" Lily asks the man called Frank. "Mark? He drowned?"

"Yes," says Frank.

"And this is him?" Lily raps the pictures in the album with her manicured fingernails, impatiently. "This is the man you call Mark?"

Frank nods. But he doesn't look convinced.

"Well," says Lily, trying hard to keep the frustration from her tone, "this makes no sense. This cannot be Carl because I am married to Carl and he isn't drowned!"

"I think . . ." The Frank man looks as though he is thinking about too many things, much too slowly. "I think I saw him. I saw him."

"Saw who?" The Alice woman asks this. Lily looks at her through narrowed eyes, evaluating her. She has something about her, something vital and proud. She makes Lily feel insecure in some way and that makes Lily feel like a cat with a dog, that she needs to show her that she is more vital and more proud.

"Mark. Carl. This man." He waves vaguely at the wedding album. "I saw him. When I was with schoolchildren. I was with schoolchildren and he was there and I . . . I dropped my coffee. And it was him. He wasn't dead."

His face has lost even more colour and Alice touches him, touches him so softly that Lily thinks she must be in love with him.

"When?" Lily cuts in. "When did you see him?"

"I don't know." His hands are shaking. "It was recent, I think. I was wearing a shirt." His fingers feel the collar of his T-shirt. "And a jacket." He mimes rubbing a lapel. "I had a coffee. I was in the city. And he was there . . ."

Lily wants to slap him. Why is he being so vague? "Please," she says. "Please. I don't want to know any more about coffee. Tell me what happened. How can my husband be one minute drowned in the sea and then the next alive in front of you?"

"Maybe he has an identical twin," says the red-headed woman.

Lily is about to sigh but then stops. This might be something worth thinking about. That would mean Carl was not this murderous, awful-sounding man from twenty-odd years ago.

They all turn to look at Frank as though he might have an answer for them. But he is just sitting there looking pale and clammy.

"Look," he says after a moment. "I understand how much you want to know what happened to your husband, but I'm just . . . I wish I could explain. It's like I'm watching two movies concurrently. On a delay. So I'm unfurling it all in my head. Scene by scene. And some bits are blending together. And some bits are coming in the wrong order. And all of it feels too loud and too bright. I just . . ."

"Do you want to go for a walk?" says Alice, "get some air, maybe?"

"No!" cries Lily. "No. Please. No. Now — I need to know it now."

The woman with the red hair has been distracted by the sound of her phone ringing. She grimaces at the number on the screen and says, "Who the hell is that?"

She looks as though she is not going to take the call but then she sighs, presses the screen and says, "Yes?"

Her phone conversation is clearly very interesting and she cups her hand over the phone a minute later and says, "It's the journalist. From the *Ridinghouse Gazette*. The one who wrote the original article. The editor passed my number on to her. She's really keen to meet up. Shall I tell her to come here?"

Alice and Frank look at each other and nod.

"What journalist?" says Lily.

The red-haired woman shushes her, rudely, and resumes her conversation. The journalist is coming here in half an hour apparently.

"Who?" says Lily. "Who is this woman?"

"Her name is Lesley Wade. She wrote a story about Frank's dad dying back in 1993. She says she knows more about the story, about what happened afterwards."

Lily nods. Good, she thinks, a person with facts rather than a confused person making it up as he goes along. Why is this man, Frank, not in hospital?

Alice turns to Frank, caresses his hand and says, "What happened to Kirsty? Did she . . .?"

Frank's eyes are shiny with tears. "I can't see her coming out of the sea," he says, looking at her desperately. "I looked for her. But she didn't come out of the sea. Kirsty isn't there."

PART THREE

CHAPTER
FIFTY-ONE

Two Weeks Earlier

Travelling into London with eight fourteen-year-olds was a little like being a circus master. Gray could only assume that these children went on trains in their out-of-school lives, that they walked on pavements and past members of the public, that they saw advertising hoardings depicting scantily clad human beings, but in the context of a school trip it was as though they'd all just been released from a sensory-deprivation capsule. They touched things, they swung from poles, they shouted — oh, how they shouted. And these were his brightest students, the top stream, virtual genii in a couple of cases, on their way to the semi-finals of an inter-school maths competition being held at a university.

It was a windy, heavy-skied day, on the brink of rain. He had the remains of a hangover and longed to grab a coffee from one of the dozens of coffee shops they'd passed since they got off the train at Victoria. But he was chained to these children; he couldn't afford to take his eye off them for a moment. Finally they approached the hall where the competition was being hosted. The grandeur of the place — towering domed ceiling glazed with stained glass, half-ton chandeliers, marble statues and burnished mahogany panelling — seemed to still the children as they entered. Gray registered them while they stood, quiet and awed. Then he herded them into their allocated section of a room filled with the territorial bristle and edge of children from different schools forced into close proximity. He set them all up with cups of water and practice papers and headed back to the registration desk. "Is it OK if I pop out for a minute or two, to grab a coffee?"

"Is everyone in your group registered?"

"Yes, they're in the prep room."

The registrar nodded and Gray fled.

The wind was wild now, sending sheets of newspaper and city dust into the air. He pulled his coat hard around him and headed in the direction of a Costa he'd seen on the way in. He ordered an extra-strong Americano and a chocolate muffin and it was as he left the shop and turned back towards the university building that he saw him.

His peripheral vision faded away into interference and his heart filled up with too much blood. The stale alcohol that he'd been trying to hold down all morning rose up his gullet and for a moment Gray thought he might be sick. He stood on the spot, his coffee in one hand, the muffin in the other, and he watched the man moving along the pavement opposite. He was still very slim, in a pink shirt with a striped tie and tight-fitting suit trousers. He looked cold and windswept, in need of a jacket or a coat. His hair was longer now — he'd kept it very short back then — and it was being blown out of shape. He seemed preoccupied by this and kept trying to pin it back with his fingers, only for it to be blown asunder again. Gray knew it was him by the angle of his jaw, the sharpness of his nose. He'd been a handsome boy and now he was a handsome man. A stranger passing him in the street might well think he was younger than his years, but Gray knew exactly how old he was. The last time he'd seen him he'd been a cocky, snake-hipped nineteen-year-old. Now he must have been pushing forty-one.

Gray's fingers lost their grip on the rim of his coffee cup and it fell to the ground; steaming coffee pooled around his feet and trickled away into a drain cover.

He looked quickly in the direction of the university and then back in the direction of the man across the street. He was turning the corner. Gray picked up his pace and followed him, stopping as he saw him run through a revolving door and into an office block.

He swayed for a moment in the buffeting wind, made a note of the name above the doors and then headed back to his students, his hangover now a distant memory, his thought consumed by only one thing.

Mark Tate was alive.

And if Mark Tate was alive, did that mean that Kirsty was alive too?

CHAPTER
FIFTY-TWO

Lesley Wade walks into the café and Alice knows before she has even approached them that she is a journalist. She is a very small, brusque woman with cropped white hair and funky, diamanté-studded reading glasses.

"So," she says now, smoothing down the sides of her paper napkin with sherbet-pink-tipped fingers and appraising Frank with fascination, "you're the mysterious teenage son."

"Am I?"

She nods. "It was the weirdest thing, that story. Just the weirdest thing. How much can you remember?"

Frank shakes his head. "Just my dad, dying in my arms. My sister, in the sea. The white house. The man called Mark. And then seeing him. In London. Going into the office. And I remembered. He attacked my sister. And I dropped my coffee." He shakes his head again. Alice's heart aches for him. "Then I don't remember anything until Alice found me, on the beach."

Lesley spreads her fingers open on the tabletop, looks down and then up again. "So," she begins, "in 1993, a young man called Graham Ross was found by a local woman sitting by the dead body of his father on the beach. He didn't know what his name was or who the man was or why he was there."

Alice's breath catches. This has happened to Frank before.

"His sister was missing, as was his sister's boyfriend, Mark Tate. Neither of them were ever found. The conclusion at the time, without any witness evidence available from Graham, was that Graham and Kirsty Ross had been at a party at Mark's aunt's house; there'd been drugs and alcohol. They'd all decided to go for a late-night swim, got into difficulties, and that having failed to find them at Mrs Tate's house, Mr Ross went to look for them on the beach and died of a massive heart attack attempting to rescue them. And that the shock of his father dying in his arms caused poor Graham to enter a temporary fugue state."

"He's in a fugue state now," Alice says.

"Really?" says Lesley, bringing her hands down into her lap. "In which case, he should really be in hospital. Don't you think?"

Alice stiffens defensively. "I told him that," she said. "Right from the beginning. But he refused. And I was taking him to the police station. Today. Literally. This was our goodbye coffee before we went."

Lesley ignores this and turns to Lily. "And remind me again," she says, "where you come into this?"

"I told you," says Lily. "I am married to the man who you say supposedly drowned in the sea here in 1993."

Lesley pauses for a minute, draws in her breath, says, "Listen. Maybe we should hold off on taking Frank . . . Graham . . . whoever . . . to the hospital or police just yet. I think, maybe . . ." Shiny pink fingernails tap, tap against the table. "I think maybe we could do something here. Something, with just us."

Derry looks up sharply. "You mean you want to run a story?"

"Well, no, not necessarily a *story* as such, more a catch-up piece. You know. Whatever happened to the boy on the beach? That kind of thing." Lesley smiles the smile of a cat upon a mouse. It's clear what she's after, but Alice doesn't care. She gets to keep Frank a bit longer.

Derry throws Alice a look of disquiet. Alice shakes her head at her. Derry rolls her eyes.

Lesley has already pulled a pad and a ballpoint pen from her bag and is sitting, poised. "So, Frank, Graham . . ." She pauses. "Which would you prefer?"

"Frank," he whispers and Alice's heart melts.

"So, Frank," Lesley says, "you left Ridinghouse, you went back home with your mum, without your sister, without your dad. What happened next? Did you get your memory back?"

"I think so. I mean, I must have. I remember my mum now. I still know her. I live virtually next door to her. I remembered my dad and my sister; I remembered being in the pub that night, with Mark and his friends and going home and letting them persuade Kirsty to come to the party with us. I remembered some of the party, too. Loud music, some weird people. Kissing a girl called Izzy. And I remembered things from before the holiday, my friends in Croydon—"

"You're from Croydon?" Alice interrupts. Just a mile or two from Brixton. All those years. They'd been so close.

"Yes," he says, "I guess I am. That's not very cool, is it?"

"But I love Croydon!" says Alice. "The Whitgift Centre!"

Frank smiles at her and then turns back when Lesley clears her throat. "When we got home I just sort of took up where I left off. Went back to school. Hooked up with my old friends. Took my A levels. I had, er, well, therapy, I suppose. For a long time. But I never unearthed the memories of that night and I just accepted the police's version of events. That we'd all jumped in the sea off our faces on drugs and that Mark and my sister had drowned. Without any memories of the other stuff, it was the only logical explanation. I did wonder sometimes if there was something big I'd forgotten, something that would make more sense of everything. But it stayed buried. Until that day in London. When I saw him."

"Yes," says Lesley, pen poised pensively over notepad, "and what can you remember about that now?"

"I . . ." He closes his eyes tightly. "God. I'm sorry. My brain is stuck on that moment, the dropped coffee. Just . . ." His head drops into his chest, his eyes still shut. "Give me one minute."

"Absolutely, Frank," says Lesley. "You take your time. We're not in any hurry."

★ ★ ★

Frank tries to recall the maths competition. Did they win? How did they do? Names bubble around his consciousness: Zach, Nazia, Muhammed, Sam, Aisha, Crystal, Hannah, King. The kids in his group. And then what? Back to school? More lessons? No. It was the Easter holidays. There was no school. Everyone went home afterwards. But how did he get home? Car? Or the bus? He sees the number 712. He sees himself pressing his Oyster card to the reader, taking a seat towards the back, resting a leather bag on his lap. Then back to his flat, the one he remembered the other night. It's on a scruffy street. A light flashes on as he passes down the alleyway towards his front door. The flat smells of this morning's cat food. He scrapes it out, cleans the bowl, refills it. The cat called Brenda circles his feet.

He marks homework. He watches TV. He googles the name of the office building he'd seen Mark Tate walking into. It's a financial services company. He clicks on the "Who we are" link and scrolls down until he finds his picture. His name, apparently, is Carl Monrose. He eats something from the freezer for dinner, lasagne he seems to recall, parcelled up by his mum when he had flu last week.

Then his thoughts take him dizzyingly from eating reheated lasagne on the sofa in his flat to a train platform, looking up, platform four, the 5.06 to East Grinstead, following the day-weary crowds, his eyes pinned to the back of Mark Tate's head. Then the timeline shifts and he's at school, sitting in someone's office. The school is strangely empty and he's wearing jeans. It's still the holidays. He's asking for compassionate leave. His grandfather is dying. Does he even have a grandfather? The man behind the desk, an older man with a weathered face and neatly cropped Afro hair, nods and looks sad and says, "Take a few days. We can cover you for a week or so." "Mr Josiah Hardman", says the plaque on his door. "Head Teacher".

Alice passes him a cup of tea across the café table. "Are you OK?" she says. Her voice comes to him like the echo of distant music.

He remembers a phone call to his mother. "I'm on a training course. Out in the sticks. You won't be able to contact me." He remembers his mother saying, "Be careful. I shall miss you." He remembers how that felt, how it always felt knowing that he was the sole survivor of his mother's little family. Knowing that every journey he took, every choice he made, every person he brought into his life caused his mother an animal ache of fear. Knowing that he could never leave her. That he was tied to her, like the owner of a loyal but life-restricting dog, until she died.

"I followed him," he says eventually. "I followed the man on to his train."

Lily shoots him a look of horror. "Carl? You followed my Carl?"

"Yes," says Frank. "I remember getting on the five oh six to East Grinstead. I sat at the other end of the carriage from him. I watched him like a hawk. He got off at—"

"Oxted," says Lily.

"Yes," says Frank. "Oxted. And I followed him. Past shops. Up a dual carriageway. Past a building site."

"And then?" asks Lily.

"And to a block of flats."

"Oh my God," says Lily, "you came to my home. My God. What did you do then? Did you spy on us? Or maybe you killed him? You took him into that building site. You took him there and you killed him, didn't you? I've seen the flashing light. The one in the window. I *knew* it was wrong."

People have turned to look at her; she's pointing at Frank aggressively and her voice is shrill. She reaches into the front pocket of her little shiny handbag and pulls out an iPhone. "I'm calling the police," she said. "They are working on my husband's missing-person case and I have their direct number. I'm calling them right now . . ."

Lesley puts a calming hand over Lily's. "No," she says, "that's not a good idea."

"It is a very good idea. Maybe he is still alive. They can go there now and see."

"No," says Lesley more firmly.

Frank's brain is processing and editing, reordering and refiling. Then suddenly he's in an empty room. There are wide glass windows covered in sticky film. He sees a phone hurtling through the air. And there's something behind the image. A noise. A voice. A fragment of something, too small to identify.

Then the scene changes; Frank has moved on again. He's following Mark Tate, following him to a coffee shop. He's wearing a baseball cap and he's watching

Mark Tate order a coffee and a pain au chocolat. His manner with the not-very-pretty girl behind the counter is brusque and offhand. He follows him out on to the street and then follows him back to his office. His heart is pounding. He can feel sweat pooling under the rim of his baseball cap. Every time he looks at Mark Tate he feels himself back in that bedroom, he hears the rending of his sister's T-shirt, feels the deep, hot throb of his broken wrist, the pounding hip hop shaking through the floorboards. His head is flooded red and black with terror and disgust, with rage and loathing. He wants, *all* he wants, is to kill Mark Tate. But he can't kill him, because he needs to talk to him first: he needs to find out what happened to Kirsty. Is she alive? And if she isn't alive, how long did she survive in those dark cold waters? Where is her body? And why? Why, why, why?

Frank pulls Lily's wedding album towards him now, and forces himself to look at Mark's face. He remembers the first time he saw that face, that warm afternoon on the beach, how he'd taken an instant inventory of the angles and the proportions of it, how his mind had processed the mathematics of that face in a split second and found it unpleasing. He feels the same way now, looking at this sharp-faced forty-year-old man marrying a girl half his age.

"Is he nice to you?" he asks, looking up at Lily.

"He treats me like a princess."

"But is he *nice* to you?"

"I don't know what you're talking about."

Now Frank's in Kitty's conservatory. She's sitting there, thin and brittle, her hand shaking slightly as she lifts the teapot. He'd taken her demeanour to be unfriendliness, assumed her to be displeased to have uninvited guests. But what if she'd been scared of Mark? What if . . .?

His thoughts spin away from him. He closes the album and drops his head into his hands.

"I took some time off work," he says. "I was due back last week. I'll probably get the sack."

"So, you had a plan?" Lesley prompts him.

"I guess, I don't know . . . I wanted to talk to Mark. I wanted to make him tell me what happened to Kirsty. I needed space. I needed time. And then—"

He's back in the empty room with the plate-glass windows. He sees his own reflection in the windows blackened by the night outside. He's alone and he has a shoulder bag filled with things. He's hiding the bag in an empty kitchen cupboard.

"I found a place and I . . ." His memories swarm and teem and he feels nauseous. "I took him there."

CHAPTER
FIFTY-THREE

Gray could not, he simply could not randomly accost Mark Tate on the street. Mark would run. He would yell. He would deny that he was Mark Tate; he would tell passers-by that this crazy man was bothering him. He would make a scene and then, once he'd shaken him off, he would disappear. Again.

And this time Gray would never find him.

So Gray made a plan.

He told his head teacher that his long-dead grandfather was dying and asked for some compassionate leave. Just a few days. Just long enough to put everything in place. He told his mother he was going on a training course. And then he began to stalk him.

Mark Tate was nothing if not a creature of habit. The same form-fitting, navy-blue suit every day, the same coffee and pain au chocolat from the same coffee shop at the same time, the same sashay through the revolving door, the same slimy greeting to the hot girl on the reception desk. He was a regular little worker bee. All that talk of being a millionaire — whatever happened to all his grandiose plans?

On Tuesday, having ascertained that Mark Tate had shown up for work as usual, Gray headed home. Here he packed a rucksack with objects from around the flat. Rope. Non-perishable food. A blanket. Some knives. His camera. A toilet roll. A belt. A pillow case. A blow-up pillow. A sleeping bag. Phone charger. Torch. Then he left three packets of cat food and a mountain of biscuits out for Brenda and took the bag with him from Croydon to Victoria and then from Victoria back to Oxted.

He followed the now-familiar route from the station to Mark's apartment block, but before he got there he stopped and peeled back the rip in the hoarding he'd discovered yesterday outside the construction site next door. He'd googled the development yesterday and, as he'd suspected, having never seen a builder at work on it, confirmed that it had run out of money and building works had been suspended while the developers looked for a new investor. The site had been sitting in a state of limbo for nearly a year, according to the report he'd read in a trade magazine. Completely abandoned.

He made his way, as he'd done yesterday, around the back of the frontline block, the only block that had been fully fitted out. There was a ditch around the back of the building, the kind of area where the wheelie bins might eventually be stored, Gray imagined, and at the bottom of the ditch was a small door into the basement level. And, as it had been yesterday, it was unlocked.

He lowered himself down into the ditch on his bum and bowed his head slightly to get through the low door. Then he took the same route he'd taken yesterday across the polished cement floor of the basement, through a pair of heavy swing doors at the other end and up a service staircase into the foyer.

There were cameras here and there in the foyer, but after nearly a year of abandonment, Gray very much doubted that anyone was watching any more. Still, he kept his face at a low angle and stayed close to the walls. Then he skipped up the next flight of stairs and pushed open the door to the first apartment on his left.

Here. Here was where he would bring Mark Tate. Here, where no one could hear him or see him, where he could keep him for as long as he liked. It was a "loft style" apartment, open plan with some exposed brickwork here and there and a shiny white kitchen built around a central island made of wood. Quickly he prepared the room. There was no mains electricity, but he'd discovered that the light on the extractor hood for the hob worked independently of the mains, as did the pale green strip lighting under the kitchen cabinets. There was no running water either and he unpacked the bottles he'd bought just now from the off licence by the station. He left the various pieces of rope in a pile by the trendy radiator that he intended to tie Mark Tate to. He blew up his pillow and spread out his sleeping bag. He unpacked the food into the kitchen: enough biscuits and crisps to last a week. He placed the toilet roll in the never-used bathroom and in his rucksack he kept his knives, the pillowcase and the torch.

Then he retraced his steps back towards the high street and found a coffee shop where he sat for four hours writing a long-overdue progress report for the head of maths while he waited for Mark Tate to return from work.

If anyone had told Gray that one day he would hide in the shadows of an abandoned building site with a knife in one hand and a pillowcase in the other, watching the minutes tick from 5:50 to 5:51 to 5:52 while a tsunami of adrenaline surged through his veins, waiting to abduct someone at knifepoint and take them prisoner — well, he clearly would not have believed them. But here he was, hand clammy on the handle of a freshly sharpened kitchen knife, and here were the footsteps of the man who had killed his father and maybe killed his sister. And here was Gray, diving from the shadows, an arm around the man's neck: *"Don't move, don't speak, I've got a knife against your throat, don't fucking move."*

He wrenched him backwards through the split in the hoarding, Mark Tate's feet dragging doggedly against the cement, his hands grasping at Gray's arm around his neck. *"Stop struggling, just stop, I've got a knife. Do you want to die?"*

Mark Tate did as he was told. Gray threw the pillowcase over his head and dragged him by the arms down into the ditch, through the basement, up the stairs and back to apartment number one. Here he flung him to the ground and quickly fastened him to the radiator with the ropes and plastic ties. He did all this without saying a word.

"I've got nothing," Mark Tate was whining through the cotton of the pillowcase. "Like a tenner. And a shit phone. But I've got money at home. Let me go home. I can get it for you."

"Mark," said Gray. One syllable. That was all. He saw Mark stiffen. "Mark Tate." As if he'd just come upon an old mate in the pub.

Gray approached him and removed the pillowcase.

Oh, it was a beautiful moment. He wished he'd filmed it. The spread of awe and disbelief across Mark's smooth-skinned, ageless face. The slight flinch. And better still, the comically disordered hair that Gray could see him aching to rearrange.

"What the . . . ?"

"Last seen on a wild summer's night, disappearing into the North Sea with my sister. Wow. Long time no see!"

Gray felt strangely high, as though he'd had a couple of shots on an empty stomach.

"How've you been?" he continued. "I see you've made a great new life for yourself! Lovely wife, good job. Wow. Got any kids?"

Mark shook his head numbly.

"No," said Gray, "probably for the best really. You being a psychopath and all."

He saw Mark gulp, his winter suntan fading to grey before his very eyes.

"Can I get you something?" he said. "Some water? A Penguin bar? Doritos? I'm thinking now I should have got some beers. But actually, since you're going to be tied to a radiator for the foreseeable it's probably best to keep your bladder empty."

From outside came the sound of the plastic hoarding flapping in the wind and the drone of rush-hour traffic petering its way out of London through the commuter belt. Gray could hear the rasp of Mark's panicked breathing and then the insistent *buzz buzz buzz* of Mark's phone buried somewhere inside his smart suit.

"What will she do? Your child bride?" Gray asked when the phone stopped buzzing. "When you don't come home from work?"

"She'll be worried," Mark said quickly. "She's new to the country. She doesn't know anyone. She'll be scared. Can I just text her? Let her know I'm running late?"

"No, you may not. Question one: what the actual fuck? I mean . . . you *drowned*."

"Clearly I didn't."

The phone began buzzing again. Gray sighed. "So, what happened? Come on, think of scared wifey wondering where you are. Talk."

Mark rearranged himself awkwardly, pulling against the plastic ties and the ropes, flicking back his head in an effort to get his fringe out of his eyes. "I got out. I was a mile up the coast. I got out and there was a phone box and I called my aunt and she came and got me and took me to Harrogate. And I nearly died. Blood loss. Hypothermia. It was all a blur; I was in and out of consciousness for days."

Gray thumped the floor with his fist. "I don't give a fuck what happened to you. What happened to Kirsty? If you got out alive, then what happened to her?"

Mark looked almost surprised to be asked. "She just . . . faded. You know. I had her; I was pulling her into shore. She was there. And then she just . . . went."

"Did you let go of her?" Gray envisaged Kate Winslet letting Leonardo DiCaprio slip into the freezing water at the end of *Titanic*, imagined the blue lips and the waters closing over Kirsty's face, felt sickened by the idea that the last thing she ever saw was the cold, hard face of Mark Tate.

"Yes," he replied, "no. I don't know. Like I said, I was slipping in and out of consciousness. I was freezing. I was holding her. And then I wasn't holding her. And she was gone. I didn't have the energy to look for her. I just kind of floated back to shore."

Gray sat up straighter. "You floated back?"

"Yeah. I think. I don't know. I'd lost a lot of blood. It's a blur . . ."

"But if you floated back, then why didn't she?"

"I don't know. OK?" And there it was, that steel in his voice, that dark emptiness which Gray remembered. It was the voice of the guy he'd seen through the bedroom window kicking the wall when Kirsty didn't want to kiss him, the guy who'd tried to barge his way into Rabbit Cottage to get to her when she didn't want to see him, the guy who'd held a knife to his sister's throat and jumped into the North Sea with her. It was the voice of the man who'd stolen Gray's life.

Mark's phone started buzzing again. Gray resisted the temptation to dig into Mark's pockets, pull it out and stamp on it.

"Did you look for her?" he said. "After you were rescued? Did you look?"

Mark shook his head, a tiny jerk of a movement. "I told you, I was half-dead. Literally. I didn't wake up until three days later. By that time the whole world thought I was dead. I couldn't have gone back. I couldn't go anywhere."

Gray clamped his hands to the sides of his head. "Fucking *hell*. She might be there. She might be there, on the rocks, right now. All these years and we might have been able to bury her. I mean, Jesus *Christ*, do you have even the slightest clue? My life has been . . . it's been *shit*. It's been *shit*. Because of you. Because of what you did to my family. What you did to my mother. To me. We were . . . we were a *perfect* family. Literally. The best family. Just boring and suburban and predictable and dull. All our furniture was brown. All our food was brown. Our car was brown. My sister was so innocent. And my parents were . . . Well, we didn't exactly have lively conversations about current affairs over the dinner table. We didn't talk about anything important, ever. And it didn't matter. Because we didn't matter. Nothing we did mattered or was ever going to change anything. In fact, you could have killed the whole fucking lot of us and it would have made no difference to anything. But we were perfect. And you destroyed us. You destroyed *me*." He stopped, aware of tears building in the base of his throat. "And what about *your* family? *Your* mum? How could you and Kitty let your mum think you were dead?"

"Because . . ." Mark sighed heavily. "My mum hated me. My father too. And me and Kitty, we had this bond. From when I was a child. And she just knew. Without me saying anything. She knew that whatever

332

had happened had something to do with me. And she wanted to protect me because that's what she always did. And then she heard via the Ridinghouse grapevine that you'd lost your memory, that the police were calling it misadventure, that they'd given up hope of ever finding the bodies. So she hid me away for two years. And all that time we were just waiting for the knock on the door, waiting to hear that you'd remembered. And it never came and you never did and bit by bit I started a new life. I moved down to Cornwall for a year, did cash-in-hand jobs, then up to Scotland, back down to Cornwall, kept as far from Harrogate as I could without a passport. Rented bedsits. Saved up enough to buy a fake identity. Got a job. Got promoted. Promoted again. And then I . . ."

He stopped, cast his eyes right, towards his own apartment block. "I met a woman. Got married. It's been hard, without a family. Doing everything by myself. Not having any real friends. But now, finally, I've got something. I've got someone. Someone all of my own." His phone began buzzing again, right on cue. He dropped his head into his chest, waited for it to stop, then looked up again. "And I love her more than I've loved anything in my life and . . ."

Gray stared at him. And then he laughed.

Mark flinched at the sound.

"Seriously? You seriously expect me to feel sorry for you? Are you fucking nuts? Oh, yes, I forgot — you are."

A muscle in Mark's cheek twitched and he tried once more to flick his hair from his eyes. "So, tell me, when exactly did your memory *miraculously* return?"

"The minute I saw you, last week."

"You saw me, last week?"

"Yeah. In town. Victoria. Going into your office. And it all came back. All of it."

"And what exactly do you remember?"

Gray blanches as the scenario passes again through his mind's eye. His voice shakes as he restates the details. "I remember it all. I remember you following us out into the garden. We were looking at the peacock. It was dancing. I remember that room you took us to. I remember you touching my sister. Trying to rape her. Then you following us down to the rocks, taking my sister into the water. My dad . . . dead . . . on the beach. All of it. All the stuff that's been locked away in there for over twenty years. All the stuff that's stopped me living my life. And now it's out. I've remembered. And you're finally going to pay for what you did. I'm going to call the police. They're going to arrest you and you'll spend the rest of your life in jail."

Mark laughed hoarsely. "Really? You think so? Based on the frankly unreliable memories of a man who was taking recreational drugs on the night in question? Who claimed at the time to remember nothing of what happened that night? Who *miraculously* regained his memory more than twenty years later? Do you really think they'd believe a man who is capable of taking someone off the street at knifepoint and breaking into private property and holding him prisoner? A man who, frankly if you don't mind me saying, looks quite, quite insane?"

"But you pretended to be dead!" said Gray. "You have a fake passport!"

"So you say."

"What do you mean, so I say?"

"I mean, if you bring the police here I will simply tell them that I must bear some similarity to some man who died a long way from here, a long time ago, and that you attacked me and that you are very dangerous and possibly mad. I will deny all knowledge of being this so-called *Mark Tate*."

"But they'll check your identity. They'll know Carl Monrose doesn't really exist."

Mark shook his head slowly. "I paid a lot of money for my ID. One *hell* of a lot of money. It's police-proof. It's everything-proof."

"Bullshit."

Mark shrugged. "I pay my taxes. I vote in elections. I travel abroad freely. I *am* Carl Monrose. Go on." He gestured towards Gray's phone with a nod of his head. "Call them. See what happens to you then. Do it."

Gray stared hard at Mark and then down at his phone. A wave of nausea passed over him as the reality of his position became clear.

"Go on," said Mark. "What are you waiting for?"

The phone was damp inside Gray's clammy fingers. He turned away from Mark. His body began to shake. He couldn't think straight.

"You may as well untie me," Mark said. "Untie me — let me go. You get on with your life. I get on with my life. Yes?"

Gray spun round. "No!" he said. "No! I haven't got a life to get on with. Don't you see? I haven't got a fucking life because you took it away from me!"

Mark sighed. His phone vibrated again. "Come on," he said. "She's getting desperate now. She'll be calling the police soon herself. They'll track my phone to here. They'll find an innocent man tied to a radiator and a wild-eyed lunatic with his prints all over a knife. Let me go now and I'll tell her some lie about a delay on the train."

Gray closed his eyes and thought of his mother. Broken, alone, entirely dependent upon Gray for any semblance of meaningful life. He thought of the small things that made him human: his job, his students, his cat, his five-a-side football team. And then he thought of the humiliation of being taken away in a squad car to a strip-lit room, trying to explain himself to a pair of steely-faced detectives, who would look sadly at him over steepled fingers as though he was mad. And then he thought maybe he was mad. Surely? What had he been thinking? Stalking this man around London and Surrey? Kidnapping him off the streets? Tying him up? What had he been hoping to achieve?

The phone vibrated again. The sound of it passed through his consciousness like broken glass. He waited until it went silent and then he turned to face Mark.

He was smiling at him, smugly, like a car salesman about to close a deal on an unsellable car. "Come on, Graham. Let me go."

Red heat descended upon Gray.

His vision blurred. His body shook. He lunged towards Mark with his arms outstretched.

CHAPTER
FIFTY-FOUR

Lily grabs Frank's arm and she almost shouts, "So? What? Did you kill him? Is he dead? Or is he still there? Tell me! Tell me now!"

He stares at her blankly, shakes his head, and she cries out, "Enough!" and pulls out her phone, but she pauses before pressing WPC Traviss's number. What if this strange man is right? What if her husband did do those terrible things? What if they take him away and send him to prison? No, she decides, not the police. Not yet. Instead she takes her phone outside the café and brings up Russ's number. He answers within one ring.

"Lily?"

"Russ, where are you?"

"I'm in the office."

"Russ, you need to leave, now. You need to go to a place. It is called Wolf's Hill Boulevard. It is a building development on London Road. Next to the flat where I live with Carl. There is no one there because it is bankrupt. You have to—"

"Lily, stop. I'm at work, I'm about to walk into a meeting."

"You must not walk into the meeting, Russ. You must go to Wolf's Hill Boulevard. It is Carl. He is there. I am with the man who put him there. He tied him to a radiator there. On Tuesday night. You must go now and find him. He is in apartment one. Please."

She hears him sighing. "Lily," he says softly, "start from the beginning. Where are you?"

"I'm in a café. In Ridinghouse Bay. I came in here to find out about the woman who owns that house. And there were these people here. And they heard me asking. And they have a friend who had lost his memory, who came here on Tuesday. And he saw the photo of Carl and he knew him. He says that Carl used to be called Mark, that something bad happened in this town twenty years ago, that Carl hurt someone. He says he followed him home last week, and took him into the building site and tied him up and left him there. So please, Russ, please go and find him! Now!"

"Lily," he sighs, "I think maybe you should probably call the police?"

"No! I can't do that, Russ. This man, in the café, he says Carl was a criminal. That he did bad things. I don't think I believe him . . ." She pauses momentarily, thinking of that night when she'd woken up with his hands around her throat, of the blackness that descended on him for no discernible reason from time to time, the fake passport, the fake mother. "But still," she rallies, "I don't want to take the risk. Not until I've seen him myself."

She hears the tone of his voice change, the acceptance softening him. "OK," he says, "OK." She hears the background noises stop, a door closing, a rustle of paper. She can tell that he has sat down. "Right," he says, "tell me exactly where this place is and what to do when I get there."

CHAPTER
FIFTY-FIVE

Alice glances at Lily through the window of the café. Then she passes Derry her door keys and says, "Can you pop back to mine — just quickly? Open the back door, let the dogs out. Ignore anything you find on the floor."

Derry shrugs and leaves. Lesley goes to the counter to buy another round of coffees. Outside the coffee shop, Lily paces and gesticulates while talking to whoever she is on the phone to.

Alice turns to look at Frank. "How are you?" she says, her hand resting on his shoulder.

He shrugs.

"Any more memories?"

He stares through the window for a moment, then sighs and shakes his head.

On the pavement outside, Lily has finished her phone call.

"What did they say?" says Alice when she walks back into the café.

"I did not call the police," she says tersely. "I called my friend. He will go to the building site. Soon we will know." She looks at them, one by one. "What do we do now?"

Lesley answers: "It's obvious really, isn't it? There's only thing we can do. We need to find Kitty Tate."

"We should go back to the house," says Alice. "See if we can find an address for her there."

"I have looked in the house already," says Lily. "I found nothing."

"It's a big house," says Alice gently. "Might be worth another search?" This girl is just five years older than Jasmine. She imagines her daughter in a strange country frantically searching for the man who brought her there. She imagines how she and Frank and Lesley must appear to her: old and other, discomfitingly unfamiliar. She smiles at her for the first time.

Lily wavers for a split second but then pulls back her shoulders and her resolve. "You can do that," she says. "I will keep asking the people in this town. I will come later."

Alice watches her turn and leave the café, hesitating momentarily in the doorway before turning left. What twist of fate brought this girl to this quiet, gently bohemian town hidden away in a dip of the Yorkshire coast? And what would she be doing now, right now, if Mark Tate had never walked into her life?

She pictures him now, tied to a radiator in an empty flat. And she thinks of what the man she knows as Frank says he had to do to put him there: the knife to the throat, the bag over the head, the tying of hands and the issuing of threats, the kidnapping and the taking hostage. She cannot conflate these actions with the soft man who has been living in her house for the past five days, the man she has slept with, who has sat with her daughter in the early hours of the morning, who has been befriended by her least trusting dog and given the seal of approval by her teenage son. She is reminded once again that the man she found on the beach last week was not a man at all, just an empty box in which to put whatever she wanted. She'd imbued him with qualities and character traits that suited her. She'd ignored the possibility that underneath the gentle, golden façade, Frank might well be a sociopath or even a killer. She'd put her children in danger. She'd put herself in danger.

And yet still, as she walks with him, side by side, towards Kitty Tate's house, her heart aches for him, her arms yearn to embrace him. Whatever he is. Whoever he is. Whatever he has done.

Frank turns to Alice and smiles uncertainly. What is she thinking? he wonders. Is she regretting every minute she has spent in his company? Is she recoiling at the memories of their night together? Is she already repainting him in her mind's eye as the twisted monster that he might well turn out to be?

From the very beginning of his slow emergence from the fugue he has felt echoes of violence, of hands around a throat, the slow burn of murderousness. What will Lily's friend find when he opens the door to apartment number one? An empty room? A dead body?

He finds that he has begun walking away from the others as they head up the hill towards the main road out of town.

"Frank? Where are you going?" calls Alice.

He looks up at them and then down towards the coastal road. "Can we . . .? Just quickly?"

Something's tugging him down the hill, down that alleyway, towards the sea. He's walked this way before. Many, many times. The others nod and follow him and as he emerges from the other end of the narrow alleyway he instinctively turns right and there it is, Rabbit Cottage. Except it's not called Rabbit Cottage any more. The engraved slate plaque outside says "Ivy Cottage". It's been painted a soft sky blue and the windows have been replaced with double glazing.

He stares at the tiny house and feels his soul opening up like a sinkhole. This was the last place they'd all been together. If he'd come home from the pub that night with his family if he'd stayed with his family instead of chasing girls, if he hadn't drunk three shots of tequila and brought those people here, they'd all have gone to bed that night, woken up together, spent another day together, and another, and another; they'd have driven back south together, spent the rest of their lives together. Kirsty would have met a man who wasn't mentally ill; Gray would have had a niece or a nephew, a brother-in-law. He may even have had a wife of his own, a child or two. His mother would have dealt with her empty nest like a normal human being instead of an anxiety-ridden lunatic. His father would have grown older and greyer and they would have been normal and boring and perfect forever and ever.

It was all his fault. All of it. *All of it.*

Derry appears then from the mouth of a cobbled alleyway, holding Alice's door keys. She looks at them in surprise. "Nice of you all to say where you were going," she says. "Just went back to the Sugar Bowl; woman outside said she saw you all heading this way."

Alice apologises and Derry shrugs and puts her hands in her pockets. They all start walking towards town. Frank finds himself side by side with Derry. For a while they walk in silence, then Derry says, "So, Frank, did you kill him?"

He starts. "What?"

"Mark Tate. Did you kill him? You keep looking at your fingers" — she glances down at his hands — "like you don't recognise them. Like they don't belong to you." She narrows her eyes. "I mean . . . it would be the logical explanation. It would explain your memory loss, your midnight flit to the middle of nowhere. Wouldn't it?"

He looks at her, trying to gauge her stance. Is she challenging him? Attacking him? Or merely trying to introduce him to some interesting concepts?

"I genuinely don't know," he says. "I might have killed him, yes. I might well have. And with my hands."

"And if you have?"

"Then he deserved to die. And I deserve to go to prison for what I did." He shrugs, feeling a sense of balance and release at this idea.

They walk the rest of the way in silence.

CHAPTER
FIFTY-SIX

Mark's phone rang again.

Gray stopped dead, stepped back from Mark, dragged his fingers through his hair. The concerned wife. He pictured her perched nervously on the edge of a sofa, a wrinkled tissue in her curled-up hands, pressing the call button, obsessively, over and over. She would keep pressing it until Mark's phone ran out of charge. He leaned down and yanked the phone from Mark's pocket and then, uttering a deathly, reverberating war cry, he hurled it across the room. It hit the extractor hood with a terrible crack, skidded across the kitchen floor and came to rest in the far corner. The bulb in the extractor hood fizzed and blinked. Then silence fell upon them and Gray felt a wave of relief.

"Nice one, you twat," said Mark. "Now she'll be even more worried. You really are a loser."

The rage, momentarily quelled, resurfaced, twice as red, twice as strong.

And then Gray finally succumbed to the primal urge that had been haunting him since the first time he'd set eyes on Mark Tate twenty-two years ago and he let his hands lead him to Mark Tate and he watched as they circled together around his neck and he mentally

346

applauded his hands as they worked together to squeeze the breath out of Mark Tate, to squeeze and obstruct and block until finally Mark Tate stopped fighting Gray's hands, until finally he softened, flopped into himself, stopped breathing, shut the fuck up, for ever.

As they approach Kitty Tate's house on the cliff, Frank takes Alice's hand and pulls her urgently towards him.

She turns and looks at him. It strikes him that her face is now more familiar to him than anything else in the world. And then he realises that he may never see this face again after what he is about to tell her.

"I remembered," he says. "I strangled him. I strangled him and he's dead."

"Fuck." She pauses. "Are you sure?"

"As sure as I can be about anything."

She puts her hand to the back of his head and strokes his hair. The gesture makes him want to weep.

They exchange a look. Frank nods.

Alice catches up with the others. "Frank remembers," she says heavily. "Mark's dead. Frank says he killed him."

There is a sharp and terrible beat of silence before Derry breaks it by saying, "Well, high five, Frank. The fucker totally had it coming."

CHAPTER
FIFTY-SEVEN

Lily sees them standing outside the house, deep in conversation. She sighs and pulls herself taller, then heads towards them with a cheery, "Hello!"

They turn at her greeting and she flinches.

"What is it?" she says.

They exchange panicky looks and then the Lesley woman smiles and says, "Nothing. It's all good. So, how did you get on?"

Lily sighs again. Her brief investigations in town had yielded very little. Kitty Tate had last been seen in Ridinghouse Bay about two years ago by the lady who owned the posh shoe shop. Kitty had told her she was here for the day to meet a buyer for her grand piano, that she wasn't staying overnight, would be heading home early evening. She'd tried on a pair of leather boots but hadn't bought anything. She'd seemed *unhappy*.

Nobody seemed to know exactly where Kitty lived now. "Harrogate way" was the general impression. And that was that.

"They say she hasn't been here for years," says Lily. "But I know that she has. That she was here yesterday. So." She shrugs. "It is all still a mystery."

"And what about your friend? The one who's going to the deserted flat? Have you heard anything from him yet?"

She shakes her head. "I called him a few minutes ago. He was on the train, twenty minutes away. We will have to wait."

"Well," says Lesley, looking towards the house. "Shall we go in?"

The man, Frank, acts strangely as he enters the house. He moves tentatively and slowly, his hands subconsciously feeling the walls and the surfaces as he passes through. He looks up and then down and she notices his hands shaking.

"It's all exactly the same," he says. "It's just like it was. Except . . ." He turns and says this to Alice, ". . . it's dead."

Yes, thinks Lily, yes. It is a dead house.

"There's one room left alive," she says. "Come."

They follow her silently up the stairs.

As they walk up the second staircase Frank starts shaking uncontrollably.

"This is where he brought us," he says. "Where he *dragged* us. And this" — he points at the step he's standing on — "this is where he pinned my sister down and tried to rape her in front of me."

He kneels down and runs his fingertips across the old carpet. "Look, blood. That's Mark's blood. From his scalp. Where I ripped it open with a coat hanger. Your husband," he says, suddenly staring right at Lily. "Did he have a scar? Under his hair? About here?" He points at the crown of his head.

"My husband has very thick hair," Lily says. "I would not know what was underneath." But this is a lie. She has felt the scar he describes, has felt it at night as she runs her hands through that hair. He has a ridge of skin there, hard, like a small piece of old chewing gum. She asked him about it once; he said it was a childhood accident. That had made her love the scar, love it both as a physical part of him and as a symbolic emblem of the personal history he so very rarely shared with her. She would seek it out during their lovemaking, let her fingertips brush against it, surreptitiously, fleetingly. And now that same scar was proof, as though she needed it in the light of so much other proof, that the man she loved above all others, the man she had given up her family for, given up her home and her life for, was a violent and evil man who hurt women.

She pushes all this down and carries on leading them to the room in the attic.

"This is the room," says Frank as she pushes open the door. "The room where he kept us locked up. Except it looks totally different."

They all stand for a while, appraising the empty room.

"Right," says Lesley. "We all need to split up. And we need to go through this place forensically until we find something with her address on it."

It doesn't take long. Alice finds it on a delivery note in the back of a drawer in an old dresser in the kitchen.

Mrs Kitty Tate
The Old Rectory

350

Coxwold
Harrogate
YO61 3FG

They all stare at it for a moment. Lily doesn't know what to think. She wants to meet this woman, this woman who for whatever reason protected Carl from the police for many years, who pretended to be his mother when they spoke on the phone on the day of their wedding, this sad, lonely woman who smells of jasmine and owns beautiful clothes and hides herself away from the people of this town in a dead house on a cliff. She wants to meet her so that she can understand everything more clearly. But she is scared, too, scared to hear things that will make her hate Carl. Because she doesn't hate Carl. She knows she should, but she doesn't. She doesn't hate him at all.

And as she thinks this her phone rings and it is Russ, and she looks at her phone and then at the other people and they look at her with a range of expressions from fear to concern to impatience. She breathes in deeply and then she answers.

"Hello, Russ. Are you there yet?"

"Yes," says Russ. "I'm here. But Carl isn't."

She pulls her hair off her face and frowns. "Are you in the right place?"

"Yes. Yes. Apartment one. Wolf's Hill Boulevard. He was definitely here, I can see the ties, the ropes — it's a mess. It's . . . Well, he must have been here for quite some time, let's put it that way. But he isn't here now. He's gone."

Her heart quickens and softens with relief. "Oh," she says, "thank God. Thank God for that."

The other people stare at her, eyes wide.

"Well, yes," Russ continues. "I suppose in one way it's good. In another way it's . . . Well, you know, where is he? What's he doing? I mean, Lily, he could be dangerous."

She breathes in angrily, knowing that her anger is misplaced but not being able to change the way she feels. "Not to me, he isn't." Then she hangs up.

The others are still staring at her.

"He's not there," she tells them.

"You mean, he's escaped?" asks Alice. She looks stunned.

She sighs. "Yes. He untied himself and escaped." She tries not to think about the fact that he has not tried to contact her, that he has not come to find her.

Derry and Alice turn to Frank and look at him questioningly.

"You didn't kill him?" says Alice.

He looks white and shaken. "I don't know," he says. "I thought . . . but maybe not. Maybe he was just unconscious?" He sighs. "I really don't know."

For a moment no one says anything.

Then Lesley looks at her wristwatch and says, "Right. It's quarter past twelve. I'm going to call the office and tell them not to expect me back. Then I'm driving to Coxwold to find Kitty Tate. What about the rest of you?"

Derry tells Alice that she will collect her child from school and then the rest of them wait for Lesley to return with her car. They sit on the front steps of the big white house in an awkward silence. It has become a pretty day; the sky is pale blue and a soft breeze scatters cherry blossom at their feet.

Finally Lily turns to Frank and says, "So. You thought you had killed him?"

He looks at her as though he had forgotten she was there. Then he nods. "Yes," he says simply. "I did." He turns away from her and looks at his hands. "The man you love is a monster," he adds quietly.

"But still," she says. "You tried to kill him. You left him there for dead. What does that make you?"

Frank sighs. There is silence for a moment, but for the distant sound of seagulls, the scratch of small birds in the hedgerow, the song of a chaffinch looking down upon them from the treetops. "It makes me wrong," he says. "But it doesn't make me a monster."

CHAPTER
FIFTY-EIGHT

Given how much there is to talk about, it is a strangely quiet journey from Ridinghouse Bay to Coxwold. Lesley uses her hands-free to make some high-octane work calls about other stories she's working on: a woman raped in Hull, three Filipino men dead in the hold of a ship berthed at Goole Docks, residents' reaction to the demolition of a well-loved pub in Beverley.

Alice zones out and stares at the countryside. It's beautiful: pale and sun-dappled, fields full of golden rape and sunflowers. Then she looks at Frank. He is still and quiet, staring from his respective window.

"Where do you think he is?" she asks.

He shrugs. "He's disappeared before. He could be anywhere by now."

She lowers her voice. "What you said, about what you did." She mimes strangling someone. "Are you sure it happened? That you definitely . . .?"

"I'm sure," he says firmly. "It happened."

She nods. What's going on in Frank's mind is impossible for her to imagine. She thinks of him that first night, barefoot and fresh out of the bath, wearing Kai's hoodie. He was empty then, and unburdened.

Now he seems different, heavier somehow, buried under the weight of so many resurfaced memories.

A sign on the side of the road says "Coxwold ½". A minute later Lesley's satnav tells her to turn right. They maintain silence for the last leg of the journey. Alice admires the picture-postcard village as they enter it: the wide street with bright-green lawns on either side sloping up to attractive, pale-stone houses, coaching inns and tea shops. They pass a handsome church at the top of the vale and then the satnav tells them to turn left and they take a tiny turning away from the village and they are there. The Old Rectory, set right behind the church. It is a beautiful three-winged house with a gravelled driveway and ancient trees, a huge magnolia in full bloom taking centre stage by the front door.

Lesley kills the engine and they all look at the house for a moment.

"I will go," says Lily, unclipping her seatbelt. "She is related to me and I will go."

Lesley starts to protest but Lily raises her hand unpleasantly close to her face and says, "No. I came here alone to find this woman. I did not ask for all of you."

"Erm, excuse me," says Lesley, "but without us you'd still be walking around Ridinghouse Bay going shop to shop with your little photo album. I'm sorry, but Frank and Alice have just as much right to hear what this woman has to say as you do. Frank's life has been ruined by what this woman's nephew did to him and his family. We're all going in or I'm turning round right now and going home."

"You only care about the story."

"Yes. Of course I care about the story. That's my job. But caring about 'the story' doesn't mean I don't care about the outcome or about the players."

"Fine," says Lily after a petulant silence that reminds Alice of both her daughters. "We'll all go."

The front door is set into the left-hand section of the house. Lesley rings the bell and there is the sound of heels against flagstones and then the door opens on a chain and there is a woman's face, pale and pretty: downy, sunken cheeks, a hopeful stain of pink on her lips, a puff of white-blonde hair, the soft scent of jasmine.

"Hello!" she greets them easily but then, as she looks from each one of them to the next, she looks worried. "Oh! Sorry, I was expecting an Ocado delivery. Can I help you?"

"My name is Lily," says Lily, "I spoke to you yesterday on the phone. I am married to your nephew, Mark."

"Don't be silly," she says, grimacing. "Mark is dead."

"Actually," says Lesley, pushing forward, "he isn't. And we know he isn't because this man" — she points at Frank — "had him locked up in an empty flat last week and your 'dead' nephew told him everything, including how you scooped him up off the rocks the night he supposedly drowned and took him home and didn't tell anyone including his own mother."

Kitty Tate narrows her eyes. "And who are *you?*" she asks Lesley.

"Lesley Wade." She offers Kitty her hand. *"Riding-house Gazette."*

Kitty starts to close the door in her face but Lesley already has her foot in the gap. "I'm working off the record," she says. "I'm helping. There's no story. Not yet. If there is it will be investigative, a big spread, full interviews, nothing salacious."

Kitty tries again to close the door.

"Look!" says Lesley. "See this man? This is Graham Ross. Remember him? He's Kirsty's brother, Kitty. The boy who came to your house; the boy your nephew took hostage and attacked, broke his arm. Terrorised. And he's lived his whole adult life in a state of limbo because he couldn't remember what happened that night." She pauses to force the door harder against Kitty's determination to shut it. "And now he has remembered. He's remembered what Mark Tate did. You owe it to him, Kitty, you owe it to him to tell him what you know."

Kitty suddenly relaxes her pressure against the door and peers through the gap. She looks directly at Frank and sighs. Her eyes fill with tears. "You poor boy."

Then she pulls herself straight and turns her gaze to Lesley. "He can come in," she says, "but not the rest of you."

"But—!" starts Lily.

Kitty ignores her and turns her gaze back to Frank. "Please," she says, "come in. I'll tell you as much as I can."

Frank looks at Alice and then at Kitty. "Please can I bring my friend in? Alice has been looking after me. She's not part of anything. Just a good person."

Kitty nods tersely and then opens the door to let them in.

They turn to Lily and Lesley and smile apologetically.

"Well," says Lesley, "I guess we could go and try a cream tea?"

"What is 'cream tea'?"

"It's cakes. Come on."

Kitty takes them through to her kitchen. It's a blend of dark wood and off-white Formica, hanging pendant lights over a central island, two large sofas at the other end and French windows opening up on to a manicured garden. She seats them at her kitchen table, makes them tea in an oversized polka-dot pot and opens a packet of Duchy stem ginger biscuits.

Finally she sits, smoothing the legs of her neat navy trousers over her tiny thighs. "I'm so sorry for what happened to you," she says to Frank. "I'm so sorry about your father and your sister and I wish that . . ." She pauses. "I knew the minute he came home from the beach that day and told me about this 'nice family', that we were to make a cake, I knew that some switch had been flicked. That it would end badly. Mark was always . . ." She pauses again, lifts the lid of the teapot, stirs it, closes it again, ". . . troubled," she finishes. "My husband's brother and his wife, they adopted him when he was quite old. Eight years, nine years, something like that. Their daughter was a teenager, becoming more independent, and I think they thought they weren't ready to end that phase of their lives. But they weren't up to the idea of a baby and starting all over again. So they had this idea of adopting an older child. And of course Mark was the most beautiful little boy, and he clung to them for dear life and they didn't think too hard about the implications of a boy who'd experienced abuse. They thought they could heal all the wounds and make up for all the hurt and unfortunately they were *wrong*. It was hard-wired."

She pours three cups of tea from the pot, places the pot back on to a mat and passes Alice the milk jug. "I'll let you do your own milk — everyone has different tastes, don't they? Anyway. They couldn't cope with him. Mark wanted everything: the best clothes, the best toys, the pick of his parents' time and attention. The sister, Camilla, she moved out when she was seventeen, to live with a friend's family because she couldn't deal with the maelstrom. But, for some reason, Mark was calm around my husband and me. I think because we had no children of our own. Because he didn't live with us so we didn't need to try to tame him. We had all this land" — she gestures through the French windows — "the dogs, the big house by the seaside. He spent holidays with us, most weekends. And I'm not suggesting for a second that he was *easy*. Mark has *never* been easy. But he was less *complicated*. And he and I in particular had a very strong bond. But as he got older . . ." She passes the plate of biscuits towards Alice. "I don't know, I just saw this much darker side emerge. Especially the way he was around girls. He was a bully, I suppose. He thought girls were just there to service his needs. I saw him behave really quite unpleasantly with these lovely girls he brought home all wide-eyed at his beauty." She shakes her head and sighs. "I did worry, even then, that something bad might happen one day. But, I don't know, he'd turn up here with his overnight bag, a box of chocolates for me, a bear hug; I did *love* his bear hugs. My husband was never one for hugging and I guess I kind of got a taste for it from Mark. Anyway, he'd scoop the dogs up and take them out and throw balls for them for hours and I'd sit here and watch him and think: He'll grow out of all his silliness, he'll meet a wonderful girl and he'll finally get it and then he'll be perfect.

"And then my husband died." Kitty sighs. "And he didn't handle it very well. Seemed to blame me for it, for some reason. The bear hugs stopped. The chocolates and the fun and the laughter stopped and, I have to admit, I started to find his presence quite oppressive, just me and him alone. He was estranged from his parents completely by this stage and living with us. They disowned him when he was eighteen, after an incident . . ."

"Incident?" says Frank. "What incident?"

Kitty smooths out her trouser legs again. "Something to do with a girl. A friend of his sister's. No charges were pressed but it was very unpleasant and his parents decided to cut the cord. Unforgivable, really unforgivable." She shakes her head slowly. "At first I appreciated him being here after my husband died, but after a few weeks, he . . . well, he became increasingly difficult to live with. We headed off to Ridinghouse Bay that summer, as we'd done so many summers before. I thought it might lighten things up a little. But if anything he was angrier there, angry with me, angry with the world. There was a . . . *malevolence* about him. I started to sleep with my bedroom door locked." She looks up at both of them, checking that they have registered the poignancy of her last comment.

"Then one day he came bounding into the house, full of joy and talk of cakes and of you, this 'nice family'. And I understood there was a girl and I suppose part of me thought, well, maybe this is it? The mythical girl who was going to fix him. And then you all turned up that day and I saw little Kirsty: so young, so pure, so completely incapable of dealing with a damaged soul like Mark. And my heart dropped."

Alice looks at Frank. What is he thinking? she wonders. He looks so closed, so numb.

"Anyway," Kitty continues, delicate fingertips running up and down the curve of her teacup. "He took her out, seemed smitten, bought her flowers, took her to the movies, then suddenly he came home saying it was over, he didn't care, 'didn't give a shit' were his exact words, that he could do better, she was just a little . . ." She stops and purses her mouth. "Well, you know, not very nice. But it only lasted a day or two and then he seemed to move on, there was a girl coming from home, he told me, a singer. He was going to watch her perform, with some friends. I was relieved. *So* relieved. It seemed as though he was finally moving on after the death of my husband. His strange obsession with your sister felt like a distant memory. And he asked me if I could go out for the night as he wanted to invite his friends back after the gig, maybe a few of the nicer people from the town. He said it would be confined to the bar. Manageable. He wouldn't let it get out of hand. And of course I said yes. Anything to make him happy when he'd been so unhappy; anything to see him behaving normally when he'd been behaving so abnormally. So I came back here for the night. It was nice, having the house to myself, not having to worry about Mark. Until . . ." A muscle in her cheek twitches and she taps her fingernails against the sides of her cup. "A phone call from a roadside box, at one a.m. 'I'm in trouble.' God. I'll never forget. *I'm in trouble*. It was as if I'd been waiting for that call from the first day I met him. And here it was. And he was breathless and in pain. 'I'm dying,' he kept saying. *I'm dying!* He wouldn't let me call the police. I didn't even ask why because deep down I knew why. Not what. But why. I got straight into the car and there he was, sitting on the rocks, down by Middlehurst Bay, in a pool of blood. He was white-blue. Like something dreadful spat out by the sea. I parked and I clambered down those rocks in the most stupid shoes, the first ones my feet found as I left the house. I cut my leg open on something as I slipped down. I still have the scar. Here." She rolls up the neat trousers and shows them a livid vertical scar up the side of her left shin. She slowly pulls the trouser leg down again and continues. "The sea was wild that night, deafening. I could see the coastguards with their flashlights out on their boats, the lifeboat pushing out to sea, the blue lights flashing in the town. Sleepy old Ridinghouse Bay was alive that night. I'll never forget it. I found my way down to him and I managed to get him to his feet. The boats were coming closer. We only had a few minutes. And then he pointed, to the slope below. Check, he said, check if she's dead."

Frank stiffens; his shoulders push back.

"So I slid down the rocks and there she was . . ."

"She?" Alice says sharply. "You mean Kirsty?"

"Yes," Kitty says. "Of course. Didn't Mark tell you?"

"Tell me what?" Frank voice emerges as a soft groan.

"Oh." Kitty looks flustered. "I assumed . . . well. What exactly did he tell you?"

"That he let go of her. That she 'faded', that there was nothing he could do to save her."

"Oh." Kitty blanches and her fingers move to the pearl that hangs from a fine gold chain around her neck. "I . . . I . . . I didn't know what had happened. I assumed at first, I don't know, drunken high jinks, that maybe he'd been trying to rescue her. So I went to her and I felt her pulse and she was still alive. But not conscious."

"And you didn't call an ambulance?" The tendons on Frank's neck are tight with rage. "You didn't—"

"He put a knife to my throat."

"Who?" says Frank incredulously. "Mark? I thought you said he was injured? That he'd lost loads of blood?"

"He was injured. Well, he seemed to be. But when I came back from checking Kirsty and he said, 'Well?' I said, 'She's breathing.' And he said, 'Get us out of here, now.' And of course I refused. Of course I did. I said, 'No. I'm calling an ambulance!' And he staggered to his feet and this knife appeared. And suddenly he had me, from behind, knife to my throat and I thought: Well, here it is. He's going to kill me."

She pauses for a moment and takes a sip of tea. "We carried your sister to my car and laid her out in the back."

"She was still alive?" Frank sounds hollow with disbelief.

"She was alive. Yes. She was."

"Did you . . . did you try to resuscitate her?"

"He wouldn't let me."

"And she died? Yes?"

Tears have turned Kitty's eyes to glass. She nods, just once. "Very soon afterwards. Before we were halfway home."

"On the back seat of your car?" he asks.

Kitty is crying now. Her tears splash on to her pale cheeks and she wipes them away with the backs of curled-up fingers. "I am so sorry. It was just . . . I was so scared. He had the knife. I didn't know . . ."

"Where is she?" Frank too is crying now. "Where's Kirsty?"

"She's — oh, God. I am so, so sorry. We parked the car in my garage around the back." She indicates the far end of her beautiful garden. "We stayed there for hours. I mean, literally, hours and hours. With Kirsty in the back. I was hysterical. Utterly hysterical. We were waiting for a knock on the door. We were waiting for sirens." She covers her face with both her hands for a moment. "We had the car radio tuned into the local news. We waited and we waited until finally, lunchtime the next day, it came across: they'd called off the search. There were still people out there, townspeople, on their own boats, but the official search was over. A sweet policeman came to my door that evening to tell me. Mark and your sister were assumed to have drowned. Your father was the hero who'd died trying to rescue them. There was no mention of you. I had to pretend to be shocked."

"But what did you do with my sister?" Frank booms. He gets to his feet. "Where is she?"

Kitty's body becomes small, as though she is trying to fit herself into a box. Then she gets slowly to her feet and says, "Come."

Alice looks at Frank and he looks back at her in alarm.

"Just come."

They get to their feet and follow Kitty to the French windows. She unhooks a key from a nail behind the curtains and opens up the door. Then she guides them across the garden, all curved beds full of meadow flowers, lichen-mottled urns and weeping willows, towards the far end where it meets the fields beyond. Here there is an oak tree, old and imposing, a giant puffball of green leaves stark against the bright blue sky.

Kitty stands next to a rose bush, bejewelled with small white buds. "Kirsty is here."

"You buried her?"

"No, I didn't bury her. Of course I didn't bury her! Mark buried her. He locked me in the house and he buried her. I planted the rose bush. Afterwards."

365

Frank sinks to his knees, on to the soft spring grass. He opens up his hands and caresses the ground with his palms. Then he glances up at Kitty with suppressed rage. "All these years," he says, his voice cracking. "My mum."

"There has not been a day gone by when I have not thought of your mother."

Franks flicks his gaze up to her again, angrily. "Where is he?" he demands. "Do you know where he is?"

"No. I don't. I haven't spoken to him since the day he made me talk to that girl on the phone and pretend to be his mother. I don't know why he made me do that. To spite me, I suppose. To cause me pain." She sighs. "I wished him luck, and then I told him I was going to remove myself from his life, not that I'd been a great part of it. Not since he changed his identity. It was too risky for him to talk to me or visit me. But I told him that I could play no more part in this subterfuge. So I sent him some money. And I hoped he would just finally settle down and be normal. The girl sounded . . ." She shrugs. "Well, she sounded like she could look after herself. She sounded *tough*. So I left them to it."

Frank is still staring at the ground where his sister was buried twenty-two years previously. He looks broken.

Alice crouches down next to him and puts her arm across his shoulders.

He looks up at Kitty. "What were her last words?" His words are strangulated with grief.

"There were no words, Graham. She didn't even open her eyes."

"I don't understand," he cries, tears rolling down his cheeks. "All these years, sitting here in your designer kitchen. Eating your dinner. Watching TV. Looking out at the view, knowing she was there? How could you?"

"But I don't live here!" Kitty cries. "Of course I don't! I live in Ridinghouse Bay, in the attic. I hate it here! I'd love to sell this place, move on with my life. But I can't. How can I sell a house with a body in the garden? And I'm only here now because of that girl, the one you came with," she says, gesturing to the front of her house. "She called me. Yesterday morning. I don't know why I answered, I really don't. She'd been trying me for hours. I assumed it was Mark so I didn't answer. Then the ringing finally stopped and another number came up about half an hour later, a mobile number, and I knew it wasn't Mark's number and I'd been expecting a call from someone else and I just instinctively, unthinkingly picked it up. Christ. And then the doorbell started to ring and I thought it was her! So I threw all my stuff into a bag and ran."

"But we were there," says Alice. "That was us ringing the bell. We didn't see you leave. There was no car parked outside."

Kitty sighs. "I went down the back way, down the cliff stairs. I keep my car parked down in the car park by the beach. I don't like people knowing that I'm there. I like to be ... *invisible*. And that's why I'm here, Graham, in this blighted, awful house. Not because I'm heartless. Because, I promise you this, my heart has not stopped hurting since the night your sister died. Not for one moment."

The talking stops but the three of them stay in position, Kitty and Alice standing, Frank still on his knees by the rosebush, a terrible vignette of grief and guilt and horror and lies.

For a moment the silence is absolute. Then Alice turns slowly towards the house and says, "We need to find the others. We need to make some calls."

CHAPTER
FIFTY-NINE

Lily studies the food in front of her. There is a large bun that sounded like a rock when the waitress put it on her saucer with silver tongs. There is a plate that is made of two plates, one on top of another with a silver pole connecting them. On here there are many small cakes, some so beautiful she can barely imagine eating them. There are also some extremely tiny sandwiches that look as if they have been made for babies to eat. One of them appears to have no filling other than cucumber.

Lesley pours tea into delicate cups and eyes Lily intrusively.

"So," she says, "tell me. What was it about Mark that you fell in love with?"

Lily shrugs. The question is not meant to be friendly. The question she is really asking is: *How could you have chosen such a monster to be your husband?* "I fell in love with him because he was kind. And handsome. And strong. Because he respected me. And my family. Because I could tell that he had hurt inside him and I wanted to help to fix it. I fell in love with him because he was everything I wanted a man to be."

"But did you never get any . . . I don't know, *vibes?* That he wasn't quite right? That he was hiding something?"

"No," she says. "Never. We were happy."

"So, I wonder why he hasn't come for you?"

"We do not know when he escaped," Lily replies primly. "He may have escaped last night, this morning. He may have been to the apartment, looking for me. And found me not there."

"Has he called?"

"No."

Lesley raises one eyebrow and looks at her pityingly.

"He is trying to protect me," she says. "That is all."

"Well," says Lesley, "that may well be true." She selects one of the tiny sandwiches and eats it. Then she looks at Lily and says, "Eat."

"I am not hungry." This is a lie. She is starving.

"Come on. We could be here for hours. And it's delicious. Try one of these." She places a tiny sandwich on Lily's plate. "Roast beef and horseradish. It's gorgeous."

"Horse — radish?"

"Horseradish, yes. It's a root, like ginger, you know. Mixed with cream. Beautiful."

Lily pushes the sandwich across the plate with her fingertips and sneers. "No. Thank you."

"Oh, well, just eat your bloody scone then."

Lily fiddles with the rock bun thing, breaks a bit off and puts it in her mouth. It tastes of cement.

"You need to put some clotted cream on it. And some jam."

"Clotted? Cream?" Her lip curls.

"Oh, for God's sake." Lesley passes her a small dish of crusty yellow stuff. "It's just cream, for fuck's sake. Christ. I mean surely you must eat all sorts of grim stuff in the Ukraine? This is just a bun and cream. It's not going to bite you."

Lily gingerly does as she's told; she takes a scrape of crusty yellow cream, a scoop of jam. She puts it in her mouth and decides she likes it. She does not say this though.

"What will you do?" Lesley asks. "If they find him? If he goes to prison? Where will you go?"

Lily sighs. "I have not thought. I will probably have to go home. After all, my marriage certificate is not legal. I will not be allowed to stay."

"Do you want to stay?"

"Yes. I think I do. I think I was ready to leave Kiev, ready to be somewhere else. I do not feel as though I have had this experience yet. That I am not finished. But" — she shrugs — "that is life."

"What are your qualifications?" Lesley asks.

"I'm training to be an accountant."

Lesley raises her brow again, this time with surprise not scepticism. Clearly she does not think that Lily looks like an accountant. Maybe this is a good thing.

Lesley's phone rings and once again she is shouting down the phone, telling people what to do. She takes her phone out on to the pavement and Lily watches her pacing the pavement, gesticulating. As she watches her, Lily has a strange thought, that maybe she would like to be like her, one day, when she is old.

Lily eats her scone and then investigates the other elements of this *cream tea*. By the time Lesley comes back she has had three small sandwiches and a cake with tiny purple sugar flowers on it. Lesley looks at the diminished spread and smiles knowingly.

"I wonder what is happening?" asks Lily.

"Yes," says Lesley, sighing unhappily. "So do I."

And as she says this, the little brass bell above the door jingles and they are there, Frank and Alice. They both look shocked and as though they have been crying. Alice helps Frank into a chair and orders them a pot of tea.

"What?" says Lily. "What is it? Did you find him?"

"No," she says. "No. He's not there and Kitty doesn't know where he is. But he's out there somewhere and he's dangerous. Seriously dangerous."

Lily narrows her eyes at her. "Dangerous?" she says. "What do you mean?"

And then Alice patiently recounts a story that is so sad and so horrifying and so dark, yet so believable, that Lily almost forgets she is talking about the man she married. About halfway through, she already knows what she needs to do next. By the time Alice has finished the story she already has her phone in her hand. It is over. Her love affair. Her marriage. Her adventure. Her love for a man she never really knew. What was it her mother had said last week, something about onions? About how you needed to see the worst of a person before you could decide to share your life with them. She had not given herself the time to see the worst of Carl Monrose but now she has been shown it

372

and no, she cannot love a man like that or share her life with a man like that. And neither can she let a man like that disappear into the ether, free to live his life.

She dials in WPC Beverly Traviss's number and she says, "Hello. Mrs Traviss. This is Lily Monrose."

She hears the familiar, forbearing intake of breath. "Ah, Mrs Monrose, good afternoon. I'm really sorry we weren't in touch earlier. We're still waiting for the—"

"Please. Take some paper. Write this down. My husband's real name is Mark Tate. He was reported as drowned in the town of Ridinghouse Bay in August 1993 when he was nineteen years old. He is responsible for — at the very least — the death of two people and a physical assault on one more. He changed his identity to Carl Monrose a few years ago and he was last seen on Tuesday the fourteenth of April at around seven p.m. in apartment number one, Wolf's Hill Boulevard, London Road, Oxted. He is very dangerous. I and various other people will require protection while you search for him. Thank you."

She listens to the silence on the other end of the line. She imagines Beverley Traviss's pen suspended above her notepad, her jaw hanging slightly ajar.

"Where are you?" WPC Traviss asks, and Lily can hear an unfamiliar tone of concern in her voice.

Lily tells her.

"Don't move," says WPC Traviss. "Stay where you are. I'll liaise with Yorkshire Constabulary. Get them to send a squad car right away."

Lily hangs up and looks at the others.

"There," she says, "it is done."

She rests her phone on the table and feels her heart break in two.

PART FOUR

Ridinghouse Gazette

Friday 24 April 2015

Local Man Arrested Twenty Years After "Drowning"

by

Lesley Wade

Former Coxwold and Ridinghouse Bay resident Mark Tate, 40, was arrested late on Wednesday night on historical abduction and assault charges after an intensive police search spanning three counties that ended in a hostage-taking situation in a bed-and-breakfast establishment in the Highlands of Scotland.

Tate was believed to have "drowned" twenty-two years ago in a tragic accident off the coast of Ridinghouse Bay in the early hours of Monday 2 August 1993. Reports at the time claimed that a party at his aunt's house on Ridinghouse Lane had got out of hand and he and one of his guests, Kirsty Ross, 15, had drowned during a late-night swim whilst under the influence of drugs and alcohol.

Kirsty Ross's father, Antony Ross, also died that night after suffering a fatal heart attack while trying to save the youngsters from the sea. Her brother, Graham Ross, suffered long-term memory loss as a result of the trauma and was never able to recall what exactly had led up to the drownings.

However, in an extraordinary series of events earlier this month, Graham Ross, 39, recovered his memories of the night of the drownings after seeing a man he believed to be Mark Tate on the streets of Victoria in central London. He subsequently followed the man home from work and imprisoned him in an empty flat near the accused's home, where, under duress, the accused confessed to faking his own death on the night in question.

Mistakenly believing that he had killed Tate, Ross fled to Ridinghouse Bay where he suffered another episode of severe memory loss. Local artist, Alice Lake, 41, rescued him from the beach outside her house on the evening of Wednesday 15 April and has been helping him try to recover his memory ever since. A chance meeting between Ms Lake and Mr Ross, and Mark Tate's current wife, Liljana Monrose, 21, in the Sugar Bowl Café on the High Street on Monday morning led them all to the home of Tate's aunt, Mrs Katharine Tate, 62, of Coxwold.

It was here that the full story of the events of 2 August 1993 was finally revealed, leading to Mrs Monrose calling the police and the subsequent nationwide police hunt for Mr Tate.

Mr Tate was recognised by the landlady of his remote bed and breakfast in Loch Hourn, Invergarry, in the Highlands of Scotland from a photo she'd seen in a newspaper that morning. Unaware of the police hunt due to lack of internet or television access, Mr Tate was taken by surprise by the police and, according to local reports, took the landlady and her daughter hostage in a locked room. The siege lasted for three hours before police managed to knock the door down and disarm Tate. He is currently being held for questioning at Invergarry Police Station, on historical charges of assault, sexual assault, abduction, unlawful burial, identity fraud, blackmail and drug dealing.

After receiving his DNA test results, it is also possible that police will be questioning Tate about a string of sexual assaults on women over the preceding twenty-two years, but this has not yet been confirmed.

In Next Week's *Ridinghouse Gazette*:
Lesley Wade's **exclusive** report from the day that Graham Ross met Katharine Tate and finally found out what really happened to his sister all those years ago.

CHAPTER
SIXTY

Lily lets herself into the flat. She has not been here since she left on Sunday but it is clear the moment she walks in that he has been here. He has rearranged the cushions on the sofa. He has taken things from the wardrobes in the bedroom. His overnight case is gone. He has showered and rehung his bath towel in the very particular way in which he always used to hang his bath towel. His toothbrush is gone; the tap is shining extra brightly. He has eaten lots of the unhealthy food she bought last week and carefully disposed of the wrappings in the recycling bin. He has emptied the waste bin and put a clean bag in the container. He has taken the cash she left behind, about five hundred pounds, and he has taken his phone charger, his Puffa jacket and his walking boots.

And there, tucked into the frame of the mirror over the fake fireplace, is an envelope, with her name on it. She takes off her coat and hangs it in the hallway. Then she returns and plucks the envelope from the mirror. She sits and she opens it and she reads it, her heart pounding hard beneath her ribs.

Darling Lily,

I have had to go somewhere far away. I want you to know that I have not been away from you all this time out of choice. A man took me, tried to kill me, left me for dead. I wish I could explain to you what happened, but I can't. It's very complicated and it's to do with things that happened a long time ago. I see my passport has gone. I assume the police needed it when you reported me missing? It is possible they may tell you something strange about my passport. Don't pay any attention. I am Carl Monrose. I have always been Carl Monrose, the man you fell in love with, the man who fell in love with you. Whatever they try to tell you about other people, that's not me. Carl Monrose is a good person, who has a good job and married a good woman. Anything else doesn't matter.

I'll try to call you — I don't know when. It might be a long time. Please don't look for me. You won't be able to find me. And if a man called Graham Ross tries to get in contact with you, please don't talk to him. He is mad and he is dangerous and he is a liar.

There is a small amount of money in our bank account, a few hundred. I've enclosed the card. The PIN is 6709. I'm sorry there's not more. And I'm sorry I had to take the cash. Also, and this is hard to say, the flat is rented. I wasn't entirely honest with you about that and I know I may have given you the impression that I owned it. So I'm afraid unless you can pay the next rent instalment, which is due on 13 May, you may need to find somewhere else to live. I'm sorry for this slip in my transparency with you. I just wanted you to feel secure.

Every minute I have spent with you has been perfect, Lily. I wish I had met you twenty years ago. Maybe none of this would have happened. I love you more than I have ever loved anyone or anything in my whole stupid life.

Stay amazing, my love, and forgive me,
Carl

Lily folds the note back into a rectangle and slides it into the envelope. She puts the cash card into her handbag and she sighs. *A slip in my transparency.* She could almost laugh out loud. Here he is, lying to her from beyond the mists of time. Or is he? Maybe her husband truly believed he was Carl Monrose, all-round good guy and enigmatic everyman. Maybe she had cured him of his badness, if only temporarily. She thinks of the poor woman in Scotland, with her teenage daughter, and how they must have felt locked in that room with Carl for all those hours. And then she realises that those people weren't in a room with Carl Monrose, they were in a room with Mark Tate. And this comforts her.

She slides the note into the outside pocket of her handbag. She will give it to Beverly Traviss. She doesn't want it, not even as a souvenir. Then quickly she packs a suitcase, with as much as she can squeeze into it. She can come back for the rest another day. She peers from the window in the living room and waves at Russ, sitting at the wheel of his people carrier, reading the Saturday papers. He waves back at her and she gives him the thumbs up.

She's going to be Russ and Jo's au pair. Russ had the idea on the way back from Ridinghouse, he said. Mooted it to Jo who, in a moment of sleep-deprived desperation, agreed to a trial few days, and Lily has been staying with them since leaving Yorkshire, while the police searched the flat for evidence. It is a ridiculous turn of events. She doesn't even like babies. But, actually, Darcy is quite a pleasant baby. She didn't even cry when Jo first put her in her arms, just stared at her as if to say: *You look all right*. Jo said, "She likes you!" and then, "Did you know that babies are genetically programmed to prefer people with pretty faces? It's because they look more like babies." Which Lily took to be a compliment. But it might not have been. Jo is perfectly nice, if a bit brittle. But more than that she is so very grateful to Lily because now she can go to the gym sometimes and have a little lie-down during the day and meet a friend for lunch every now and then. They will give her fifty pounds a week. That's fine. And Russ has given her his old laptop so she can continue her distance-learning accountancy course. Also, Putney is lovely. Much nicer than Oxted. Eventually, hopefully, when she has graduated, she would like to have her own flat here. And maybe, one day — not yet — marry a nice Englishman. She likes Englishmen very much. The women, she is not so sure about, but she is getting used to them. Or maybe it is the other way round.

There is one more thing she needs to do before she leaves this flat. She opens her jewellery box in the bedroom and she searches through the tangle of tacky costume jewellery that she'd brought to England with her from the Ukraine in anticipation of the nights in ritzy nightclubs and celebrity-filled restaurants she'd foolishly imagined might be waiting for her over here. She pulls out a small suedette pouch and peers inside. There are the wedding rings she found in Carl's filing cabinet. She knows whom they belong to now. They belong to a woman in Wales called Amanda Jones. She married Mark Tate in 2006 after a whirlwind four-week romance. He told her his name was Charles Moore. When she started asking him too many questions about who he was and where he came from, when she started going through his personal belongings trying to find clues to the man she married, he walked out, taking her rings from her finger and calling her a whore.

Amanda Jones recognised his picture from the newspaper reports and turned up at her local police station. She's remarried now and has a small child. Lily will send her the rings. The money will come in useful for her, Lily is sure.

Then she takes one more look around the flat where she spent ten days of her life married to someone called Carl Monrose and she closes the door behind her.

As Russ pulls away from the car park, they drive past Wolf's Hill Boulevard and Lily looks up at the flat on the first floor. The light is still flickering. She wonders again what it was about that light that had so troubled her in those days when she was here alone. And then she remembers sitting on the sofa, calling her husband's phone, frantically, insanely, again and again, and then the sound of an animal roaring, so loud that she'd thought of the wolves that disturbed her sleep sometimes in Kiev. And then . . . silence. Her calls stopped going through. It was the sound, she now knew, not of a displaced wolf but of Graham Ross throwing her husband's phone against the cooker hood, just before he tried to strangle him to death. It was the sound of a tortured man finally acknowledging his pain.

She'd heard it and she'd buried it, deep inside her subconscious.

A sign by the road says: "Central London 12".

She turns to Russ, a kind man, and she smiles.

CHAPTER
SIXTY-ONE

Alice turns the lights down in her bedroom, leaving just the kind light of a black-shaded lamp to illuminate her face. She places a large glass of wine on her desk and then goes to the mirror where she prods at her disastrous hair with blunt fingernails. The time is 7.58p.m. For two minutes she paces back and forth, stopping at the mirror every few seconds to check that her appearance hasn't suddenly deteriorated further. Then it comes, the lullaby plip-plop-plip of a Skype call. She rushes to her desk and breathes in hard, clears her throat, presses reply.

And there he is: "Hello, Alice."

"Hi!"

He looks tired.

"How are you?" she continues.

"I'm . . . aaah, well, what can I say? Not so good."

"No?"

"No. Turns out I'm not very good at being Gray Ross. Turns out I suck at it."

"Oh, Frank . . ."

He smiles. "I do like being called Frank," he says dreamily. "I miss it."

"You'll always be Frank to me," she says.

"I know. I know. That makes me feel . . ."

"What?"

"Kind of sad."

"Why?"

"Because I don't like being Gray. You know, the kids at school call me Fifty Shades." He sighs and Alice laughs loudly.

"That's hilarious!"

"I suppose so. But it's not that. It's everything. I mean . . ." The image on the screen moves as he picks up his laptop and moves it around. "Look at my flat, Alice. Seriously. Look at it."

He pans the webcam around a square room with yellow walls. There are piles of paperwork everywhere, a scruffy cream sofa, a cheap ceramic table lamp. Then he takes her into an unmodernised bathroom with a threadbare bathmat hanging at a slapdash angle on the side of the bath and a dead plant in a pot on the windowsill. His kitchen is piled with dirty dishes and his bedroom has an unmade bed at its centre and broken Venetian blinds at the windows.

"Everything was as I left it. Seriously. This is how I live."

"I've seen much worse," says Alice. "Where's Brenda?"

"Hold on . . ." The image jerks as he searches his flat. Then: "Hello, gorgeous, there you are." The camera zooms in on a stripy red cat sitting curled up on a pile of dirty sheets.

"Oh," she says, "she's lovely!"

"She hates me," he says. "She's been sulking ever since I got back."

Alice laughs; she can't help it.

"It's not funny!" he protests. "As far as I can tell she was the only friend I had in the world. Seriously, Alice. You wouldn't want to know me."

She laughs again.

"No. I'm being serious. I'm pretty much an alcoholic. Or I was — the fugue seems to have knocked that on the head, thank God. But, Christ, the recycling is ninety-nine per cent beer cans and vodka bottles. I don't know how I hung on to my job for so long. I'd been given warnings about coming in late and unprepared. Had a reputation for smelling of stale alcohol. And, according to my mum, I'm distant and I don't call her enough. So." He shrugs, makes an L out of his thumb and forefinger and holds it in front of his face. "*Loser.*"

Alice smiles. "Well, then," she says, "that just about makes us quits."

He sighs and his face becomes serious. "Listen," he says. "I've made a decision. Pretty monumental. I'm in a really bad place. I'm guilt-ridden and I'm angry and I hate my life and I can't move on. I just can't. I've been seeing my therapist again but it doesn't seem to be helping so he's recommended some time away." He pauses and his eyes drop to his lap. "He's suggested admitting myself into a psychiatric ward. Just for a little while. Get to the bottom of this memory issue I seem to have. Get to the bottom of *me*. And I think he's right."

388

"How long?" Alice feels panicky She'd been going to invite him up for a weekend visit, had deliberately left the next four weekends clear to ensure that he'd be able to come.

"No idea. Four weeks minimum. Maybe longer. I just . . ." He sighs loudly. "I can't be around anyone like this. I can't be around *you*. And I'd like to be around you. I really would."

Alice smiles. "I'd like to be around you, too."

He brightens and straightens up. "Show me the dogs," he says. "I want to see the dogs."

"OK!" She lifts the laptop and takes it to her bed where Griff is stretched out and yawning. The dog wags his tail lazily when he hears Frank's voice coming from the laptop. "Ah," says Alice, "look! He remembers you!" She moves the laptop on to the landing where Hero is sitting looking grumpy because Griff doesn't let her in Alice's bedroom and then downstairs where Sadie lies shivering in front of the fire in a knitted jumper. Kai and Jasmine wave at him from the sofa. Romaine appears from the kitchen with a toothbrush between her teeth and kisses the screen, leaving toothpaste drool all over it.

Franks sighs. "I love your house," he says. "I miss your house. I miss you. I . . ." His voice cracks. "There'll be a funeral," he says, "for Kirsty. Not for a few weeks yet. Will you come?"

"Of course I'll come."

"Good," he says. "Good. Then that's a date. I'll be better by then, Alice. I'll be . . . Well, I don't know what I'll be. But I'll be better. I promise."

"Don't make promises," she says, "just do what you can do. Just be what you can be. However flawed that is. I have very low standards," she jokes. "I swear, I'll go with anyone."

Finally Frank laughs and it's beautiful to hear.

"Good luck, Frank," Alice says. "I'll see you on the other side."

Frank kisses his knuckles and places them against the screen. Alice does the same. They stay like that for a moment, their hands touching across the ether, their eyes filled with tears.

"I'll see you on the other side," says Frank.

"I'll be waiting," says Alice.

And then the screen goes blank.

CHAPTER
SIXTY-TWO

Two Months Later

They bury her in Croydon. Where else would they bury her? Not in Ridinghouse Bay where her short, unsullied life came to such a horrible end. And not in Bude where her grandparents lived, where her mother grew up, now it has been revealed that her killer lived there for a few years in the late nineties, date-raped two different women during his time in the town and stalked another into a state of near-suicidal depression.

There was only Croydon. And at least it is a beautiful day.

Alice feels a surge of homecoming as she negotiates the London transport system. She feels her salty seaside mamma persona fall away and she imagines herself in hipster pavement cafés and graffiti-daubed playgrounds and corner shops run by people with foreign accents. She loves Ridinghouse Bay, but she misses London.

Frank meets her off the train at East Croydon. He looks well. He has kept the beard that had begun to grow during his days in Ridinghouse Bay and it is now a hefty chin-covering wedge of copper and brown. His hair is short and he is dressed in a well-cut black suit with a dark checked shirt and sensible black lace-up shoes. He looks exactly like a trendy urban maths teacher should look. Except that he is not a maths teacher any more. The school gave him extended sick leave when he came back to Croydon but after six weeks on the psychiatric ward he decided that he didn't want to go back to work. So now he is unemployed. Which is bad, because he won't be able to take them to the Ritz. But good, because it leaves them both with options.

"Hello," he says shyly, kissing her softly on her cheek and hugging her lightly. "You look gorgeous."

She touches her hair, embarrassed. It would be true to say she has made a very big effort. The badger stripes have gone at some not inconsiderable expense and she is wearing strange twangy pants that hold in her tummy. She is also wearing make-up applied by her daughter, who is quite skilled in make-up application, being a member of the YouTube tutorial generation. And a dress.

"Thank you," she says.

He leads her to his car, a crap Vauxhall with dirty upholstery. He apologises for the dirty upholstery and she tells him not to worry, reminding him that he's seen her house, that dust doesn't really figure on her personal landscape. It's strangely awkward for a while. Alice hasn't seen him for such a long time and she's torn between wanting to sit on his lap and cling on to him for dear life and wanting to pretend she really isn't bothered either way.

"How are you feeling?" she says.

"Sick," he says.

392

"Well. You've been waiting for this for twenty-two years."

"Exactly," he says, eyes on his wing mirror as he goes to overtake a parking car. "Exactly."

"How's your mum?"

"Nuts," he says, eyes on the other mirror, pulling back into his lane. "Totally and utterly nuts. No wonder I was such a mess. I'm hoping that this will finally calm her down. Burying her baby. Give her some peace."

"Yes," says Alice. "It must have been . . ." She thinks of her three babies. "I can't imagine. I really can't."

She's nervous about meeting Frank's mum. She's nervous about all of it. The aunts and the elderlies, the grief and the pain and the coffin full of delicate girl-bones.

"I brought something for your mum," she says uncertainly, touching a plastic bag at her feet. "I'm hoping . . . I don't know. It's risky. She might like it. She might hate it. I wanted to show it to you first."

"Sure," he says, his eyes going to the bag. "Is it one of your pictures?"

"Yes," she says. "How did you guess?"

He smiles. "Because you wouldn't have brought something unless it came from your heart. And your pictures come from your heart. Also, I can see a bit of the frame."

She nudges him and laughs.

"I tell you what," he says, "I haven't had any breakfast and I don't suppose there'll be any food on offer for quite some time." He rubs his stomach. "Shall we stop somewhere for a bite to eat? We've got plenty of time."

She nods, grateful for an excuse to defer the moment of meeting Frank's family.

He pulls on to a side road and parks outside an old-fashioned café furbished entirely in orange-stained pine. "Bring your picture," he said. "I can pass judgement."

They order sandwiches and jacket potatoes, Diet Cokes and cups of tea. They talk about Mark Tate's court case, about the chances of any convictions being brought in the face of so little physical evidence. They talk about all the women who have come forward since his arrest claiming to have been assaulted by him, about the "other wife" who came out of the woodwork. They talk about Lesley Wade's surprisingly fairly-written *Gazette* exclusive which has been syndicated by all of the nationals and is going to be expanded into a ten-page feature in the *Sunday Times Magazine* once Mark Tate has been tried and sentenced. They talk about Kitty Tate, how she was arrested shortly after Mark's arrest on charges of joint enterprise and is currently on bail awaiting trial and how, within days of the disinterment of Kirsty's body, Kitty had sold both her houses to a property developer at a knock-down price and was currently living in a rented flat in Ripon. They talk about Alice's children and her dogs, about how all the teachers at Romaine's school now treat Alice with a kind of star-struck awe after seeing her name in all the newspapers every day for a week. They talk about Frank's time in hospital and about his plans for the future. They talk like old friends who once went on a remarkable journey together and have no one else with whom to share the memories. Their eyes meet across the table and there is nothing but warmth between them. She wants to take his hand but she waits for him to take the lead. He is the one who has been broken and glued back together again. He is the one burying the ghostly remains of his sister today. He needs to dictate the pace.

"Are you better?" she asks.

He smiles. "I think so. I feel . . . I feel like . . . not like Gray. But also, not like Frank. I think . . ." he says, "I feel like Graham."

"And who is Graham?"

"Graham is the man I was supposed to be. All along. You know . . . *Graham.*" He widens his eyes at her, urging her to get it.

She laughs.

"*Graham,*" he says again. "You know? He's solid, but ambitious. He's loving and family-minded. He has a dog—"

"You have a dog?"

"No! No. Just a metaphorical dog. But, you know. Graham has interests and friends. Graham can draw and is quite good at football. Graham is a good man. Not exciting, but good. Graham is good husband material."

Alice laughs again. "I like Graham," she says. "I really like him. But can I still call him Frank?"

"You," he says, running his fingers around the rim of his mug of tea, "you can call him anything you like."

"Will you come and see us?" she says, racing ahead of herself, cursing herself as she says it.

But she needn't have worried. He nods and smiles. "I want to come. I really do. I want to come and see you. When can I come?"

Alice feels herself flood with relief. "Whenever!" She laughs. "Come now."

Frank laughs. "Maybe not quite now."

"No," she says, "no. Obviously. Christ, I'm a desperate old hag, aren't I?"

"You are neither old nor a hag. And I have no issue with the desperation. None whatsoever." He smiles and finally his hand reaches across the table for hers.

"So," he says, releasing her hand a moment later. "Let's see this picture."

She feels nervous pulling it out of the bag. She's had sleepless nights agonising over every detail of it, trying to strike the dreadful balance between sentiment and mawkishness. "Here." She slides it to him across the table. Her fingernail goes immediately to her mouth. "What do you think?" she says.

It's a picture of a peacock, tail feathers spread wide open, its head held at a playful angle, one foot off the ground.

"It's dancing," says Frank softly.

"Yes!" she says. "I'm so glad you could tell. I wasn't sure if it didn't look like it was having a fit. Jasmine said it looked like it was trying to fly. She said she felt sorry for it."

"No," says Frank, running a finger over the glass. "It's dancing. It is most definitely dancing."

"And look," she says, turning it slightly towards her, "see the maps. This" — she points at one section — "this is Croydon. For obvious reasons. But this" — she indicated another bit — "I don't know. I started to think of what she might have done if what happened that night hadn't happened. I tried to imagine where Kirsty Ross might have gone with her life. I thought . . . here, this bit is Sussex: maybe she'd have gone to university there? And here . . . Crete, maybe her first holiday with friends? Then this bit is Thailand — you know, backpacking in her gap year. Then Clapham — maybe she'd have shared a flat there with friends for a while. Then I thought maybe she'd have got married, bought a house close to Mum and Dad, maybe here . . ." Her finger slides across the picture. "Norbury. Not very glamorous, I know. But from what you told me about Kirsty, I got the impression she was quite a simple girl. She would have lived within her means. Within her comfort zone." She shrugs, unsettled by Frank's silence. "It was just a crazy idea I had. This idea that I could somehow recreate her lost life. Give her the history she never had. Make something real."

Frank looks at her and then down at the picture. He breathes in hard and Alice sees that he is trying incredibly hard not to cry.

"It's perfect," he says. "Really. Just incredible. And beautiful. And right."

"Will your mum like it, do you think?"

"Mum will love it," he says, taking her hands again. "Mum will love you. *I* . . ." He stops and shakes his head. "Come on." He pulls a twenty-pound note from his jacket pocket and leaves it on the table. Then he holds out his hand to her.

The sun shines kindly on the grey streets of Croydon that day. In a funeral home half a mile from here, Kirsty's casket is being placed in a white hearse, upon which her name is spelled out in pink roses. Half a mile in the other direction Kirsty's mother is adjusting a pink rose on the lapel of her black jacket while her grandparents unwrap blocks of cheese and packets of crackers, arrange wine glasses on the dining table, pour peanuts into bowls and nervously check the time.

The press are already gathering around the crematorium, dressed in black, setting up cameras at discreet but workable distances. The funeral of the girl who spent more than twenty years buried under an oak tree 250 miles from home, the girl who died at the hands of a man who has been branded Britain's Most Evil Man, the girl who was finally found by a lost brother who hadn't known his own name, is a big story indeed. The country will want to see the close-ups of their faces as they inter their lost girl's bones in the ground.

In a large, genteel flat in Ripon, with tall windows overlooking the grounds of the cathedral, Kitty Tate unpacks yet another box of possessions. She stops for a moment as the cathedral bells chime the half-hour and thinks that in an hour and a half Kirsty Ross will be buried by her mother and that in an hour and a half she will finally, after twenty-two years, be able to breathe properly again. She thinks of her upcoming trial, of the possibility of going to jail, and she feels numb. Then she thinks of her nephew, awaiting trial in Brixton Prison, completely alone, horribly convinced of his own innocence, blaming the world for every wrong thing he has ever done, incapable of real love or empathy, damaged to his very deepest core, and her breath catches again.

In Putney, Liljana Mazur sits with her ten-month-old charge on her lap in a café with a friend called Dasha who is also a nanny to a baby, who is also twenty-one and who is also from the Ukraine. She is telling her new friend that today a girl called Kirsty Ross is to be buried twenty-two years after she died. She tells her that she was invited to the funeral but that she couldn't face it because the people there would hate her for being married to the man who had killed her. She tells Dasha that sometimes she even hates herself for being married to a man who could do that to a woman. And then she turns away so that Dasha cannot see that she is crying. The baby turns to look up at her and places a small hand against her cheek. Lily takes the hand and kisses it.

And here, in a dirty Vauxhall, parked outside Pam Ross's Croydon semi, Frank and Alice turn to each other and smile.

"You OK?" says Frank.

"Sure," says Alice. "You?"

Frank nods. "I'm glad you're here," he says. "Really glad."

"I'm glad I'm here, too."

"I talked about you a lot. In therapy."

"Oh yes," says Alice. "How did that go down?"

"The general consensus was that I should wait. That I'm not strong enough to be part of someone else's life just yet." He pauses and Alice holds her breath. "But that's not the issue. I've been part of your life already and I know it's good for me. The question is: Is it good for you to be a part of my life?"

"Do you want me to be?" she asks, too fast, her words ending on a sharp gulp.

"I want you to be. Yes." He turns and glances at the small semi to his left. "But it's not just me any more, is it?"

She leans forwards and peers at the house. It's an innocuous-looking place. Well kept. A shiny green Peugeot 107 on the driveway, patterned curtains at the windows, purple hydrangeas in the flowerbeds.

"I can do family," she says.

"Family with baggage?"

"I can do most things."

He smiles. "I know," he says. "I know you can."

"What did you think?" she says suddenly, wanting to delay the onslaught for a few moments more, wanting to hear something light, something hopeful. "The first time you saw me. On the beach. In the rain. What was the first thing that went through your mind? Honestly."

He smiles. He takes her hand. He says, "I thought you looked wet. And a bit scary."

She taps his arm and tuts. But she can see why he might have thought it. She'd been acting the role of the scary woman for years because deep down inside she was scared. Scared of being alone. Scared of being an outsider. Scared that she'd had all her chances at happiness and blown each and every one of them.

He puts an arm around her shoulders, brings her head into the crook of his shoulder and says, "I thought you were magnificent."

"That's nice," she says. "For what it's worth, I thought you were handsome. And also very wet."

He laughs and kisses the crown of her newly high-lighted head. "I'm glad it was you who found me. I'm glad it wasn't anyone else."

"So am I."

"Shall we go?"

"Yes," says Alice. "I'm ready."

Other titles published by Ulverscroft:

THE GIRLS

Lisa Jewell

Clare and her two pre-teen daughters, Grace and Pip, move into Virginia Terrace, a cluster of flats and houses surrounding a communal garden. It's a place where families feel safe and children can run free. Neighbours have known each other for years, and trust each other implicitly. But then, after the annual garden party — a glorious summer's day of getting together and enjoying a barbecue, listening to music, having a few glasses of wine, letting the children play — the unspeakable happens. Grace is found by Pip, unconscious and half undressed, her face a bloody mess. And as a police investigation is launched, the secret games that the residents of Virginia Terrace have been playing for decades are about to be horribly, brutally exposed . . .

THE THIRD WIFE

Lisa Jewell

In the early hours of an April morning, Maya stumbles into the path of an oncoming bus. A tragic accident? Or suicide? Her grief-stricken husband, Adrian, is determined to find out. Maya had a job she enjoyed; she had friends. They'd been in love. She even got on with his two previous wives and their children. In fact, they'd all been one big happy family. But before long Adrian starts to identify the dark cracks in his perfect life. Because everyone has secrets. And secrets have consequences. Some of which can be devastating . . .

THE HOUSE WE GREW UP IN

Lisa Jewell

The four children of the Bird Family have an idyllic childhood: picture-book cottage, cosy kitchen filled with love and laughter, sun-drenched afternoons in a rambling garden. But one Easter weekend a tragedy so devastating strikes the family that it begins to tear them apart. The years pass; the children become adults and develop their own separate lives — it's almost as though they've never been a family at all. Almost. But not quite. Because something happens that will call them home, back to the house they grew up in — and to what really happened that Easter weekend all those years ago.

BEFORE I MET YOU

Lisa Jewell

Having grown up on the quiet island of Guernsey, Betty Dean can't wait to start her new life in London. On a mission to find Clara Pickle — the beneficiary in her grandmother's will — she arrives in bustling and grungy 1990s Soho. In 1920s bohemian London, Arlette — Betty's grandmother — is starting her new post-war life, soon drawn into the hedonistic world of the Bright Young People. But less than two years later, tragedy strikes and she flees back to Guernsey for the rest of her life. As Betty searches for Clara, she is taken on a journey through Arlette's time in London, uncovering a tale of love, loss and heartbreak.